ERIC JORDAN

OPERATION
HEBRON

International Media Group Ltd.
London

In association with Mosaic Press

OPERATION
HEBRON

Published by International Media Group Ltd.
Ten Stratton Street London W1X 5FD, UK.
For information about permission to reproduce selections from this book
or obtain secondary rights, contact Permissions/Rights,
Email: operationhebron@hotmail.com

Distributed to the trade in the United States by Mosaic Press
4500 Witmer Industrials Estates,
PMB145 Niagara Falls, NY 14305-1386
Email: mosaicpress@on.aibn.ca
Distributed to the trade in Canada by Mosaic Press
1252 Speers Road (#1 & 2) Oakville, Ontario L6L 5N9 Canada
Email: mosaicpress@on.aibn.ca

Canadian Cataloguing in Publication Data

Jordan, Eric, 1931-
Operation Hebron

ISBN 0-88962-777-0

I. Title

PS3560.0715063 2000   813'.6   C00-930001-5

Printed in Canada by Webcom Ltd.

MP 10 9 8 7 6 5 4 3 2 1
FIRST EDITION

The publisher wishes to acknowledge Rebecca Brite and Sophie Alvacete
for their valuable editorial and production assistance.

A David Applefield Production

Visit www.operationhebron.com

Copies N° 1 - 100 have been numbered and signed by the author.

AUTHOR'S DEDICATION

*T*o my mother and father in that big publishing house in the sky. Thank you for your selfless and unquestioning love and support over the years as I wandered the world thousands of miles away on adventures – major and minor – and always returned, often years later, to your continuing encouragement to use my God-given talents to the maximum. This work of pure fiction, another of my efforts in that respect, is a tribute to you both.

Royalties that I accrue from this work will therefore go to a special scholarship fund for needy secondary students which has been established in your name.

ACKNOWLEDGMENTS

I wish to thank my close friends, family members, and editors around the globe who over the years have encouraged, cajoled, helped and even provoked me to produce this first novel. Without this input and encouragement to keep writing and trying I truly could not have done it.

In particular, I wish to thank my first tutor, Dawn Kolokithas, an ex-Berkeley writing professor in Paris; Josephine Quintero, a free-lance writer/editor in Marbella; Laila Khalil, an editor in New York; and Shari Leslie Segall, a writer/editor in Paris; who have all provided professional advice at different times during the decade it took me to finish *Operation Hebron* while otherwise earning a living. Thanks also go to London novelist Janet Ingles, who labored through my rough text; and Duncan Thompson, who gave me a short course in script-writing, which better enabled me to picture the scenes I was trying to describe. I owe much to my well-published, long-term friend John Barron, a retired giant at *Readers Digest* and *bête noire* of the "Evil Empire," who gave me his most objective, in-the-face, comments on my earlier drafts and encouraged me through to the end. Thanks also go to my old high school buddy James Powers, SJ, now a master professor of English literature at Gonzaga, who took an early look at my pages and recommended I persevere; to Sheila Lavey who convinced me years ago that this book could be an exciting read and offered me several good ideas; to Don her husband who made sure I said nothing factually incorrect about the FBI.

I'm grateful to the Scottish editor, Hunter Steele, who helped shepherd late stages of the manuscript; and finally to David Applefield and IMG, my publishers, who have had the courage to accept *Operation Hebron* and run with it... after only a few hundred more suggestions! I also want to thank Kent Carroll, a pillar of New York publishing, who agreed to take a last look before the manuscript went to press; and to Jodee Blanco, the heart and lungs of our ongoing effort to get the word out that *Operation Hebron* lives!

Finally, I wish to thank my dearest daughter Christina, who not only helped me to enrich my text – particularly with her multi-language skills – but who ultimately provoked me into becoming an author when she suggested that I either stop talking about "my book" or finish it. Thank you Christina for speaking up bravely and constructively to your father at the right moment.

Last but not least, I want to thank my close friend Renato Casaro, the star of modern film illustration, for taking time out of his hectic schedule to honor my wish that he paint the jacket cover for *Operation Hebron*.

Now, I turn over my first novel to you, the Reader. I hope that *Operation Hebron* will entertain you as I intended, as fiction, while at the same time it provides a more realistic feel and sometimes frightening picture as to what is going on out there in the world of international politics and intrigue.

Eric Jordan (*eric@operationhebron.com*)

ERIC JORDAN

OPERATION HEBRON

International Media Group Ltd.
London
2000

Chapter One

Washington, D.C.
November 7th – Election Night

Two shots rang out from the seventh floor of the apartment building across the Potomac River from Georgetown in the Rosslyn area of suburban Virginia. The sharp cracks shattered the peaceful night, sending out a ripple of consequences that would shock the world. Light feet, calmly but hurriedly, left the building. Four blocks away in a motel parking area they stopped, then climbed into a waiting rental car. The vehicle proceeded along the almost empty highway to Dulles International Airport, never exceeding the sluggish speed limit imposed in this country. *Steady, sure, was the best way out. Never draw attention to yourself or compromise on the details.*

A much heavier pair of feet pounded up to where the bullets had resounded. Their owner flung the apartment door open and burst inside. At the sight before him a man let out a hoarse scream, half rage, half disbelief, and felt as if his heart might burst a valve. Three men lay on the floor soaked in a mixture of blood and the debris of torn flesh.

The man went to his knees next to his boss, heedless of the streams of blood that still flowed. He searched for a pulse. There was none. He bolted upright and glanced at the other two bodies. No sign of life there either.

The man reached into his pocket, withdrew his cellular phone, and dialed his embassy. As he waited for the connection, a white folded piece of paper near his boss's open right palm caught his eye. He cradled the phone between his chin and shoulder, picking up the paper delicately so it wouldn't be covered with blood. He brought it forward and started to read to himself. Its contents didn't make much sense to him. But, then, he had not understood a lot of what his boss did. He spoke.

"Stay put, Abe," barked an agitated voice from the embassy. "We're calling the police now. They'll be there quickly. You return to the embassy as soon as they arrive. But, remember, you have diplomatic immunity. Say nothing! Do you have your passport? Your diplomatic ID?"

Abe replied in the affirmative and turned off his mobile.

In the distance, approching sirens wailed. Abe rose to his feet, pocketing both the phone and the folded paper. Whatever the paper meant was not the Americans' business. As instructed by his embassy, Abe waited, aching with disbelief and sickness, guarding the body of the man who would have been alive, if only...

The stairs echoed with racing feet. The elevator bell announced its arrival at the seventh floor and its doors slid open. More feet pounded their way toward the apartment. Abe sighed and dug into his inside coat pocket for his diplomatic passport, his ticket to immunity.

The call came in from the Arlington, Virginia, Police Department, reporting an apparent shoot-out in a Rosslyn apartment. Of the three murdered men, one had been identified by the caller as a diplomat.

Special Agent Brenda Straus of the FBI Counter-terrorism Section alerted her team. They jumped into a car and wheeled though the streets, tires squealing, lights flashing.

The sight that greeted the FBI team could have been out of a special effects horror movie. The diplomat lay on the floor, a gaping bullet hole in his left side, which kept dripping out his little remaining life. Uncooperative and hostile, his chauffeur, who was also his bodyguard, insisted that he had no idea who the other two dead men were, and demanded the immunity that came with his diplomatic status. The second body belonged to a swarthy man whose wide-open eyes still registered the angry shock of unexpected death. The third man, in jeans and a hooded parka, was lying on his side. He had been shot in the face, leaving a messy plum of flesh and gore. He was unrecognizable.

"Holy shit!" cried Lieutenant Ford of the Arlington Police Department. "Agent Straus! Take a look at this driver's license," he said, pointing at the faceless man, and handing her the small plastic card.

Brenda read it carefully and let out a horrified gasp. "My God!" was all she could say, before firing orders at her team. "Jack, call the White House on the secure car phone. Tell them to get the Secret Service over here right away. We need positive ID." She shuddered. "Holy shit," she echoed, under her breath.

She turned to Ford. "Make sure no one knows about this. Keep everyone away from those bodies until the Secret Service arrives. And I mean everyone. In fact, seal off the entire floor."

Then the FBI and the Arlington Police waited.

They would not have to wait long...

A Few Hours Later
Over the Atlantic Ocean

The 777 glided over the Atlantic, advancing swiftly toward Frankfurt.

The first rays of golden sun broke the barriers of darkness and early morning haze to embrace the jet in a soft halo. The voice of United flight 978's pilot came over the speakers, trusting, with mid-fifties male assurance, that his passengers had had a restful flight and wishing them a pleasant German breakfast. Then he broke the incredible news from America that had reached the cockpit by radio.

Two hundred and sixty-three passengers, some wide-awake, others shaking off the lingering web of sleep, were first rendered speechless. Then suddenly they came alive with the shock of what they had heard, voicing their astounded reactions. Even the non-Americans screamed questions and roared speculations, as if shouting would give credibility to their premature theories.

The peaceful morning was transformed as passengers buzzed for the flight attendants, demanding that the pilot kept them abreast of the news as soon as he received it. They wanted to know who was responsible and whether the killer had been caught.

Passenger number 264, a lovely raven-haired Serb with an Austrian passport, occupying seat 3C, didn't share the others' excitement. She didn't need to speculate. Her eyes opened slowly to a world of incredulity. And for a second she was amazed to learn the identity of the third man she had gunned down. But then she shrugged. If he had been a contact of the diplomat, he had deserved the bullet that disfigured his face. As a professional assassin, the green-eyed beauty had no regrets. She had accomplished her objective with precision and success. She was not in the regret business. An outstanding bill had been paid. She was also safer than she had been at any time in recent months. Her getaway had been impeccable.

Too bad, she mused, smiling. *That's one murder I'll never be able to claim unless I'm ready for my place in the history books.*

No. Jackie Markovic would never know just how stunning that thought actually was, nor that she had unwittingly disrupted the most audacious covert operation ever aimed at the United

States, an operation only one intelligence service would have dared to undertake. The operation its authors referred to as "Hebron," perhaps the greatest success story in the history of espionage.

Jackie checked her makeup and buckled her seat belt as Frankfurt/Main's sprawling airport came into view.

Chapter Two

Jerusalem
Earlier That Year – April 21st

The blue incoming-call light on his private line interrupted Prime Minister Aharon Eshel's musings. He stared at the phone for a few moments to redirect his focus. When he picked up the handset, he heard the clipped, raspy voice of his intelligence chief, General Benjamin Stern, the director of Mossad.

"Stern here."

"Yes, Ben."

"First, more bad news. The Americans are getting pissed with our stonewalling on the final peace deal with the Palestinian Authority. The White House intends to go public and blame us for the delay, as usual. Ditto with our recent high-tech sales to China and Russia. We've got big, big troubles. I hope the Americans only know part of what we offered to the Chinese. If they knew the whole story they'd go ballistic." He seemed unaware of his pun. "In a few hours I'll have more on what's happening in Washington. When I do, I'll call you immediately. After you get the details, you can decide if you want to make a personal call to President Douglas tonight to stop him from going public."

The intelligence chief hesitated for a second before continuing in a more positive tone. "Now, as we agreed, boss, I've called a

16

meeting of The Five for tomorrow. Given developments in Washington, it's urgent that we move our Hebron proposal decisively. The Five can assemble at twenty-one hundred hours, if that suits your schedule?"

Eshel skimmed his desk calendar for Tuesday evening. "Okay, that's fine. Where're we meeting this time? It has to be absolutely secure."

"At Jerome's farm. My sister-in-law and the kids are in Haifa, so the place is vacant. That farm is still one of our most discreet sites. Even the American satellites won't be lookin' for us there."

That last remark had Eshel gritting his teeth. He remembered that Gershon Yahav, the minister of finance and the newest member of the Israeli cabinet, had been anything but discreet about the farm after The Five's last meeting there.

"I'll be there, Ben. However, make sure that everyone, especially Yahav, understands the necessity of absolute security. The last meeting was Yahav's first at the farm. Frankly, I got the impression that he takes lightly the restriction that no one, and I repeat, no one, should know about The Five, whether friend or foe."

"I appreciate your concern, boss. I talked to Yahav after that last session, and I think he has a better understanding of the role of The Five now. He understands its importance to Israel's survival, although he claims to suffer sleepless nights since! I welcomed him to the policy-making level of government.

"Poor bastard. I know how he feels!" responded Eshel with a gruff laugh.

Stern continued, "I'll bring the Hebron dossier with me. Tiron will be in from Washington tonight; he'll bring us up to date on the pre-election climate in the US."

"I hope Tiron's exposition, your briefing, and my exhortation will persuade our brothers to kick-start our operation. But I've

17

got to have their concurrence. This one I won't risk on my own. And your agent? You say he's ready?

"That he is, boss. He's champing at the bit, as they say. Well, that's it for now. I'll be at my brother's farm an hour before the meeting in case someone arrives early. Expect a call from me in two hours on the Washington situation, and I'll see you tomorrow."

Without comment, Eshel returned the phone to its cradle. His racing mind was robbing him of his energy. Exhaustion was aggravating his weak back. Pain, hot and piercing, shot through his spine. He drew in his breath. No use dwelling on something as paltry as back pain. He popped another painkiller and swallowed it with half a glass of seltzer. He would need all his wits to launch the most daring covert political action considered by any Israeli government since the nation's foundation.

Just then, the high-pitched voice of his executive assistant, David Hazor, jolted his thoughts back to the present.

"Sir! The minister of aviation telephoned. He insisted that you address the El-Al strike threat immediately. Also, he would like us to arrange a meeting with you this evening for himself and the El-Al managing director.

"Secondly, Kurt Baden of the German Social Democrats called asking that you ring him back in Berlin. Then, the chief of staff wishes to see you before he leaves for Washington tomorrow morning. And lastly, I have the civil service appointments, promotions, and retirements for you to sign, sir."

"All right, all right!" snapped Eshel. "Just leave everything on my desk and I'll get to it when I can. Okay? Sometimes you're worse than my wife, the way you nag," he added with a forced smile.

When Hazor retreated, Eshel leaned back in his chair, then winced. He had a flashback of that last parachute jump during the Suez Canal operation. He knew the pain was going to be with him the rest of his life. Anxiety and tension exaggerated his reaction. He would have to rush the evening's work if he hoped to get some rest and be ready for the long meeting tomorrow night. Still, he had to hear his private secretary out and attack Hazor's list before he could entertain such a blissful thought as a warm bed. But he needed a break. He rose and went to the window.

He looked out the window of his office, his gaze fixed on the citrus trees dotting the court yard, two stories below. Iron bars on the window partially hid the trees from his view. From where he stood, one would have thought the trees were locked behind the window's iron bars if their leaves hadn't been moving gently with the breeze.

For a few minutes he let the sway of the branches soothe him. *A tranquilizing sight befitting the Holy City,* he thought. *A sight that belies the harsh reality of a land torn by violence.* He studied the sky. The spring day had been mild and the sun was strong, lending comfort to a region in a world that knew only brief moments of security. And, as if reality had finally sunk in, the sun smeared the sky with bloody stripes on her way to comfort the other half of this wretched world. Eshel had these philosophical lapses from time to time, the makings of a true statesman.

Swearing under his breath, the prime minister pulled away from the window and walked to his desk, frowning deeply. Thoughts sprinted through his mind. That was normal; Eshel was accustomed to making decisions. His job was to resolve his country's problems, domestic and international.

What was unusual this time was the critical context of Israel's current quandary, the most challenging encounter that the young nation had faced since its War of Independence. The solution that Eshel had chosen was audacious. It not only had the potential to resolve Israel's immediate problem, but if it worked it would guarantee the country a healthy future for decades to come. True, conducting such a covert operation risked waves of consequences that would spread across international borders. But, for Israel's survival, the end always justified the means, and Eshel never hesitated to make that clear to friends and enemies alike. He said it in public and he said it even more pointedly in private, even to heads of state. And in this case he was convinced the nation's survival was once again in question. Just as it had been at its birth, when he fought as an underground guerrilla. *When it comes to survival, principles are a luxury,* he repeated to himself.

He slumped heavily in his high-backed black leather chair, then reached for the onyx digital clock on his desk. As if searching for inspiration, he fiddled pensively with the handsome bronze stand. The clock had been a gift from Rabbi Weinbert, president of the American Jewish Congress, during Eshel's visit to Washington two years earlier. The prime minister hadn't returned since. Or, more accurately, he hadn't been invited back by the American administration since he had frozen the peace process. With another curse, he slammed the clock onto his desk, convinced of the righteousness of his daring plan. Consequences to the world be damned.

For the last few days, he had had a peaceful interim, a rare luxury during which he could think clearly. The so-called peace talks with the Palestinians were, as always, off and on. This time, more off. A temporary though undeclared cease-fire was supposedly in effect. The human bombs and border skirmishes never ceased. But battles were fewer this week. Excessive street clashes and their resultant bitterness had declined for the moment, as had the associated tensions. Yes, it was a relatively peaceful interim. *Peace? Would there ever be permanent peace in this part of the world?* he wondered.

Publicly, he pronounced his great hopes for a permanent peace with the Palestinians. Privately, he had no intention of giving them a square meter more of Israeli land than necessary. He had resisted the American president's effort to push Israel into concessions with the Arabs in the formal peace talks when they had begun long ago in Madrid. Later they moved to Oslo, and then to Wye. *Peace talks by which,* Eshel scoffed, *the US had used her political pressures to force all parties to participate and compromise.* Eshel had played along but never compromised Israel's basic positions.

He hoped that the Iranians would keep the Arabs in the Gulf and Arabian Peninsula – and, of course, in Lebanon – sufficiently busy and worried. *And the Arabs are still warring among themselves, à la Iraq. Israel counts on these two factors.* Eshel was enveloped in this crucial thought when there was a single short knock and the PM's door opened. In came Lev Eglon.

"What do you have for me, Lev?" asked Eshel.

The tall, angular Eglon was Eshel's loyal private secretary. For the last five years he had been the backbone of the prime minister's office. Eshel considered him efficient, witty, and reliable. Furthermore, he labored quietly and never sought public acclaim. He handed the prime minister the file of outgoing letters and cables and incoming personal messages.

"Sir, your letter to President Douglas is ready for you to review and sign. Also there are the confidential notes you wished the chief of staff to carry to the chair of the American Jewish Appeal and the American Israel Political Action Committee. Next, the miscellaneous letters I've prepared for your signature: the ones in the green file are minor, so no need for you to read them before signing.

"You've also received a message on your sterile line from an American, at least he sounded American, who gave his name as Charles and said he'd call back."

Eshel's lips tightened, but he didn't respond. "Charles" was the telephone alias that the Mossad chief in Washington, David

Tiron, used in connection with Operation Hebron. Eshel had given Tiron strict instructions to deal with Jerusalem only through Mossad channels and never to call him directly. For Tiron, with his American-accented English, to call him directly in an emergency was a serious mistake. He had to be careful with this Tiron, Eshel reminded himself.

He suspected that Tiron, taking advantage of Eshel's previous service with Mossad and his key role in the Stern Gang during Israel's War of Independence, was trying to develop a political kinship with the prime minister. Now Tiron apparently felt he could phone the prime minister to discuss a major secret intelligence operation such as Hebron. Eshel made a mental note to remind himself to quash this notion when he met with Tiron the following night.

He nodded to his secretary and opened the correspondence folder to review the final version of his letter to the American president. He felt a twinge of uneasiness. The president's almost legendary toughness with Israel regarding West Bank development financing, the Gaza airport, and the Arab-Israeli peace negotiations had strained the relationship between the two leaders. The fact that the president had declined to come to Jerusalem or any of the subsequent meetings meant he still expected Eshel to make concessions. *Concessions that, damn it,* Eshel reminded himself, *I will not consider. I will not give up more land.*

Unfortunately for Eshel, the president was very popular with the American voters despite his cool, aloof personality. The Israelis knew well that he could, given time, bring the majority of the American people with him on nearly any issue.

This was vividly demonstrated when Eshel had once threatened to go over the president's head and approach Congress directly regarding Israeli loan guarantees. Douglas hadn't budged an inch; he had in fact called Israel's and the Jewish lobby's bluff and had won, costing Israel and its American supporters a major loss of face. *A lost battle in a bigger war.*

Eshel sensed that Douglas was unswayed by domestic political influence peddlers even though he was only in his first term. Moreover, public opinion made this US president an awesome player in the world of international politics. Most heads of state and government officials refrained from crossing him.

Eshel knew from his service in Israeli intelligence that US-Israeli relations had deteriorated since Israel invaded Lebanon at the end of the Reagan administration. The bilateral relationship was strained even further after the discovery of the Israeli agent Jonathan Pollard in the US Defense Department, and the revelation of Israel's theft of atomic-weapon parts and enriched uranium from the US.

Now the Americans were firm with the Israelis, and had offered them an ultimatum: "We supported you militarily and financially. Negotiate peace with the Arabs, or you'll never see another dollar during the lifetime of this administration!"

Intolerable, thought Eshel. *Something radical has to be done.*

He had made his decision. The ground had been prepared, and he trusted that The Five, Israel's key body of policy-makers who were by tradition called on to approve major covert actions, would agree with him. In a decade The Five had acted only a dozen times. Although technically he needed their approval for the political risks involved, he especially needed them to sign off on the money. He would have assumed the political risk without The Five, as he was at ease doing so in other dangerous and risky Mossad operations, but such large sums of money could not be released by the minister of finance without their approval. That had become part of the unwritten culture of covert action in the State of Israel.

The letter to President Douglas could wait until he returned from the meeting tomorrow, when he would know if The Five had agreed to his plans. He might even change the near-pleading tone of his letter about the necessity for the US to help Israel out of its disastrous financial situation.

"Hold the Douglas letter until Thursday, Lev."

"But, sir, the American ambassador called a few minutes before you came in to say he's leaving for the States tomorrow. He expects to have a letter from you with him. He'll be staying home all evening to be sure you can reach him quickly."

"Lev, this is Israel!" snapped Eshel. "We don't want any American ambassador getting the idea that he's our main channel to Washington. That would confuse our Jewish friends in the States, wouldn't it, and reduce our ambassador's access in Washington. It would also give those damn State Department types the impression that they have some role to play in Washington's relations with Israel." He paused before adding, "Let the ambassador enjoy a sleepless night at home. If he calls, tell him you delivered his message to me. Nothing more."

"Yes, sir."

"That'll be all tonight, Lev."

"Yes, sir. Good night, sir." Eglon collected his file. He then asked, "Excuse me, sir. Should I know who this Charles is, sir? I sense something special there."

"Nothing of concern to you. Forget it."

"Yes, sir."

When Eglon left, Hazor re-entered. "Sir, I wish to draw your attention to the matters I raised a few minutes earlier."

"David," the prime minister sighed, closing his eyes for a brief second. "Tell the minister of aviation to come to my house for breakfast tomorrow to discuss El-Al. This evening's out of the question. My back is pure torture tonight."

"Sorry, sir. Of course." He left the office.

The prime minister turned his attention to the scores of letters that his secretary had left for him to sign. As fatigue fought with tension and pain, Eshel scribbled his name on documents without reading their words. Once again he had to trust his aides implicitly.

April 22nd

Jerome Stern's farm was small, seven hectares. Situated near Holon, between Jerusalem and Tel Aviv, the farm served as the Stern family's weekend retreat. General Stern had given his brother the cash to buy the getaway, both to serve his brother's needs and for his own or government business.

This was the fourth occasion that The Five had met at the farm. When the property was first bought, they gathered there for a pro forma meeting to test security. Everyone arrived with ease, their unexplained appearance remaining undetected and undisclosed. The farm was hailed as ideal and they unanimously approved it for future use.

General Stern arrived with his wife for dinner at 6:30, ostensibly a normal family visit. An austere official of medium build, Stern wore casual slacks that failed to disguise his military bearing. Most Israelis believed he would look the general even in a bathing suit.

A few minutes later his Washington station chief, David Tiron, tapped lightly on the door. He had flown into Tel Aviv two hours earlier, his first trip back to Israel in twelve months. Dark-haired and olive-skinned, he could pass for an Arab. His black, alert eyes and hooked nose made him look more like a Bedouin warrior than an Israeli intelligence officer.

The minister of defense, Natan Mintz, arrived next. He had driven himself in a blue unmarked Land Rover borrowed from his military intelligence section. The prime minister and Mintz were military comrades. They were also like-minded political allies. They supported one another almost without question, a fact well-known by any Israeli politician or officer who had ever risked a confrontation with either.

Mintz had a limp from a wound in the 1967 war, and more sense of humor than most Israeli policy-makers. A bachelor, he was known as the Marlboro Man by friends because of his casual attire, his rough, outdoor appearance, and his old Jeep, which he had had re-upholstered in denim.

As he usually worked late, any evening he disappeared from the office was like a religious holiday for his staff. When he asked his aide to arrange a car and said he'd be leaving earlier than usual that day, the rumor spread rapidly that the "old man" had a hot date.

After Mintz had settled in the farm's small library with a beer, another member of The Five arrived – Gershon Yahav, minister of finance. He came in his cabinet car with his ministry driver, who was dismissed at Stern's angry insistence.

Yahav was an academic economist from Berlin. His colleagues considered him more German than the Germans because of his precision and lack of flexibility or subtlety. Still he was completely aboveboard, and the cabinet knew from experience that he found it extremely difficult to conceal his position on any matter, minor or grave. As bright as any man who had ever served his country, he was a genius at incressing the value of every currency unit in Israel's possession. He did this so well that the world wondered why the small nation was not bankrupt several times over with its hyperinflation, ever-expanding military budgets, and costly international maneuvers. This financial wizardry gave Yahav his seat on The Five, despite his colleagues' reservations about his discretion.

Next came Edmund Rothberg, the polished diplomat who was Israel's foreign minister. An Oxford graduate, he had studied at MIT in Boston. He had served as Israel's ambassador to the United Kingdom and the United Nations, and his political vision was generally regarded as larger than that of a mere civil servant. This talent had caught the attention of the prime minister when Rothberg was in New York with the UN. Particularly noteworthy was that – unlike so many ambassadors – Rothberg never forgot that Israel and its objectives were foremost, whether or not its policies met with the approval of the host nation. And that included the United States.

Deep down, though, he was seriously pro-American, which he hid as only a polished diplomat could. His close friends, including the prime minister, recognized this aspect of his political personality. Eshel hoped eventually to exploit such an attitude, one he appreciated more as relations with the Americans worsened. Rothberg's day might come, Eshel often thought, but when and how remained uncertain.

The prime minister arrived late. He was driven in a shiny red Chevrolet by his old friend, bodyguard, and general factotum, Harry Golden, a transplanted Brooklynite.

The Five relaxed with a drink, chatting briefly about inconsequential events. After fifteen minutes, the prime minister called the group to order in the living room while Golden and the other drivers stood guard outside the small farmhouse, watching all approaches to the area as the sun disappeared behind the surrounding hills.

Except for the prime minister, who positioned himself in a large, heavily brocaded armchair near the stone fireplace, Israel's key leaders sat around the living room without any attention to protocol. These meetings did not officially exist and so protocol was suspended.

Eshel opened the meeting at precisely nine o'clock. He asked that it be considered "extraordinary," even given the unscheduled, special nature of The Five's top-secret sessions.

"My friends, the subject we're considering tonight is weighty. It will, for good or bad, affect our nation's future and the Jewish people like no other political operation ever considered in our history. We cannot guarantee success, but the potential gain is more than worth the risks, as you will hear.

"In brief, I am asking you tonight to authorize Mossad, politically and financially, to lay the groundwork for our nation's most important covert-action program ever: Operation Hebron. The objective: to elect our agent – a serving US senator – as the next president of the United States of America." Eshel stopped to let that sink in. He watched his advisers sit stone-faced.

"Up to now," he continued, "the very existence of Hebron has been one of our most closely guarded secrets, even more closely guarded than the existence of our nuclear arsenal. This longtime veteran agent should have an opportunity to run for president this year. If that proves true, a few months from now – depending on operational progress, the primaries in the United States, and other factors – we'll meet again to decide whether to give Mossad the final go-ahead. At that point, and only at that point, will I allow Mossad to brief you on the identity of Hebron. There will likely be three American presidential candidates, as in the past two US elections, and one of them – God willing – will be our man. Our agent, our Hebron. In political terms, our modern-day Messiah.

"The point to keep in mind, as we assess the risks together, is that if Operation Hebron succeeds, it will radically alter our ability to control American policy for a decade. And in that decade we will arrange mutual agreements and treaties which will last Israel another generation. No more Camp Davids, no more Oslo negotiations, no more Wye agreements. We will do what we damn well please, not what the *goyim* want. And the next time an Iraqi dictator or anyone else raises his ugly head, we'll lop it off the face of the map. Or rather, we'll have the president of the United States amputate it for us.

"Finally, I promise you that your decision, first tonight, and again for the final go-ahead at the next stage, will influence the security of your children, of your grandchildren, and of generations of Jews to come. So there's no easy way out of this one." He paused. "I'll take comments now."

Rothberg spoke. "Aharon, do I dare point out that just last Sunday the *Washington Post* published an article on US-Israel relations that quoted one of our journals as saying, 'Eshel owns the US Congress.' And I think we generally agree: you do. If so, why do we run a high-risk operation involving the presidency of the United States itself? Too risky, too expensive. My God, the crazy Americans spend one hundred and fifty million dollars in an election. Are we suddenly that rich? We have social projects, and our people need that money."

The prime minister hesitated. He looked each person in the eye. None spoke further. They waited for his response to the foreign minister.

He spoke. "We have influence in Congress, whether or not the press claims so. We always have. That's certain. But do you understand what I'm saying? I'm not saying 'influence.' I'm saying 'control' of the most powerful office on the face of the earth. Also, I'm not asking you to spend one hundred and fifty million dollars. Ten to twenty million, yes. But we'll let the Americans throw the money around. We'll judiciously spend a few million here and there, where and when it'll make the difference. Yes, the difference. And only then." He stopped as he caught Yahav snickering.

"Yahav, what's so funny?"

"Excuse me. I didn't mean to interrupt you but the arithmetic of my good friend Rothberg does not do justice to an Oxford man. We receive over four billion dollars in American aid each year, including the more than one billion we received from the Wye agreement. It doesn't have to be repaid. And Rothberg is

29

worried about spending ten to twenty million on an operation to control the US presidency? Why, we can take that out of the hundred-million-dollar 'Special Emergency Fund' in the prime minister's budget, all of which I took from our American grants. So, Rothberg's worries about the cost of this operation to Israel are irrelevant. Sorry. We can use American money to finance the election of our own guy. Not bad, huh?"

Eshel nodded appreciatively and continued. "As I was saying, before our colleague Yahav contributed his most pertinent comment, if Hebron wins, we – and not the American taxpayers who paid for the election – will control America. And through the White House we'll control the international scene. Trade, arms, industry, technology, Jewish security. More comments?"

No one spoke. When he was sure there were no other objections or questions, Eshel turned to General Stern and ordered, "Brief them, Ben."

Chapter Three

Brussels
May 28th

A black Lincoln limousine made a sharp right turn off the Grand-Place onto a narrow side street, stretched against the curb, and paused. The driver killed the lights but kept the motor humming. His eyes searched the sidewalk, but his vision was limited by the rain beating relentlessly against the windshield. He turned a knot and the wipers gained speed.

In the rear seat, the American ambassador to the European Union, Richard Sorensson, was also watching the sidewalk. Pushing a button, he lowered his darkened right window a few inches, then leaned forward to peek through the slim opening. He wiped his condensed breath off the cool pane with impatient strokes, while cold droplets wet his forehead.

His Belgian driver-bodyguard, Gérard, gripped the steering wheel. The ambassador could see him frowning and knew his servant was concerned about the poor security of the situation, and probably cursing his employer for being the promiscuous bastard he was. But that was his nature and his staff had to tolerate it or move on.

Both men checked their watches almost simultaneously. It was 9:30.

At that precise moment a woman walked into view at the corner.

31

A dark hooded raincoat covered her from head to calves; a blue umbrella decorated with a circle of yellow stars, representing the European flag, deflected the raindrops. Her strides were long and sure, signaling a confident woman. The ambassador shifted in his seat as his eyes strained through the opening.

"That's her! Let's go," he rasped, his eyes following those long limbs.

"Yes, sir."

The chauffeur turned on the headlights, pulled the vehicle smoothly away from the curb, and advanced the thirty meters to where the woman had slowed her pace. Braking beside her, he got out, walked around the limousine, and opened the back door.

"Madam," he murmured.

Without comment she handed her umbrella to the driver, then climbed into the rear seat, next to Sorensson. The driver could not see her face inside the hood, dripping with rain.

"*Chéri*," the woman cooed. "You were right on time."

"So were you, baby doll."

She kissed him on both cheeks, and snuggled close to him. When she crossed her legs, her short skirt rode upward to reveal her lace-top hose and purple garter belt. Sorensson chuckled, threw his arm around her, and pressed her closer. She smiled at him, happy that she was in command. She just had to take care with the driver, who, she knew, was armed.

"Home, Gérard."

"Yes, sir."

Gérard glanced in the rear-view mirror at his passengers. He frowned, sighing audibly.

Sorensson's head snapped up and his eyes met the driver's in the mirror.

"We'll talk about that tomorrow, Gérard," he said. "Keep your fuckin' sighs to yourself, or I'll see to it that you're counting furniture in the administrative warehouse."

The driver's face froze at the harsh admonition made in the presence of the woman. He looked straight ahead and, without comment, did as he was told.

The sexy woman gave the ambassador a quick wink, obviously approving of his forceful repremand of the insolent chauffeur. "Chic," she whispered.

The ambassador winked back. This was early foreplay. Dominance was a favorite game.

She knew he was proud of having pleased her by showing his driver who was boss. She now felt totally in control – *the way it had to be*.

Back in his master suite at the ambassadorial residence, Sorensson gazed at the reflection that stared at him from his dressing-table mirror. He still had a full head of hair, even if it was silvery. The years had been kind to him – his skin hadn't sagged yet and although in certain light it looked weather-beaten, his features retained much of the boyish charm that women found endearing. He helped that impression by daily exercises including moderate weight-lifting. He told everybody who would listen that he was addicted to strict exercise and diet regimes. Reaching for a comb, he began to smooth his graying hair once again.

Behind him a feminine voice purred, "Hurry, lover! I'm wasting away out here." He liked that accent. That, the eyes, and a perfect pair of breasts had clinched the deal in that wild bar several nights before.

His eyes released his own image in search of the one belonging to the voice. The reflection of the raven-haired woman smiled back at him. A sexy, tanned woman of thirty, she lay against the pillows of his king-size bed, costumed in purple lingerie and black stockings, fondling her full breasts with her silk gloves. *Someone loves me tonight*, he thought. Catching his stare, she stretched full length, threw her arms over her head, gripped the headboard, then wiggled her toes. Beautiful and willing. *Penthouse material*, his male mind thought.

He was drawn again to her eyes. A cat's eyes: detached, cold, slightly slanted, green. They followed his every move. "Honey, you look absolutely dangerous but my cock won't let my goddamn brain heed the warning signal. So, pussycat, I'm on my way," he teased as his tanned form turned away from the mirror to move across the ochre wall-to-wall carpeting. "Just a quick shower and I'll be ready?" he continued, shrugging off his blue silk robe like a muscle-bound boxer ready to lace up for the bout.

"Hurry, *chéri*," the black-haired beauty whispered, curling with coyness against the pillows.

Sorensson turned, smiled, and clumsily blew her a kiss before closing the bathroom door behind him, allowing his date a teasing sight of his firm buttocks.

She rolled her eyes and smirked with delight that he had left her alone for a few minutes. That was all she needed.

This man was certainly meticulous in his routine, she thought as she heard the shower splatter against the marble walls. She knew that his habits were well-established and didn't change for anyone, no matter how enticing.

She had to admit that Sorensson was in amazingly good physical condition for a man in his early sixties. Like many wealthy men she had met, he had the means to stay in shape, including a personal fitness room in every home. And he went regularly to Luxembourg to the Aqua Vita Mineral Spa. Money gave him an advantage on most men in stemming the insidious onslaught of age.

Smiling smugly, the woman eyed the closed door, knowing that none of his muscle toning and skin treatment would serve him well for another evening – not even for another hour. By then she would have finished her business. The American ambassador to the European Union, Richard Sorensson, was her contract. Nothing more, nothing less. The thought made her orgasmic, without the aid of a man – or a woman. She took a sip of the champagne he had poured.

The fact that he was a notorious womanizer, despite his position, enabled her to outwit his security shields of bodyguards and the armored limousine. The human libido was the most irrational of instincts and thus the most useful when manipulated. So far, this contract had been one of the easiest of her professional career.

Now, she was here, and everything on her agenda was moving forward with exquisite timing.

From the bathroom a discordant operatic strain rose and swelled. The woman reached into her purse for the little blue bottle disguised with the banal label *bicarbonate de soude*. She poured the white powder into the tall glass of champagne. The liquid fizzed to the top as the chemical mixed, then quickly settled back, retaining its original appearance and taste. Once swallowed, the drug would strike within two minutes. Her handsome target would sink into a deep sleep, his lifeline a bare thread until she cut it.

Having thoroughly cased this residential quarter of Brussels, the woman was confident that her escape tonight would be smooth. This contract would mark her third hit in Brussels in three years. She was convinced there was not a less threatening major city for a contract killer to work in. Yes, the heart and pulse of the European Union, Brussels was her favorite: easy to enter and, more importantly, easier to exit. Its hopelessly fragmented police system ensured her that response would be slow, inconsistent, and, more likely than not, ineffective. She'd be on a plane before the authorities even suspected what had happened.

Nevertheless, as a professional, she knew that carrying out an assignment in the field was never as simple as planned. She had been taught that operatives almost always met with surprises. For that reason she had devised unusual backup systems. And she always succeeded because like a modern alchemist she mixed new technology with her extraordinary imagination and clandestine techniques. Security guards and police investigators were chasing shadows. The criminal mind complemented the brilliance of scientists and engineers.

Tonight was no exception. *Here he comes.* She pointed those nipples at him.

Her target emerged from the bathroom exuding whiffs of expensive after-shave, his gray hair combed into place. He wore the blue robe and an open expression of lewd anticipation. His catch for the evening swung her elegant long legs over the side of the bed to greet him. Holding his eyes, she adjusted her garter belt, then reached for the champagne glass and offered it to him, smiling coquettishly.

"I'm happy to see you, Mr. Ambassador," she crooned. "A toast. That your cock is stretch-size like your limo. That gives me a lot to work with, *n'est-ce pas?*" She patted the bed then stroked her left thigh up to her crotch, still locking her catlike eyes with his.

Sorensson took the champagne glass from her and quickly downed its contents. "Okay, sweetheart, I'm ready to devour you and your purple pussy – and now!"

He pulled her roughly into his arms and covered her mouth with his, driving his tongue inside. She tugged him backwards toward the bed, which both encouraged and excited him.

"Lie back, *mon chéri*, and I'll give you a little massage," she whispered, nuzzling the base of his neck.

"Ah, that I could take, babe, but not for too long. You're torturing me!" He was getting hard.

He removed his robe and let it slip to the floor. Then he lay across the bed. She laughed deep in her throat before rolling him onto his chest. Straddling his buttocks, she began gently to massage his lower back, letting her hand rest for a second or two on a slight fold in his waist. With a low groan he turned around, pulled her to one side and kissed her on the bend of her arm.

"Come on!" She laughed again, but with urgency in her voice. "Let me finish, will you! I want to relax those muscles of yours."

"Not all of them, I hope!" Grudgingly, the ambassador rolled back onto his front, burying his face in the pillow. "Mmm, is that some kinky thing of yours, massaging me with silk gloves on?"

She smiled and continued kneading his neck. "Relax, you sex fiend! Just lie there and close your eyes. You boss others around all day long. Let me boss you tonight. I'll show you how to get that VIP stress out of your system. You'll see," she purred.

"I know I will, I know. But, still, I'd rather feel y-o-u-r f-i-n-g ..." Sorensson's voice suddenly grew weak. His breath growing heavier, his chest heaved in the effort to breathe. He then slipped into a deep sleep, his face still buried in the pillow.

The woman felt his body go limp, detecting the exact moment he lost consciousness. He was now utterly vulnerable. She swung her silk-clad legs around him to get off the bed. Next, she rolled him on his back, threw his right arm over his eyes, then covered his nude body with the sheet. His thick member was losing its girth. "Poor prick," she muttered. A perfect pose for someone who appeared to be comfortably asleep, which, for the moment at least, was more true than not.

Now for the final episode. She opened her small black evening bag and carefully peeled back its lining, revealing a secret compartment. Inside was a hypodermic needle loaded with enough pure heroin to kill three men. She lifted Sorensson's left arm to expose his hairy armpit. Then, with a short sharp stabbing motion, she plunged the syringe directly into the vein leading to her victim's heart. The deadly drug would travel the shortest route, killing Sorensson in a few minutes. She placed the syringe back in her purse. She'd leave no trace. *They'll have the body; that's enough. Let them work.*

Next, she fastened a pulse monitor-transmitter disguised as a digital watch to Sorensson's right wrist. The transmitter would give her an accurate reading of what was happening in his body while she departed from the area.

She stepped back from the bed, dressed carefully, and fluffed out her short-cropped hair at the dressing-table mirror. Looking and feeling as composed as she had upon entering the room less than an hour ago, she glanced around for a last check.

"Oh yes, *les pommes frites*," she murmured. She couldn't resist the temptation to taste one french fry, now cold, a remnant of the dinner they had not touched. Ever wary, she picked it up with a napkin so as not to stain her purple gloves, *the poor fool's sexual fetish*, she thought with amusement.

Jackie Markovic cautiously opened the door to the hallway. The Do Not Disturb sign hung on the bedroom doorknob. The ambassador had bragged to her about how he had adopted this hotel system in every house he owned. The staff, he had pompously informed her, knew it would mean immediate termination if they bothered him when his sign was hanging outside. She blew the dying man a kiss, turned off the room lights, stepped into the hallway, closed the door behind her, and confidently descended the stairs.

She found Gérard in the reception hall at the foot of the stairs, a brooding look on his face as he watched television, popping one potato chip after another into his mouth. She was on full alert, her finger on a small automatic pistol in her raincoat pocket.

"It looks like the ambassador worked too hard this evening," she said, with a tart wink, in her deliberate French-accented English from underneath her rain hood. "Better let him sleep late tomorrow. No, don't disturb yourself," she added, moving to the front door while pulling the hood tighter around her face as if against the dampness outside. "I've already called a taxi from the bedroom. It should be here any moment now."

Since his retirement from the local police force five years before and his subsequent post with Ambassador Sorensson, Gérard had seen scores of women come and go from the master's bedroom. She noticed his bored and disapproving frown. He escorted her to the front door and opened it without comment, watching her uninterestedly as she walked down the wet steps, slipped through the tall gates of the residence, crossed a street that sparkled with rain puddles in the streetlights, and got in the waiting taxi. "Another *pute*," he thought, and turned back. The heavy iron gates closed as he pushed a button.

She glanced back. He was already returning to his television. She was sure he hadn't noticed the ripped scrap of crumpled newsprint she had dropped on the wet stones of the residence's interior driveway.

Peter, Jackie's assistant, was waiting in a taxi he had hot-wired a few minutes earlier. Middle-aged, of average height and square bulk, Peter had been working with Jackie for nearly a decade. This mission was different; she realized it was robbing Peter of many a night's sleep. *So far*, she thought, *he had done well in hiding his consternation.* Like now, as he struggled to keep his generous-featured face from betraying his nervousness. But Peter's face telegraphed his fears nonetheless, and perspiration trickled down his forehead. She watched like a deadly cat as he tried to conceal the signs of anxiety by greeting her with a smile as she walked toward him with her sure, long *I-DID-IT* strides. His smile didn't fool her, but she said nothing and climbed in the back seat. Peter eased the taxi away from the curb, drove to the end of the tree-lined street, and stopped.

He handed his boss the radio receiver connected to the monitor-transmitter on the ambassador's wrist. The digital reading showed that her victim's pulse rate was falling rapidly. Jackie smiled, satisfied that the death process was now irreversible. As Peter drove on, she kept an eye on the receiver until they were out of range.

They turned onto a narrow side street off the Boulevard de Waterloo, the chic shopping street of Brussels, where they abandoned the stolen taxi. She got out first, motioned as if paying, and walked away. He followed. Their rented Mercedes awaited them. The woman quickly scanned the area. The only sign of life was a stray cat that scurried across the narrow road into a darkened doorway, where it sat motionless, its ears flattened and its alert eyes watching the pair intently.

Peter unlocked the Mercedes door, put on a chauffeur's hat and slid behind the wheel; Jackie climbed into the back seat. They followed the city's back roads. Destination: Maastricht, the Dutch city across the Belgian-Dutch border, made famous by the treaty that had changed European Community to European Union in the 1990s.

En route, Peter pulled into a parking area off the autoroute. There he changed into a business suit and Jackie changed into her latest Escada outfit before joining him in the front seat for this portion of the trip. She was confident that when they arrived at the General Aviation terminal at Maastricht Airport, Peter would look like a wealthy businessman traveling with his girlfriend.

Their leased executive jet from Geneva sat with its two-pilot crew waiting for them. It was a sleek orange-red Lear 55. Two wide white stripes were painted along its wings and body, while its tail displayed a white cross flag. The aircraft was fueled, cleared, and ready to fly.

Peter suddenly grabbed at his stomach.

"Is your ulcer playing up?" Jackie asked. "You don't look too good today."

"I just want to get airborne and the hell out of here," he replied.

Jackie had the exact opposite desire. She would have liked to stay in Brussels long enough for some mussels and more *frites* and her favorite white wine near the Grand-Place. And it would have been worthwhile to stop by her favorite back-street bar, seedy and down-and-out, filled with decadent characters and great underground contacts. However, because of their Geneva interim destination, time ruled. She had accepted, though reluctantly, that she would have to wait on the mussels and wine for a subsequent visit to her favorite European city. That was fine with her – she was used to the small sacrifices that came with this line of work.

Peter, however, was another matter. From the minute she contracted for this hit, she had watched him grow uneasy and nervous. Another agent who felt the way Peter had about this mission would be miles away by now. Not Peter. He was too faithful to let her down or turn his back on her. But now she was concerned that his anxiety could give them both away. It had been drilled into her since childhood that a skilled operative always displays a composed demeanor and a poker face. She'd have to come up with a cure for his case of nerves – *top priority, that one*, she thought.

One and a half hours later, the two conspirators peered out of the rain-spattered window of their jet. The winds and storm clouds which had greeted them as they were cleared by the tower were still with them over the Jura mountains and into Switzerland. The weather had improved by the time the aircraft made its approach to Cointrin Airport in Geneva.

From the jet window Jackie could hardly see through the menacing shades of gray and black. She knew this bad weather meant they were in for a few bumpy moments before landing. Always a fatalist, Jackie was surprised that her palms were prickling with beads of sweat.

"Peter, in this kind of weather I'm relieved and apprehensive at the same time. Do you feel the same way?"

"You look tired and irritable, Jackie," he answered evasively. "Now, don't start asking me questions. Wait until we are safely in the car." His voice was tight and serious.

"Sorry," she mocked, reaching to run her fingers through his hair. "I must have forgotten that you don't like talking about danger while an operation is still in progress. But, darling, you know it gives me a high. It's stimulating to discuss the danger. It excites me." She turned to face him. "And you've done well, too." *At least in the past*, she added to herself. "It was so satisfying to plunge the needle into Sorensson's vein."

"Come on, knock it off! Don't be a bitch. Leave it till we're in the car. Okay?" Peter's heavy jaw drooped and his face lost its color. Again, she was irritated by his behavior. *No longer the cool partner he used to be*, she thought.

"Oh, sorry to bother you, sir. But keep one thing in mind, darling Peter; we've executed successfully a hit against a superpower official. Something which you told me was too dangerous to try. What's with you these days, anyway?"

Peter kept his gaze forward and didn't respond.

Jackie didn't press him further. He'd relax, she decided, once they cleared immigration and the customs checkpoint. She herself was always attacked by waves of apprehension at that aspect of her mission – even if the immigration checkpoint was on familiar ground. Whatever the cause of Peter's nervousness, she decided he had to overcome it to be of continued use to her.

Peter and Jackie exchanged a quick glance as they prepared for their landing in Switzerland. Once through Swiss immigration at the Geneva airport, they were safe. From the airport, it would be a few minutes to the French border. Their arrival had been carefully timed. Geneva's airport closes at midnight, except for emergencies, allowing the locals a good night's sleep.

The sleek orange-red Lear 55 skipped onto the wet runway. Water sprayed from its nose-wheel as if from a Riva powerboat. Blue lights marked the way.

Peter turned to his companion and smiled. "*Hamdallah sallama*," he said, borrowing the Arabic expression to thank God for a safe arrival. She replied by blowing him a kiss. It was her mark, a signature of sorts.

The small aircraft rolled to the west end of the airport, close to its home terminal. The ground staff was waiting – efficient, concerned, and eager to clock out for the day. Smartly dressed in tailored, dark blue suits, two young men helped the couple down the four-step ladder extending from the sleek jet's exit door.

Jackie stood in the doorway. She was pleased that her long, shapely leg caught everyone's eyes. Those legs were her ticket to so many places. They were truly her built-in *laissez-passer*.

The party dashed across the rain-soaked parking ramp to the charter terminal's one-man immigration office. This would be the last stress point. Peter's leased car was waiting. After the Swiss clearance, they would disappear for a few days on the French Riviera to cleanse their trail even further. From there they'd go to their respective safe havens – hers in Palma de Mallorca, his in his native Athens. They would rest for a couple of weeks, and make sure they were safe, before meeting again in

Geneva. There she'd verify that her numbered bank accounts had been appropriately boosted by Ibrahim, the new contact with their primary Middle Eastern assassination contractor.

Chapter Four

Washington, D.C.
May 29th

Brenda ignored the elevator and took the steps two at time to the fifth floor. She opened the door to her office, simultaneously flinging her briefcase to the floor next to her desk, slid into her chair, and jabbed her computer on. A scant second later, her monitor demanded a password. Brenda Straus, special agent in charge of the Middle East Unit of the FBI Counter-terrorism Section, stabbed the keyboard impatiently. WATSON, and her birthday. At times she resented the seconds it took for the mainframe to respond to her code. She needed every second this morning, for in ninety minutes she was to face an angry president and a shocked world. The screen scrolled, then stopped, waiting for her next command. She was in. Additional keystrokes sent the computer on a search errand into its memory bank.

She glanced at her digital watch – 05:45.

Forty minutes earlier, the shrill of the phone carrying the agitated voice of her section chief, Bob Hutchins, had awakened her at her Georgetown apartment.

"Brenda? It's Bob. Get out of that bed. Now! And get your *derrière* down to the Bureau!"

"Bob? What's up? World War Three?"

45

"Close. Sorensson's dead, for Christ's sake."

"What happened? You were in Brussels last week to interview him. Dear God. Don't tell me the Libyans got him?"

"Could be, but Jesus it's weird. And we don't have a scrap of evidence yet. Our Belgian police friend, Guy, will fill us in later today. We'll talk more later. Just get down there. Right now the dear prez has summoned the director to the White House. Judge Baker is to see The Man at 8:30 sharp. You know how close the president was to Sorensson. He wants answers. That means answers from us. Me, and you! Judge Baker wants a briefing memo on Sorensson. We meet him at 7:00. That should be just enough time before he leaves for the White House. So haul ass, young lady!"

"Okay. I'm up, and I'll be out of here in five minutes. What about Guy in Brussels? Should I...?"

"I've already called. We tracked him down in his favorite bar and followed with a flash cable. We need his initial impressions within the hour. It's gonna be a long day, Brenda."

Now, in the quiet of her office, only the computer hummed and beeped. Still reeling from Hutchins's call, Brenda swirled around in her chair to peer out of the window onto Pennsylvania Avenue. Sunlight was beginning to brighten the sky as a *Washington Post* truck driver dropped off the morning edition at a corner kiosk. The nation's capital was beginning to stir.

Sorensson dead. No! Assassinated! No question about that. Her gut knew it. It had just been a matter of time. Soon, speculations about his death would bounce from one edge of the USA to another. From one corner of the world to another. This was big. The wording of her report would be crucial to the investigation. The report must also help calm the fears and confusion of every American diplomatic officer abroad.

The director's request for her presence meant that a Middle

East connection was suspected. But who in the Middle East? Libyans seemed obvious. Too obvious, maybe. Why Sorensson? Why now?

These days, whenever the Bureau faced a tough case with even the hint of a Middle East flavor, the director assigned her to it. She had earned that distinction. But now the pressure was on. Sorensson had been one of the president's closest friends. The chief executive would not let this blow over.

The FBI had recruited her at the age of twenty-six, shortly after she had received her doctorate in languages and linguistics from Georgetown University. Initially she had been hired as a contract translator for telephone taps and electronic eavesdropping operations, but was quickly promoted to super-analyst. In 1986 she was allowed into the Special Agent program because of the role her analysis played in the identification, arrest, and conviction of Jonathan Pollard, the Israeli espionage agent in the US Defense Department. It was the Pollard case, in fact, that put Brenda on the map.

During her ten years at the Bureau, Brenda had constantly been reminded that she had broken records in climbing the rungs of the FBI career ladder. The Bureau management told her frankly that she was earmarked to rise far and fast. But she knew that while her performance often left management proud, it also made not a few agents envious. The resentment her successes provoked in some of her colleagues, male and female, was the only problem she found at work. The marginal special agents mumbled that she was always ahead of them because the Bureau wanted to look good, pushing a woman forward. But Brenda was confident that the top agents knew she was one of their best.

While she had broken professional-advancement records, it was only too clear that she had not broken many hearts – which was her plan. She kept her frizzy hair coiffed like a mop, and never relinquished her brown-framed glasses. She refused contact lenses, hiding her pretty green eyes. She wanted to be judged wholly on her achievements, and so pushed to the background any underlying prettiness. The fact that she could be a pretty woman would have no consequence on her career.

Her plain apparance didn't bother Brenda. The intellectual and emotional challenges she faced nearly every day at the Bureau were a lot more important and much less superficial than looks. Her profession as a law enforcement officer was everything to her. She was a natural. Born to the job. She wanted to be the best special agent the Bureau had ever had. With her brains, her languages, her instincts, she was convinced all she needed was a few breaks. No one would ever be able to accuse Special Agent Straus of sleeping her way up the ladder.

Brenda also compensated for her lack of natural beauty with considerable effort at accentuating her physical strength. During the many years she spent at Georgetown she swam daily, and worked her way up to a black belt in karate. This physical prowess had helped her excel at the tough FBI Academy at Quantico, Virginia. Plus, it kept her weight under control and her energy levels high.

Her life would have been almost perfect at this stage if her father had not broken with her over the Pollard affair. A dedicated Zionist, Democratic Party activist, former political appointee, and lawyer, in that order, Sidney Straus had made it clear to his daughter that he couldn't stomach the public disclosure of her role in convicting Pollard. After she had testified against Pollard, her father told her she had betrayed her Jewish origins and faith. *The man had compromised our national security, dad*, she had pleaded with him, but he refused to hear it.

She had always admired and loved her father dearly, despite

his patriarchal manner. His unreasonable reaction to her federal police duties devastated her, while her mother's understanding and support only fueled the explosive situation further.

Although heartbroken by the feuding at the Straus home over her career, Brenda was determined not to apologize to her father for doing what any patriotic American in her position would have done: defend the United States against a traitor. Even if that nation was Israel. Particularly now that the Israelis had admitted Pollard was their agent.

She shook her head to clear the web of thoughts that distracted her from the crisis at hand, and focused on the flickering screen instead. Sorensson's profile stared back at her.

He was a good-looking man. Or perhaps distinguished-looking was a better description. Well-dressed and well-groomed, with a physical appearance implying culture and affluence. Reading his biographical information confirmed this analysis.

As Brenda punched a few keys, Sorensson's close relationship with the president scrolled before her:

Roommates at Yale Law School.

Best man at Congressman Douglas's wedding.

Godfather to Senator Douglas's first-born, Amelia.

Supportive friend to the widowed Vice President Douglas.

Campaign manager for Douglas's presidential election.

A picture of a beaming Sorensson, looking on as Douglas took his oath of office, spoke of his deep feelings for his president.

After that came Sorensson's ambassadorial post in comfortable Brussels. President Douglas had bestowed this coveted post on Sorensson partly to reward him and partly to remove him from Washington and its vulture-like media corps. They were ever eager for a good old-fashioned scandal, and Sorensson had a near-compulsive appetite for beautiful women.

Still, the fool never gave up this vice, thought Brenda, her lips thinning. *When it came to females, he was a real liberal!* He loved them all, and was a true multiculturalist.

A couple of paragraphs down, the screen displayed data on Sorensson's Libyan contacts. The FBI was deeply concerned about those contacts and had sent Special Agent Robert Hutchins to Brussels both to interview Sorensson and to caution him against possible assassination attempts. *I wish he had listened*, Brenda thought, then brightened as her thoughts veered into a different channel. *Time to call Guy. He must be in his element now.*

Guy van den Heuven, Belgian Judiciary Police commissioner, had the demeanor of Inspector Clouseau and the effectiveness of James Bond – one of Europe's most celebrated crime busters. Brenda was always amused by his flamboyance and impressed with his results. Her smile broadening, she imagined Guy in Brussels fighting off the media with relish and making good use of his countless influential contacts to uncover the facts surrounding the murdered ambassador. She warmed to the idea of working again with him. Secretly she acknowledged that he was one handsome man, and figured she didn't stand a chance with him. *Don't mix things*, she was perpetually reminding herself.

Brenda had met van den Heuven a few months before when he made an official trip to Washington. His dark combed-back hair and his mustache and square jaw gave him a raw sexuality – which he was well aware of, and used to full advantage as a divorced man in Europe's capital. Apart from having a long professional history with the FBI, Guy was close personally to Bob Hutchins. Their friendship went back to Bob's days as legal attaché at the American Embassy in Brussels. They had shared many a bottle of wine.

Guy and Bob had worked together on several international criminal and terrorist cases during the latter's overseas stint. Bob saw in Guy an acutely perceptive investigator with a terrific sense of humor. "Guy has the best instincts of any police official in the world, even when he is distracted by the skirts strutting by," he had told Brenda. Hutchins was fond of the somewhat dated term *skirt* and for him a woman was always a *gal*.

Van den Heuven was rarely surprised by human vice or frailty. It could even be said that the source of his passion for the profession was human weakness. His father had hoped he'd follow in his footsteps as an anthropologist, but Guy gave the lineage a little twist. *"Cherchez la femme"* was his favorite expression: "Look for the woman," which translated into the practical tactic of looking for the suspect's vice to uncover the motivation. Guy's only failing, which to Brenda was excused by his background and surroundings, was his vanity. "A typical continental" was how Hutchins described him to Brenda before they had all met in Washington. Americans were so naive, so simple, but so much fun, according to Guy. He was perpetually impressed with the American capacity for trust. To him that was the American Achilles' heal, their propensity for believing another person's word – so un-European, so unlike the way almost every other culture functioned. So endearing. "If I were a crook, I'd definitely pick the United States as my home. So easy to work. 'He went that-a-way,'" Guy would mock, "and all the cops run the other way."

Brenda had been struck both by Guy's charm and his keen professional instincts.

After a moment, while the international phone lines tried to connect her, Brenda got through to Guy's office in Brussels. But her luck wasn't any better than Bob's. Guy was still out.

What was taking him so long? She needed his preliminary

findings, limited though they might be. Sorensson's assassination had put the Bureau in an embarrassing situation. The murder a few days after Hutchins had interviewed him was going to raise questions as to the efficiency of the Bureau's Counter-Terrorism Section. Where was the protection? the president would ask.

A political pressure-cooker that could explode, the case had the potential of becoming a media disaster. Brenda realized its potential political fallout. The Pollard case would pale in comparison.

With those unruly thoughts, Brenda momentarily lost objectivity. Then she gathered herself and continued to take data from her computer files and add them into her report. It was almost 7:00 a.m. A meeting this early in the morning was highly unusual. Obviously the old man wanted help in facing President Douglas. Russell, the national security adviser, would be present, and he'd have questions too.

Brenda hoped, for the Bureau's sake, that Judge Baker had already briefed the president and secretary of State on the FBI's conviction that Sorensson maintained an unacceptable level of contact with foreign hoods. Sorensson's contacts included Hamed bin Fezzani, the Libyan ambassador to Belgium. He was a cousin of the Libyan leader and known in certain circles as the head of Libyan intelligence operations throughout Western Europe, using his ambassadorial position as a pretext to travel unimpeded in his Falcon 50 executive jet. Sorensson had met with him on numerous occasions.

After Bob Hutchins got off the phone with Brenda he began dressing for his meeting with the director. He held two socks in his hand – one black and one dark blue – as he whispered aloud, "Brenda and Guy, you guys better save my butt on this one."

He went into his kitchen and groped for the can of Maxwell House to fill his automatic machine. A confirmed bachelor, Bob could make toast and coffee. He could even squeeze oranges in his electric juicer. After that, his cooking repertoire fell off rapidly. Grilled cheese, if he felt inspired.

He had just switched on the coffee-maker when the phone rang. He dashed into the living room to pick it up.

"Bob Hutchins here."

"Bob!"

"Guy!"

"Mon ami, how are you? Long time we did not speak – I hear you were in Brussels and did not call. Too busy, I suppose. We'll catch up this time. I know why you're calling. Why you don't come over, my friend, for a good dinner? Monique and me – you remember Monique, my assistant? We found this new restaurant, Le Petit Lapin, *magnifique*! It's even better than the ones you and I visited too much!"

"Guy, I already feel better, just hearing your voice." Hutchins slumped his 6'2", 210-pound frame into the armchair near the door, one sock on, the other in his hand, giving full attention to his European counterpart.

The two men exchanged a few more pleasantries before Guy continued in a professionally urgent tone.

"Brenda called me too. My regrets for the death of your Ambassador Sorensson. I already went to the house. What do you Americans always say? All hell broke loose? This is big news, *mon ami*, and Guy van den Heuven is here to find answers soon!" Guy chuckled softly, knowing Bob accused him of being conceited. "I think, Bob," he said more seriously, "this was a hit, maybe a Middle East operation. Also, no strange fingerprints; all the marks of a professional. You should come *tout de suite*, my friend. That means today, tomorrow at the latest. Your new legal attaché is little good. Nice man, but no experience in international crime and as ready for terrorism as Donald Duck. He and your embassy security officer fight now for authority over the investigation. So come quickly, *mon ami*, and save me from these American pencil pushers! And bring *la petite,* the brilliant Brenda. Do not let them force you to bring the usual too many investigators. We only need you and Brenda."

"Consider it done, Guy," said Bob. "I'm so damn glad you're working with us on this. We meet with the director this morning to prepare him for his meeting with the president. You know Sorensson was Douglas's closest friend. We may wind up spending the morning in the Oval Office, helping the old man explain to the president how and why his buddy could get whacked. If you can't find me, stay in close touch with Brenda. We'll get to Brussels – probably tomorrow, okay? Do you have anything else?"

"Give me a few hours."

"As you get more send it the safe way. I'll check in every hour."

"*Oui! Oui*, Bob. *Pas de problème*. Remember Françoise, my secretary? She'll find me wherever. Send me details on your ambassador's contacts with those Libyans. I know this was a problem for you at the Bureau. We must work together, my friend, with what you have and what we find here. *D'accord?*"

"*Oui, monsieur*! I already have Brenda at the Bureau pulling data together from the central file. We'll get it out to you today through our office in Brussels." Trailing the long phone cord, Bob walked back into the kitchen for his orange juice; he refused to get a cordless, sure he'd forget where he'd laid it down. "Just ignore the bureaucratic games in our embassy. Their pretensions have little to do with the policy-level realities you and I are going to have to face. Oh – what's the piece of evidence suggesting it might've been a Middle East operation? I'll need to know that when I see Baker this morning."

"Mon cher Robert, it was a small piece of newsprint from an Arabic newspaper, found just inside the gate. *Entre nous*, my men missed it. I saw it when I arrived after them. We are checking to see which journal this is from. We think Baghdad. But hard to know when this piece was dropped, or if someone left it there on purpose. So, we do not know how important this is. I do not want our bosses to get excited about something we are not sure of. I think no need to mention this now, but it is up to you." Guy paused for a few seconds to give Bob time to digest. "We do not know for sure what killed the ambassador. No apparent wounds. We took blood samples and I will have the results in an hour. I will get back to you on this. Try to calm your embassy monkeys. I don't want anyone trying to nab the body from our morgue."

"Leave that to me, but you'll only get seventy-two hours before we'll have to yield to the family wishes. So move."

"Seventy-two hours is an eternity, *mon ami*."

"Good. Let me know the minute you have anything solid. By mid-morning Washington will be berserk over the news, wanting answers and making absurd guesses. All of that shit'll be on my head! So keep the information coming. I'll speak to you in a few hours. *Bonne chance*, Guy."

"Au revoir. Courage! Guy van den Heuven will help you find the bastards!"

Laughing at Guy's humorous audacity and his keen affection for American-style cussing, Hutchins put the phone down and strode out of the apartment. No one would notice the two different colored socks.

FBI Headquarters

Six a.m. at the Bureau headquarters on Pennsylvania Avenue, and Brenda Straus was still fixed to her screen. She had assembled everything she could find on the victim. On her PC she pulled that information together into a fuller dossier, then affixed to it the FBI files on the Libyan whom Sorensson had been meeting in Brussels over the past six months – much to the consternation of the State Department, the FBI, the CIA, and the Israeli government.

Most of the text was in English, but some information from the Belgians was in French, which Brenda easily scanned. Her language talents also included German, Spanish, Hebrew, Greek, a smattering of Dutch, and elementary Arabic. As she was unit chief for the Middle East, she was working on bringing that last up to the same fluency as her main languages.

Contemplating the information displayed on her monitor, she found it peculiar that the White House, while claiming to be deeply concerned about Sorensson's personal diplomacy efforts, had not ordered him to terminate his Libyan encounters. *We have to get to the bottom of that,* she thought, *even if he's dead. That's one question for the president.*

Hutchins, as chief of the Counter-Terrorism Section, had urged the director to speak with the president regarding Sorensson's Libyan interlocutor. Brenda had also written an urgent memorandum to the director, stressing Hutchins's recommendations and hoping the director would communicate her concerns to President Douglas. Her memorandum had stated unequivocally that Sorensson's meetings with the Libyans were dangerous and should cease, that US policy prohibited a direct representative of the president from meeting with a terrorist chief. Thus, fortunately, she had covered herself and the Bureau.

According to the Bureau's information from the White House and from State Department officials, Sorensson had explained these contacts to the president and claimed to have had his approval to continue them. She had always assumed that Sorensson had argued that such a confidential, unofficial exchange was necessary to persuade the Libyans to abandon terrorism, to convince them that that was the only way to establish favorable relations with the United States – something the Libyans had been actively seeking for years.

At meetings she had attended, however, the State Department and the FBI had agreed that the Libyans would gain more from these conversations than would the US. Furthermore, on behalf of the FBI, Brenda had warned that the Libyans might be conducting the sessions to size up the ambassador as a target. And that was the part that bothered Brenda and her boss the most.

Brenda was engrossed in the political complexities of the case when Hutchins arrived, startling her. "Brenda, I hope you realize this is it. The case of our lives! As I said, the director wants to see *you* there. More than he wants *me*, I think."

"You're the specialist in terrorism," Brenda protested, adjusting her glasses. She swiveled her chair to face her boss. "But I agree. I had that sensation this morning on my way here. And my intuition tells me that this is even bigger than we think. But, we first have to identify the killer or killers." She patted the PC and frowned slightly as if the answer was on the hard drive.

"For instance," she continued, "I pulled the file on all the assassinations in Brussels over the past three years. There have been four. Sorensson is the fifth. First victim was a Syrian diplomat. Two Muslim sheiks went next – they were involved in the Salman Rushdie affair. Probably a hit by the Iranians. The fourth was Dr. Bull, the ballistics scientist." She paused, chewed on her lip, took her glasses off, and rubbed her eyes.

"None of these killings is close to being solved," she continued. "Did it ever occur to you, Bob, that there's someone out there – or more than one – who believes Brussels is a pretty easy place to eliminate enemies?" She put her glasses back on and re-examined the information on her screen.

"Clearly, the killer's a professional, hired by the Iranians, the Iraqis, or the Israelis – though somehow I doubt the last."

"Could be because you're biased?" Bob laughed teasingly.

Brenda nodded, smiling. "Could be. The trouble is we won't know who's behind these hits if we don't find the killers. So instead of getting lost in endless speculation about why anyone would want to kill good ole sleazy Richard Sorensson, we should concentrate on finding the hit man." She could tell from the look on Bob's face that the note of sarcasm in her voice concerning White House feelings was not lost on him.

He rubbed his temples with his fingertips, apparently trying to relax the tension already building. "You're right. That's obvious," he replied, glancing at his watch. "But first we have to stop theorizing and get that damn memo for our meeting with Baker. As factual as possible, with no assumptions or conclusions. Very clinical. Okay?" He then told her what Guy had reported about the scrap of Arabic newspaper.

"The first draft is almost finished. All I need is Guy's preliminary report."

"Jesus! Brenda, you're a life saver! Run off a copy of what you got while I send a message to Brussels to speed things up. Have we received anything from our people there?"

"Yes, but nothing of value. Guy's information is what we need the most."

Fifteen minutes later Guy called again and, as promised, provided more details. With his information Brenda had gained a crucial degree of credibility in her memo for the director and brought it "up to the minute," as Judge Baker was fond of saying. She started printing the final draft.

As the pages slid from the laser printer, Bob grabbed them to proofread.

"I like the heading – 'Death of Ambassador Richard Andrew

Sorensson in Brussels.' You don't beat around the bush and yet you haven't used the word 'assassination' in a formal document. You're right. No place this morning for assumptions."

At 6:45 Hutchins signed the briefing memo. He put on his jacket and opened the office door. "Great job! Ready to roll?"

"All set?" She picked up her briefcase, locked both the inner and outer doors, and joined him in the corridor.

The elevator ride to the ninth floor was silent. While Brenda was mentally checking the important points to cover in the meeting, Bob looked distracted. She wondered what he was thinking.

On their way out of the elevator on the ninth floor, they spotted Chuck Borland, assistant director of the Criminal Investigation Division, and Austin Phillips, assistant director of the Counter-Intelligence Division, both in shirtsleeves and suspenders. Engaged in a hushed conversation, the two men were heading toward the director's door. Hutchins opened it graciously, waving the two senior officials in first.

"Good morning, gentlemen," Hutchins ventured.

"Good morning my ass, Mr. Hutchins!" responded Borland, his thin, elongated face flushed. With a cursory nod in Brenda's direction, he continued. "Bob, your butt's on the griddle! You better have some good answers this morning, or we'll all be transferred to the Okefenokee Swamp."

Phillips said nothing, but smiled thinly. Brenda knew that smile, dreaded by all FBI agents. She had long ago learned that agents gave Phillips's oversized body more room than it needed. His narrow black eyes, shiny black, bushy hair and eyebrows, and beaked nose associated him visually with the vulture he was in human affairs. Brenda saw him as a ruthless professional who never granted an adversary a second chance. Like a vulture he would circle and wait for his prey to make a critical error; then he'd strike, splattering as much bureaucratic blood and guts as possible. She'd heard plenty of stories in the corridors to confirm her assessment of him.

Phillips's eyes narrowed to slits as he studied Hutchins's surprised, flushed face, but Bob did not rise to the bait. Phillips would have to wait for another opportunity to draw blood.

"Good morning, lady and gentlemen. Please have a seat in the conference room." Bob and Brenda were saved by the peppy greeting from Kate Sumner, the director's secretary.

Kate had been with Baker since his judgeship in South Carolina. A sun-weathered veteran executive secretary of fifty-six, Ms. Sumner had reportedly adjusted to the Washington bureaucracy much better than the Judge. Brenda had heard that her counterparts around town considered her "one tough bitch," a woman no one should ever cross. Rumor had it that she was responsible for initiating FBI investigations to pay back social slights in Washington.

The four of them walked into the conference room and stood at a side table bearing coffee and pastries. Hutchins promptly poured himself a coffee, then took his cup to the conference table and waited for the others to join him.

Phillips pounced on Hutchins the minute everyone was seated.

"I read the report of your interview with Richard Sorensson earlier this month, Hutchins," he began. "I have the feeling – intuition, I might say – that something is missing." He paused.

No one reacted.

He proceeded. "Did you, for one reason or another – shortage of time, confusion, perhaps – leave something out of your report? Try to remember what's missing, it might help us," he added.

Spearing Phillips with a contemptuous look, Hutchins replied in a cold, flat voice, "Austin, I remember quite well. I was the guy who became concerned about Ambassador Sorensson's contacts with the Libyans in the first place." He calmly took a few sips of coffee. "True, I didn't have much to go on at first, including from your shop. Then, when more evidence surfaced, I became convinced there was more to Sorensson's contact with the Libyans than he was telling State. Maybe even more than he was telling the White House." A few more coffee sips.

"Then we had the surprise of a Belgian surveillance report last month, confirming my suspicion. In fact, when the Belgians tailed the Libyans, we learned that Sorensson had at least one contact with Hamed bin Fezzani that he *didn't* report to anyone. So, I got permission, via a memo to Judge Baker, which Brenda here prepared – then I flew to Brussels for an initial interview with Sorensson.

"The key revelation from that interview, which I deliberately left out, was that by the time it was over I had serious doubts about my initial suspicions. I was no longer sure they'd been valid. Not that Sorensson cleared up any factual points – it was his manner more than anything else. He was extremely cool. He was also co-operative, forthcoming, and anything but worried.

"That left me so damn confused and off balance that I couldn't trust my instincts on this case. I opted to take extra care to be factual in my interview report – no speculative comments."

"Did we have taps on his office and home phones? I can't remember if we had, but I do know we discussed the issue." Phillips, obviously annoyed that Hutchins was fully in control, waited for the answer.

"Yes, we discussed it. And no, we didn't tap his phones. That had been turned down."

Brenda was sure he'd deliberately used the passive voice to remind Borland and Phillips of their refusal to sign off on his written request to the director to tap Sorensson's home phone – a precaution that would have been for Sorensson's own protection. It would also have caught members of his household staff who might be in contact with the Libyans.

Kate Sumner entered the conference room. "The director's ready for you all, lady and gentlemen."

They entered Judge Baker's lush office. Pale blue deep-pile carpet covered the wide expanse. Mahogany shelves lining two walls of one corner held an impressive collection of leather-bound legal tomes. The entire wall facing the door was a floor-to-ceiling window covered by a heavy satin drape in ascending shades of soft beige. In front of the window stood an imposing antique mahogany desk and a high-backed black leather chair, while a long black leather sofa, matching love seat, and a round table occupied rest of the room. Behind the sofa hung a splendid array of the judge's professional and personal honors and awards, including a historic photograph of himself and the Supreme Court chief justice in baggy shorts and Budweiser cap flanking a five-foot marlin.

To Brenda, Judge Baker seemed a kind man, level-headed, mild-tempered, and fair. It was clear to her he was also suave, canny, and astute. This rare combination of traits in a man of such power, balanced the predatory likes of Austin Phillips. Clearly, the judge had gained the respect and admiration of everyone who worked for him. Brenda thought him the perfect director. The ideal to aim for. *Maybe one day...*

When the group entered, Judge Baker was still in an animated conversation with Bruce Talbot, his political-appointee aide. Talbot was a public relations specialist to whom the director always spoke first on any high-profile case. Everyone in the Bureau knew his job was to ensure that the judge's public image was akin to those of Sir Lancelot – always saving the crown from an insidious enemy. Talbot told anyone who would listen that, in public relations, he who hits fust wins – a philosophy he considered a rarity among current public relations advisers in the government.

"Good day to you all," the director greeted them, as he moved over to the sofa and motioned for the four to follow. Talbot quickly seated himself next to his chief.

"Good morning, sir," replied Chuck Borland, while the others mumbled a similar response. Borland continued to lead the meeting. "It looks like a long day ahead for all of us, sir."

The director nodded impatiently.

"Mr. Hutchins," he said. "I want you to be the responsible agent in the Sorensson affair. And as agreed earlier over the phone, you have my permission to assign Special Agent Straus to this case." He turned to face Brenda. "I'm continually hearing good reports about you. Keep that up, Agent Straus."

"Thank you, sir," replied Brenda.

"Very well." The judge shifted in his seat and gave Hutchins his full attention. "I don't want to speculation on how the ambassador died – suicide or murder. Apparently, he died in his bed. Instead, please refresh my memory with some detail on why we placed the ambassador under investigation in the first place."

"Well, sir, back in July of last year," Hutchins began, "we were confidentially advised by a senior Belgian police contact that Sorensson was having a series of private meetings with the Libyan ambassador to Belgium, Hamed bin Fezzani. As you know, Fezzani is a cousin of the Libyan leader, Tarek Fezzani, and behind his ambassadorial cover he is the head of all Libyan intelligence in Europe, including assassinations and other terrorist activities." Hutchins inched to the edge of the love seat, resting his elbows on his knees. "I made an initial check with the Assistant Secretary of State for European Affairs to see if these contacts were being reported to Washington through routine embassy reports, as the Bureau had no independent intelligence to support this. The assistant secretary confirmed to me that Sorensson had forwarded no such reports.

"Next, I approached the White House chief of staff through official channels, to ask if there had at least been some reporting from Sorensson to the president's office on this Libyan contact. The chief of staff said Sorensson's reports to President Douglas were by telephone – there's no written record except White House notes. Our guess was the president had suggested to Sorensson to drop the contact, discreet as it apparently was, on the grounds that it was not consistent with US policy and might be misunderstood by our friends and the Congress if it leaked." Hutchins looked at each person seated.

Everyone was listening intently to his account. Brenda was ready to interject if he forgot anything.

"If you remember, sir," Hutchins said to Baker, "the reports from our liaison contact advised that the Sorensson-Libyan contact was ongoing. The Israeli minister of the interior mentioned the matter to our ambassador in Israel and asked for an explanation. That showed these meetings had the potential to erupt politically, because the Israelis themselves could make it known. I checked again with the White House and suggested we investigate.

"I summarized that in a memorandum to you and you signed off on the investigation, which allowed for at least one interview with Sorensson. However, my recommendation that we put a tap on his home phone was rejected by the Bureau."

"Hold on! I'm unaware of a request for a tap on Sorensson's phone," spluttered Judge Baker. "When did you make that request?" He turned to his secretary, frowning. "Did you see anything like this?"

"No, sir. I definitely did not!" Ms. Sumner looked at Hutchins with an air of incredulity that surprised Brenda. Brenda remembered the memo well. She had helped Bob compose it, but bit her lip as he continued in the same calm tone.

"Sir, I forwarded it through channels last November but it was returned to me." Hutchins purposefully avoided looking at the men sitting to his right.

Borland cut in hastily, "I returned that request to Bob because I didn't see how we could do it without bringing in the Belgian police. I didn't wish to share our problems with them more than necessary, at least not at that stage."

Openly distressed at the apparent bureaucratic bungle, the director waved his hand impatiently at Hutchins, directing him to continue.

"So you see, sir, what started as merely a potentially embarrassing situation has turned into something far more serious," Hutchins said, relieved that Judge Baker realized now that Borland had blocked telephone taps on this case.

"All right," resumed the director, "so that and a few other things led to your interview with Sorensson." He gestured to Ms. Sumner, who handed him a file.

"I've read your interview report and see he was cooperative and gave no hint of being upset by your leading questions," he said thoughtfully. "So why on earth would he kill himself a week later? Or, was he murdered? What's your best guess at this hour? Any chance of natural causes? That would save us all."

"Sir, I'll leave that response to Agent Straus. She's the one who did the research and prepared the report," Hutchins said in a rush. He slid Brenda's memorandum across the coffee table toward the director while she gave copies to Borland and Phillips.

All eyes shifted to Brenda.

She opened her copy and chose to address the question in Judge Baker's eyes. "Sir, first, I must stress that, based on the latest information we've received from the Belgians, Richard Sorensson's death looks like murder – a professional one, in fact.

"To this memorandum I've attached an analysis of the blood work done on Sorensson. His blood carried an abnormally high heroin level. Enough to kill a couple of men. This eliminates the possibility of accidental overdose, which we didn't suspect anyway. At first the Belgian authorities couldn't detect normal needle marks on his body to explain a drug injection. But a closer inspection exposed what appeared to be an injection wound in his left armpit. This is a sophisticated form of murder. Whoever killed the ambassador is a trained professional – knowledgeable in effective ways of killing."

Brenda flipped a few pages.

"This photo was transmitted electronically from Brussels a few minutes before our meeting. It's a picture of a watch found on Sorensson's body. But, gentlemen, it turns out not to be a watch – it's a small transmitter. The transmitter – perhaps to monitor the pulse – had been worn for several hours. His bodyguard and servants had never seen it before. The assassin attached it so he could be out of the house while the victim was still alive and yet monitor his victim till the end. This is no low-life killer, clearly!"

She turned some more pages. "Turn to page six – Sorensson had been dead for close to twelve hours when he was found at 10 a.m. Brussels time. We have three initial theories about how he could've been murdered. One, the killer's a woman who visited him the previous evening – certainly the last person known to have visited him. Apparently, an escort or prostitute. Two, it could be someone working in league with her who entered through a terrace door off his bedroom, which was left unlocked, perhaps by the woman. The third immediate possibility is that one of the domestic employees left the door open to allow the killer to enter while Sorensson was asleep after the woman left."

Brenda scanned her memo. "Based on the early information we have on hand, I'm convinced Sorensson's murder was planned, cased, and executed. And yet there is no apparent motive for doing away with Sorensson. So far, no one has come forward to claim responsibility for killing him. Nor were any papers or money taken. Several thousand dollars in cash and sensitive documents he had at home were left in place in the ambassador's clothing and in his desk drawer. Just like the hit against Dr. Bull, also in Brussels."

Judge Baker interrupted. "So, it seems I was right in alerting the president that the Bureau should brief him about Sorensson's death. But what exactly do I tell him and Russell? That's what I want to know. I can assure you, this won't be easy for the president to hear." He leaned back on the sofa, frowning.

Talbot cut in, now that the professional reporting was over. "Judge, I recommend," he started earnestly, "that you tell the president that, while tracking a dangerous terrorist, the Bureau found that Sorensson had been his target. And that in the process of our surveillance of the Libyan and his operatives, we discovered that they were moving in on Sorensson, using sexual ploys to set him up. Accordingly, we sent Special Agent Hutchins to Brussels to meet with Sorensson and warn him. He took the advice well and was most appreciative. At the same time, it must be emphasized that he have been a target of terrorists. Naturally, we should stress that the media be told only that an investigation is under way. Nothing more. We sure as hell don't want the press speculating if we can prevent it."

Phillips's light, whispered voice was heard next. "I couldn't agree more with what Mr. Talbot has recommended. I must add, however, that we have to get to the bottom of the Sorensson case, regardless of who murdered him. I sense there is a counterintelligence component here and our primary job is to discover who hired the killer – if, as Agent Straus believes, the killer is a professional."

Judge Baker nodded. "I agree. But I want Agent Hutchins to have overall responsibility for the investigation, with the assistance of Agent Straus.

"Thank you, gentlemen. I now have to prepare for my meeting with the president. Hutchins and Straus, please stay behind in my outer office. You and your memo will be going with me to the White House in a few minutes."

As Hutchins, Straus, and the others departed, Bruce Talbot remained for a private conference with Judge Baker.

In the outer office, Hutchins sighed. Brenda reminded him that they had survived the first round, but she realized he was now under greater pressure than before. They would soon hear what the president had to say about his knowledge of the Sorensson-Libyan connection. It was important to get that clarified with the president, however sensitive it might be for him.

Just as everyone was leaving the director's office, a young woman came into the reception area, her hands clasped nervously around a fax.

"Well, Jennifer, don't just stand there. What is it?" snapped Ms. Sumner.

"A secure transmission from the National Security Agency for Brenda Straus. I think it's urgent, or I wouldn't have interrupted."

"Okay. So you thought it was important! Instead of standing there, wringing the message, why didn't you give it to her!" said the older woman, taking the document from the young female messenger and handing it to Brenda, who was watching the scene with amusement.

Brenda read the top secret intercept quickly then silently passed it to Bob. "Interesting development," she whispered to him as they filed out of the room. "The Libyan ambassador in Brussels is reporting Sorensson's death to Tripoli by enciphered cable. And he is hysterical – saying they have to find out who did it or they'll be blamed because of their Brussels meetings with him. This complicates matters."

"Brenda, the answer's in Brussels. Guy's dinner guests will arrive for breakfast."

Chapter Five

Washington, D.C.
May 29th

The Executive Service guards saluted the FBI director's limousine as it pulled into the west rear gate of the White House. Ahead, at the White House entrance, a short stout figure was waiting. Dressed in an immaculate pin-striped suit and holding a leather briefcase, the man craned his neck to see which car was clearing the gates.

"It's that arrogant SOB Russell," muttered Judge Baker.

Bob and Brenda exchanged amused glances. Although they both agreed with Judge Baker's assessment of the assistant to the president for national security, they kept quiet, hopped out of the car and joined their boss, who was already walking toward the West Wing door at full speed.

Bill Russell spoke first, extending his hand. "Good morning, Judge Baker." He gave a nod in Bob and Brenda's direction as they followed the judge into the White House.

Russell, a fleshy, balding man in his early sixties, bore a remarkable likeness to the actor Telly Savalas. His background was purely academic: he had a doctorate in Middle Eastern affairs from George Washington University and prior to his appointment to the White House staff he'd been a political science professor and head of Middle East studies at the

University of Michigan. Brenda knew he was by nature not very practical, more theoretical, and thus had a hard time in the White House, dealing with fast-moving international events.

"The president sent me ahead to advise you that he's asked Senator George Johnson, Chairman of the Senate Armed Forces Committee, and Congressman Paul Owens, Chairman of the House Foreign Relations Committee, to sit in on your briefing," said Russell as if he were rehearsing a press release. "And, of course, our new Secretary of State will be here."

"That senator from New Hampshire is always around here, isn't he?" commented Baker. "I guess he's got his feelers out for the president's endorsement at the Republican convention. He'll be closest to the president now that Sorensson's dead."

The FBI director turned to Bob and Brenda as they entered the White House and walked into its main hall. "Since Johnson won the first primary in January, he's the man to watch."

Russell ignored the interruption, cleared his throat, and continued, "The Washington press corps badgered both congressmen earlier this morning to get their reaction to Sorensson's death and it will only get worse. The news arrived too late for their morning editions, but it'll be covered in the evening editions. CNN ran it live. Having both here will keep the investigation bipartisan" – Johnson was a Republican and Owens a Democrat – "without letting the meeting get too large."

"That's the president's prerogative," commented Judge Baker in his Southern drawl. "The facts, as the FBI collects them, won't change to suit who hears them, no matter how many parties are present!"

Bill Russell frowned. Brenda could see he was annoyed at not having received due credit for trying to defuse a potentially explosive partisan situation. Russell said nothing further as he led the group up the stairs that would take them to the East Wing and directly to the Oval Office.

President Howard Lee Douglas was standing behind his desk, his back to the door. He leaned forward, one arm outstretched, a hand resting on the curtains of the window in front of him. The other hand was buried in the pocket of his dark brown, snug-fitting trousers. He had taken off his jacket, revealing a light-blue shirt stretched taut across his chest. Brenda could read grief in his stance – head downcast, wavy gray hair in disarray, broad shoulders drooping. Anxiety, maybe anger, caused the fist in his pocket to open and close repeatedly.

Only once before had people seen Douglas this way – when he lost his wife a few years earlier. But then he had Sorensson by his side, giving him comfort, lending him support. Now once again he was suffering feelings too powerful to veil under the political mask. Brenda realized this was not going to be an easy meeting; she had been worried about fact and neglected the power of emotions at play here.

The new Secretary of State, George Bates, stood next to Douglas, speaking in low tones. The president seemed in a world of his own, turning his head when the door opened and the sound of footsteps entering the room reached him.

"Judge Baker, Agents Hutchins and Straus, and Dr. Russell," announced the president's secretary.

Douglas pulled away from the window, straightened to his full six feet and turned to face the three men and the woman who had come to try to explain how the American government had failed to protect his best friend.

Forgoing his usual warm greeting to visitors, he motioned for them to be seated in the middle of the large office. Then he went to the winged chair behind his desk and sat while the others jockeyed for the best seats. He fixed his tie, ran his hand through his hair, and rubbed his whiskery face.

"Judge Baker," he began, finding he must clear his throat. "I trust Bill Russell has already informed you that I felt it best to invite these two friends from The Hill to sit in on this briefing, as well as the Secretary of State. This way the two primary branches of government will share your initial information concerning the circumstances of the tragic death of my friend Dick Sorensson. Personally, I'm still having difficulty believing this could have happened. Go ahead, Judge."

Baker unzipped his black leather briefcase and took out several printed reports, among which was the summary memorandum Brenda had given him.

"Mr. President. First, on behalf of the Bureau and myself, I'd like to extend our deepest sympathy for the loss of your friend. We all know he was very close to you. I know this briefing will be difficult. But, given our official responsibilities," Baker said softly, "it must be done if we hope to get to the bottom of this."

He put his glasses on, opened the memorandum, and continued in a clear, strong, authoritative tone. "To save time, Mr. President, I'll read aloud the 'eyes only' memorandum which I will leave behind for you. After which, I'd like Special Agents Hutchins and Straus to add a few words. Bob and Brenda are our top specialists on terrorism."

"Terrorism?" the president said sharply.

Adjusting his glasses, the judge nodded and began to read from the memo, pausing only occasionally to glance up at the president. Brenda had always admired his cool, studied style in controlling a meeting, particularly a potentially explosive one like this.

"At approximately 10:00 a.m., Brussels time, on the twenty-ninth of May, Richard Andrew Sorensson, US Ambassador to the European Union, was found dead in his bed at his official residence. It is believed he had been dead for approximately twelve hours. At this time the Bureau has no firm information concerning the exact cause of death. We do, however, have unconfirmed information from the Belgian police that Richard

Sorensson died from an extraordinarily large dose of heroin..."

Several people in the room gasped.

"...most probably injected by an as-yet-unidentified assailant. As there is not a shred of evidence that Sorensson was a habitual user, the strong circumstantial evidence indicates that he was murdered.

"We are working in tandem with the State Department and the Belgian police to determine whether his murder was a personal or a political affair. And, in the case of the latter, whether it was the act of a state or a terrorist organization. We will suspend judgment on those two questions until we have enough facts to confirm one or the other."

Looking up from his briefing paper, Baker interjected, "Special Agent Hutchins will follow my comments with some informal observations, which we can't yet put into official report form."

Baker continued, the weight of his statement visable on his face. He knew the president was hanging on his every word. "We can unequivocally state, however, that Ambassador Richard Sorensson had been a subject of protective surveillance by the Bureau for the past three weeks. He had been informed last week, in Brussels, by Special Agent Hutchins, of this surveillance."

With his usual exquisite timing, he paused to allow the impact of this statement to sink in.

"The protective surveillance of Ambassador Sorensson had become a necessity because of his cultivation of a Libyan diplomatic contact in Brussels who, we suspected, had targeted him. Essentially it was a Catch 22 situation, with this Libyan contact being of potential benefit to the US while, at the same time, presenting a potential threat to a key American official.

"The exact nature of the Libyan official's interest in Richard Sorensson has yet to be determined, but, as the Arab official in question is suspected of playing a role in Libyan international terrorist operations, we had no recourse but to stay in close contact with Sorensson – at least until we determined the nature of the threat to him."

Judge Baker lowered the paper, indicating the end of the official text, and removed his glasses. "Now I would like to introduce Special Agent Robert Hutchins, who is in charge of our coverage of international terrorism and, as such, was assigned to interview Ambassador Sorensson."

"Thank you, sir," replied Bob, moving to the edge of the sofa. "First, some new information. Before we left the Bureau this morning, my colleague Special Agent Straus received a note from the National Security Agency. According to code-word intelligence in that message – about which I was unable to inform Judge Baker," he threw an apologetic glance at the judge, "the Libyan ambassador in Brussels appears to know absolutely nothing of Sorensson's death. He sent a wild message this morning reporting the news and telling the Colonel that the Libyans had to find out who did this or they'd be blamed because of his contacts with Sorensson. Therefore, we might not have such solid grounds for suspecting a Libyan terrorist involvement in this incident. We will, of course, work to confirm this sensitive information.

"At the same time, as I'm sure Judge Baker will agree, we must exercise extreme caution in commenting publicly on the ambassador's death. There remains a slight chance it could be the result of his personal lifestyle. Therefore, this issue must remain a 'No Comment' situation – until we've confirmed the facts."

"I agree wholeheartedly with Special Agent Hutchins," commented the judge, "and would go so far as to recommend, Mr. President, that all statements be issued from the State Department, to keep the media away from the White House. I also recommend that such statements be coordinated with the national security adviser and myself.

"In essence, the department's initial public statement should read more or less as follows: 'Out of concern for the investigation, and to ensure the privacy of the late ambassador's family, all statements will be withheld until the police and coroner's reports are available to the Secretary of State.'" Baker went on, "I also suggest that only the State Department spokesperson handle the media. The media vultures would love to drive you crazy on this, Mr. President. This procedure should prevent that." He nodded to indicate that he had concluded.

There was a long pause.

"Let me get this straight," said the president, holding his left hand extended. Using his right index finger, he started to count off the fingers on his left hand.

"The FBI knew that Richard was in danger – " his right index ticked off point one. "The FBI put Richard under protective surveillance – " another was counted. "Mr. Hutchins then flew to Brussels to interview the ambassador and to warn him of the alleged danger." He ticked off finger number three. "Am I missing anything so far?" he asked, his face reddening.

Silence. Everyone realized it was better not to interrupt the president when he was in such a mood.

"Okay, then," he continued. "A United States ambassador has been under FBI protection. He was also fully aware of a probable assassination attempt on his life. His personal Belgian bodyguard was handpicked, as was every member of his security staff. Richard was not a wet-behind-the-ears politician. He was one of the best. These facts are indisputable!" His voice grew louder. "I knew the man for a lifetime, as both a friend and a colleague." He turned to Bob. "Now, Mr. Hutchins. Explain to me how the assassins could slip through embassy as well as FBI security. Who is responsible? I need answers, not theories!"

Though the room seemed to shake with the anger of the

president's words, Brenda felt it was clear to everyone that he was trying to keep the volcano within him from erupting.

In the hush that followed, the piercing eyes in the president's flushed face inspected each person, one at a time, waiting for an answer.

Brenda sat forward in her leather chair and raised her hand. "I'd like to answer these concerns, Mr. President, if I may. I'm the one who analyzed everything the FBI has on Ambassador Sorensson."

What she was about to say required courage. She had to choose her words carefully. This president wasn't prepared to hear bureaucratic boilerplate. So, she reached for the glass of water which had been left on the small table next to her chair. She drank slowly, emulating her director, allowing herself the few precious seconds she needed to steady her nerves.

"True," she began, "the FBI had Ambassador Sorensson under surveillance. We were watching him closely, but he wasn't under our full-fledged protection. Not yet. Our assertion that the Libyans had marked him for a hit wasn't conclusive. It was only speculation. That was why Agent Hutchins believed we should warn the ambassador of the danger of his contacts. Gérard, the ambassador's personal guard, was dependable. Nevertheless, as a US mission employee, he could not challenge a direct order from Sorensson. He could only explain to him the probable danger, and suggest alternatives."

Brenda took a deep breath before plunging into the sensitive subject everyone suspected might be coming. She looked straight at the president, then dove in. "Ambassador Sorensson was well-known for his excessive fondness of women. I am sure, Mr. President, you are aware of that. This has been widely known for years, long before he went to Brussels."

The president merely stared angrily at Brenda. He did not comment.

She went on. "When the FBI learned of the murder a few hours ago, we narrowed down our theories as to who could have done such a thing. These are only theories, of course, at this early stage. However, the more information we receive, the closer we get to the answers we're seeking..."

At the president's stormy expression, Brenda trailed off. More seasoned agents had failed to withstand that Douglas mood.

The FBI director commented, "Mr. President. It is of course a great loss..."

"It's more than that, Judge!" stormed the president. "Those killers have made a mockery of US power. Our embassies in every damn country are frantic – doubling their security, re-evaluating their personnel, reinforcing new measures to secure their offices, their homes, their goddamn cars! Ask our new secretary of State here, who now has to deal with this mess. The world is laughing at us. They think – no, they see – we can't protect our own people!"

"We'll do everything in our power to resolve this situation as fast as possible, I assure you, Mr. President," the judge put in quickly. "But, please, don't forget that although the Libyans claim to be clean, we're not crossing them off our list. We also have to consider that the media might bring up the issue of the ambassador's meetings with the Libyan. Please keep in mind that several people in our embassy and the State Department knew about these meetings, as did the Belgians and the Israelis. That issue might not reflect favorably on the White House..."

Baker, too, lost his nerve when President Douglas shot to his feet and began to pace in front of his audience.

"You know damn well," began the president in the slow, deliberate voice that everyone in the White House dreaded, "how I feel about the press! I didn't build my political career by buttering up the media bastards who think they rule the country. They're so goddamn arrogant they now interview each other as

77

stars. No, my presidency is built on sweat and hard work and producing for the citizens of this nation." He stopped pacing. "I don't work to impress those who think they can make or break politicians. I leave that to the TV moguls! I've always been true to the people. What I promise, I try to deliver. If I fail, I tell them where I went wrong. You underestimate the American people!" he said, pointing his finger at Baker. "They're not stupid. They'll understand any issue if you care enough to explain it to them!" Douglas walked to the judge and stood in front of him. "If you have a question about Richard's dealing with the Libyans, and why I had allowed it, then come out with it!"

Baker rose slowly to face his angry president. Brenda saw that standing put him in a better position to defend himself. Sitting, he had been like a canary about to be devoured by a cat. She admired his ability to deal with this emotional confrontation.

Now eye to eye with the president, the FBI director said, "I meant no disrespect, Mr. President. My intention was to draw attention to a delicate matter that might harm our investigation." He paused until Douglas's expression softened. But what he wanted to ask had to be asked, and the president had given him an opening. "However, as you've suggested, Mr. President, it's my duty to search thoroughly, wherever that leads, to resolve this murder. Particularly to find out if there's a larger threat to our nation. And certainly, sir, I'd like the White House's explanation of Sorensson's dealings with the Libyans."

"Done!" replied Douglas. "I'll have my secretary call you to set up a session on that point. Not now." He turned around, went to his desk, and sat heavily. He looked up and spoke again. "I expect a daily report on your progress, Judge Baker. I want the Bureau to put every available agent on the investigation – both here and abroad. No lame excuses. It's our responsibility that all Americans retire at the end of each day feeling safe because someone out there is watching over them. I can't emphasize this enough. Do I make myself clear?"

"Yes, Mr. President! In fact, Agents Hutchins and Straus are off to Brussels tonight to get to the bottom of this atrocious act. Our people in Brussels are already working closely with the local authorities on it."

"Okay, then. As Judge Baker suggested earlier, all press statements will be the joint responsibility of the secretary of State, in co-ordination with Judge Baker and Bill Russell.

"Now, if there is nothing more, good day." Douglas made a few notes before beckoning to Senator Johnson. "George, please stay behind. There are a few things I'd like to talk about."

After the departing officials closed the door behind them, Johnson walked to the president's desk and took one of the chairs immediately in front of it.

"Mr. President, I'm truly sorry about Dick. He was a friend of us both. He'll be missed."

"Thanks. I'll feel his loss even more with the coming election. That's what I wanted to discuss with you. As you know, Dick managed my campaign. He'd offered to help with your nomination this year and he would've been of great help."

"I'm truly sorry."

"Thanks, George," Douglas said, shaking his head and sighing. "Now we need to focus on the election. I'm very pleased you proved yourself in the New Hampshire primary. Now I'm prepared to back you all the way for the presidency.

"This coming Friday, I'll announce that on account of my health I won't be seeking a second term. I can't wait much longer to make this announcement – the rumors are getting too loud and too frequent since I didn't campaign in person in the primaries. My main concern is Hayes. I don't want him declaring himself a candidate for the nomination – whether he's VP or not. And he's getting ready to do just that. No, I want him to be your vice-presidential candidate instead." Douglas paused. Tilting his head back, he closed his eyes for a moment. The tension of the early hours was taxing him.

He breathed in and out before opening his eyes to look at Johnson. "Hayes is a solid personality but he just lacks that fire in the gut it takes to get elected president. And I think, deep down, he knows it. On the other hand, he's a loyal, effective vice-president, and I'm confident I can persuade him to go along as your VP. At least then he won't be running as an independent candidate, threatening your power base. And he is an experienced vice-president. That's worth something." Douglas walked to the bay window behind his desk and stood gazing at the expansive green lawn, his back to Johnson, a hand in his pocket.

"Although the party machinery might support Hayes, on the assumption I'll back his nomination, I want you to be the Republican candidate," he said before he turned around to look at Johnson. "I'll back Hayes only if necessary. That is, if you decide at some point prior to the convention not to go through with it. So I'm relying on you, George, to be our new Republican leader in the battles ahead."

"I'll do my best, Mr. President. The Democrats are demoralized and disorganized and they have several loose cannons rolling around their decks, like that stooge Senator Westlake."

Hearing that name, Douglas clenched his fist angrily. "Yeah, that bastard is more Israeli than the Israelis. And, given Israel's blatant violation of our recent agreements banning sales of the Patriot missiles to a third country, and their gall in confronting me directly on the West Bank housing finance issue, they won't be on our side! And God knows what technology they're selling to China. At least the Middle East is one issue where Hayes agrees with us, George."

"Good! But you're right – Westlake will certainly have the support of the Israeli lobby. We have to factor that in. I still think the economy will be the key issue, though.

"Speaking of the Israelis, our Republican turncoat Senator Dan Kramer, from that great state of New York, and his new Reform Party have a lot of Jewish money behind them. Keep in mind his wife is Jewish and her father is one of the top fund-raisers in the Jewish community in this country. With his father-in-law bringing in the cash, Kramer has a chance of doing relatively well, for a third-party candidate. As I see it, his big problem is that he'll be behind from the beginning because he will not get the federal funds that Westlake and I will have. That should be over twenty million dollars for each of us. In any case, Kramer's going to be tougher than the usual third-party candidate. My people tell me that he could pull close to twenty per cent, even though the public polls predict much less. The winner will be a minority president, almost for sure. Dick Sorensson was right in his conviction that the Israelis are the ones we have to worry about."

"Yes, we'll keep a close watch over Kramer," the president responded. "We can't afford any surprises. I don't want everything I've accomplished this term to be rolled back by the Democrats or anyone else. That's why you've got to run – and got to win, George. I don't just want a Republican to succeed me, but a Republican whom I've picked. We've got to continue the same policies for eight more years. By then, my approach will be locked in the national psyche for a couple of decades. We'll end up with Democrats speaking like Republicans. They'll keep helping us balance the budget and give welfare back to the states. We've moved the country to center-right, George, where it belongs – including the Democrats – and we've got to keep it there. Yes, siree. The center has moved right of center. Don't lose sight of that for one minute."

"It's never left my mind, Mr. President. I owe that much to

you for all we've been through during the last twenty years. But let's not worry about the election any more today. I can see how devastating Dick's murder has been for you. Please, take it easy until you hear from the judge. There's not much we can do until then."

"Anyway, George, keep me posted on the race. But I'm not going to rest until we find Dick Sorensson's killer. Keep in contact with the Bureau on that, please." The president waved the senator out of his office, then put his head down on his folded arms.

Chapter Six

Outside Moscow
June 2nd

Splendid stands of pine, dressed in dense clusters of green needles, surrounded the dacha of the Russian president, Vladimir Stepanovich Popov. Tucked away in Zhukovka and overlooking the Moscow River, the 24-room dacha rested among the towering trees. On this night its lamps sparkled like a diamond necklace caught in a spotlight.

Hidden in the woods, machine guns and the infrared sighting mechanism of the Presidential Guard T-72's 122 mm cannon locked in its sights all vehicle entrances.

Inside the cozy wood-paneled living room of the luxurious dacha, two men had joined the president – his foreign minister, Andrei Grigorievich Stravinsky, and Boris Alexandrovich Rostov, the chief of the SVR, the new Russian Foreign Intelligence Service, or FIS. The three shared a few vodkas while awaiting the arrival of the subject of their closed session – General Yuri Ivanovich Borozov, Russia's top intelligence operative and head of American operations for the FIS.

President Popov listened closely to Rostov's brief on Yuri's background and achievements, now and again bringing another tumbler full of vodka to his mouth. On the table beside him lay a dossier filled with the operational successes of Borozov's brilliant career as a KGB – and now FIS – espionage master.

It was the Russian president's standing order that before he met a new face his aides were to prepare for him a detailed report on the person behind the face. Popov regarded a written report as a security blanket – assurance that the information he was going to hear existed somewhere in black and white. His aides knew their president was actually more receptive to oral briefings than written ones and that he only scanned the written reports he demanded. Nevertheless, they were meticulous in their research and in the details they furnished him with. Occasionally he would read them. In this case, he had just finished doing exactly that.

"What you won't find in that dossier, Vladimir Stepanovich," said Rostov, pointing at the file, "are details about Yuri Ivanovich's younger years."

"I noticed that. But I think I know about our hero," replied the president, staring ahead, his eyes focusing inward as if he were reading a page imprinted in his memory. "Wasn't he an Olympic hundred-meter track star in his youth? Great spy material, eh? To run fast?" The president burped and slugged down another vodka.

"Correct, sir. Yuri Ivanovich was a great athlete. The qualities that make an athlete a winner are also invaluable for anyone who chooses espionage as a career. Qualities such as determination and professionalism, drive, audacity, and ambition."

Stravinsky interrupted. "Sounds like a recruitment brochure, Boris Alexandrovich."

"I trust this man has brains as well as speed and a sense of adventure?" The president raised his thick eyebrows.

Rostov chuckled. "You will see first hand, sir, that Yuri Ivanovich is highly intelligent, with incredible foresight. In short, he is our best espionage operative. In his assignments he has honed his natural talents for recruiting top agents, along with his instincts for adapting to every international situation. And moreover, he thinks strategically."

"What about his family?"

"His father was none other than Ivan Fyodorovich Borozov, one of the stalwarts of the International Department of the Central Committee. Growing up in that environment, Yuri Ivanovich was destined to rise quickly in our intelligence service. Having Ivan Fyodorovich for a father would have been enough to ensure him a good career in the *nomenclatura*."

"Now, that sort of comment gets me worried," the president interrupted, his voice rising. "I want to hear that our man got where he is today through his own sweat, blood, and brains, not because he is a spoiled youth from our Communist era." He looked hard at Rostov. "Don't forget I have a good idea of how much he is costing us." He patted the file with his puffy hand. "It's listed here. He likes the Western jet-set lifestyle, particularly pretty girls. And you're always asking for more budget, Boris Alexandrovich."

"I can't deny that he's an expensive operator, but that contributes to his success, I assure you. Nor can I deny that his personal circumstances gave his career a boost. But I promise you that Yuri Ivanovich got where he is today through brains, cunning, and mastery of his profession," replied Rostov as he walked over to the table and helped himself to more vodka.

"Another thing in his favor," he continued, "is that he is married to Galina Dimitriva Zokenskaya, a former Bolshoi ballerina and daughter of Dimitri Fyodorovich Zokensky, former minister of economic planning and a member of the former Central Committee. She is not only attractive and cultured, but is also an exceptional hostess. That trend has become increasingly important since the seventies in Soviet – excuse me, Russian – society and abroad."

With this last revelation, Rostov, a slightly stooping, thin man with straggly gray hair, gave the president a shrug.

"On the negative side, however, when she was young she was an unbridled gossip with a flair for exaggeration. These days she dances less, teaches ballet more, and has the time to support her husband's professional demands. This marriage is more of a business partnership than anything else, although, according to our sources, General Borozov is scrupulously careful about covering his tracks with other women."

Popov snorted.

Rostov gave a weak smile and continued. "As I have stressed, even Yuri Ivanovich's FIS colleagues regard him as the master of the art of espionage. He is feared by his peers and, especially, by his enemies."

"That's what I like to hear!" interjected Popov. "But what about his record? I know I have it here." He once again drummed his short, chubby forefingers on the document impatiently. "But let's hear it from you, Boris Alexandrovich." For the fourth time the Russian president refilled his vodka glass.

"I was just coming to that. Yuri Ivanovich Borozov was educated at the Foreign Ministry Institute in French and English. He earned a master's degree in English in the United States. At Yale, one of their best universities. Where President Douglas studied, in fact. After his return from several successful tours at the KGB *rezidentura* in Washington, he was assigned to head the American desk in Moscow in early 1998, a position he still commands in the FIS.

"But most important, while in the United States he successfully managed two of the KGB's most valuable intelligence operations there. He gained access to American military ciphers through a network of retired and active-duty American naval personnel, and was responsible for recruiting Stardust, our key agent in the CIA. You are fully briefed on that case. These are our two best cases inside America since we got the atom bomb secrets."

Stravinsky finally spoke. His thin, high-pitched voice didn't match his round, ruddy face. "So, now we know that Yuri Ivanovich has been star material since his birth! Surely you didn't ask for this urgent meeting to waste our time singing his merits," he said sarcastically. "Why are we here, Boris Alexandrovich?"

"Andrei Grigorievich. You're always doubting our intelligence people. Sorry you don't have someone in your ministry the equal of Yuri Ivanovich?

Rostov looked back at the president. "Anyway, during Yuri Ivanovich's last posting in Washington, he forwarded an unusual operational proposal to Moscow. It was based on the well-identified power of the Israeli lobby in the United States, and its extraordinary abilities and efforts to support Israel's objectives there. He emphasized in his analysis that this network consistently gave Israel the best intelligence of any nation on US policy-level plans and decisions. Likewise, he noted, it gave Israel the best leverage for influence on US policy-making, both in the executive branch and, particularly, in Congress."

"Why do you say 'unusual' proposal?" asked Popov.

"Previously our intelligence officers, indeed our former party leaders, only considered this Israeli and Jewish influence in the United States as a threat to our national objectives there. We had never considered the possibility of exploiting such influence and intelligence in America to *our* advantage."

"What are you getting at? How could we do that?" snapped the Russian president.

"General Borozov proposed that instead of regarding the Israelis as a counterintelligence problem, we should redirect our operations to penetrate Israeli and Zionist circles in America, with the primary objective of giving our leaders the same intelligence on the US as that enjoyed by Israel. In other words, we should piggyback Israel's highly effective penetration of the American political system."

His interest noticeably hooked, Popov set his tumbler on its tray and stared intently at Rostov.

"The proposal noted that, since the creation of Israel, pro-Israeli Americans, Jewish and non-Jewish, have enjoyed – with one exception – near immunity from American counterintelligence efforts to restrict their access to either information or influence. There is an unwillingness, even inability, within American security, to do anything, even *say* anything, against Americans who act on behalf of Israel. Even when these actions were prejudicial to America, no one stopped them. Pollard is the only modern-day exception, which proves the rule."

"That's no great discovery!" shouted Stravinsky. "We all know that. The *world* knows that."

"Correct, Andrei Grigorievich," the FIS director responded calmly. "What Yuri Ivanovich did was turn these facts, known for years, into a gold mine of intelligence for us. We piggybacked their operations in the US by penetrating the government in Jerusalem. For instance, in the Pollard spy case, while Pollard gave the Israelis truckloads of documents, we got them all via our agent Volga in Jerusalem. In fact, at one time Pollard's product was so voluminous and so sensitive we had to send special diplomatic flights to Jerusalem to bring back the documents Pollard had stolen for his Israeli masters. And except for the cost of translating the documents, it was all free. Enough to fill a basketball gymnasium from floor to ceiling.

"Even since Pollard's arrest by the FBI, the Borozov operations in Israel have continued to uncover the most secret operations of both Israel and the US, as our recent reports to you have shown.

"Our new indirect sources in Washington, via the Israelis, enjoy near immunity from investigation and arrest, which is unique in our global intelligence operations against the Americans. And this leads us to why we're here tonight. We have discovered the most daring covert action that Israel has ever embarked upon. And believe it or not, it's against the United States. Yuri Ivanovich will brief us in detail. It's incredible in scope and imagination. Only the Israelis, only Mossad, would have dared."

"Enough! Let me meet this hero!" the president shouted. He reached for his vodka tumbler, now standing refilled on the tray next to him.

As Rostov left to get Yuri Borozov, he noticed that the foreign minister had moved closer to speak confidentially with Popov. Stravinsky had been Popov's closest adviser on several state visits to Washington, so his views on the Russian intelligence presentation would be seriously heeded by the president.

Borozov's official car approached the stone gatehouse that guarded the main entrance to the presidential dacha's grounds. Lights from the gatehouse and roadway flashed on, flooding the curtained Lada sedan and forcing it to a cautious stop. The hulking camouflaged cannon in the woods was aimed with computer precision, ready to fire.

A guard officer, alerted ahead, approached the driver's window. Though he knew who the driver and passenger were supposed to be, he asked to check their credentials. Yuri Borozov well understood that nothing was taken for granted when it came to the security of the Russian Federation's first elected president, who had already survived two coup attempts. A third attempt was always a possibility, though most of the president's opponents were simply waiting for him to keel over from ill health.

"My number is 193764, renewed this year on the 29th of January," responded Borozov curtly.

The guard officer verified the figures on his guest log and, satisfied, stepped back and gave a sharp salute. Simultaneously, the officer behind the bulletproof windows of the guardhouse pressed a button to open the massive iron gates.

It was drizzling by the time the black Lada moved onto the grounds of the dacha. Borozov was suddenly yearning for the clear skies he had left behind on his recent covert trip to the Middle East. He would return there someday, hopefully as the FIS resident in Israel. *But that can wait,* he thought.

Borozov was jolted out of his musing when the car lurched to a stop at the inner-perimeter gate. Here a black Volga sedan and three uniformed guard officers were waiting to escort the visitor's car to the dacha's inner sanctum.

After another check of credentials and an electronic search of the car, they were on their way to the main house. Upon hearing the echo of the doorbell, the presidential guard officer inside opened the heavy double doors – just as Yuri was smoothing down his wavy blond hair.

A second later Rostov strode across the large entry. "Yuri Ivanovich! Right on time!" Rostov slapped him on the back, steering him into a small waiting room.

"Listen! I just finished telling the president what a genius you are. By the way, he wants to know what's behind the assassination of the American ambassador in Brussels."

"Fine," replied Yuri seriously, patting his briefcase. "I can give the president some further details on that, based on a clandestine signal I received from Volga in Tel Aviv."

"Perfect. Follow me. He's with the foreign minister." Rostov strode quickly back to the main room with Borozov at his side. As they entered, Popov looked up expectantly.

"Is he here? The famous one?" The president glanced at his watch. "He's punctual, that's good. I feel like an early night. It's been a long day." He stifled a yawn as the vodka continued to work its magic. "Well. Continue, Boris Alexandrovich. I'm taking all this in. Besides, regardless of the Israeli business you just mentioned, I had to meet the man who recruited Stardust."

Yuri felt his throat go dry as he entered the president's salon. But his nerves were under tight control – the result of years of training. He went directly to where the president was sitting and snapped to attention before his leader.

"Well, well. So, you are the hero who recruited Stardust. And I hear you have new secrets for us," the Russian president said, casually saluting without rising.

Yuri again snapped to attention as a return of salute. He then moved toward the easy chair indicated to him by Rostov. A waiter immediately offered him a tray with glasses of vodka and orange juice. He took the juice, wanting to be at his best for this important briefing.

But before the waiter could leave the room, the president grabbed him by the coattail and pulled him back. "General Borozov needs a *real* drink. Give him a vodka!" The waiter, still held by the coat, offered a vodka from his tray to Borozov, who diplomatically rose to accept it.

Releasing the waiter's coat, Popov raised his glass in salute and roared out, "Yuri Ivanovich, before anything else, I want to congratulate you on Stardust. You have succeeded in preventing serious American penetration of our government and in giving us many delicious opportunities to feed disinformation to the White House. It has been expensive, yes. My God, over five million dollars, I understand. But worth every one. I long wanted to meet you personally. So, that done, I understand you have new intelligence about America from your sources in Israel. Another outstanding operation on your part. So, sit and tell me, Yuri Ivanovich." The president gulped down yet another vodka.

At that command, Borozov drank his compulsory vodka and took a deep breath to launch into the most important political briefing of his career.

"Thank you, Sir. As you know, for the last several years we

have been engaged in a major new program to obtain intelligence on the United States government at the highest levels. We do this by means of agents in Israeli and American Zionist circles. They not only have significant access and influence in Jerusalem and Washington, but are nearly untouchable by American counterintelligence services.

"A few days ago, Boris Alexandrovich briefed you about the murder of the American ambassador in Brussels – their ambassador to the European Union." He paused to open his briefcase and take out a briefing note with dates and secret cable references. "Well, we can now confirm that the Israelis were behind that operation. But, it was not a formal government operation. It was a renegade operation approved solely and privately by the prime minister upon the recommendation of Mossad."

Popov blinked.

Yuri continued. "Eshel did not seek the formal approval of his cabinet committee for covert action, known as The Five, because he knew they wouldn't give it. He took the risk himself, as he was furious that the American president allowed this ambassador in Brussels to continue to meet secretly and negotiate with the terrorist chief, cousin of the Libyan leader, Fezzani. Eshel accepted the Mossad's proposal that this murder would produce a double advantage for Israel – it would put an end to any American *rapprochement* with the Libyans and, at the same time, it would cripple Douglas personally, as Sorensson was one of his closest associates. As you know, Eshel considers President Douglas less than friendly to Israel. Further, the Mossad claimed it would be easy to blame the Iranians for the murder. And that's the way they set it up. So far, it's working."

"Yuri Ivanovich," responded Popov, "how did the Mossad accomplish this operation to make it look like the Iranians did it?"

"The Mossad chief in Washington contacted a double agent of

theirs, one Ibrahim, and instructed him to hire, ostensibly on behalf of the Iranians, an international hit man named Peter Dimitriopolis to have the American ambassador killed. Actually this Ibrahim is a triple agent. He also works for us. So, he advised us.

"Fine, Yuri Ivanovich. Now, this secret Israeli operation regarding America and its election?"

"The American president is not sympathetic to the Israeli cause, to say the least. He's got no use for them, although he hides it. In fact, Sorensson was the primary source of the president's feelings about the Israelis. The Israeli prime minister considered that when he approved Sorensson's assassination."

Borozov continued. "A few days ago, our intelligence sources informed us that the ruling circles of Israel were considering a covert action of unprecedented ambition relating to this year's elections in the United States."

Yuri paused for a second before continuing in his slow and calculated voice. "First, I should emphasize that only a handful of Israeli policy-makers are aware of this operation. These men, The Five, convened in secret this past April to authorize the Mossad to lay the groundwork for it, and they will meet again in the coming days to give the final go-ahead. It's an operation of incredible boldness. We certainly know that the Mossad is one of the best intelligence services in the world, but this surpasses anything even they have ever considered, not least in its potential payoff for Israel. And it was all the prime minister's idea. The Mossad code name for the operation, and the agent involved, is Hebron."

Yuri surveyed his small audience. He had their full attention. Taking a deep breath, he added, "As incredible as it sounds, the objective of Operation Hebron is to get this agent, a US senator, nominated by his party and elected this year as president of the United States. Our only serious gap in information is that we do not as yet have Hebron's identity. Only the prime minister of Israel, the Mossad chief in Washington, and Hebron himself know who Hebron is. Of course there are, as we know, three probable candidates. All three are senators: Westlake, Johnson, and Kramer. One of these men is the Israeli agent Hebron."

The Russian president shook his head in disbelief, laughed, then coughed and slammed his empty vodka glass hard on his side table like a gavel bringing order to the secret session. "This is not intelligence, Yuri Ivanovich! This is nonsense – a hashish dream by one of your Middle Eastern sources, or else just the usual Israeli messing around in US politics through their Zionist friends." Popov waved his hand in the air to negate the possibility. "Are you going to try to convince me that what you are saying is actually true? That we are going to have to deal with an American president who is an Israeli agent?" He gave a disbelieving grunt. "Get me another vodka," he shouted at the FIS chief.

Rostov jumped up and reached for a nearby bottle.

Borozov paused respectfully, but retorted with confidence, "Sir, you will be proud, once again, of our nation's intelligence service. Our top agent in Israel was able to record a small portion of a sensitive meeting of The Five. The topic of that meeting was the Hebron project. I brought a typed transcript of that tape, as well as a copy of the original tape itself."

"I want to listen to it. I mean, read it," ordered the president. "And, Boris Alexandrovich, get that damn waiter back here with the vodka. Where is he? Screwing the maid?"

Rostov left the room to get the waiter and more vodka.

Borozov resumed. "I have the tape and Russian transcription. But allow me to say, in summary, that the Hebron project, although still in the planning stage, is the most daring Israeli operation of all time."

Stravinsky broke in. "You said that already. Okay. Let's say your intelligence is worth considering. What do you propose we do?"

Yuri stared back at Stravinsky. "In the past the Israelis have involved themselves in overt meddling in the American political scene. We are now facing something way beyond that. Something of unprecedented scope. And we have to consider how we might exploit the Hebron operation ourselves. We have time on our side and top-level penetration of the Israelis and the US. Of course we have other agents in Israel, but only one who has immediate, direct access to details concerning Hebron. And we have Stardust in the CIA. He has recently been offered a temporary posting with the National Security Council staff in the White House, in Dr. Russell's office. We have already instructed Stardust to accept the assignment."

"Tell me, Yuri Ivanovich," Stravinsky persisted sarcastically, "how did we build up this network in Israel when for decades we suffered from knowing next to nothing about them?"

The president looked at Yuri expectantly. Yuri chose to address Popov.

"As we have reported previously, in the late eighties and early nineties one of the main Mafia organizations in Russia established itself in Israel. The American FBI calls it the Racmiel Brandwein organization. We call it the Kosher Dish. This Russian-Jewish Mafia controls networks operating primarily through Moscow, Tel Aviv, New York's Brighton Beach, and Antwerp. As Israel had no money-laundering laws, and easy immigration for Jews, I directed, beginning in 1989, a major operation to place our agents inside this Jewish Mafia network in every city where it operates. That has been accomplished."

Stravinsky shifted in his seat and looked at Popov. Yuri had obviously gotten the president's attention. Stravinsky wasn't pleased.

"The success was immediate, as we could help our agents in the Mafia outwit and outperform their competitors. What's more, some of the Mafia émigrés weren't really Jewish. They had bought fake documents to get out of Russia and into Israel. We knew all of them and blackmailed some of the better-quality ones into working with us."

Yuri pulled another file from his briefcase. "It's all recorded here, sir, knowing your preference for written reports." At the president's nod, Yuri continued. "With our clandestine support, our agents rose to key positions in this network, centered in Tel Aviv. They bought off Israeli officials, even ministers. In the process we picked up several high-level personalities as agents, who initially thought they were working with gangsters. A few were relieved when we advised them they were working for Russian intelligence. They assumed we would provide them with better protection. In fact our top agent in Israel, code name Volga, is the primary source on the Hebron operation. His control officer is an FIS staff member posing as a Jewish Mafia leader in Israel. Despite this, Volga's position in Israel makes him untouchable, and his communications with us are perfectly secure."

Yuri looked at Stravinsky with a triumphant challenge. "So, Andrei Grigoricvich. In effect we have Israel penetrated at all levels. This effort has culminated with the revelation of Operation Hebron."

Impressed with this summary, Popov, slapping his knee and getting to his feet, said, "Yuri Ivanovich, if you are right about what you reported tonight, and continue to succeed in tracking this Hebron operation, you'll have a great future ahead of you. Now, let me read the transcript of the Israeli tape."

As the president read, Rostov said sardonically, "We will know the truth, and the truth shall make us victors!" It was a Russian spin on a biblical quotation, which he had been told was carved on a marble wall in the entrance hall of the Central Intelligence Agency.

Outside the dacha, a clap of thunder boomed and lighting flashed. Heavy summer rain followed, pounding the windowpanes.

Yuri thought, *Another shadow – that of the Russian bear – is now about to join the dramatic events building around Operation Hebron.* And he told himself, *You did it.*

Chapter Seven

Brussels
June 3rd

"Ladies and gentlemen, this is your captain." The deep, friendly voice came over the speakers of Sabena flight 467. "We should be landing at Brussels National Airport at Zaventem in approximately eighteen minutes. We're experiencing clear skies and warm, pleasant weather, 23 degrees Celsius. I hope you've enjoyed your flight with us today."

Brenda smiled at Bob as she fastened her seat belt. "Welcome back to Brussels."

"I'd forgotten how damn long it takes to gct across the pond."

"That's the easy part, Bobby," said Brenda, her eyes twinkling. "I imagine that once we land we won't get much sleep or enjoy our visit like our friendly pilot hopes."

"Right!" grunted Bob. "And stop calling me Bobby! I've told you a million times!"

"Right!" laughed Brenda. "But it did the trick, didn't it? You're wide awake now!"

Bob shot her a teasing frown before he turned his head to peer out the small window to his right, and saw the runway rising to meet the plane. A few minutes later a jetway connected with the aircraft. Yawning passengers stood, fumbled with their carry-on bags and backpacks, and waited to disembark. The round old satellite terminal, hooked onto the new terminal, looked familiar as they came out of the ramp into the gate area.

"Hold on a second," said Brenda, heading toward an airport newsstand.

Sorensson's picture dominated the front page of every newspaper and magazine. Brenda bought two papers, one in French, *La Libre Belgique*, one in Flemish, *De Standaard*. She began to translate the French for Bob.

"They portray him as the epitome of charm, comportment, and ambassadorial dignity – what crap! Look!" she said, raising two fingers. "Two full columns. Talking about his life's achievements and his impeccable diplomatic service. And of course they're elaborating on his close friendship with President Douglas."

La Libre Belgique directed its readers to page three, where Brenda found herself staring at another large photo of Sorensson flashing his winning smile.

She read on. Nothing was revealed of how he was murdered. No speculation as to who was responsible. She put the newspaper down and picked up the *De Standaard*. Almost identical coverage. It was obvious that the US government had influenced the media.

"The only official comment I see is: 'A thorough investigation is under way, headed by the Federal Bureau of Investigation.'" Then Brenda let out a snort that made Bob raise his eyebrows.

"What?"

"A couple of paragraphs of sentimental bullshit from Albert Thornton. You know, Sorensson's second-in-command. The Chargé."

"Yeah. I'd imagine he's playing for a promotion. We all know what he thought of Sorensson and how he tried to backstab him with the department. Like they did with our lady ambassador in Bern. Remember?"

Brenda turned her attention to another news item on the third page. Nothing in it seemed particularly unusual except the coincidence: another murder. The same date. This time a hooker, found strangled and dumped by the roadside in a Brussels suburb, Stockel.

Taking a pad out of her briefcase, Brenda made a note to ask Guy to talk to the Stockel police about that case.

Located near the Grand-Place, *Aux Armes de Bruxelles* was one of the city's most popular eateries. Famous for its old-world atmosphere and its rich Belgian cuisine, the restaurant counted Guy van den Heuven among its frequent diners for lunch or supper. The *maître d'hôtel* had reserved the usual corner table for the police commissioner.

Guy arrived early. Knowing it was Brenda's first visit to Brussels, he was almost as eager to show off his city to her as to see his old friend Bob.

Glass of Bordeaux in hand, he spent the free minutes going over his notes. So far his investigation hadn't produced much. The search of the ambassador's residence had yielded nothing. Guy would have liked to have questioned Sorensson's staff. But his hands were tied with that idiot American chargé d'affaires, Thornton waving a State Department limited-search authorization in his face. *Didn't that pompous bureaucrat know that I'm on their side? And that Guy van den Heuven was better placed to crack this case than anyone!* The killer had planned the murder to perfection and had covered his tracks well. But Guy did not believe in such a thing as a perfect crime. This was because perfect human beings do not exist. *There is always a slip. Always a lead. It may be missed by the police, but it's always there.*

He looked up to see Bob and Brenda weaving their way toward him between the heavy oak tables.

"Good to see you again after all this time," said Bob. A huge smile lit his face as he pumped Guy's hand.

Guy had jumped to his feet, his smile equally wide. "Bob, *mon ami*! And brilliant Brenda too! As I asked. We need all the brains we can get to crack this one! And I finally get to show you Brussels."

Brenda flushed at Guy's flattery. She smiled modestly and sat between the two men, then took her notebook out of her briefcase and placed it on the table.

"*Non, non*! *Ma chérie*, Brenda!" Guy said, laughing. He closed the notepad up and returned it to her. "Here in Brussels, we drink first, then we work, *d'accord*? This Bordeaux is excellent." He raised his glass in a brief toast, then sipped, savoring the taste for a few seconds before letting the wine slide down his throat.

"Perrier for me, please," said Brenda, but she was smiling. The man was such a charmer, and absolutely enamored with himself!

"I'll go for a double whisky and water, myself," said Bob. "It was a hell of a long flight. I'm still recovering. But it's great to be in Brussels again – reminds me of the good old days!" *Don't know what he sees in Brenda, but he sure seems smitten*, Bob privately noted.

"It's fantastico to see you here again, my friend. Too bad I do not work well with your legal attaché," Guy said with an expression of exaggerated disappointment that made his guests burst out laughing. "No matter, you and Brenda are here now and we should begin the real work. But that starts later. Your first hours in Brussels, we take it easy, *n'est-ce pas*? After all, Mr. Sorensson is dead and we can't change that." Guy's voice picked up energy as he cheerfully commanded, "First, we eat!"

When Brenda had placed her order, she had not expected the lavishness of service or the richness of the national dishes. *The Belgians certainly know how to enjoy food*, she thought. They started with appetizers of duck-liver pâté and mussels in a cream sauce. For the main course Brenda had veal in a rich, gravy with

101

sliced mushrooms, while Bob had lobster soaked in a cream-and-cheese sauce. Guy savored his favorite dish of ravioli with crab.

After the *crême brulée* and a second round of drinks it was time to talk about Sorensson.

Guy became serious as Bob asked, "What have you gotten so far?"

"Not much. It's the same as when I spoke to you on the phone."

"That's it? Nothing new?" urged Bob, glancing sideways at Brenda, who remained silent.

"Well," said Guy, "first of all, this murder was, *certainement*, the work of a professional. It was too – how would you Americans say it?"

"Too clinical, too precise, too expert..."

"*Exactement*, Brenda!" nodded Guy.

"You said on the phone that you were sure the Libyans were not involved?" she queried. "That and the NSA intercept came as a surprise. Sorensson's close contact with Fezzani was no secret. It raised a lot of questions and had us squirming." She looked at Hutchins, then back at Guy.

"Brenda, I received a definite response from my Libyan Embassy source. It confirms your NSA fax. So I have tentatively ruled out the Libyans. Also, Brenda, *chérie*, do not forget that no terrorist organization has claimed responsibility. No, Guy van den Heuven has his own theory!" he added with a smile.

"Let's hear it," replied Bob.

"*Certainement*! Here is how I see it." Guy took out his notebook. "*Numéro* one, your ambassador liked women too much!" He threw an apologetic glance at Brenda, who remained stone-faced, though she felt herself blushing. It was as if Guy had somehow caught the underlying prettiness that she fought to hide.

"Yes. He was an asshole," she muttered.

"So?" asked Bob.

"Very simple, my dear Robert. We already know that he had a

'lady of the night' with him the evening he died. My theory is based on this indisputable fact."

"You think she was the murderer? But you said it was a professional hit?" Brenda asked.

"At this point of the investigation, she has to be the one who let in the assassin, distracted Sorensson for the assassin, or *was* the assassin, though I can't imagine how a woman could have overwhelmed a large man, in good physical condition, to inject heroin into his armpit. There is no evidence he was struck with anything."

"That leaves us with the only possible motive," mused Brenda, deep in thought. "A political motive. But it doesn't add up," she said as if alone in the room. "If it's political, our main suspects would be the Libyans. Guy received definite intelligence that negates this theory. If not the Libyans, then who?" She looked up as if suddenly remembering she had company.

"Yes, Brenda?" asked Bob.

"So, Guy's reasoning is that the killer was a professional assassin who used this woman as an accomplice to get close to Sorensson. Or..."

"Or...?" asked Bob.

"Or this woman herself is the killer. I tend to lean toward the latter theory – that our killer is the woman who was the last person seen with Sorensson."

"Well, *ma chère* Brenda, I agree with you on one point."

Brenda threw him a questioning look.

"That the motive had to be political. There is no other explanation. We still have that small piece of Iraqi newspaper, a Baghdad daily, which I found in the driveway," Guy turned to Bob. "I hope you did not bring this up with your boss, Bob. At least for the time being. It could be a false lead left by the killer. But whether it is a valid clue or a planted clue, it indicates the political nature of whoever is behind the killing."

"There must be more to that piece of newsprint," said Bob.

Guy paused for a few moments, allowing the waiter to clear away the plates and take orders for coffee.

"I can't be sure, my friend," he answered, looking directly at Bob. "Does it even implicate Iraq?"

"Would an Iraqi be so unprofessional as to leave a piece of his daily newspaper?" Brenda's tone was disbelieving. "A little far-fetched to me."

"Weeeeell," Guy replied. "We're shooting darts in the dark, as you Americans say. It's possible that the suspect is an Iraqi working for his president – to avenge America's role in the Gulf War. It is also *possible* that a new group – one we know nothing about – did it and decided to keep quiet. We do not understand all people, you know."

"Or it could be that Iran is behind all this," suggested Brenda. "The piece of newspaper could have been dropped on purpose, as you suggested. By the Iranians to incriminate the Iraqis." Brenda paused and looked at Guy. "However, these are only speculations that lead us nowhere. One fact remains unchanged – for us, at least. It's immaterial whether the assassin worked alone or for someone else. Either way, the act of assassinating an American diplomat constitutes terrorism."

"Whoa, whoa, there. Take it easy!" said Bob.

"Bob, remember our meeting with the president? He was right. He was genuinely concerned for Americans abroad and I was feeding him some bureaucratic rubbish! I thought a lot about that during our flight here. My gut tells me that our suspect is a woman. A woman who pretended to be a hooker, and who did the killing herself. It's what Sorensson's profile would have suggested to any pro." Brenda turned to face Guy. "And the woman, in my theory, *is* a pro. She's the key to this crime. Not just an accomplice, as you suggested, Guy. But *the* killer."

"You sound pretty certain, as though you already have a

suspect in mind," Bob said. "Although we've gone with your gut feeling before and found you on target, I'm not so sure this time. There are just too many variables. Too many motivations. It's too early to zero in on a single scenario."

"I think, dear Brenda," said Guy, "that, although it is very possible that a woman is involved in this crime, her involvement was more indirect." Guy flashed her an apologetic smile. "Perhaps she was followed by our killer, or she could have left the terrace doors open for the killer to enter while she distracted the target."

"For now, I know a woman's our key here," insisted Brenda. "You guys don't buy it. But so far there's simply no evidence – not a shred – that a man's involved. It's just your machismo that seems to demand it must have been a man."

Guy frowned. "I think it is time to contact the guys at Interpol and NATO intelligence to see what they can come up with. Right, *Bobby?*"

Bob glared at Guy, who by now was shaking with laughter. "Absolutely," Bob replied, his voice controlled.

"Okay, gents. Let's get out of here and get some rest," insisted Brenda as she laid a credit card on the table and waved for the waiter.

"Please, *mes amis*. You are guests of the Belgian Judiciary Police tonight. No credit cards. Only good old-fashioned Belgian francs – untraceable."

A few minutes later, the investigative threesome left the restaurant pleased with the three-hour meal turned business meeting, and agreeing to meet the next morning.

When Bob and Brenda arrived at their hotel, the embassy's FBI secretary was waiting in the lobby. She put down her book and hurried toward Bob to hand him a sealed envelope.

"Mr. Hutchins, this arrived today by courier from Washington

– it's from Judge Baker. I was instructed by the legal attaché to hand it over to you personally."

"Thanks, Linda." Bob edged over to the side of the lobby to read the message, then said: "Brenda, let's go to my room to discuss this. Our techs swept our rooms today, so it should be safe to talk there."

"It's a directive for me to return to Washington immediately," Bob said when they'd closed the door behind them. "It seems the White House has insisted that an intergovernmental task force be established to handle our hostages in Peru. I'm to chair it. The judge wants you to take over full command of the Sorensson investigation." He handed her the letter to read for herself.

"That's great for you, pal. But I've never managed anything this big before on my own." Brenda plunked herself down on the nearest chair, her eyes wide in disbelief. "All this on me? Bob, I'm flattered but I don't need it."

Bob smiled warmly. "You'll have to learn fast. That's the way it goes. It's like war. The commander's suddenly gone and the next officer in line is in charge. And Brenda – do you think for one minute the judge, of all people, would've assigned you a task he didn't think you could handle? He's too smart for that."

"It's just too much, too soon." Brenda was suddenly exhausted. "Besides, we have to find out what gave in the Sorensson-Fezzani contacts. Knowing that will bring us closer to solving this. Oh, God! I'm so tired, and now the judge goes and drops this on me!"

"Just get a few hours of shut-eye, Brenda. It's been a hell of a grind these last two days. You have everything you need. You speak French like a native, and more important, you have those gut feelings working overtime for you. Besides, Guy is the best cop in Europe. And he'll give you any help you ask for. Poor Guy!" Bob chuckled. "I felt sorry for him. You almost bit his head off!"

"Joke as you please, Hutchins," Brenda said. "I'm going to my room to review my notes and think this through. See you later."

"I'll say *au revoir* now. Tomorrow I'll be back on our side of the Atlantic focusing on llamas!"

June 4th

The tapping of rain against windowpanes awakened Brenda from a troubled sleep. She opened her eyes, looked around, then gathered her bearings. The illuminated digital clock read 04:45. Through the wet window, she saw a gray sky. Grunting a few words which would have earned her a round of applause at the Bureau, she brought the pillow over her head and decided to wake up at a more civilized hour.

The next time Brenda opened her eyes it was 7:30. The dark sky was changing color and the pink stripes that crept onto the horizon lifted her spirits considerably.

Showered, dressed, and ready to tackle the day, she rang for room service. Over a delicious croissant and an aromatic Belgian coffee, Brenda opened her notebook and recorded that Bob had been summoned to Washington.

Time to get started.

She picked up the phone and dialed. "Commissioner Guy van den Heuven, please. This is Special Agent Brenda Straus calling."

A few seconds later Guy's voice came over the wires. "*Bonjour*, Brenda! What can I do for you?"

"Hi! It's early but I need to see you right away. Bob was called back home. He's left already. That leaves you and me to crack this case."

"*Oui, oui, ma* Brenda. I will be at your hotel in thirty minutes. But Bob called home? Why?"

"Come straight up to my room – 965. I'll fill you in."

While waiting, she pulled out yesterday's paper, read page

three again, and poured more coffee. Exactly thirty minutes later she heard a knock.

"*Bonjour*, my friend Brenda!" Guy proclaimed as he swept through the door. "Guy van den Heuven at your service!" He gave her a succession of *bises*, those little cheek-to-cheek kisses used for greeting in the French-speaking world. *Nice aftershave*, she thought.

"*Bonjour*. Want some breakfast? Some coffee?"

"Coffee, *s'il vous plaît*." Brenda noted he was still using the formal *vous*.

As they sat in the small seating-area of Brenda's room, she showed him the article reporting the hooker's death.

"I found it in yesterday's paper," she said. "The more I think about it, the more curious I am. For some reason I feel there is a lead here. What do we know about how Sorensson lined up his call girls?"

Guy the flamboyant was immediately replaced by Guy the efficient police commissioner. Suddenly Brenda barely recognized the man sitting next to her.

"Not much. He'd have his driver take him somewhere and wait in the car. He'd go off to some bar or street corner and either come back with a lady or have one lined up for the following night. That's all. We've looked for leads with dating services, corporate escorts, that kind of thing. When it came to girls, the ambassador was no snob."

He read the news piece once, then again. He lowered the article and stared into space. After a few seconds he said, "Stockel is a suburb of Brussels. It is very close from here. Maybe ten minutes' walk. Hmm. A hooker is strangled and her body dumped in a shallow ditch in a park." Guy looked out of the window. "Let me think about this. First, I ask myself who would want to kill a hooker? It doesn't happen here." He looked up.

"Her pimp, her drug dealer – or someone who wants her silenced."

"*Exactement*! *Question numéro deux* – what do we do next? Only one answer, my friend. We go to Stockel police station and ask questions, if you like."

"It's a long shot, but at this point, they all are. If we can eliminate her pimp and her drug dealer then we might be able to connect her to the woman with Sorensson the night he died. If so, that could put an end to our search for the green-eyed one Gérard described."

Guy jumped to his feet and hurried to the door, taking the article with him. "I'll go now to talk to the Stockel police. I'll get a photo of the hooker, then meet you at the ambassador's residence." He stopped at the door, his hand around its knob. "Give me one hour. I will meet you there in one hour!" Then he let himself out.

Half an hour later, Guy called Brenda to tell her three things. The hooker's pimp had an airtight alibi, the hooker had never touched drugs, and she was murdered somewhere else: her body was moved and dumped in Stockel. It didn't look interesting. But yes, he was able to get photos of her and would bring them to Sorensson's residence.

Brenda sat in her taxi while the residence guard checked her papers. The black iron gates opened and the taxi drove up to the main door. Stepping out of the vehicle, Brenda stood for a few moments marveling at the lush scenery around her – a palatial turn-of-the-century house, its front yard an expanse of manicured grass. A shallow stream running downhill, complete with softly gurgling waterfall, lay at the far end of the lawn. She inhaled the scent of jasmine. *Impressive*, she thought, *impressive and seductive*.

Unfortunately, she wasn't there to admire the luxurious edifice or its picturesque landscaping. But she did imagine what it might have felt like for a young woman to be escorted here by the American ambassador.

She went looking for Gérard.

He was sitting in a small office just off the lobby, empty bags from several snacks littering his trash basket and desk. When she entered he stood hastily. Then he looked over her shoulder to the man arriving behind her. It was Guy.

"Here," Guy said, reaching into his breast pocket.

It was a color shot of a girl in her early twenties. Scantily dressed, she was standing at what appeared to be a bar counter.

"You must be Gérard," said Brenda, flashing her badge. "I'm Special Agent Brenda Straus, FBI. And you know Commissioner van den Heuven. We're here to ask you a few questions."

Upon Gérard's nod, Guy bombarded him with questions in French.

Gérard replied, "I want nothing more than to help you solve this horrible crime and punish whoever is responsible." He looked disturbed. "You know how much I hated to see such an important man waste his time in the worst streets of our city? How can you protect a man who uses his authority to keep you from protecting him?"

"We understand, Gérard. It wasn't your fault," Brenda said, feeling sympathy for the proud retired cop.

Within a few minutes it became clear just how vehemently Gérard had disapproved of the ambassador's penchant for prostitutes. And he repeated how absurdly difficult it was protecting such a man.

"His private life invaded my ability to protect his public life," Gérard went on. He seemed to take it as a personal failure.

"What about the night he died?" asked Brenda. "What more can you tell us about that particular girl? Was there anything memorable about her? Was she different in any way? Did you get a good look at her? Where did she come from?"

Gérard replied that the woman who accompanied Sorensson that night had been a stunner, *très belle*. Although she wore a long, hooded black raincoat, Gérard had caught a glimpse of short black hair and striking green eyes. She had seemed as giggly and dumb as the usual lot. Except this one hadn't been impressed with the place, as had the other girls.

"She just strode right in on the ambassador's arm. Barely glanced around as you'd expect her to. I mean, the girls were usually flabbergasted. People can't help it. Look around – the furniture is Louis XIV, the chandeliers were bought at Sotheby's, and the floors are Carrara marble. Even the plants are exotic and their pots are antiques. That's from the Ming Dynasty. All the paintings, the ambassador brought from his Park Avenue apartment. That's a Renoir. It's hard not to stare at all that. But this one just marched right in. It was almost as though she'd been here before," Gérard concluded, then his face grew thoughtful.

"Or it could mean she had come with a mission and was too preoccupied to notice all this," said Brenda, gesturing around her.

"*Bien*," said Guy. "Now, look very closely at this photo, please, Gérard. Have you seen this girl before?"

"Well, she wasn't here the night the ambassador died. But she does look familiar. But where? Let me keep this print for a while? I'll get back to you."

"We'll be in touch in a day or two," said Brenda. "Thank you for your cooperation. Oh, and we'd like to know more about how the ambassador made these arrangements with women."

"That's easy. He found them in bars and on the street. There must be some service, too. But Mr. Sorensson didn't let any of us in on who he'd be spending his evenings with or how he had arranged his dates. I'd drive him to some corner and a girl would appear."

Brenda and Guy left Gérard in the house and headed for Guy's unmarked Peugeot, walking silently, each deep in thought. Guy fired the ignition, shifted into gear, and stepped on the gas. The car took off with a squeal. Brenda glared at him. *If there's one thing I can't figure out about Europeans, it's their driving. Why do European men love to do that?*

Two turns and a traffic light later, Guy said, "*Bon*, Brenda. What's your next step?"

"Let me out there, at the taxi stand. I'll go to the embassy. Meanwhile, please stay on the dead hooker's case. Or any other such murder you can find in this time frame. I'll call you when I finish."

"*Très bien.* I will also check out the Interpol records at headquarters. *Au revoir.* I'll call you at the embassy if I find anything."

She got out with a parting wave and walked to the first taxi in line. To the Moroccan driver slouched over an Arabic newspaper she said, "*L'Ambassade des Etats-Unis auprès de l'Union européenne, s'il vous plaît.*"

As she sat across the desk from Ambassador Sorensson's private secretary at the US Mission to the EU, Brenda sized her up. A woman with a permanent smile fixed on her round face, her tailored blue suit perfectly pressed, her hair carefully coiffed, Sue Parry seemed the very model of Foreign Service efficiency.

"How long have you been working for the ambassador?"

"It would've been three years this August."

"And how would you describe Ambassador Sorensson?"

"As a boss? Well, he handled the mission fairly well, I guess. As bosses go, he was, let's say, demanding. Tough, and sometimes even rude. He wanted everything perfect. He kept us working long hours, but I have to say he made sure we were well compensated – he was generous with leave time. But ruthless – devastating, even – in his reprimands."

"What about his private life? Have you heard, or were you aware of, how he spent his time?"

"If you're asking if I knew about his wild side, the answer is yes. Everyone in the building knew he was a lady-chaser. Not that I'd describe most of the women as ladies. I'm surprised Washington never talked to him about it," she said, poker-faced.

"So he didn't have a kept woman?"

"No. Nothing like that, or I would've known."

"Well, did he, for instance, favor any one woman? Particularly one he kept inviting to his home?"

"I don't think so. Probably only Gérard, his personal guard, would know that."

Brenda took a copy of the photo of the dead hooker out of her briefcase and set it on the desk between them. "Have you ever seen this girl before? With him, or around any of the bars in this vicinity?"

"No, I certainly have not! I don't frequent bars as our late ambassador did," retorted Sue indignantly. "Nor did I go to his residence late at night." Then she thought for a few seconds and asked, "Why don't you look at his personal datebook? He kept it locked in his desk drawer. And yes, I do have a key."

"Thanks for the suggestion."

They moved into the ambassador's private office. The luxury Brenda had witnessed at his residence was evident here as well, although on a smaller and more conservative scale. He had spared no expense in surrounding himself with antiques, from the Tuscan inlay table to the Isfahan rug. *He had exquisite taste*, she thought.

Sue Parry unlocked the right-hand top drawer of the ambassador's desk and handed Brenda a leather-bound agenda.

"If it's all the same to you, I'll just sit in here for a while and have a good look at this and whatever else is in his office," said Brenda, taking a chair near the fireplace.

"Of course. Can I get you a cup of coffee?"

"Yes. Thank you."

Brenda took her time with the agenda, and decided to carry it with her for an even more thorough examination. She might send it to the FBI lab, where her efficient pals might discover something everyone else had missed.

It took her a few minutes to decipher the ambassador's handwriting. Most days included similar mundane entries – meetings, lunches, official functions. But she noted an entry that was repeated in recent weeks. Fezzani, the Libyan ambassador. Several of those meetings were at Sorensson's residence. Could Fezzani have been casing the place? she wondered. Despite the information that the Libyans weren't involved, she wasn't so sure. Gérard had remarked how the woman hadn't seemed interested in the residence, almost like she knew the layout. Perhaps Fezzani had briefed her. Or had she been there before?

When Sue returned with the coffee, Brenda asked whether she was aware of Sorensson's close relationship with the Libyans.

"Oh, that! I certainly was," replied Sue, as she set the cup in front of Brenda. "Cream and sugar?"

"Black, thanks. Tell me about it."

"They often held meetings. Even became fast friends, I thought. Fezzani was a bit of a womanizer himself, you know. I'll bet he introduced the ambassador to some women. I overheard Ambassador Sorensson once on the phone hinting about that to him. Could that have had something to do with it?"

"I have no idea," replied Brenda. "But it's a thought. I'll take a look around, if you don't mind. I'll sign for anything I take."

"Of course." The secretary left Brenda to do as she pleased.

Half an hour later Brenda emerged from Sorensson's private office carrying his datebook, a few files, and two audio tapes. She handed Sue Parry a signed receipt for the items, thanked her for her cooperation, and gave her the hotel phone number in case she remembered anything that might help the investigation.

The next couple of hours Brenda spent speaking to various senior officials at the mission, including the chargé d'affaires, the political counselor, the CIA station chief, and the security officer, all of whom were aware of Sorensson's contact with Hamed bin Fezzani.

Michael Hawthorne, the political counselor, stressed that Fezzani was well-known by the US as leader of the Libyan terrorist operations in the West. "He wasn't just any old Libyan."

"What justification did Sorensson mention for this liaison?" asked Brenda.

"He'd insist that this contact had the approval of the president," replied Hawthorne derisively. "So there wasn't a whole lot we could do, or say, to dissuade him. Although we tried."

"You'd be wise to put together your documentation of those attempts," Brenda advised.

At 12:45, before leaving the mission, she called Guy and asked him to meet her at the *Armes de Bruxelles*. *I need another session with him*, she told herself. *Maybe it'll clear my head and give me a bright idea.*

Although the restaurant was crowded, Guy's favorite corner table was reserved. It was a warm and muggy day, so while waiting for Brenda, he had ordered a Duvel to sooth his dry throat.

Ten minutes later she arrived.

"So what have you discovered, *ma collègue préférée?*" Guy asked eagerly.

She nodded at his beer, saying, "I'll have one of those, thank you," then reported: "Basically everything we came up with earlier regarding the ambassador's Libyan connection has been verified. I know you have an inside source on this one, Guy. However, I have Sorensson's calendar, which lists all his rendezvous with Fezzani. We should check that against what your source says."

115

"Good – and I also have something here for you to see. A list and mug shots of professional hit men. But, Brenda, I have a much bigger surprise for you! Gérard called me just before I left the office."

"Really?" inquired Brenda. "What did he say?"

"He recognizes the dead hooker and thinks he saw her with Sorensson. We are going to see him again tomorrow."

"Why tomorrow? What's wrong with right now?"

"*Eh, ben!*" sighed Guy, getting slowly to his feet and looking ruefully at his half-full beer.

Gérard was waiting by the mansion's iron gates, gorging on pastry and dropping crumbs on the driveway. His small round eyes darted repeatedly – left, right; left again. Every now and then he would stop munching long enough to wipe his wide, perspiring forehead.

Upon seeing the commissioner's Peugeot approaching, Gérard straightened, shoved what was left of his pastry into its wrapper, then wiped his mouth, leaving a few crumbs clinging to his thick mustache.

"Let's have a talk with our Monsieur Gérard," said Guy, closing his car door as Brenda exited hers, and gesturing toward the residence.

Once in the house, Guy pulled out an enlarged photo of the murdered prostitute and handed it to Gérard. "Look. It's clear – the girl's image is sharp. Have you seen her or not?"

"*Oui*. That's her all right."

"Are you one hundred per cent certain this is the girl you saw?" Brenda persisted.

He nodded. "As if yesterday. The photo brought it back. She was here several days before the ambassador was killed. There were four..."

"Four women?" Guy signaled for Gérard to stop. He reached

into his pocket for a mini tape recorder, switched it on, then gestured for the man to continue.

Gérard was obviously relishing the attention. Used to asking the questions during his days on the force, he was now on the other side and the experience was gratifying.

"There were the four of them," he was saying. "The ambassador, another man they called Peter, and the two girls. The men seemed pretty drunk. The girls were giggly, but not so bad off." Gérard was itching to impart the juiciest tidbit of all. "The other girl – not the dead hooker – had short black hair and was all over the ambassador that night. And I remember, just like the night of the murder. She wasn't interested in the place, just the boss." Pausing for a few seconds, he closed his eyes and massaged his forehead, as if willing his mind to bring the scene into focus.

"Then?" prompted Brenda.

"The other man, this Peter guy, wanted to make a phone call and the ambassador asked me to show him to the library."

"That means this Peter had a chance to get a good idea of the floor plan?" said Guy.

"It seems so," replied Brenda. "We'll have to retrace his exact steps. Can you get from the library to the ambassador's suite through the garden?"

"Yes, madam."

"*Exactement!*" Guy turned to Gérard. "Can you describe Peter for us?"

Gérard thought for a few seconds. "He was a dark, swarthy type. Thick mustache. You know, the Mediterranean kind. He spoke French with a heavy accent. Looked Turkish, maybe. Or Greek, or Italian. Maybe Balkan."

"Okay. You'll have to take us to the library – the same way you did Peter."

"Sure, but there's more. The big point is..."

"Cut it out, Gérard!" yelled Guy. "If you weren't a former *flic*,

117

I'd have your balls! Come on, don't waste our time."

"Sorry. The black-haired girl – she's the same one who was with the ambassador on that last night. I think."

"You think?" pressed Guy.

"I'm pretty sure. She had green eyes and they keep reappearing in my sleep. And, as I said, she was not the least interested in the house. And that happened both the night of the murder and the earlier night, when there were four. I used to enjoy watching the reactions of these tramps he brought in here. She gave me no pleasure at all, this one."

"Thanks," said Guy, and he shook the other man's hand vigorously. "You've been extremely helpful. Now show us the library."

After the tour, Brenda asked, "What do you make of this 'Peter,' Guy? A pimp or a professional killer? Of course, 'Peter' might be an alias – it would've been pretty foolish of them to use this guy's name in front of a bodyguard."

"The only thing we can be nearly sure of, dear Brenda, is that this woman with the green eyes was the last person to be seen with the ambassador. So, she and her swarthy friend are our only suspects. Now, I would guess Peter did the dirty work. The woman got him access to the target. And then it was easy. When Sorensson was home, the alarm on the grounds was off. Pretty flimsy security, if you ask me. Let's get going, Special Agent Brenda." He turned and approached Gérard.

"Gérard, you come with me to headquarters to look at some photos. We need to identify this 'Peter.' At least we have a name, genuine or not."

Later that afternoon Guy knocked on Brenda's hotel-room door. She was seated at her laptop, bringing her notes "up to the minute," as the judge liked them.

"*Ma chère* Brenda..."

"*Oui. C'est moi.*"

Guy grinned. "I have no great news." He smiled, looking behind her glasses and into her serious eyes. Brenda thought of the word *dragueur*, somewhere between "flirt" and "seducer." The moment passed.

"Gérard was unable to recognize any photo from our books on known hit men and terrorists. I have to admit I had some hope. But he's sure none of them is the Peter we're looking for."

"Too bad. So, what's next?"

"I'll get my people searching through our archives on every professional hit and terrorist incident. That will take time. And luck. I'll also check with some friendly services around Europe, give them Gérard's description of Green Eyes's boyfriend and see what comes out of that." He again looked at her more personally, smiled, and added, "As much as I will miss you, you're probably better off going back to Washington."

She frowned.

"But my dear Brenda, don't worry, I'll find an excuse to get you back here, and very soon."

"I'm getting to like Brussels," she said. Then, focusing back on Peter, "I agree he's the one to track. We find him, we find the girl. Still, I can't help feeling, since she's the last one to see Sorensson alive, the chances are high that she's the one. She knew his Achilles' heel."

"His Achilles' hips, rather," Guy joked.

"In any case, we have to get one to find the other."

"My dear Brenda, we will look, and look again. It's like you Americans say – *It's not over...*"

"*Till the fat lady sings*," finished Brenda, her laughter joining Guy's. I leave in the morning. I await the results of your search. Our suspects are Europeans, and probably still moving around Europe. So, go get 'em, Commissioner, *s'il vous plaît.*"

"Nothing would please me better than to deliver Green Eyes and our boy Peter to you on a silver platter."

Chapter Eight

Geneva
June 6th

He hardly felt the wheels of the white Swissair Airbus 320 from London touch down on the dark carpet-like runway of Cointrin Airport. William Russell, US national security adviser, traveling on "private business" without an entourage, admired the Swiss for many talents, but particularly for operating the world's best airline and airports. In an age when airport terminals increasingly resembled cattle yards, with recessed lighting and Visa and MasterCard emblems everywhere, Russell regarded Geneva's and Zurich's spotless terminals as way stations to paradise.

With his recent appointment to the White House and the hectic whirlwind of the upcoming conventions, he had had little time to travel, and it was this he missed the most from his days as a college professor. As a specialist in Middle Eastern affairs, he had been able to write off frequent trips and, although they were mainly to the Gulf, he always managed to squeeze in a couple of days in Europe. He found fhe contrast between Geneva and Cairo exciting.

It's good to be back, he thought, smiling warmly at the blonde stewardess as he disembarked. Hit on the aircraft steps by blasts of surprisingly cool air for June, he wished he had a topcoat to throw over his shoulders as he boarded the airport bus.

It took him six minutes to get from the plane, past immigration, and out through the green doors of Swiss customs. *About normal*, he reflected with admiration. He glanced at his Omega and walked to the main entrance, relieved to see Alfredo standing next to the silver Mercedes 600 that had whisked from this terminal so many of Mansour Cherif's special visitors.

Russell's carry-on luggage disappeared into the immense trunk of the powerful automobile. Seconds later Alfredo put the automatic shift into drive. The car passed Palexpo, turned right into the Route de Ferney, and headed for downtown.

"Vesenaz today, Alfredo?" asked Russell.

"No, sir. We're going directly to Megève."

"Ah, our Moroccan pasha has moved to his Alpine headquarters, has he? Well then, I have time for a good cigar after that damn commercial flight. They don't let you smoke anymore."

Alfredo winced. Russell immediately knew he was worried that the car would reek of smoke long after the hour-long drive. There were few things his boss hated more than tobacco smoke. Russell had seen it many times – Mansour forbade it in his presence and berated any member of his family or staff who polluted his house, offices, or automobiles with the abhorred odor. Perfumed sprays were everywhere. In this instance, though, Alfredo would not deem it appropriate to say anything to his passenger, who, he knew well from previous visits, was close to his boss.

As the car neared the Inter-Continental Hotel, home of many OPEC conferences, Russell asked Alfredo to stop so he could pick up a box of Montecristo No 1's from the Gérard & Fils cigar shop. While at the hotel, he got a quick haircut from Jean-Claude, his favorite hairdresser on earth. Mansour was always neat, and besides Russell knew he would not have a relaxed moment for a haircut back in D.C.

Within minutes, as he luxuriated in the rear seat with one of Cuba's best cigars – a bit tricky but not impossible to get in the US – they reached the Pont du Mont Blanc, linking the right and left banks of Lac Léman.

The silver sedan cut through the center of the city to Route de Malagnou. In a few minutes they were at the French-Swiss border post before the Autoroute Blanche, the French superhighway to Mont Blanc, Europe's highest mountain. The French customs officer waved the Mercedes through. Russell surmised the customs officer had seen the Geneva plates and approved of rich people spending Swiss francs in *la belle* France. *Sorry, about that*, mon ami, *only a poor American government employee inside*. He chuckled to himself.

After a thirty-minute drive at 160 kilometers an hour, Alfredo took a right turn to the small industrial village of Sallanches, home to some of the best ski factories in France. He then began the drive up the twisting mountain road to Combloux and then Megève, the ski resort developed by the Rothschilds.

After winding up the mountain for twenty minutes, they reached an exquisite chalet on the crest of Mont d'Arbois that overlooked Megève. Russell stepped out into fresh mountain air filled with the scent of lavender. He noticed nearby the small creek cutting through the Mont d'Arbois area, which he remembered from previous visits; the locals referred to it as the "River Jordan" to mark the presence there of Jews and Arabs.

The door was opened by a butler. "*Bonsoir, monsieur, soyez le bienvenu au Flocon, le chalet de Monsieur Mansour.*"

Russell's mind, fogged by the flight, smoke, booze, food, and fatigue, searched for the appropriate French response: "*Merci pour votre chaleureux accueil.*" He chuckled inwardly at his halting, heavily accented but error-free French. He loved the warm greetings of the French and Arabic languages, both of which he had learned during his childhood in North Africa and the Gulf. Although he spoke Arabic better, his French was sufficient to impress women around the world and to cope with temperamental Parisian headwaiters.

He was escorted to the den, where the butler, identified upon request as Jean-Pierre, poured him a freshly mixed *kir*. Although he seldom thought of it when not in Europe, Russell enjoyed the white wine with its sweet hint of *cassis*. He relaxed in front of the warm fire, content to be back in Megève.

Though the spot was now one of his great loves, he had first come here by chance in 1978, having failed to get a holiday hotel in nearby Geneva. To the rescue had come his wealthy Moroccan friend, Mansour Cherif, suggesting Megève and arranging a chalet apartment for Russell and his companion, a 38D-cup brunette beauty from Louisiana. Russell had been finishing his history of the Ottoman expulsion from the Arab world, and it was the perfect spot to contemplate the challenges of syntax and draft footnotes by day, and dive into Sandra by night.

The few minutes of pleasant recall were interrupted by the entry of the tall, striking Mansour, regal with his graying hair and goatee. Russell always thought it must be the Berber strain, rather than the Arab side, that gave Mansour the intimidating handsomeness which seemed to unnerve those meeting him for the first time. *Some things never change*, he thought, as he watched Mansour survey the room, checking his guest's general health, and the adequacy of the logs in the fireplace.

"My good friend. I trust the drive from Geneva was comfortable?"

"Of course, Mansour. Everything was perfect, as usual. Alfredo, the car, the view, the chalet, even the *kir*. All to remind me of that fateful first visit to Megève. What more could I ask for?"

"Ah," his host laughed in his sly, polished way, "you must want something badly to flatter me so. But you have yet to enjoy dinner and a good rest. Then you will be happy, far away from those journalists, politicians, and government officials who ruin your days and are after your job."

Russell could, indeed, think of several and nodded soberly. *"Eh, oui."*

Jean-Pierre came into the room to refill Russell's glass from a crystal-and-silver pitcher and to ask the master of the house if he cared for a drink.

"Water," Mansour demanded. "One must never forget one's origins and, as a Bedouin, I must be ready to return to the desert if need be and drink only the water of the oasis." He smiled. "That keeps me ready for all eventualities."

"You're always the philosopher, my friend," Russell said. "I miss your worldly wisdom when I'm back home."

"So tell me, Bill, what wicked affair is your great superpower about to unleash on the world for the summer season? Are you going to destroy India and Pakistan now that they are testing their bombs again? Should I perhaps take refuge in the desert?"

Russell smiled. "As the world knows only too well, the boys back home are getting ready for serious electioneering. It will be a pretty close race among the three senators. In fact, we might have some real – as opposed to imaginary – political problems ahead as far as the Middle East is concerned, especially if this Westlake character gets elected." Russell spat out the senator's name with contempt. "We also have Kramer running, and you know where his money comes from!"

"Good!" Mansour put in with a slight nod. "Allah sends us problems every day to test us. Without them we would become soft and the enemy would defeat us. Tell me more – specifically, where the problem is, so I can solve it!"

124

"It's Westlake I'm most worried about. He's going to win the Democratic nomination with considerable ease next month and, as you well know, he's one of the most pro-Israeli members of the Senate. One thing's for sure – he's...," Russell hesitated, then finished, "fucking dangerous." And he added, "What can we do to stop him?"

Mansour smirked. "Frankly, dear friend, it's hard for me to see what will be different. Throughout recent history, most of the American presidential candidates have competed to outdistance each other in bowing and scraping to the Zionist lobby in the United States – you know, the lobby that doesn't actually exist!" He laughed and took a long drink of water. "Remember that scene in '84 when Mondale, Hart, and Jackson appeared before a Jewish group in New York and each tried to prove he had done more for Israel than the other. Or Gingrich in Jerusalem." He smiled with a touch of irony from within that perfectly trimmed beard. "You would have thought they were running for president of Israel." Russell returned the smile. "But they're all history now."

"Sure are," the American nodded.

"Besides, my friend," continued Mansour, "the Zionists in the United States have made more money for me than anyone else. By blocking congressional approval of more F-15 sales to Saudi Arabia, they've enabled me and my Saudi partners to push through a sale of Tornados – to date, over a twenty-billion-dollar project, with commissions you'd never believe! I'll be rolling in commissions for life. Now you understand why I love those Zionists of yours." He laughed heartily. "They are so blindly determined to control your lousy Middle East policy that they throw away the richest foreign sales, not to mention jobs, of their own nation. Every time my Geneva bank statements arrive, I toast Zionism. God bless them!" Mansour then motioned to the dining-room and asked his friend to join him. "*Allez*, now for a small meal."

Russell was familiar with Mansour's "small meals." He feasted his eyes on a tantalizing oriental salad with a dozen rows of fat *dolmas*, stuffed peppers, calamari tentacles, and slabs of goat cheese.

Mansour could never wait more than ten seconds for his food to be served, so salad and bread were in place when they went to the table. Russell bit into a stuffed grape leaf and waited for Mansour to bite into a tomato before steering the conversation back to what he was there for.

"Wonderful salad." Mansour knew what was coming.

"My financial advisers have informed me of several good investment possibilities which may be of special interest to us both." Russell paused and looked steadily at his host. Mansour nodded; Russell's statement was loaded with innuendo and he listened intently.

"The buyout of a select handful of American companies, a hot real-estate development project in California, and a small offshore oil company are all up for grabs. But more important than all of this is my concern over Westlake running for the presidency. It could hurt us."

"Bill, you of all people should know every politician's a whore. You're there in the middle of them. Only whores are more honorable because at least they deliver what they promise. Getting into power and staying there are two different games. Why do you continually insist on wasting your time trying to put one group in or keep another out?" Mansour tore off a piece of pita bread and dipped it in the large bowl of chickpea purée that had been placed in front of him. "Try the humus; it's excellent."

Russell was silent.

"The point is merely to work around them, or over them, to keep the nation prosperous despite them, for they can never make money for the citizens, but only spend their money, or devalue it, as one of your secretaries of Treasury did so well in the late '80s."

"Mansour, I wish politics had as little effect on our nation as you sometimes pretend. The fact, is you know better, so let's talk seriously, okay?" It seemed to Russell that his retort soured the smile on Mansour's handsome, tanned face.

The Moroccan spoke. "*D'accord*, my dear visitor. Politics it is. But is Senator Westlake really that evil? True, he's a bit more pro-Israeli than most of the Senate – even more than Kramer. But, from over here he doesn't seem nearly as competent as the others. This means that he might be more easily handled on the Arab-Israeli question than a more intelligent man who might initially be more evenhanded, if such a phrase is applicable to any American's appreciation of the Middle East."

"You still don't seem to quite grasp what I'm telling you," Russell sputtered in response. "That pro-Israeli son of a bitch sailed through the Western states' primary in March and now is on his way to winning the fucking nomination. For Christ's sake, we want you to do something about it. And now! The Israelis always win because you guys sit around and eat chickpeas."

"Bill! Calm down. I was just pushing you! To see how bad Westlake is for us."

The butler suddenly entered the dining room and whispered something in French to Mansour, bringing a sly smile to his face. He responded in a clear voice, "Well, invite them in. Don't make them sit out there like idiots."

The butler nodded obediently.

Russell could guess. "Please, Mansour. No bimbos!" he whispered peevishly. "I thought we could have a serious evening."

"Be calm, my friend. This is only an interlude to stop you from talking politics. Otherwise, how would you get any rest? I must force you to rest, at least when you're here. High in the Alps!"

Russell gave up as two classy blondes in stunning white silk dresses walked into the small dining room. One of them, clearly Swiss, smiled warmly at Mansour and introduced her Austrian friend to him. She then turned to the American guest and introduced herself. "My name is Ursula. This is my friend, Andrea."

"Pleased to meet you, ladies," Russell replied in a resigned voice as he turned to Mansour. "Remember, tomorrow we talk shop."

"We will – that is, if you perform well tonight. I'll ask the girls to grade you, to see if you're still a person worth dealing with. As you know, I never trust a man who doesn't screw well – and often." Mansour waved the Austrian girl toward Russell, and a quick step brought her behind his chair. Her arms around him, she began to loosen his tie.

He put down his fork; this meal was clearly over.

Mansour stood and suggested they go into his sitting room for Turkish coffee. He and Ursula relaxed on the plush cushions of one sofa, Bill Russell and Andrea on the other. Mansour started playing with the remote control for his 55-inch-screen Sony, scanning the world of images beaming in from satellites. He picked up his phone and asked the butler to bring him the new films on video which he said had just been delivered to his bedroom suite. Mansour had a passion for movies, particularly postwar American comedies.

Several seconds later the waiter entered with coffee and a dish of white chocolate truffles. He placed them on a six-foot-diameter brass and silver inlay tray, which sat on a low foot between the two sofas.

"Mr. Mansour, don't you have a porno film we could watch?" asked Andrea. "Something to warm us up." This was her first time at Mansour's and she didn't want to come across as timid.

Ursula knew this wasn't a good approach and tried to warn Andrea with her eyes, but it was too late.

"No, Miss Vienna. If you want some sex films, I suggest you go back to your native *Oesterreich*. This is a proper house and you're here to welcome my friend, Dr. Russell, and to have a free cup of coffee, not to start demanding things." Mansour stopped abruptly. He sipped his cup of Arabica – audibly, as befitted a good Middle Easterner – while regaining control of his temper.

Russell decided to use the chill in the atmosphere to get back to the point of his visit. "Look, why don't you ladies go upstairs and get comfortable while Mr. Mansour and I finish our coffee. We'll be up before you can count to..."

Before Andrea could figure out what had happened, Ursula leaped from her end of the sofa. "That's a good idea! We haven't even had time to comb our hair since we arrived. See you later, gentlemen."

Andrea took her cue, jumping up like a frightened colt to join her friend, and the two of them glided out. Russell tried not to notice the beautiful swaying buttocks under the rustle of white silk.

"We won't take too long," he added, now feeling the weight of his jet-lag.

As the women left, the butler arrived with the videos. Mansour had Jean-Pierre insert an old Dean Martin and Jerry Lewis comedy. "Forget the girls. Let us watch the movie. It's a good one."

Mansour's behavior began to irritate the American. It was more erratic than usual – *first, tempting me with beautiful ladies, then insisting on a mindless comedy*, he thought. *Okay, Mansour loved movies, but this was overdoing it*. Russell's eyelids were growing heavy and his mind returned to the high-octane blondes. Secretly, he was relieved Mansour had banished them.

He wasn't sure he could perform tonight.

Twenty minutes later, Mansour was roaring with laughter and Russell could feel the fatigue sweeping through his body and mind like a gas cloud settling on an unsuspecting victim. He decided to make his move toward the bed for which his whole being cried out. "Old buddy, I'm going to leave both blondes and Dean and Jerry for you – just to show you how generous I am. I'm fading fast and better find the bunk assigned to me before I end up snoring here on the sofa and ruining this classic."

"Bill! You always underestimate me, no matter how many years go by – and how many is it now? I have something for you to take to bed – some light reading in case you wake up at three in a different time zone. My lady friend from Zurich will bring it to you in your bedroom. It is a bit of pure gold – one of my best efforts – and will remind you that your old friend Mansour has yet to lose touch with the world of international operators. Good night, my friend." *Operator for sure*, Russell thought, centering his weight over his legs. "*Pourquoi pas, Monsieur Mansour.*"

Russell looked up to see James, the upstairs butler, already waiting, evidently summoned by the buzzer near his master's seat.

James was the only English butler in Mansour's entourage. Mansour had hired him away from Buckingham Palace during a Moroccan state visit to London. He led Russell up the deeply carpeted stairs to the bedroom hallway, lined with modern paintings which contrasted with the rustic antique furnishings. Russell saluted the dancer in the pastel print on the landing.

At the far end of the hall, opposite the master suite, James opened a door and led Russell into a bedroom suite warmed by an open fire. In true five-star style the butler showed the honored guest around the two rooms, reviewing the operation of the radio, television, and video controls. James pointed out the bath and dressing room – where the visitor's suits had already been pressed and hung – and finally the welcoming bed, where Russell's pajamas lay next to a white terry cloth bathrobe with an embroidered golden M. The bathroom boasted several brands of eaux de toilette, after-shave lotions, shampoos, and soaps. The clear bottle of a cologne called Boss caught Russell's eye and he chuckled.

"Just dial me on 17 if you need anything during the night, sir. Have a pleasant sleep." James backed out of the large suite, closing the door behind him.

Fading fast, Russell undressed impatiently and shuffled into the shower, where he alternated hot and cold water to keep him awake. Minimally more conscious, he lumbered back into the bedroom, the terry robe soaking up the hot moisture from his shoulders. He stopped at the sight of the beauty from Zurich, draped in a white satin dressing gown, reclining on the small sofa. She was sipping a glass of champagne she had poured for herself from the bottle that had been left cooling on the wet bar.

"Excuse the intrusion, Dr. Russell, but His Excellency Mr. Mansour wished you to have a dossier to read in case you have trouble falling asleep, or if you wake up early. If you need a massage or anything else before going to bed, I'll be happy to be of service. Any friend of Mr. Mansour's," she added, with the sexiest modulation of her voice, "is such a *very* special friend of mine."

"Thank you, dear lady," he whispered with a gaping yawn, "but I'll be damn lucky just to get into my pj's tonight, let alone anything else. See you at breakfast." He smiled, pleased with his line. *To think that I'm turning this down. Unthinkable twenty years ago. Ten, even.*

"In that case I'll leave this file with you." Ursula reached behind a sofa pillow to reveal a plain, letter-size, sealed envelope, slightly perfumed. She left it on the bedside table and moved toward the door. "Call me on extension 32 if you wish to discuss the file – or just want to reconsider. Any hour. I'm quite proud of the dossier. It's the best I've produced for Mr. Mansour in a long time." She walked out of the room, again showing off her satin-covered *derrière* to maximum advantage, which was about the easiest thing she had done all day.

Just before switching off his light, he turned over the envelope and, as he was fading away, made out the label – "The Life and Loves of Wes Westlake, US Senator." *My God. Damn Mansour's done it again. He was way ahead of me! Fucking Jerry Lewis.* He grinned as his head sagged to his chest and he drifted into sleep, the envelope gripped in his hands.

Washington, D.C., June 7th

It was 10:00 p.m. and Senator Westlake was sitting at his desk at home writing explicit instructions for the transfer of several thousand dollars from an offshore savings account in the Cayman Islands to his local Washington bank. He was pleased with his image in the press lately and there were still five months before the election. His carefully contrived visits recently to AIDS victims at City Hospital had received just the enthusiastic media response he had wanted. Luckily he had the money to ensure that he was backed by a team of smart, hardworking assistants. He had already appeared on the cover of *Time*, the emblem of success in America.

He also had timed a press release about restricting the cutting of hardwoods by the timber industry to coincide with a major ecological convention to take place in Brazil. Since his father owned one of the largest timber mills in Washington state, Westlake had never had to work for a living. Nevertheless, he had inherited a savvy business sense, which he used when there was serious personal gain involved. He knew wood well.

On the Republican side his main threat was George Johnson, senior senator from New Hampshire. Like Westlake, Johnson had won his primary hands down, and had a certain polished charisma that made Westlake uneasy. He was a strong favorite bet to win the Republican ticket in August, especially with the president's backing. Westlake wasn't so concerned about New York Senator Dan Kramer, the third-party candidate, despite his heavy financial backing. Third party was third party in America.

Six feet three inches tall, Wes Westlake was a ruggedly handsome man and he knew it. His salt-and-pepper hair was very thick and straight and he was constantly brushing it back off his face, a gesture the political cartoonists loved to capture. His slightly flushed complexion gave him an almost cherubic look. Good looks combined with money, political power, and nerve created an attraction which helped with the women's vote. As his marriage had lost what he called "zip," he found considerable solace in female companionship, particularly Jeri, long his favorite hometown girl, with that cascade of red hair and killer figure. He glanced at his watch. 10:30. She would be in bed. He reached for the phone.

"Hi, honey. Hey, I miss you – especially right now." He heard a sleepy giggle.

"Oh, Wes. You're dreadful. Here I am huggin' my lil' ole teddy bear, just dreamin' that he was you."

"Mmm, pleasant thought." He heard a door creak upstairs. "Listen, gotta go – be in touch soon, okay?"

"The last time you said that was a good two weeks ago! I'm gettin' just a bit antsy, dear Senator Westlake. Just remember I deserve a hellava lot more. *More!* Got it?"

The telephone clicked and Westlake sat staring, a tad puzzled.

What the hell did she think she was going on about? She wouldn't dare, he thought uneasily. He would have to start being more careful, he lamented. *Shit.*

Chapter Nine

Washington, D.C.
June 11th

Just back from Brussels, Brenda had found on her screen a bold message from Judge Baker – "CONTACT ME NOW. The President is waiting." She guessed Douglas was ready to discuss the Sorensson-Libyan connection. *The judge's delicate challenge of the president worked. This is getting to be fun.*

Mary Maloney, the president's secretary, led the FBI director and Brenda into the Oval Office. Douglas was scribbling a last remark on the document he was reviewing with Bill Russell, who stood beside the oak desk.

Without looking up, the president acknowledged his guests. "Have a seat, Judge. I'll be right with you." He put his pen down and lifted his head. "Redraft that and let me see it at tomorrow's nine o'clock," he instructed Russell. Douglas then joined the judge, Russell, and Brenda in the seating area.

"So, Judge, we have unfinished business to take care of, don't we? Let's get on with it." Russell quietly took a seat as well.

"Mr. President," Judge Baker began, "allow me a moment to explain how this line of questioning got started. It's not easy for any of us to go into this delicate matter..."

"Oh, come off of it, Judge. We're not children," retorted the president.

"No, Mr. President, of course not. Well, our chief concern has to do with the question of why Ambassador Sorensson was meeting with the Libyan ambassador in Brussels. He told the State Department and Dr. Russell that he had your approval for these contacts." The judge paused. "We have yet to find any written approval. Naturally, if you gave the ambassador your oral approval, that's good enough for me. But, if you didn't, we need to look further into why he was seeing the Libyans." He stopped again. The president remained silent. He wanted to hear more.

The level of tension in the Oval Office seemed to mount. *Why was the president so sensitive whenever anyone mentioned Sorensson and his Libyan contacts*, Brenda thought. *That's why they were there. Why not get on with it?*

Brenda considered trying to draw the president's ire away from the judge. She might be overstepping her bounds; hers was a delicate place, in which one basically spoke only when asked to. Hesitantly, she decided to take the chance.

"Mr. President, excuse me for breaking in, but, as the Special Agent in charge of this investigation I must tell you that solving this murder is not going to be easy. The slightest, smallest detail could make a difference. We have no choice but to follow up on even the least nuance. The Libyan-Sorensson connection is an enigma to everyone we've talked to. I've been pressing Judge Baker to insist on this session with you. You seem the only one who can shed any information on this. We need your help, sir."

"Yes, yes. Let me tell you the whole story and put an end to all this guessing."

Oh-oh, he's in a frosty mood again, she thought. But she slid to the edge of her seat, hoping that an answer was finally forthcoming.

"Damn it, Judge. If Dick said he had my approval, you shouldn't question it. He was extremely loyal to me," Douglas said between clenched teeth. "I did approve his contact with the

136

Libyans. He persuaded me and I agreed. The question's not whether Dick had my approval. The question should be why I gave it."

Douglas stared around his office. That photo of himself with a past president on a fishing trip in the Keys was crooked. He needed to collect himself. For several moments he didn't speak. Then, abruptly, shifting his gaze, he addressed the group.

"It'd been over two years since our countrymen disappeared in Lebanon. Again! As you know, the kidnappers' demands were, as usual, completely out of the question. The United States could not and would not meet them. We'd been playing for time ever since." He suddenly stood up and walked to the window, staring at nothing in particular. A bird, a Fed Ex truck on the far side of Pennsylvania Avenue. Then he spun around and looked pointedly at Baker. "Not one damn agency in this town could tell me where the two kidnapped Americans were being held. Not the CIA, not Defense and the NSA, not State, not even you guys. Nobody, but nobody! Everybody around town had a thousand and one reasons why they didn't know. I faced the same frustrations Ronald Reagan had back in the eighties." He turned again to look out at the South Lawn of the White House. *It just isn't as pretty with those freakin' baracades*, he thought. *What a world this has become!*

"Mr. President, I well remember your sense of frustration," remarked Baker.

"Yes." He turned back. "Well, I was getting more furious at this lack of action with each passing day. So were the American people. We were all desperate for answers." He walked over and settled back into his chair. There was exhaustion in his gestures.

"Then one day a Moroccan friend of Bill's," Douglas waved his hand in Russell's direction, "called him to suggest the Libyans were so anxious to develop better relations with us that they might provide information about the kidnapped Americans.

The Moroccan knew the Libyans well – did a lot of business with them, it seemed. We were ready to try anything."

"How did we know we could trust this man, Mr. President?" asked Brenda.

"I'll respond to that, sir," Russell chimed in. "I've known Mansour for a long time. He's given me many good tips over the years. If you're interested I can forward a full dossier to your office. He's credible."

Brenda nodded her willingness to receive his file.

Russell nodded back and continued, "The Libyans have been trying to improve their relationship with us ever since Reagan sent the B-111s with those smart bombs over Tripoli and scared them to death. But subsequent administrations refused their approaches. Mostly because of Lockerbie, even after we got those thugs tried in The Hague."

"Bill kept saying that, from past dealings, this guy was trustworthy. Considering I had no apparent options other than taking a risk with the Libyans, I raised the issue with the Secretary of State, without revealing the source of the idea. He scoffed and suggested that it would cause considerable political embarrassment if we got caught. Asking one terrorist nation to give us information on another doesn't make for great PR." Douglas was fidgety and got up. He went to the refreshment table and poured himself a glass of Poland Spring. He took his glass to the window, seeming to derive energy from the broad, immaculate green lawn.

"'Why not?' I asked the secretary, reminding him that thieves rat on one another all the time. That's the key to most of our best police work. Well, to make a very long story brief, the secretary refused to even consider it. The same with CIA. So we dropped the idea." He shook his head and raised his hands and water glass in the air.

"Then one day, Dick was in town and we had dinner in my

private quarters. I ran the idea by him, certain that he'd laugh it off too. But he didn't laugh. Good old Dick. He couldn't stand to see me so damn frustrated about anything." The President's voice cracked a bit and his eyes briefly revealed his sorrow.

"As you know, he was an international attorney before he came into government – was used to getting results, and fast. He wasn't about protecting his ass. So he thought about the idea for ten minutes, then told me it was worth trying. He suggested the best way to commence relations with the Libyans might be through their ambassador in Brussels, whom he recalled having met at a reception at the Egyptian Embassy. There were hints about improved relations if the Americans were amenable. But the deputy chief of mission and political counselor at the mission had convinced Dick it'd make him look bad at State to even report the idea as worth considering – another great assist from our senior bureaucrats trying to cover their butts. Always better to do nothing than risk anything. Right?

"So Dick volunteered. I was surprised he'd want to get involved in such a scheme – to risk his good name by trying out the idea. He wanted to accomplish for me what this whole damn bureaucracy couldn't do. I guess he risked a whole lot more in that try than his good name." The hurt in the president's eyes spread to his face. He nervously put down his glass and rubbed his arms, then got to his feet, jammed his hands into his trouser pockets, and walked to his desk, his back to his guests. His drooping shoulders gave away his battle with his emotions. But, as everyone watched in silence, his shoulders straightened, regaining their strength. He was back in control. He turned around and continued.

"Contact was made. Their ambassador in Brussels, who's related to Fezzani himself, told Dick he was sure they could help us find the two Americans in Lebanon. And then the guy went further. He suggested to Dick that maybe Libya could get them out – and at no cost to us. I remembered when Sadat got a couple of imprisoned Americans out of Aden for Nixon in the late seventies. So I agreed to Dick's request to let him try. After all, Dick wasn't a kid. He was an international operator of some repute. I told him to do what he had to but not to promise them a thing in return. And I'm sure he was working it that way." The president went around his desk, pulled out his leather chair, and sat squarely, as if about to address the nation. "Of course, they didn't like it in Foggy Bottom. The State Department people could only think of protocol and policy restrictions. Like most presidents before me, I found that getting something really done is beyond them. But I swore an oath to protect America and its citizens. And I gave Dick the approval he requested. If he paid with his life for talking to the Libyans, it was for that reason and none other."

My God! Brenda thought. *He's blaming himself. No wonder he turns into a bear whenever anyone mentions Sorensson.* She cleared her throat. At least she could ease his mind on that score. All eyes turned to her, but Baker beat her to the words.

"Mr. President, like Dr. Russell, I know the frustration and sense of powerlessness you feel here. I can't say I blame you. As you know, Dr. Russell and I even tried a couple of private American channels in the hope of freeing the hostages. I believe this was before you agreed to Ambassador Sorensson's suggestion."

Brenda added, "Mr. President, we don't yet know why Ambassador Sorensson is dead, and so we can't conclude that the Libyan contacts led to his death. In fact, as you know, there's intercept intelligence that the Libyans, too, are puzzled about why he was murdered. Now I can see that they're upset because this channel to the White House has been cut off."

"Well, it's certainly cut until you people find out whether the Libyans were involved in Dick's death," said Douglas. "Judge

Baker, I want you to give Ms. Straus whatever she needs to solve this case. And Ms. Straus, if you need to talk to me directly, pick up that phone and call. This was not just an American ambassador. Richard Sorensson was my best friend and I want to know who did this – whether or not we can prove it in court. When you're a superpower, you don't have to prove things in court. This time we'll literally take Tripoli off the face of the map if those guys did it. That's a promise!"

Chapter Ten

Palma de Mallorca, Spain
June 14th

Jackie Markovic was thousands of miles away in Mallorca. There Jackie always found her peace. She told her friends it was her *paraíso*, paradise on earth.

The sky was clear, the sun warm, and Jackie could not resist the inviting water. She emerged from her room wrapped in a large beach towel and headed for the deep end of the bean-shaped pool. Alongside the pool's edge she stretched her slinky 5'9" body, wearing a straw hat, a pair of round, oversized sunglasses, a bikini bottom, and nothing else. She lay on her tummy, her right cheek resting on her folded arms, her weight flatening her firm breasts. Sleepily, she let the sun work its magic on her perpetually bronzed back.

After a peaceful quarter of an hour, Jackie turned over. Her breasts pointed skyward. Several male guests, loitering around the deep end, admired the well-shaped globes, especially the dark, erect nipples. With a mischievous smile, Jackie slowly ran her palms over the taut buttons, back and forth, enjoying the muted groans from the men.

It had been nearly two months since she'd seen her Russian lover. Her smile spread wider. *A long time for a girl like me to go without sex – at least with a man.* The thrill of her latest success, however, was more than consolation for her starved emotions. Her face upward, she squinted at the unending blueness, and began mentally spending the francs she had just earned from the Brussels hit.

It should be in the bank by now. She was going to fly to Switzerland to make sure it was all there, then call Peter. After giving Peter his share, she'd take a long-overdue vacation. Maybe she'd call her lover and ask him to join her. They had such great sex, and for that he'd find a way to see her, regardless of where his assignments had taken him. But first, she would make sure the Iranians finally had replenished her account. *Hell, I took out an ambassador.* The deposit was overdue and she was getting edgy. The Iranians had always been prompt and reliable before.

Her flight to Geneva was already booked for the next morning, Iberia Flight 984. Once there, she would go directly to the Wilhelm Friedrich Bank, withdraw fifty grand worth of Swiss francs and treat herself to a shopping spree on the Rue du Rhône. There was a Patek Phillipe that she'd been eyeing for months. Now she would please herself with the regal toy. Jackie closed her eyes, a pleased smile curving her full lips. Mindful of the admiring gaze of the dark man in the Cerruti suit to her left, she dozed off. *Let him dream.*

Geneva, June 15th

Jackie left Geneva Airport, turned right from habit – even though she knew from arduous training that any pattern was often dangerous – and walked a few steps to the covered taxi stand. She took the first Mercedes taxi to her private bank just off the Rue du Rhône. She never had it stop right in front of the inconspicuous door, but always got out half a block away. She thought of the seven-figure payment awaiting her and excited herself with the

143

thought of seeing the sum appear on the pink slip the bank's computer would generate. This was the largest single payment in her career. For several years she had been rich, but this payment, combined with her savings and her "pension plan" of small apartments around the world, propelled her into the league of the filthy rich. She had earned the adjective. She was the best at what she did, and her fees reflected it. After the Macao job a year ago for that Hong Kong group her price had gone up.

This time, too. It was a lot of money, but the job was worth it. Many would have turned it down. Too big, too risky, too political.

Because of the importance and nationality of the target, she had insisted that Peter triple their usual fee. She and Peter would probably have to go into hiding for a year or more, and she had factored the cost of semi-retirement into the price.

After all, it was high-risk indeed to murder an ambassador – particularly an American, given their usual high-tech defensive barriers, massive manpower, and determination to hunt down such a killer. By now the most efficient and determined police operatives in every nation would be looking worldwide for the assassin. That thrilled Jackie more than the deed itself. Though the professional in her would not allow her to underestimate the danger in which she had placed herself this time, eluding the Americans would provide another exhilarating challenge.

The taxi stopped in front of a drab concrete office building. Jackie got out, paid, and blew the coffee-colored driver a kiss. Two Swiss women walking by frowned. Such brashness on the part of a young lady just wasn't right. Jackie grinned to herself as she walked to her bank. *Garce*, her lover liked to call her, the French equivalent of "bitch," but with style.

She had chosen this small, family-owned private bank because it was even more discreet than the big Swiss banks. The postcard-sized brass nameplate near the understated entrance was the only indication that the building housed a bank.

In her new black-and-white Chanel suit, Jackie rang the small buzzer beside the brown wooden door. The electronic latch unhitched and the door swung open. She approached the poker-faced blonde receptionist, who gave a neutral smile without uttering a word and pushed a small form across her desk. Jackie filled in the name of her bank officer, her identification number, and a quickly scripted *J* on the bottom line. The receptionist made sure she could read the handwriting, scanned the signature for a cross-check clearance, and said, "Please take a seat."

No names had been mentioned, even though there were no other clients in the waiting area. This was a matter of policy. No names spoken in the common space. Your banking matters were strictly personal. It made Jackie feel protected. The receptionist went into another room to call Mr. Luc Bonnaire, youngest of the senior partners.

As Jackie sat in the large oak chair, she admired once again the decor of one of the oldest private banks in Geneva. Persian carpets lay on a stone-white marble floor. High-back oak chairs rested against the walls, their plush red velvet cushions depicting German hunting scenes. Matching velvet drapes covered five tall windows, and a modest but high-quality crystal chandelier hung from the hand-painted ceiling. *This is where I belong*, she thought.

The receptionist returned. "Follow me, please." They entered one of the small interior rooms where Bonnaire always received her. Furnished with a small meeting table, four chairs, and a bookcase, the room's only connection with the outside word was the simple telephone resting on the top shelf. Not even a cordless.

"Good morning, Mademoiselle Markovic. Good to see you again," Bonnaire said as he entered, extending his hand from a cufflinked sleeve.

"I am expecting some good news from you." Jackie's green

eyes sparkled with anticipation.

"What would that be, mademoiselle?"

"A *very* large deposit. Larger than usual." She smiled with satisfaction. But the smile began to fade as she heard Bonnaire's next words.

"Sorry, mademoiselle," he said cautiously. "There have been no new deposits to your account. You could have called me to ask about such..." And then he caught himself; Mademoiselle Markovic preferred no telephone conversations. "How much was it you were expecting?"

"One million eight hundred thousand dollars. The money should have been deposited into the three accounts and might be in mixed currencies, German marks, Swiss francs, US dollars...," her voice, which had gradually intensified, suddenly trailed off, while her bronzed skin flushed as shock traveled through her nervous system.

The small room fell quiet. Apprehension, thick and menacing, occupied the short distance separating its two occupants.

"Again, mademoiselle," the banker said uneasily, "I have received nothing in such quantities for you. According to the information I have here, your last deposit – two hundred thousand dollars – was in January of this year. When the receptionist informed me that you were here, I assumed you had come to review the progress of your investment portfolio. I brought that with me."

Jackie's famous smile, which had charmed many a banker, faded like the colors of a caught fish. Her eyes were puzzled. "There must be a *mistake*," she whispered. "No, I don't mean you, Mr. Bonnaire. I know you're always impeccable with details, but could you double-check with your colleagues to see if the bank has received any deposits since May which they've been unable to account for? Perhaps my account numbers were incorrect in the transfer. I don't know, but there's a mistake somewhere." Anxiety finally reached her throat; the calm and discretion of the place were no longer sufficient to stem her irritation.

To satisfy her, Bonnaire immediately agreed to double-check; he suggested that, meanwhile, Mademoiselle Markovic should have an expresso. He ushered her out, eager to put some distance between himself and this woman. Her anger – and something else which he could not define – he found unsettling. His chest tightened, constricting his breathing. Some people conveyed danger, and she was one of them. Once they had lunched at a beautiful lakeside café in Geneva. Sipping her coffee, the woman had reminded him with little ambiguity that if he ever slipped, or whispered her account numbers to a nosy bank authority or government agency, he would never again have to worry about his pension plan; retirement would come early. This was an unecessary thing to remind a banker of in Switzerland, but she was new at the game and took no chances. He understood, and although bringing in a new client with a sizable first deposit pleased him, the conversation ruined his lunch. She had softened the threat by also offering him the use of a string of comfortable, well-furnished apartments in leisure spots and major cities – a luxury of which he had eventually availed himself, and had come to prize. The week in Cyprus had been glorious. *Sacré Mademoiselle Markovic*, he thought.

Bonnaire returned to confirm that the bank had received no unresolved deposits of this type in the past few months. "But rest assured, Mademoiselle Markovic, that in the coming days I will be doubly vigilant on your behalf. You may call me – ask for Léman – to inquire if there's good news. If the funds have been located, I will say, "Yes, let's set up an appointment." Is this agreeable to you, mademoiselle?"

Bonnaire's suggestion did not appease Jackie. *Where is my fucking cash*, her mind screamed. She nodded curtly before rising.

Confused and shaken, Jackie left the bank, her mind reeling. *What had gone wrong? What?*

Over the next week Jackie disregarded her usual overcautious nature and phoned Bonnaire daily. But the repeated inquiries revealed that her Brussels hit had not been paid.

Sorensson's death had been confirmed and reported worldwide one day after she killed him. Then why hadn't her fees been paid? Her confusion gradually turned into barely controllable anger.

She had to inform Peter of the situation. He'd be shocked. Then the shock would quickly be transformed into distrust. Distrust of her. Was she holding out? Jackie knew that would pass through his mind. She had to be careful.

Peter's initial panic agitated Jackie further, for she had always depended on him to be an assertive and resourceful front man and backup. Her right hand for many years, Peter had once been mean and tough. A turbulent, destitute childhood in Salonika had taught him a few things. And his training with Henri Curiel, the infamous founder of the Egyptian communist party, had cultivated his ruthlessness and channeled his talents into clandestine operations, where his lessons were put to good use.

But lately there had been a change in Peter. Gone was the sly, crafty partner. In his place was a brooding, nervous, unsure old man. As to what had caused this alteration, Jackie hesitated. The change was slowly eating at his core.

She watched him try to cover up his nervousness but she could sense the change. He now seemed physically unwell, overstressed. She could handle his fatigue, but his suspicious inclination toward her was intolerable. *Where was the bloody payment?*

The fool, she thought. *There has never been reason for him to suspect me.* She had made sure of that by giving him the responsibility of negotiating all their contracts. This way Peter had first knowledge of all payments expected, and the exact amount of his cut. The two of them had designed their own built-in monetary control system – he controlled the contract; she controlled the receipts. It was in the interest of each not to cheat or play foolish games.

The month of June was closing and her inquiries at the bank continued to yield disappointing responses. Now Jackie could wait no longer and decided to take the matter up directly with the client.

"Something is seriously wrong. We have to fly to Paris and check with Kavir. There is no other way," she insisted one morning as they took their coffee in a small *patisserie* on Rue des Alpes, near the Quai du Mont Blanc.

"Oh, god," sighed Peter, popping another half a Valium and two magnesium capsules into his mouth while Jackie stared blankly at the garden. The statue of the Duke of Brunswick was still there.

She turned to him as he swallowed. "Listen. I know you're tired, I know you're upset. So am I. But I promise you that when this is all over we'll both take a long vacation. So let's get on with it, get our asses to Paris and find out why those bastards haven't paid us. They've never missed a payment before, so maybe it's just...," she wanted to say "an oversight," but stopped short. One point eight million dollars is a sum hard to forget. "Maybe they're short of cash – the newspapers claim Iran is having a cash crisis. In any case, we have to know the reason."

"Yes, yes. I am tired of this stuff. So tired. After Paris, it's a long holiday. You promise."

"*D'accord*, dear Peter. *On y va.*" She pointed in the direction of the central station. The TGV, the fast train to Paris, left in less than an hour.

Paris, June 24th

The next morning in the City of Light, Jackie stood at the window of her third-floor hotel room. The Hôtel Quatre Trèfles was modest and banal, perfect for the task. She positioned a chair so she could watch the Café La Terrace across the street without being seen from outside.

Sitting leisurely near the open window, Jackie wore her headset, a device disguised as a Walkman or *balladeur*, as the French insisted on calling them. With this gadget, she could communicate with Peter as he held this crucial meeting in the café across the avenue.

Jackie had contracted a Swiss expert known simply as HS to have this useful little toy developed. He lived in a village on the far side of the Zurich airport, called Bachen-Blach. HS was rumored to be the world's foremost developer of clandestine communication techniques and security objects. Most of his clients were underworld organizations, but there were a few freelancers like Jackie. She paid well for the expertise, and was convinced that he was worth every cent. Or thousand. With the advantage of his wizardry she was equal to any superpower warrior. Technology did have its democratic benefits and was now international, exclusive to no one power.

At 10:30 a.m., three hours earlier, Peter had used a phone booth to call the Iranian Embassy. A heavily accented French voice had responded and Peter had asked for Shadar Kavir, the religious affairs officer. Kavir's real function was local representative of the Revolutionary Guard. He had been the contact between his organization and Peter for several sensitive assignments requiring assassination, which Jackie had carried out. Among those eliminated were two Muslim sheiks at the Brussels mosque who had protested the death threat issued against Salman Rushdie. Another victim was an Arab diplomat in Brussels who had worked for the Iranians as a secret agent; later, he had changed alliance and fed the Iranians false information. That didn't last long.

150

Kavir was powerfully connected to the Tehran regime. He conveyed a sense of authority and danger, despite his modest attire and humble beard. He liked to think that people feared him and recognized his authority. But he had always been scrupulous in dealing with his contract help, and when it came to payment, he was honorable. "We have our own set of principles, and that you refuse to understand," he often repeated to Western journalists.

Thus, when Peter had called that morning for an emergency meeting, Kavir was noticeably wary. He had no outstanding task for Peter, nor was any payment overdue. Yet Peter made it clear by his tone of voice that a meeting was essential.

They had exchanged the usual signal, after which Kavir replied, "You will have your manuscript back in three days to the address on the envelope." That meant they would meet in three hours at the same place as last time, a small café in the seventh *arrondissement* on the Avenue Bosquet near the Ecole Militaire.

Kavir arrived with two of his men. Their function was to assure the security of the outdoor meeting – a precaution against a possible setup by Peter or, more unlikely, a police trap. As Kavir had diplomatic immunity, he wasn't concerned about arrest, unlike his professional contractors. This meeting had taken him by surprise, and he didn't like surprises. But the contractor, Peter, was so important that he couldn't refuse to meet him. Intelligence was a matter of knowing.

Jackie spotted the countersurveillance from her hotel window.

"Hello, *monsieur*," Peter said, rising to his feet and extending his hand as Kavir approached the sidewalk table. He sat down at the small table.

Without accepting the handshake, Kavir gave a curt nod then glanced around suspiciously, trying to figure out what was going on. "What do you want?" he said in an angry whisper.

"Take it easy, my friend," responded Peter with surprise. "I just want to get paid for our last assignment. What do you think I want – do you know how long it has been? Your credit is good, but we're not used to waiting this long."

"Payment? We owe you nothing," the Iranian snapped back. "You were fully paid for the last project. Why do you come here? If you're up to tricks with us, you are a dead man. Understand?"

"What are you talking about? What about Brussels – you know, the ambassador? Ibrahim used your code and we did it as he ordered. His instructions were very precise. He even mentioned the last operation we had done for you, the Arab diplomat in Brussels."

"I have no one by that name working for me," responded Kavir, "and I ordered nothing. Nothing at all. My God! Are you talking about the murder of the American ambassador in Brussels? Are you crazy enough to think for one minute that we would do such a thing? Don't you know, you imbecile, that killing an ambassador is treated by international law as an act of war? You're crazy, insane, to have carried out such an assignment for anybody. You were set up. It certainly wasn't us and don't you ever *dream* of connecting us to this crime, or I shall see to it personally that your life ends. *Vous comprenez?*"

Having heard this exchange over the receiver, Jackie was in a state of rage. Worse still, she believed Kavir. Instantly, she knew she and Peter had made a mistake – a grave mistake. *"Merde!"* she muttered grimly, gritting her teeth and pressing the headphones tightly to her ears.

Peter sputtered, "B-but, how could this happen? H-ow could this man know our code and our previous arrangements?" He pushed his wrought-iron chair back and blurted, "You are penetrated. You people have no security. Lots of motivation, lots of money, lots of hatred – but no security!"

Kavir quickly decided to end the session for fear that this meeting was a gimmick to push for some kind of confrontation.

His Middle Eastern mentality led him always to expect duplicity. All too often his suspicions were valid.

"Mr. Peter, listen carefully. For us, you should never, do you understand me, never, take orders from anyone but me. That was a stupid move on your part. The breach of security could be from one of your team. I don't know. It is not us. You have been used by somebody. I suggest you find this Ibrahim and break every bone in his body, one by one, until he tells you who used you. You know as well as I do that our side has always paid you as agreed when you performed as agreed. We have nothing to gain from not paying you. I consider this conversation concluded and never again do I wish to discuss the matter with you. Never!"

A whispered woman's voice came through on Peter's concealed earpiece. "I believe him, Peter. Thank him for the clarification and tell him you consider the matter closed and will await any further work he may have in the future."

Peter repeated the message as though the comment were spontaneous. Kavir nodded acceptance in a superior manner, rose, and left the table without touching his coffee – another security precaution.

Sinking deeper into her chair, Jackie stared out the hotel window. *Damn*, she thought. *Damn, damn, damn! I've been set up – used. Fucked! For the first time in my professional life. And now I'm going to find out who's responsible. The bastards will pay. How they'll pay! I have a reputation to uphold and I won't allow myself to be used by any man. Never again! Not after my father...* An image of her father flashed on her mental screen with an X over his face, like the black mark her computer flashed when the application for a file could not be found.

Jackie decided to do what she always did when she was depressed: spend money and pamper herself. It was her favorite defense. She opted to stop by the Carita beauty parlor; the relaxation would do her good and would clear her mind before she met Peter several hours later. They always kept a safe distance after an important rendezvous.

A shampoo, hairdo, and manicure later, Jackie felt better. Her mind was sharp and her thoughts focused. She would unvail this scam and have her revenge. Like the Mafia, she felt she could not afford to have anyone walking around bragging about tricking her. Beyond the money, this was a matter of honor. Furthermore, she despised the idea of having done the dirty work for an unknown client and an unclear cause. No, she promised herself, the ultimate price would have to be paid to re-establish her credibility.

But by whom?

At four that afternoon, feeling more herself, Jackie met Peter in a lingerie boutique on the Faubourg Saint-Honoré. If he were tailed, it would look like he was meeting his frivolous mistress after conducting a day's business. At all times Jackie made sure she was protected from any suggestion that she was the ultimate assassin, even if Peter himself fell under suspicion.

But more important than being careful, she had a score to settle. She bought a low-cut Rosie brassiere, black with bows and a matching garter belt, paid with two crisp 500 franc notes, and flounced out, vengeance in the swing of her hips.

Chapter Eleven

Jerusalem
July 9th

Dry wind rising from the desert accelerated and swirled. It picked up tiny sand particles and carried them away, impairing visibility in its wake. The bodyguards keeping watch over the Israeli farmhouse on the outskirts of Jerusalem squinted into the haze, trying to see through its thickening vail. Every now and then they would press handkerchiefs against their nostrils or wipe the sand off their faces. The weather made them even more cautious, they tripled their sentry efforts.

The six men who had gathered in the small library of the farmhouse were well protected from the sting of the wind. They were also protected from prying eyes by the heavy curtains drawn and fastened over the windows. The door to the library was shut and locked. History held the pages of a new chapter in suspense, waiting for the final episode that these men were about to write.

Prime Minister Eshel presided over this meeting of The Five. The sixth man, an ad hoc member for this session, was their Mossad man, David Tiron, who'd flown in from Washington.

For the moment, the group was at ease, enjoying wine and Dominican cigars. The library where the meeting was being held had once been a sewing room. A cheap wall-unit bookcase had been placed to the left of its door; a well-used three-seater couch, matching chair, and a scratched coffee table were in the center; at the far end, opposite the door, stood a modest wooden desk and a cane-back chair; covering the floor was a hand-woven wool rug. Humble furnishings for such an elite group. But the unpretentiousness of the room didn't bother anyone. They were there for a reason.

David Tiron was standing by the bookcase, briefing Benjamin Stern, his boss, on the latest developments in the US presidential election. As always, General Stern's military bearing was in evidence, yet he seemed relaxed. He nodded at intervals as Tiron talked, and the faint smile that softened his thin, hard lips was an indication that he was pleased with what he was hearing.

Defense Minister Mintz, wearing his customary cowboy attire, limped to the makeshift refreshments table against the wall. After refilling his wineglass with some half-decent rosé from Haifa, he limped back to the couch and dropped his bull-like frame next to Foreign Minister Rothberg.

Sitting on the chair that faced the couch was Finance Minister Yahav. He was subdued, staring ahead, feeling completely out of place in such an intense political atmosphere – very different from the finance world in which he reigned supreme.

Eshel, immaculately dressed in his trademark blue pin-striped suit, was sitting behind the desk, pen in hand. He stared into space as if searching for inspiration before jotting down his notes. Rereading what he had just put on paper, he crossed out some words, edited others, and rewrote the rest. Finally, he gathered the pages, bent them in two, stuffed them in his breast pocket, and looked up. That was the cue – the meeting was about to begin.

Eshel was at the desk, facing the couch. He was joined by Stern on his right and Tiron on his left. They sat in rough farm chairs. Mintz, Rothberg, and Yahav, all of whom remained where they were, adjusted their positions to fully face the three.

"We're here this evening," Eshel began, "to make a final decision regarding Operation Hebron. As I explained in April, this summer we must decide whether to grant Mossad the final go-ahead. So, the time has come." He paused, choosing his words for maximum impact. "A decision not to act, just as surely as a decision to act, will determine our nation's fate for the coming years. So, inaction does not reduce our responsibility in this critical affair."

Everyone realized the implications of this remark – indecision or abstention would not excuse them, individually or collectively, from the consequences of the evening's session. Yahav reached for his water glass. Tiron stared at his brown shoes.

"I want – no, I *have* to speak with brutal frankness. It's imperative that you give me your best judgment, based on your experience and dedication to Israel."

Becoming aware that he would have to carry the burden of a new state secret, Gershon Yahav shifted uneasily in his chair. He wished he were home reading an economic treatise or playing with his new Macintosh.

"I have asked General Stern," said Eshel, turning his head and nodding at the director of Mossad, "to brief you on the proposition that faces us tonight. Hear him out, then each of you will be given the opportunity to comment. Keep in mind that the proposition and vote must go with us to our graves. There will be no written record of tonight's session, giving me and our nation plausible denial – that ageless *sine qua non* of secret political action. Unlike in Washington, there will be no files to uncover or be leaked. No history to rewrite." Eshel paused, accentuating the power of his rhetoric. "Benjamin, begin."

Wearing a short-sleeved khaki shirt without insignia, and

khaki field pants, Stern stood up, stepped forward slightly, and began, his clipped, raspy voice conveying authority and his own personal style.

"First of all, as you've noticed, David Tiron is here to give us a last-minute briefing on Operation Hebron and the election process in the States before we consider the proposals of today. For several years, David has been keeping us current with policy changes in Washington. He knows firsthand the setbacks we've recently suffered in the States and elsewhere and how they're affecting Israel's future. As you must be aware, some of those setbacks are almost insurmountable. We are being isolated politically on the world scene." He paused, casting a brief glance around the room. Everyone was with him.

"Lebanon, for example. The Gulf War. The radical changes – the mess, even – in Moscow after the Cold War and civil unrest. The bleak situation facing our allies in the new South Africa. The insolent and unprecedented American denial of our request for an immediate loan guarantee for the West Bank settlements. Our problems with Arafat and the new Palestinian state. Saddam's determination to level us with mass destruction weapons. New, younger, inexperienced heads of state in the Arab world from Morocco to Jordan. And so on, and so on..."

A murmur of understanding filled the room.

"During the past year our critical economic situation has pushed us into a serious problem vis-à-vis the United States. Our image in Washington has suffered and our influence, at least with the White House, is clearly eroding," Stern's voice rose.

"We must now pause and assess our strategic position. The time has come to develop some major moves to reverse our dwindling influence. The simple fact is this..." He stopped, swallowed, and marched on. "Without the United States's determination to ensure our survival, we will disappear as surely as we are meeting here today." The last sentence was spoken with such dramatic emphasis that the hum of perfect silence vibrated through the room. "But first, let's get David's update. David?"

Tiron rose. His skin seemed darker than ever that night, as if stress had a tanning effect. He came forward and, with a quick glance at the Mossad chief, continued in the same vein.

"Prime Minister and cabinet officers, I've been with our embassy in Washington for ten years now, so I'm privy to the subtle differences in America's treatment of Israel. The gentle erosion is not so gentle anymore. Any way we look at it, we know that in the end it's the US that makes the difference. US emergency military assistance in '73 saved us from being overrun by the combined Syrian-Egyptian forces – although we could never admit that publicly. But the Americans know it, as do the Arabs. Our ammunition was nearly exhausted when the Americans came to our aid."

It was time to deliver the punch line.

"We all know that Israel's survival is dependent on how effectively we can influence the decisions taken in the White House. In the American system, the Congress can talk in our favor, can appropriate aid for us, but it is the executive branch of their government that must act. In the next decade, we'll be vying with the residual financial power of the oil-rich Saudis, the anti-Israel factions in Iran, and the growing influence of the rest of the Muslim world, as we venture deeper into this young millennium." Tiron turned toward the general, who nodded in approval.

"Right, David," Stern said, looking around the room. His next words were silky smooth, but had the effect of a roar. "Our situation is bleak and getting worse. Many factors contribute to this reality. One is the Arabs and their damnable oil. Oil and its price affect the way the world deals with us. We all know this. And let us not deceive ourselves about the long-term influence of petrodollars. Just because OPEC suffered relatively low world prices for a few years, does not mean we can count on long-term weakness among the oil-producing nations, any more than they could count back in the early '80s on long-term wealth. And, trust me when I state that it will be countless years before alternative energy sources seriously diminish the influence of our oil-producing friends." Everyone understood the irony of his last word.

"Case in point – our economists agree with Sheik Hamdani, the OPEC Secretary-General, that in the next few years, with China becoming an economic superpower, a world shortage in oil will exist, giving OPEC the chance to raise prices once again to the forty-dollar level. Also, environmental pressure to reduce use of atomic energy will help support the ballooning prices." He stopped, took a drink of water, and proceeded.

"On the global scale, there are a few setbacks that will surely affect us. First, the vote in the United Nations has already turned against us. Then, there's South Africa, where our good friends have turned over power over to a new reality. I don't have to tell you that this means our close military ties with Pretoria are now and hereafter seriously jeopardized, particularly our cooperation on nuclear weapons development and testing."

Nat Mintz interrupted. "Sorry, Ben. But please, why do you paint such a black picture? You and I have been through some pretty rough times together, have we not? We can rise above all this political game-playing – it's what makes us the resilient nation we are."

"Well said," chimed in Rothberg. "I stand witness to Nat's comments."

"In my own way I also agree with you, Nat," responded Stern. "But we have to present our global situation as we see it – not as we'd like it to be. David, you continue."

"Thank you, General Stern. We're here to decide if Operation

Hebron is worth the risk and expense of trying to reverse our precarious situation. Actually the picture would be even blacker than we have painted it, except for the opportunity presented by this operation.

"Now, it's important for us to realize two other factors. First, although the largest Jewish population lives in the US – nearly seven million as of the late nineties – we shouldn't assume that the strong Zionist influence on American foreign and defense policies is in direct proportion to the demographics. Second, we can't presume the automatic support of American Jews for Israel." He ran his index finger down a page of his notes. "Jews represent only 2.5% of the total US population. Statistics also show that in the last three presidential elections American Jews voted for the Democratic party. But in spite of the Jewish endorsement that party suffered some of its worse defeats in history. It lost Congress for the first time in forty years back in 1994.

"In 1984, a study at Brandeis University concluded that ethnic-group votes did not factor in the overall outcome of elections. It was clear that both the Jewish and the African-American votes were inconsequential. They were perhaps slightly more important in the 1998 congressional elections. We've worked hard with our Zionist colleagues in the US to bury the findings of this study, but election results have eroded the myth of the 'Jewish vote' – a myth we've worked hard to maintain for decades. That's why President Douglas dared to call our bluff on the loan guarantee and more money for technology development." Tiron stopped, ran his fingers through his dark hair, and took out a handkerchief to wipe his brow. He knew the future of Israel rode on his ability to convince them.

"The 1971 election law and all its amendments since have reduced our impact on the US elections. That's certain. One, contributions are now restricted to one thousand dollars for individual campaigns. And two, the law put a cap on the total funds an individual can donate to any combination of political candidates in one year. Now so-called 'soft-money' is on its way out in US politics.

"With that rewriting of how American political campaigns are funded came the birth of the PACs in the United States. This allowed us to make some subtle changes in how we work through the Zionist organizations. But in the end, our influence has been diffused. We must admit that we're facing a serious loss of influence in the American political system. The good news is that this is not obvious to everybody, even if they know it in the White House – which brings us to our moment of truth. I think that about sums it up." Tiron withdrew to make room for Stern.

"Thank you, David. You've covered the pertinent points. In sum, gentlemen, to meet our national objectives, it's no longer enough to influence members of Congress and the media in the United States. We've got to look for more drastic measures to maintain the gains of past years. Allow me to be so bold as to say that we must, from now on, strive whenever possible to assure absolute control over key members of the United States government."

There was an involuntary murmur.

Stern turned his head and said, "Yahav, I see your face. You think I'm off my rocker. But the fact is, we have the potential to do just that, and that is why we are gathered here tonight."

"Ben, wait. If you're determined to continue with such a heady proposition, I suggest we pause to refill our glasses," Mintz interrupted, disturbed by the intensity and tone of self-importance that filled the air.

"Why not?" responded the Mossad chief. He folded his dossier and invited the group to join him at his brother's liquor

162

cabinet. Stern poured himself a whisky. Two others joined him. The rest stayed with Israeli wine.

Stern resumed the briefing. "To bring us back from our current state of affairs, on the brink of financial disaster, with diminished political and military power, we must consider a daring gamble, one worthy of our national reputation for risking the impossible and succeeding. The prime minister has authorized me to present the final details of this operation to you tonight." He paused for his first sip of the whisky.

"For over twenty years, our service has controlled a prominent American senator. He is not, I repeat, *not* Jewish. He was recruited as an agent during his early days in the Senate. In recent years due to his political manœuvrings he's become increasingly influential and we've used him selectively as what is called, in our profession, an agent of influence – although his main value has been as an espionage agent covering top policy decisions in Washington. As this committee knows, he's not our only agent in America, but he is by far our most secret and highly placed political asset there.

"And I stress," Stern said in a lower voice, his right index finger pointing slowly around the room, "this man is not just another sympathizer, but a controlled, paid agent, like Pollard. His first loyalty is to us – we've tested that under pressure many times over the last two decades. Now a political situation has developed which offers this individual a chance to run for the presidency of the United States. His party is sure to nominate him as its candidate for president."

Hardly a breath could be heard in the room.

"There's no question as to the advantages to Israel if this man is elected. Given the problems we face in America, we'd have the ultimate agent – the president of the sole remaining superpower. This would win us four to eight years for regrouping and rebuilding our long-term position of influence there and elsewhere." He stopped, pleased with the prospect in front of them, gloating a bit from the brilliance of possibility, proud of his ultimate act of *chutzpah*.

"These are the facts. Knowing this, it's time to talk and then vote for – or against – backing Hebron in the presidential race." Stern reached for the briefcase beside his chair and withdrew a folder. "This dossier will, for the first time ever, identify this agent to persons other than the prime minister. Even our agent himself is not informed of his code name, Hebron, which is only known to our service and those in this room. The Hebron summary dossier contains no compromising operational reference in case any copy should go missing.

"Afterward, you will be asked to give the prime minister your initial reactions. He is indeed the real author of this idea. We in Mossad are merely the operators, executing his instructions."

"Which reminds me," interrupted Eshel. "I need to talk to David Tiron about this very point."

"Certainly, sir," replied Stern, then continued. "Finally, to confirm the obvious, we'll use only the code name Hebron in talking to each other about this case."

The single dossier identifying Israel's most important secret agent since its foundation was passed to Rothberg, who was flushed with anticipation. When he opened the first page and saw the photograph his lips parted and his tongue pushed against his teeth.

Speechless, Rothberg handed the file to Mintz, who opened it and with a pleased smile gave it to the chief of staff. The latter, in turn, glanced at the photograph then offered it with a poker face to Gershon Yahav.

Yahav accepted the dossier shakily, looking at its cover for a few seconds. He passed it back to Stem without opening it. "Colleagues, I'm honored to be included in The Five. However, my function is finance. That's my duty and I accept it. I do not need to know the identity of our agents or the details of our operations. I would sleep much better at night not having to bear the responsibility of that knowledge, so please excuse me from it."

Eshel replied, "You are always prudent, Yahav. Nervous, but prudent. I accept your request. Now I await your votes. Do you vote to give Mossad the green light to launch the final stage of Operation Hebron? Rothberg?"

"Yes."

"Yahav?"

"Yes."

"Mintz?"

"Yes."

"Stern?"

"Yes."

"And, I, Aharon Eshel, vote Yes also. That's unanimous for The Five. General Stern, I turn the meeting back to you."

"Good, that's settled," said Stern. "I'll pass around Yahav's financial statement, which requires everybody's signature. It calculates the covert funding required for the Hebron election operation at twenty million US dollars."

The paper was duly signed by The Five, without comment.

With the approved file of Hebron clutched to his chest, Stern stood and began the second level of his briefing.

"We learned last year that President Douglas, upon his doctor's advice, would not be seeking a second term. He may require a heart operation by late summer or early fall. His doctors have reportedly advised him to conserve his strength in anticipation of the pending surgery. Clearly, a political campaign is out for him.

"Until this summer the president had told only a few family members and personal friends – and of course the chairman of the Republican National Committee and his re-election committee chairman. But it leaked to the Democrats. When we first heard of this, we decided Hebron might have the opportunity to win a wide-open election, especially with our backing and financial support.

"He'd heard the rumors about the president's health but, like nearly everyone, assumed Douglas would run and win. He was therefore flabbergasted by our proposal to put him in the Oval Office. He'd never realized his agent role might go beyond keeping us well informed. But after delicate handling by David here, Hebron has agreed to a scenario which in our thinking will work. We've reviewed his proposal and modified it using our experience in the US electoral system, and we've completed a full-blown operational plan – taking advantage of all of our capabilities in the US – which'll give Hebron a good shot at being elected. David, would you like to take over here, please?"

"Certainly," responded Tiron, self-importantly.

He glanced at his notes, then went into a lengthy and detailed discussion of the political situation in the United States, discussing the Democratic, Republican, and Reform parties, their current strengths and weaknesses, and the various personalities running in state primaries. He ended with a profile of the many Jewish organizations in the US which Israel could count on to influence a presidential race. He presented his ideas on how Hebron must remain covert while complementing the overt activity of the American-based Zionist groups.

He concluded:

"We're making history today by directing a secret agent of our nation to win the presidency of the United States. We must remain determined to succeed. Seeing this feat accomplished is worth any risk – even the rupture of relations between Israel and America."

Rothberg spoke. "But how are we going to work with an agent as president? If he is too obviously doing everything we favor, he'll be criticized to no end."

Tiron replied. "I've discussed this with him. Hebron suggests that what we have to do is fix our bottom line position clearly with him in advance and then propose something more demanding and outrageous in public. He as president could then reject our public position and propose instead an 'American' plan which would in effect be what we are aiming at. We would publicly moan and groan about this and even reject it. We would tell the world the Americans were pushing us around. But later we would accept the 'American' compromise – which would be the end result we were seeking."

"Sounds eminently sensible and feasible," said the prime minister. His voice captured the tone of conclusion. He had got his vote and would now wrap up his historic meeting. "Gentlemen, I propose a toast." He raised his glass in the air; the others followed. "To Operation Hebron and the making of our own American president." They all smiled at the sheer audacity. "May God bless us and the nation of our children and their children."

"*L'chaim.*" They all echoed with the toast that had bound Jews for five thousand years. "*L'chaim tovim,*" Eshel repeated.

He called the meeting to an end, thanking all for their confidence, and asked Stern and Tiron to join him privately in an adjoining room. The others headed to their waiting cars.

Once the three men were seated, the prime minister leaned forward for emphasis and rapped his left knuckles firmly on the polished mahogany coffee table in front of him. "Listen – both of you. Now that Hebron has now been launched, your wet operations must stop immediately. It's just too risky." Eshel turned to Stern, sitting to his left, then to Tiron, standing on the other side of the table. Both men remained expressionless.

"I mean it, Ben. I want all files, all correspondence, any

computer data destroyed – anything to do with your wet operations must be eliminated, shredded, burned. I don't care how you do it, just make sure it's done thoroughly and immediately. No leaks."

"I understand, sir. But I still think the assassination was necessary. The man posed a major threat to us, with his liaison with Fezzani. Who knows what that could've led to?"

"The Americans are still laying the blame on Iraq or Iran," put in Tiron. "A bonus for us."

"And tell me," asked Eshel relaxing slightly, "have we paid the assassin any moneys through this Ibrahim?"

"Yes," David Tiron replied. "Two hundred thousand dollars cash, deposited in a bank, non-traceable, as an advance. We owe one million eight hundred thousand more. But since we used Ibrahim as an Iranian false flag, the assassin will blame those Iranian bastards if we don't pay – and we won't. So you see, Mr. Prime Minister, sir, despite what you say, we've gained a lot and lost nothing."

"Now look here, Tiron," Eshel continued, the veins on his neck pulsing visibly. "You're just too hellfire confident to say we can't lose. With all your years of intelligence experience, surely you realize that there is always a danger of exposure."

Tiron listened, but a tinge of arrogance crossed his face as he waited for the moment to break in. "Sir, we've eliminated all risk of exposure because the assassin doesn't know who he's worked for. Brilliant, no?"

"I'm just grateful the other members of The Five are not aware of those events. So we can halt right now. Is that understood?" He looked at one man, then the other, long and penetratingly. He was serious.

"Absolutely, sir," Stern was the first to respond. "We'll act on your instructions immediately."

As the two Mossad officers left the prime minister and headed outside, Tiron turned to his boss. "Ibrahim has to have an accident. He's the only one who can connect us with Sorensson."

Without flinching, Stern replied, looking straight ahead, "We'll send him to St. Peter." They smiled.

Chapter Twelve

Paris
July 10th

Yuri Borozov arrived at Charles de Gaulle Airport on the early-morning Air France flight from JFK. He was using his real name on a diplomatic passport identifying him as a counselor at the Russian Foreign Ministry. After passing by the immigration police post in Aerogare 2B with his one light overnight bag, he stepped out past the sliding doors and proceeded to the first Relais H newsstand to his left, where the FIS officer from the Paris residency was waiting. She was browsing a tennis magazine, as previously arranged, a shopping bag at her feet.

Yuri stopped beside the shapely Russian agent and reached for the July issue of *Motocross Magazine*. He let it slip from his hands and swore in a stage whisper ostensibly to himself, in English: "You idiot!"

With that brief exchange of indirect recognition signals, the FIS officer moved her right leg to nudge the paper shopping bag against Yuri's left shoe. She then replaced the magazine she was scanning and departed without looking at Yuri. Mission accomplished.

Yuri, while picking up the magazine he had dropped, gathered the handles of the paper shopping bag. He went to the cashier to pay for the magazine, then continued down the airport hall and ducked into a men's room. Inside a closed toilet stall, he pulled from the shopping bag a gray Armani suit, size 54 jacket. In its breast pocket was an envelope containing 3000 French francs and a perfect American passport and driver's license. A second envelope held Europcar rental keys and a parking stub with the number of a spot in the underground level 2 written in pen.

He checked his new identity. He was now George Cavanaugh, an American businessman who ran an import-export agency based in London. He changed suits. There was a pair of non-prescription glasses in a hard case in one pocket of the Armani suit. Once he put them on, he matched the photo in the new passport. He checked his Russian suit for anything that could connect it with Yuri Borozov, placed his Russian passport in the folded plain brown envelope that had contained the American one, and laid it flat in the bag. On top of that he folded the suit he had worn from New York.

Leaving the men's room, with rental keys and parking stub in hand, "George" rode the elevator to the level 2 parking area below. He was alone. He found a new metallic green Peugeot 306, used the key to unlock the rear of the small hatchback, deposited the shopping bag, shut the hatch, and locked it, then slipped the key through the inch-wide opening of the driver's window. He turned, as if he had forgotten something, and hurried back to the arrivals level where he proceeded to the Europcar desk and picked up the car that was waiting for George Cavenaugh. He showed his passport and New York state driver's license, and within minutes was steering a blue Renault 21 onto the A1 *autoroute* toward Brussels. An hour and ten minutes later he was on the Belgian side of the open border on his way to the European capital, where he'd catch the Sabena flight to Barcelona, followed by an Iberia hop to his final destination – Mallorca.

Yuri Borozov had no trouble moving freely around Europe. He looked and sounded every bit the forty-eight-year-old American businessman he claimed to be. In the dark gray, double-breasted suit, his athletic six-foot build was not conspicuous. The disguise was impeccable, and felt natural. There were moments when he felt as though he truly was a native New Yorker.

Once in Brussels, Yuri made easy contact with an FIS support officer for illegal, deep-cover agents. On a street corner he accepted a McDonalds hamburger sack through the window of his car and headed out of the city toward the airport. In the place of a Big Mac was a wallet with a Sabena ticket to Barcelona and an Iberia ticket from there to Mallorca, as well as 50,000 Belgian francs, 10,000 American dollars, 200,000 pesetas and a plastic-card passkey to a Mallorca hotel room.

Palma de Mallorca, July 11th

The apartment was small but well-appointed like the cabin of a yacht. Located in the port area, it had one tiny bedroom, a kitchenette, an oval teak dining table that seated two, with matching chairs and a yellow brocade sofa that Jackie had placed under the bay window so that she could beam out over the harbor. It might have seemed like tight quarters to many who knew her means, but to Jackie Markovic it was cozy, a nest where strategy and pleasure cohabited. Of the seven apartments she owned worldwide this was her favorite, even more than her larger home several miles away.

Known in Mallorca as Jackie Bergen, here she had absolute privacy. She made a point of not associating with anyone, not even her neighbors, who considered her distant and snobby. Her mobile telephone number was known only to her real estate office, her housekeeper Maria, and the two men in her life. One was Peter, the other her lover, who was already twenty minutes late for dinner. Her cover life as a real estate agent in Palma was kept separate from this safe apartment.

Jackie drummed her immaculately manicured crimson nails on the dining table, set for two. In the center a cluster of perfect white water lilies floated in a crystal bowl of water perfumed with tiger lily essence. That always loosened up Yuri. Two fragrant candles glowed softly in sterling silver holders, and in a wine cooler was a chilled bottle of Dom Perignon.

She had taken great pains over her appearance. Her short raven hair was combed back, revealing the true beauty of her face. Her almond-shaped green eyes were treated with smoky-gray eye shadow, and jet-black mascara lent her lashes thickness and length. Her full lips were colored crimson to match her nails.

She wore a short, black chiffon halter dress that left her back bare to the waist. In front the dress formed a deep V, accentuating her alluring bosom. A diamond solitaire hung conspicuously in the valley between her breasts. The skirt gently flowed, ending abruptly just above the knees. She was dressed to evoke desire.

She looked good, and she knew it.

Jackie was about to go into the kitchenette to check the salmon *en papillotte* when she heard the three short telltale peals on the downstairs intercom. She stopped, pressing her hand to her chest. She felt a warm flush creep over her cheeks.

Forcing herself to relax, she opened the door.

Filling the space, wearing his irresistible smile and thrusting a bunch of red roses toward her, stood her *wunderkind* lover, Yuri Borozov. She tried to scowl at him to show her displeasure for having been made to wait. Instead, she broke into a huge smile, flashing perfect ivory teeth. "*Hola hombre*, welcome to our modest nest for the night," she said with a dramatic sweep of her left arm.

173

"More modest than the owner, I hope!" replied Yuri, pulling her into his arms, one hand pressing her close to his full length, the other dangling the forgotten flowers behind her.

"You're late!" she protested even as she drew him inside the apartment.

"How about fetching a vase?"

"I suppose flowers make it all right making me wait. Huh!" She took them and went to find the beige and gold Lenox vase he'd brought her from some duty-free shop once, Gander or Shannon.

"Truce, Jackie. Come here and give this bear a kiss," Yuri teased.

She laughed then. He is becoming more of an American every day, she thought. Bear, really! Grizzly, more like. Throwing him an exasperated glance, she tossed the flowers on the dining table and walked back into his arms. "Yuri, where have you been? I need to talk to you. It's terribly important."

"I know, my sweet. Otherwise you wouldn't have risked signaling me like that. Headquarters wanted an explanation about who you were. So I had to come up with an operational emergency."

"And did they buy it?"

He threw her one of his most seductive glances. "I was convincing, but you never know what they'll believe or what they'll do to check out their suspicions. They still think Peter is the hit man. They don't know your connection with him. They just think you're a special source on terrorism. Better that way. For you, and for me."

Yuri walked with her to the sofa. "But that's my problem. I'll take care of it so you won't be exposed to Moscow." He looked out the window. Brightly colored boats and yachts punctuated the horizon which shimmered in a translucent haze against a red-and-orange-smeared sky.

"Quite a view you have here, Jackie," said Yuri before he sat on the sofa. "So what's troubling you, my sweet? Come here – tell me all about it." He stretched out his arms and she sank gratefully onto his knee, resting her head on his shoulder. Then, too wound up to stay still, she jumped to her feet. "Let me pour you a glass of champagne, while I pour out my woes." For the first time since he had met her, Jackie's facial expression seemed momentarily unguarded, betraying inner torments. Then Yuri saw her mask of steely calm fall back into place.

"First, there's something you must know."

"Who did you kill this time?" he joked.

"That's not funny."

"That bad, huh? Sorry, Jackie. Go on – I'm all ears. Why do the Americans love to say that?"

She took a deep breath and said on one word. "Sorensson."

Yuri bounded to his feet. "You?"

"You heard me. And anyway, who else has the guts? Do you think Peter would have dared?"

"Or the stupidity!" Yuri yelled. "Are you out of your mind, Jackie? You stop at nothing? What's it going to take to put some fear and sense into you?"

"Nothing," she replied easily, turning her back to him. "Oh, do put a lid on it, Yuri, will you? I didn't ask you here to grant me absolution. It's done. Over. Finished! And to perfection."

Yuri walked over and stood silently, watching the proud tilt of her head, knowing the challenge he was about to see in her incredible green eyes. He put his hands on her shoulders, turned her around to face him and was met with the expected gleam. He was vulnerable to such beauty and daring. "Then why did you ask to see me, Jackie?" he asked gently.

For Jackie it was hard sometimes being a woman. She hated the tears part. Most women used them as a weapon. She did, sometimes. But at Yuri's soft smile and the concerned look, her feminine side took over and real tears came. She buried herself in his arms, annoyed at her own dependence. For a few seconds she let herself enjoy having a man absorb her weak moment. Her very rare weak moment. *But dammit.* Everyone deserved an occasional weak moment and the comfort and understanding that a lover should be able to offer. Even though love for this couple was more of a sport than a sentimental journey.

Only for a moment. She withdrew, stepped back, and went to attend to the wine.

"Jackie...?"

"Well, I blew it," she said, pouring tall glasses for them both and taking a sip of hers. "Yup, I really was taken for a fool this time." She slammed her glass on the table so hard that the narrow stem shattered and fragments littered the surface. "Shit."

"What the hell happened? You said it was perfect, and from our intelligence they have no suspects yet." He didn't mention that the Russians knew who had arranged it. This was precisely his domain, and now this luscious lover-monster of a killer was deeply involved.

"That's true. It was a perfect hit. So easy..."

"So how were you taken for a fool?"

"We were never *paid*!" Jackie shrieked. "I mean, except for the up-front money. And what's worse, we were tricked. You know how I hate that. The Iranians were not behind it. We don't even know who the fuck ordered it." She poured another glass and gulped a mouthful of the sparkling vintage. "It doesn't matter to me *who* orders a hit. That's irrelevant. I don't take sides – I just do the job. *And* get paid. I don't care why anyone wants a hit. But I'm always careful who hires me. So I'm sure to get paid, or know where to collect a debt." Yuri knew she'd be particularly energetic in the sack tonight. Anger worked its way into her hormones.

"This time I wasn't careful enough. We made serious

mistakes. Got too greedy – too eager. I didn't double-check our contact, Ibrahim. Assumed he worked for the Iranians, just like he said. So I paid the fucking price. Ripped off by some bastard pretending he was from the Iranians. And now I don't even know where to find him. How could I let this happen to me?"

Yuri sighed, walked back to the sofa and sat on its edge. Hunched forward, his forearms on his knees, he cast his head downward and sat in silence. He appeared to be contemplating the geometric design of the yellow carpet. Jackie stood watching him bring his glass to his lips. After some time he looked up and met her tormented eyes.

"There's a lot of speculation going around about who killed Sorensson. Many theories – no concrete evidence. We're no exception in Russia," he lied. "If I had known you were involved I would've looked into it more thoroughly." He leaned over to put his empty glass on the table. "I'll check this out for you, Jackie. I'll come up with something, promise." Yuri closed his eyes for a second, then rubbed his forehead. "It's been a hell of a week – and right now the only contact I want is right here!" He patted his lap invitingly. "Problems and dinner can wait."

Though Jackie was eager to find out what he knew, she surrendered to the fact that a well-sated man is a relaxed man – a man ready to cooperate. Nothing like the combination of sex and food to get Yuri to tell her all.

"I have a better idea," she replied, pulling him to his feet. Looking straight in his eyes, she began unbuttoning his black silk shirt. He watched her long, tapered fingers free one button at a time. Spreading the shirt wide, she bent her head and rained small kisses on his broad chest. He groaned and drew her roughly against him.

"Hey, kitten, I need you!"

She raised her head. "Mmm, that's good. Very good," she said, cupping her hands around his chin and kissing him full on the lips. Then, teasingly, she planted more small kisses on his neck and around his ear.

"Stop that." He twisted his head away. "You're driving me insane." She drew back and blew him a kiss before walking toward the kitchenette.

"Come back here!" he said laughingly. "Look! What a state you've left me in!" He started to pull off his shirt.

"I love watching you undress. Finish the job," teased Jackie, admiring him through the serving window of the kitchenette. Yuri's wavy hair was slightly tousled and his firm muscular frame now revealed. Around his neck hung a fine gold chain with an orthodox cross; *a present from whom?* she wondered. She'd never asked.

Jackie turned the oven down to warm, and from a drawer nearby, which also contained a Walther 9 mm automatic, she took out a vial of her favorite perfume – Yves Saint Laurent's Opium – and dabbed a micro drop on her finger, then rubbed it into the V between her breasts.

When she walked out of the kitchenette Yuri wasn't there. From the bedroom she could hear one of her favorite Ravel CDs. Taking off her shoes and tossing them aside, she entered the bedroom.

Yuri was on the bed, naked, waiting. Jet-lagged, but eager.

Jackie stood at the end of the bed and, without breaking their eye contact, unzipped her dress and let it drop on the floor. She had nothing on beneath. She threw him one of her long-distance kisses, aimed at his engorged cock, then swayed teasingly back and forth, playing with her hair, then her breasts, then her thighs.

"You have such a perfect body," said Yuri huskily, sitting up and reaching for her.

In response, Jackie threw herself on him and began to claw at him like a starving cat. Yuri flipped her over on her back, raining kisses on her face, her neck...down to her eager breasts, which in turn he took in his mouth, sucking and squeezing.

She responded beneath him, clutching his head to her breasts. Her hands frantically glided up and down his back, her nails dug into his skin. Without warning she gave him a shove and pushed him on his back, then climbed on top. It was her favorite position; she loved "fucking, not being fucked," as she described it. What Yuri didn't know was that she had not learned this dominant role with men.

Surging with lust, she groaned as she forced him to enter her...and began riding. She was a cowgirl, and after a day of travel over six time zones, Yuri felt great being driven. He thought of the stick shift of his Fiat Spider parked in a Moscow garage as Jackie shot him into overdrive. He came, and she came twice. Then she stopped and purred with her chin on his collarbone. *Still the best?* she thought.

They had made a pact; condoms with the others – except his occasional obligatory nocturnal visit with Lina – and that way skin to skin would be reserved for their infrequent and intense rendezvous. Exclusivity of a sort.

Yuri lit a cigarette. "I only smoke after sex." He told her that each time. She swung her legs out of the bed and disappeared into the kitchenette, returning a few minute later with the half-finished bottle of Dom Perignan and two clean glasses.

"Then how come your pack is almost empty?"

"I've had it for a while, my beautiful impish goddess," he retorted.

Sitting on the edge of the bed, her back to him, she asked, "Do you smoke a cigarette after fucking your wife?"

"I don't fuck my wife. I maintain domestic security. Lina has nothing to do with us. You know that, Jackie. It's a marriage of convenience. She helped my career. I lend something to her reputation, and it works fine."

"Calm down, Yuri. Really, I couldn't care less."

"Listen, Jackie. Remember what you told me? No secrets between us."

"And do you really think I believe you believe that? You, an FIS officer. How many thousands of secrets do you know that I don't? Don't forget, bastard, that my father was an agent for the KGB." Jackie stood and reached for the red silk robe which she always kept on her bed and which had slipped to the floor during their erotic rodeo. Wrapping it tightly around her, she turned to face her lover. "Face it, darling, we both thrive on danger, power, and – for me at least – money, which is why I'm fucking pissed off. Who has my money?" she screeched.

Yuri sat up on the pillow and blew a smoke ring. "But with me it's more understandable," he said. "I have a political motive as well as a selfish one – you've no idea what life's like in Moscow." His voice raised; he was looking away from her now, frowning. "Life for most Russians is so banal, so ordinary. I need to move in different circles. To be stimulated, challenged, stretched. To break away you have to take risks. For me, there's no choice." He lowered his voice and looked at her with a gentle, puzzled look. "But you? Why do you do it? I don't understand. With your looks, your intelligence, all your languages, you could do almost anything. Why this?"

"Because I'm the best!" she said dramatically. "Plus the adventure, the danger, the challenge. And of course, I told you, the money. When I get a job, I'm like an animal stalking the conquest. I follow my target, his every move – never let up for one moment. I get inside the target's skin, feel his pulse, and then wield the power to stop that pulse! If you think sex gets you high, you should try murder." She threw her head back and laughed raucously.

Yuri sighed, disappointed. He had hoped Jackie would confide in him about her past. He knew there was some painful secret there, some tinge of evil with which she had had to cope. He tried again.

"But how do you keep your profession a secret? What about your family? Close friends?"

"Family? What a laugh! My father's dead, and a good thing too. The bastard. And I have no close friends. I keep trying," she thought wistfully of her latest pick-up. "But why do I need anyone else? When I have everyone I need in the world in one man!" She slipped out of her robe in one graceful motion and snuggled up beside him in bed. "And you will help me now, Yuri? Like a good friend, I mean. Help me find out who set me up in Brussels? I mean it. I'm being serious now. Dead serious." Jackie wrapped her arms tightly around Yuri's neck and nuzzled his shoulder. "You'll find out, won't you? And soon, darling?"

Yuri could sense her green eyes on him, narrow and piercing, waiting for a response. He met her gaze steadily, his expression serious. "Yes, I think I can help you, Jackie, but you've got to give me a little time. To think, to rest. Let me sleep for a half hour, okay? And we can talk again."

"All right," she pouted. "If I've no choice." Then she scrolled down his body in an avalanche of dramatic bravado, swirling her tongue around him. He shook.

"Afraid not, my sweet." He rolled away from her and stared at the blank wall, thinking hard. *What on earth have I gotten myself into here?* he mused grimly, before falling into a deep yet troubled sleep.

"See what happens when you get carried away!" Jackie pushed the food distractedly around on her plate and refilled her glass with some fancy white wine. He smiled and tore off a wedge of bread, covering it with a thick slice of Manchego cheese.

"Hey, the salmon was great..."

"But overdone," she laughed, pushing back her chair. "Listen, Tiger – leave all this, I'll get to it later. We still have some talking to do."

"Not just talking, I hope. You are particularly adorable with a tousled look, Jackie!"

She gave a coquettish shrug before turning to face him, suddenly serious. "Yuri. You promised."

Not for the first time that evening he noted how Jackie could turn from a warm and passionate woman into a steely cold professional at the drop of a fork.

As if reading his thoughts, she drew a hard-back chair up to the sofa and settled into it, assuming a stern and commanding manner which reminded him fleetingly of his elementary school teacher back in Moscow.

"Well?"

"You don't give me much time," Yuri responded, putting his glass down on the side table and meeting her eyes steadily.

She stared back unflinching. "No one gets away with cheating me. This is my career. I've helped yours along. It's time for you to help mine. You know my lifestyle requires regular paydays."

He could imagine, though this was his first time at her Palma port apartment. He had once visited her main residence on the island, a swanky, four-bedroom villa near the beach, which was surrounded by a six-foot wall and boasted the largest in-suite Jacuzzi he had ever seen. Yuri's mood and tone now matched her own. "The Iranians, I tell you, weren't behind it. In fact they knew nothing about it."

"Yuri, I know that. Peter found out firsthand, and I was there. But who set me up? What the hell's going on?" Jackie's voice crescendoed while fury blazed in her eyes.

Yuri went silent. He knew he was about to do what he shouldn't. The words turned in his head. He eyed her near-perfect breasts. How could he tell her without telling her. He had to protect his key source.

"Well?" snapped Jackie, glowering at him and seething. She was angry enough to bite the head off a snake. She stood up, moved to the window, made a furious motion out at the port, then took a deep breath and sat down again. "Go ahead – and don't worry. I'm not taping this, you moron. You're not afraid of that again, are you?"

Yuri was relieved to see a faint smile return to her lips.

"Okay, here it is. You asked for it. But, watch out, girl. You forget how you know it, this instant. We said no secrets, but this is more than secret." Like a little girl about to get candy, she sat straight up. "This is as covert as it gets. The Israelis were concerned about a secret channel between the US and Libya which Sorensson had been promoting." He paused as the disturbing image of this beautiful woman assassinating the American ambassador sprang to mind.

"Israelis." Her eyes bright now, she leaned closer to Yuri and placed a hand firmly on his crotch. "As in Mossad?" To him, that hand was saying, *Tell me everything or I'll rip it out at the root.*

He nodded. "For a long time we've been running a highly placed source in Israel." Yuri raked his fingers through his hair, collecting his thoughts. How much more could he tell her? It was tempting to let her see just how important his role had been in the development of this intelligence coup.

"Interesting," Jackie hummed, her mind racing to fill in the scenario. As if reading his thoughts, she continued. "You Russians...crafty SOBs! Crafty, and you, Yuri Borozov, you're the fucking best there is. And that's why you're with me." Comprehension filtered into her eyes, and Yuri momentarily was glad he'd let it out.

"Jackie, it was Mossad, a rogue Mossad operation that got a

bit out of control."

"In other words, you don't want me to go after the Israeli prime minister on this one!" She chuckled at the thought.

"Don't be facetious, Jackie. If you dare use any of this, we're finished. I'm finished and you're dead." Yuri sat up straight, not allowing his gaze to stray for one second from her face. It was vital for him to gauge her every reaction to his words. "It didn't get the nod of their top-level policy group. They sidestepped the rules."

"So I was set up by Israeli intelligence? The bastards! For God's sake, why didn't you tell me all this before?"

For an instant Yuri saw her composure crumble, her vulnerability exposed, as she considered how she and her partner had been duped by the Israelis. And now Yuri. He knew.

Yuri patted the sofa seat beside him and motioned for her to join him. "Like I said, this intelligence, for obvious reasons, is very sensitive. And I hadn't put two and two together – I had no idea it was you. And now that I know," he swiveled to face her, "I'm worried. Damn worried. For God's sake, do you realize the mess your greed's gotten you into?" He squeezed her firm round ass. This was the closest he'd been to the emotion of love.

"Okay, okay – but what else? Come on, Yuri. I need facts and names here. I need to get this right."

"Hold on, Miss Assassin, I don't know if I trust you not to do something foolish." Yuri wanted to divert her from his agent in Tel Aviv. It'd be a colossal mistake letting her get close to Volga. He couldn't share that.

"Trust, trust, you asshole! You're the only man on earth I fuck without a condom. Isn't that trust?" she yelled. "Look, we're talking about a lot of money here." Sitting closer to him now, Jackie laid her head on her lover's shoulder for a moment before murmuring in his ear. "A lot of money that we could use, my love. Just imagine. A getaway, somewhere exotic, where we could make love on the beach and sleep under the stars." She'd regauged her tactics.

Yuri's expression was deadpan. "Sorry, Jackie – no amount of money's worth the risk of you going after Mossad. It would be a no-win situation. For you, and for me. It's bad enough the Americans are looking for an assassin who – I now learn – happens to be you."

"You still haven't told me who," Jackie purred as she leaned over and delicately ran her tongue over the outer rim of his left ear.

"Knock it off. Stay serious for a minute, you cat."

"A name, Yuri. A *name*. I won't do anything foolish. I just need to know where to go for my money."

"No names, Jackie, but if you use your brain you should be able to figure out that the Mossad chief in Washington handled this."

"The name, Yuri."

"Jackie, I've given you everything you need. You're a big girl. What else do you want? I can't write you a blank check."

He was close to saying "Tiron" but stopped. It was important for him to be able to say he hadn't named a name. Jackie was deep in thought. *How stupid, how fucking stupid of them to think they could double-cross me. It would've been smarter letting me think the Iranians had paid me.*

Gently Yuri stroked her forearm. "I told you this because I trust you won't do anything to hurt me, to hurt us." He took her hands in his. "You're used to danger. But when I think of what you've done..." He felt a surge of panic when he thought of her role in the Sorensson hit. "You're too confident by half, Jackie. And making hits against the US government – well, it's insane."

She looked at him in surprise as he raised his voice angrily.

"And what exactly do you do, then?" She raised her voice to match his. "What is that, if not just as dangerous? You Russians work against the Americans, the Israelis – fuck, you work against every damn country. Let's face it, Russians and Serbs, we're alike. We even argue well together. That's why we fit so perfectly."

The insinuation was not lost on Yuri, who raised his eyebrows as his mind flashed back to their lovemaking. "Well, that's certainly true," his voice softened. "But still, you're playing with lava. How do you know the Americans won't eventually ID you and burn your cute ass?" He ran his hand over her roundness. "What a shame that'd be."

"Why? Are you going to tell them? If not, who will?"

"Be serious! My advice is, lay low for a while. And keep in mind that if the Americans ever find Peter, what's to guarantee he won't tell them about you? For a deal? Don't fool yourself about that."

"All right, all right. I'll sit this one out for a few months. Or years. Maybe it'll give me something to do in my retirement – chase round the world after some circumcised Mossad prick and try to persuade him to pay me. I mean, pay Peter." She laughed at the afterthought and Yuri felt a cautious glow of relief.

She snuggled closer to her Russian, enjoying the closeness but still acting. Seething inside, Jackie wanted to change the course of the conversation. Not since she was a small child had any man gotten the better of her, and she was not about to sit back now and be jerked around. She liked strong men, but, more important, she would allow no one, man or woman, to abuse or control her. Not since her father...

It had been a long day and evening and Yuri struggled against a wave of fatigue. But Jackie was far from sleepy; her mind was busy scheming.

"I can only guess what risks you've taken in telling me all of this, Yuri," she whispered, "and I want to show you my appreciation. Right now."

"I didn't tell you anything, my dear. You guessed." Fighting the wave of sleep, he thought how ironic it was that what he had passed off on the FIS as official business, when it was only his favorite pussy calling him, turned out in fact to be connected with the most critical of all his covert business anyway.

Caught between exhaustion and arousal, he let himself be led to the bedroom. Gently this time, Jackie unfastened the buttons of his shirt and he flopped back gratefully onto the bed. A minute later he felt her slip naked beside him, lightly scratching his thigh, and he turned to face her.

"You promise me, Jackie, you won't do anything foolish?"

"Shhh – I want to do something particularly foolish, right this very minute." She entwined her legs around his waist and pressed her body close to his. He was now fully aroused and she pressed into him. The bed shook with the force of their mounting rhythm.

"What have you done to me?" Yuri murmured softly into her hair.

"It's called loving you," replied Jackie, and without uncoupling they sank into a deep slumber.

Momentarily unsure where he was, Yuri awoke to the tantalizing smell of freshly brewed coffee. Mallorca. He heard Jackie in the kitchen clearing the scraps of salmon from the dinner plates. Despite the amount of flying and the wine, his head was impressively clear. Closing his eyes again, he mulled over the previous night's conversation, wondering whether his disclosure about Tiron had been a grave professional mistake. Undoubtedly, it was. He hoped that emotionally it was worth the risk.

As Jackie touched his shoulder, he opened his eyes with a start.

"I have to go, darling. I promised to call Peter first thing this morning – he'll be waiting. After that, I have to be out all day, I'm afraid – I have a ton of things to do. I've made some coffee and there's bread. The cereal's in the cupboard next to the sink. Will I see you tonight?"

Yuri rolled over and squinted at his Rolex on the bedside table – 8:30. His route onward to Moscow was back via Brussels and Paris, and he would be on the Sabena flight at four in the afternoon.

"Sorry, kitten. You know how much I'd like to stay."

Jackie was actually pleased but nodded regretfully, pretending she hated to see him go. She had work ahead of her and there was no time to lose. After a long kiss at the doorway, she shot him her customary wink. "Just shut the door when you leave. It locks itself." And she strode out into the morning sunshine, stopping for a moment to admire the view she never tired of. The morning after Yuri always felt good. "Nothing foolish," he called after her. "We'll get this worked out."

Glancing around quickly, a diehard habit, she slipped into a small bar which was empty except for a couple of wizened old men who stared at her hard for a few seconds before returning to their brandy and coffee. Satisfied with the security, Jackie strode straight to the telephone in the corner of the dark room. Impatiently, she punched out the twelve-digit number.

"Hello, Spartacus, it's me." This was a safety signal between the two partners; if she ever used the name Peter in addressing him at the beginning of a call, he was to assume she was making the call under duress or police control. Likewise, she would presume the same if he addressed her as Jackie when he initiated a call. In such a case, they would conduct the conversation as though they were lovers.

"Listen," she continued, "we have to meet, and soon. I'm

going to catch the early afternoon flight to Geneva tomorrow. Can you pick me up at the airport? I've some very hot info on our last invoice."

"I'll meet you, of course. But don't count me in on anything more till we've talked, okay?"

"Of course," replied Jackie dryly. "See you tomorrow." She hung up and ordered a Spanish-brand cola, which she sipped slowly, deep in thought. The clock above the bar read only 9:20. Yuri would undoubtedly still be at the apartment.

Now she was formulating a plan quite contrary to what Yuri had made her promise. Jackie decided she would wait a while before returning to the apartment. Even though guilt was not one of her characteristic emotions, she didn't trust her conscience around the Russian. To detach herself completely, she decided to take a walk, the long way around the bay.

As she reached the steps leading to the beach, she gazed at the horizon, just able to make out the shadowy silhouette of the distant mainland. Carrying her shoes, she began to stroll by the water's edge.

With her dark hair gently whipped by the sea breeze, Jackie appeared casual and carefree to the lone runner approching her. As he jogged so close that he almost brushed her shoulder with his arm, the stranger missed the transformation of Jackie's expression as her face broke into a beaming smile. She sat down cross-legged on the sand, her head tipped back, her eyes closed, her breathing deep and rhythmic.

As usual, her process of analysis and elimination offered up the perfect plan. She filled her lungs with the fresh sea air and lay resting her head against her hands while watching the white trail of an airplane etch out its route across the sky. For a fleeting moment she remembered Yuri. He was such a hopeless romantic.

But now, with the name of Mossad's Washington chief within

reach, she had something a lot more exciting than an orgasm to work on. She had to move fast. Everything else was on hold. A seagull dove for a fish not far from the water's edge. She cheered as it came up with a skewered herring flapping in its sharp beak.

Chapter Thirteen

Moscow
July 13th

George Cavenaugh, en route to Moscow, had converted back to Yuri Borozov. The Aeroflot IL-86 zipped through skies of swelling clouds, consuming miles and bringing the agent closer to his homeland. His apprehension was growing by the minute. The cabled message that had reached him as he transited through Brussels had requested – demanded – that he return at once. "A matter of utmost urgency," his assistant at FIS had underscored.

In all the time Yuri had worked for intelligence, "urgent matters" could be counted on one hand and were usually resolved across continents through a "flash" coded cable or the embassy pouch. Rarely had Yuri been ordered back to Moscow so abruptly.

He leaned back into his seat and observed the other first-class passengers, who were sharing the journey but not the urgency. Each flight these days he noted more of the rich young entrepreneurs of the new Russia coming from their business deals, legal and illegal, throughout the West. Capital flight at supersonic speed! *The changes I've seen*, he thought.

He lifted his left foot and rested it on his right knee. A water stain on his shiny new shoe annoyed him. He wiped it off with his handkerchief before spreading the latest edition of *Pravda* on his lap. More economic pessimism draped in promising language.

Hours later, in Moscow, Yuri turned the key to his fifth-floor apartment and gingerly sidestepped the pile of letters on the doormat. The apartment was stuffy. He drew the curtains and opened the windows. Moscow's weather was chilly for July. Gathering his mail, he went into the living room to find his Toshiba answering machine persistently winking. He pushed the play button, went to the sofa, and sat, tossing the pile of letters next to him. Stretching out his legs, he propped his feet on the coffee table and listened to the messages, including two from his wife demanding that he be at their dacha over the weekend as promised.

Yuri stared into space. It had been a while since he had been with Lina. They had bought the large country house two years before. Lina had understood and conceded to her husband's need to retain his bachelor pad in Moscow, for it was conveniently located near his office. The dacha was a good two-hour drive from the capital and Yuri was often late or, worse, unable to be there for his wife's social events.

Lina was headstrong and spoiled, unwavering in her insistence that Yuri accompany her on weekends of social engagements that left him bored with the trashy gossip of her circles. He was tired of pretense. He had nothing in common with either her *nomenclatura* or nouveau-riche friends. Yuri found both groups, the old and new establishments, vacuous and dull. But to keep the family peace he would keep his promise and attend his wife's elaborate dinner on Saturday. Deep inside he had another motive for being among those people.

Jackie. Nearly every time he was forced to think of his wife he thought of his lover, back in sunny Spain. He was beginning to worry that she would stop at nothing to avert the threat to her reputation or retrieve her loot – no matter the danger involved for herself or those around her. A true Serb. A sharp tug in the pit of his stomach hit him as he relived the stupidity of having poured out one of his deepest confidences to her. He was afraid he had gone too far. Only time would tell. With determination Yuri pushed all thoughts of Jackie to the edge of his mind, lending his full attention to the recorded messages.

The voice of his male secretary was urgent and curt, but the message was clear and to the point – at ten sharp the following morning a driver would pick him up for a meeting at headquarters, where none other than President Popov and the foreign minister would be present.

On hearing this, Yuri felt a rush of pride. The fact that Popov wanted to meet with him again was proof that his achievements and expertise in the world of international espionage were being recognized.

The clandestine recordings from Tel Aviv which Yuri had submitted to the president as Russian summaries must have impressed him, he surmised. The clear references in the tapes to Hebron and to Israel's hopes of putting an agent in the Oval Office had evidently wiped out Popov's skepticism.

After two generous tumblers of vodka, Yuri collapsed into bed, exhausted but pleased.

At ten sharp he exited the main door of his apartment building. The distinctive FIS black Lada sedan was waiting for him. Nodding curtly to the driver, he climbed into the back seat and was soon lost in thought, his musing lasting all the way to Foreign Intelligence headquarters.

Yuri hurriedly climbed the steps to the lobby and was met by an aide to the director. The aide slung his arm warmly around his colleague's shoulders as they walked toward the elevator. "So how was your trip? You must tell me all about it later." He pressed the button to the third floor. "But right now we don't have much time – we have a serious situation here."

"Tell me straight, Ivan Nikolayevich!" urged Yuri.

"The president's come up with a crazy idea we have to stop. The chief wants you to stand your ground and support him. I've a feeling you could make the difference. Most of all, we have to keep the foreign minister from controlling every fucking thing that happens these days."

The elevator doors slid open and the two men stepped out, Yuri's feelings of eager anticipation were quelled by this latest development. They shook hands, then Ivan turned left to go to his office and Yuri's quick, sure strides took him to the director's suite at end of the corridor.

Boris Rostov rose from his desk. "Come in, Yuri Ivanovich, come in. Always on time. Glad you're here. This is a big one." His clipped sentences were an indication that he was worried about the outcome of the pending meeting with the president.

Rostov waited while Yuri took the seat facing the desk. "The president should be here any moment. The reason I've sent for you, Yuri Ivanovich, is that I'm told our great leader has a crazy idea of giving the Americans our intelligence about Hebron. Probably Stravinsky's idea. Has to be. We've got to persuade the president not to do such a thing. It's insane. First, the Americans'll never believe us, and second it'll blow our sources in Israel."

Yuri nodded. He had no problem with blocking such a dangerous idea. His first priority was to protect his Israeli sources. *What were they doing, these policy jerks, jeopardizing sensitive Russian intelligence this way?* He breathed deeply and tried to consider all the arguments to ward off such lunacy.

A moment later both men jumped to their feet as a secretary opened the door to allow the Russian leader to enter, trailed by his foreign minister.

Impatiently, Vladimir Popov waved his right hand in the air, urging them to sit. "So, let's get down to the matter at hand," he said. "Because of our recent improved relations with the

American president and our need for the Americans' support to get more money out of the G-7 and the IMF, I've decided to inform President Douglas of this crazy Israeli covert operation they call Hebron." Popov turned to Foreign Minister Stravinsky, who smiled encouragingly. "Stravinsky agrees wholeheartedly with this decision and feels this move will benefit us most in the long term with the Americans. You see? We're good capitalists – we sell our information. Should bring us billions." He smiled.

"I see," replied Rostov, his color rising. "And of course, I must respect your opinion." He paused, trying to conceal his disgust at how easily Stravinsky could manipulate the president. "However, and I am sure I speak for General Borozov here as well, we feel that informing the US about Hebron at the present time would be imprudent. Not least because it could threaten our national security by endangering irreplaceable agents.

"Also, we must consider that the American election campaign is already under way. The Democratic convention starts today. To bring the Hebron operation to their attention would provoke panic and confusion among their policy-makers. Of course," he added hastily, noting Popov's skeptical expression, "perhaps this is why you have called this urgent meeting."

"Sir," Yuri's voice was slow and sure, "by revealing this information we would be seriously endangering our policy-level sources in Israel. As you know, our agents in Israel are also our best sources on US policy. Their invaluable intelligence has been proven time and again. This is how we know about the Hebron plan. With our sources there, we will always have an information feed between the United States and Israel, and inside the United States itself. It's doubtful that we can protect our sources once this sensitive information is released to the Americans. It is certain that the leak to the Israelis will be immediate, and they will know they've been penetrated. We'd have to start again from scratch."

Popov continued to look straight at Yuri.

Realizing he had the leader's attention, Yuri felt marginally more optimistic. "Secondly, from my personal experience in America, I doubt the Americans would believe our story of the Hebron operation. The 'not-invented-here' syndrome in American intelligence and security services is alive and well. They'd take this as a provocation on our part, and suspect something. Furthermore, we don't know for sure who Hebron is. Actually, until the Republican convention's finished on August twentieth we won't even be sure who the candidates are." Yuri paused.

The Russian leader turned and look at the foreign minister questioningly. Yuri decided to give Stravinsky something to think about also. "In fact, passing the Hebron information could actually endanger US-Russian relations."

"And how exactly do you deduce that?" barked the foreign minister defensively.

Yuri turned to look at Stravinsky. "Some American officials would instinctively claim that any information from Moscow putting Israeli policy in a bad light has to be an attempt to poison Washington's relations with Jerusalem."

"If I may interrupt for just a moment," said Rostov, leaning over his desk for emphasis. "Apart from all this, I doubt Hebron will remain a secret very long in any case. This is clearly a more consequential and daring political act than Watergate or Irangate. They are child's play in comparison."

"I agree," said Yuri vehemently, though well aware by now that the foreign minister's tight-lipped expression and rigid body language meant that neither he nor Popov was to be swayed. Yuri also realized some of his arguments were beginning to be contradictory.

"I will comment on what I know best, Vladimir Stepanovich," Stravinsky said to Popov. "While I always respect the reporting of our intelligence, I cannot agree with their guessing or opinions about what the Americans might or might not do. As we discussed earlier, the rewards of being the first to inform President Douglas about Hebron are immeasurable – both in a tangible and intangible sense."

Yuri's eyes strayed to the bulging briefcase by the foreign minister's chair and wondered exactly what it could reveal about the "tangible" returns he had just mentioned.

Popov drummed his fingers on his heavy thigh and ran them through his thick head of white hair. He left his chair and paced the room as three pairs of eyes followed his moves, awaiting a response. "I agree with Andrei Grigorievich," he said. "I did not say I had an idea. I said I had made a decision. Keep in mind, Boris Alexandrovich, that when your sensitive sources informed us that the Israelis had arranged the Sorensson assassination, I accepted your position that we should not tell the Americans what we knew."

Rostov nodded uneasily.

Popov stopped at his chair, clutched its back, and leaned forward. "There were very good reasons for me to go along with your recommendation. First of all, the incident was over and done with. Second, to say we knew who and what was behind the assassination would have raised speculation that we had something to do with it. Third, it was important to protect your sources in something which literally had nothing to do with us. So I accepted your counsel."

He straightened, walked around the chair, and sat. "But I have since realized that in this case," he warned, his voice discouraging opposition, "our vital interests are at stake. We must stop this Hebron, whoever he is. Can you imagine what would happen to Russian-American relations if we knew an Israeli spy was chief of state in Washington? Worse, commander-in-chief of American military forces. No, no! We could never allow that to happen. We'll give our best information to the Americans and insist they stop this – which they will be eager to do. So. Who will do it?" He looked expectantly at Stravinsky.

Yuri and Rostov sat motionless, aware that their influence and powers of decision were no match for the manipulative foreign minister, whose personal agenda was driven by a fierce determination to control Russia's relations with the Americans. Struggling to contain his mounting frustration and disgust, Rostov did what he'd been used to doing throughout his career in the former communist regime: locked his jaw shut, preventing words he'd later regret from jumping out.

"I've thought about this," said Stravinsky. "And I feel it would be a mistake to pass such delicate intelligence through normal channels. We can't afford the suspicion of American counterintelligence, which I agree with Boris Alexandrovich will be there. So I think we should go right to the top – to the White House. We want to be sure Douglas gets this unassessed – before his experts have time to start telling him how it couldn't be true, or worse, God forbid, decide he shouldn't be told. They're capable of that, you know."

"Go to President Douglas himself?" asked Yuri with surprise.

"Why not? That's easy, through Russell, their national security adviser."

"Good thinking, Andrei Grigorievich," said Popov, smiling. "I understand Russell would like to reduce the influence of Israel. That's why he encouraged Douglas to call their bluff on that West Bank thing."

"Which is one reason why he works so closely with the president," chimed in Stravinsky.

"If we must inform the Americans," said Rostov, his voice barely controlled, "then we must stipulate that the Russian government will deny any such report if it leaks."

"Naturally," replied Stravinsky. "Anyway, Stardust will

inform us if it gets to the CIA. Won't he, Boris Alexandrovich?"

Rostov flushed, clamped his lips tight, and nodded.

Yuri took over quickly before his boss gave in to temptation and delivered a right hook to Stravinsky's teeth. "We'll direct Stardust to monitor how the Americans are swallowing this. I'll also task Topaz in Brussels to keep us informed on any leaks to NATO."

"Good. That's what we need. But tell me, there's one element here I find particularly intriguing."

"Yes, sir. What is it exactly?" asked Rostov, raising his eyebrows in Popov's direction.

"Well, who do you think Hebron is? Can't we figure that out?"

Yuri's blue eyes sought and held his boss's steady gaze. The two men seemed to have developed a code; Rostov unerringly read the message that Yuri's eyes transmitted. The FIS director kept his face devoid of expression. But before they could deny any knowledge of Hebron's identity, the foreign minister struck again.

"All I can tell you, Vladimir Stepanovich, is that we suspect Senator Westlake," Stravinsky insisted. "He's the most vocal pro-Israeli of the three likely candidates and as of yesterday he's the Democratic choice. Senator Kramer is an unlikely possibility. He's Catholic, although married to a Jew. And Johnson, who'll probably win the Republican nomination next month, is a conservative, Protestant politician – distant from all ethnic groups in the United States. Further, Johnson is close to President Douglas and shares his hostility toward the Jewish lobby."

The Russian president glanced at his watch and with a grimace pushed his chair back and stood up. "I must leave. We end this discussion here." He looked expectantly at the foreign minister, who saw his opening and took charge.

"Certainly. I'll work on the arrangements immediately. To

personally deliver the Hebron intelligence to Douglas through Russell."

"I trust our embassy or FIS people in Washington will not be informed," ordered Popov.

"They won't be. And I'll ensure there are no liaisons with the CIA or FBI on this," replied Stravinsky definitively.

"I don't see how you can do that," said Yuri, his right hand clenching in a fist, "when it's primarily a US security problem. President Douglas will surely call in the FBI and probably the CIA too."

"Whether you agree or disagree, Yuri Ivanovich, I think that this is the correct strategy," said Popov. "Andrei Grigorievich, I give you permission to act accordingly. General Borozov, you keeping collecting intelligence. We'll take care of the political side."

Yuri nodded, his face reddening at being put in his place so soon after being told by the president he was a hero.

Again the foreign minister spoke, cementing his advantage. "Thank you, Vladimir Stepanovich. Let's see. This is Friday. I'm in New York on Monday for the Security Council meeting about the Balkans. I'll arrange to see Russell in New York on Sunday. Monday at the latest."

Yuri, realizing that he and the FIS had lost this round, kept quiet and exchanged glances with Rostov.

"That's decided, then," Popov snapped. He left the room, followed closely by the triumphant foreign minister, who smiled back over his shoulder at Rostov and Yuri.

In the ensuing silence Rostov walked around his desk and extended his hand to Yuri. "Well," he said smiling, "good thing you recommended from the beginning that we keep Hebron's identity to ourselves. Real foresight. At least they and the Americans don't have that jewel."

"Right, but this is bound to be a disaster in any case. I feel it in my gut." Yuri shook his head in disbelief at what had just transpired.

Rostov commented, "No. It's our challenge to be sure it isn't. We'll wait and see how the White House reacts. Then we'll decide how to act – quietly," he added.

"That's easy to figure. The Americans won't believe it. Coming from Moscow? I assure you, their cold-war mentality isn't that far in the past. It'll backfire for Stravinsky, you'll see. I know the Americans."

"Keep me informed, Yuri Ivanovich. You must return to Washington right away. There is much to do. Much damage to be limited."

"I'll do my best. I was planning to spend the weekend with Lina, but I'll call her. She'll understand; she'll have to."

Rostov laughed, slapped Yuri's back, and walked him to the door. "No, she won't!"

Yuri smiled thinly. "I guess not. Anything else?"

"Yuri Ivanovich, we have two immediate worries. How to protect our top agents from exposure, and how to get *that* bastard," he gestured in the direction Stravinsky had taken, "out of the picture. But the deeper reality is that this Hebron affair could finish us. All of us, including you. So, jump on it, as if we were still the KGB!"

Chapter Fourteen

Washington, D.C.
July 15th

On this Saturday morning, Dr. William Russell was on his knees in his backyard with several flats of zinnias beside him, awaiting transplant into their new beds. Nothing relaxed him more than working in his garden. Though recent events had put him far behind schedule, he was confident these late-bloomers would be spectacular. In the study on the first floor of his Alexandria town house, rows of blue ribbons adorned the walls in testimony to his horticultural achievements. He took almost as much pride in that expertise as much as he did in his distinguished position at the White House.

In blue jeans and a checkered short-sleeve shirt, Russell dug and aired the soil, and separated the young plants. The ringing of his private phone took him by surprise, interrupting the first hours of his peaceful weekend. His head snapped up. He paused, but did not react immediately.

Then he frowned and cursed as the rings persisted, seeming to turn into shrieks. "Damn it!" He shoved his trowel into the fertile ground, yanked off his gardening gloves, dusted off his jeans, and hurried through the house into his study. He snatched up the receiver, wondering what sort of news warranted ruining his first day in the garden in weeks.

"Russell here," he said curtly.

"Dr. Russell, this is Andrei Stravinsky calling from Moscow."

The slightly accented English grated on his nerves; as unexpected as was the call, even more so was the caller. Caught totally off guard, Russell stuttered and tried to gather his thoughts. "You're calling, ah, on behalf of Foreign Minister Stravinsky? Is that right? Well, what can I do for you?" he asked diplomatically. But his mind was racing at receiving a call at home from a high-ranking Russian. It had never before happened.

"No, Bill, this is Stravinsky, not an aide. I'm calling you in person. I apologize for the interruption on a Saturday, but it is an extremely urgent matter."

"Oh, Mr. Stravinsky! Sorry for the confusion. Of course, I gave you this number." But Russell was thoroughly perplexed; he in fact had no recollection of ever giving it to the Russian minister. "So, what can I do for you?"

"I will go straight to the point. President Popov has entrusted me to deliver a private and confidential message to your president. You and I must meet as soon as possible. Because of the nature of the message, we – my president and I – are not involving our usual diplomatic channels in Washington."

Russell was uneasy. "Can't you give me some idea what this is all about?"

"Not over the telephone. The confidentiality is as critical as the urgency. It's a matter that can't wait. And because of its delicate nature, our meeting must remain wholly undetected. Do you follow what I'm saying, Bill?"

"Not really," Russell said cautiously. "At least tell me why the urgency."

"It's a private message from my president to yours and must be handled by direct conversation, not on paper. And it concerns a matter even more critical to your government than to mine, I assure you. Sorry, but that's all I can say right now."

"I see." Russell was quiet for a moment, trying to make sense of the fragments of information. "Well, and how do you plan for us to meet without anyone taking notice?"

A relieved Stravinsky replied, "I'm expected in New York on Monday. A forty-eight-hour official visit to consult with our mission and attend the Security Council meeting. I can arrive in New York tomorrow afternoon instead. So I propose that you and I meet late tomorrow, Sunday, in our Waldorf Astoria Towers suite. I have stayed there before. The suite number is 2900. I thought that would be best, as it will attract the least attention. Is that agreeable to you?"

"What time?"

"I can be waiting for you in the suite at either 7:30 or 11:30 in the evening. I'll have no aides with me at those times, so you choose whichever is better for you. Call the suite before you come to the room. If anyone other than me answers, hang up. I always answer by saying, 'Stravinsky.'"

"Okay," said Russell, swallowing the urge to put the Russian in his place. "I'll be there. You realize of course that I must advise the president in advance."

"Of course you must. We understand that. After all, the message is for him. Why would you not alert him? I'll expect you then, at either 7:30 or 11:30 Sunday evening, suite 2900, Waldorf Astoria Towers. If there is a problem and you are delayed, call me at the hotel suite at those same times. Goodbye, Bill."

"It's agreed. Goodbye."

The phone clicked as Stravinsky hung up.

His frown deepening, Russell hung up the now dead phone. Half-intending to finish his gardening, he went to the back door, turned its knob, and pushed it open. He didn't step outside, but stood staring ahead. Abruptly, he let go of the door and headed back to his study. He sank heavily into his desk chair, his mind traveling thousands of miles over Europe, stopping in the heart of Russia. He wouldn't have a peaceful moment until he talked to Douglas. But the president was teeing off on the back nine of the Bethesda Greens Golf Club, despite his physician's advice. Russell would have to wait until the afternoon – the president didn't allow himself to be bothered on the course unless it was a question of war. If he was distracted, his putting game went into the crapper, and there was nothing like double bogies to get Douglas in a bad mood. Russell had to occupy himself with something or he'd go batty with anxiety. He headed toward the zinnia bed, determined to concentrate on his projected floral design. But he knew it wouldn't work. "Shit, they managed to ruin a perfect day," he grumbled, finding his planted trowel.

President Douglas had to return to the White House earlier than he had hoped, shortness of breath having interfered with his enjoyment of the game. After a shower and a light, healthy snack, sprout salad with yogurt dressing, he retired to his private upstairs study to catch up on his paperwork. Seated on a maroon leather La-Z-boy, his feet propped up on the extended footrest, he opened his date book for the coming week. Frowning and nodding, he scribbled notes in the margin. *What new crises await me here*, he mused, laying the calendar on the side table and reaching for the pile of folders.

Russell's call came through just then on the secure phone. Douglas's brows drew together and his eyes narrowed as he reached for the receiver.

"Mr. President, it's Bill." Russell's tone conveyed urgency. "Hope I'm not interrupting, but I have something rather pressing."

"What is it, Bill?"

"The Russians." He could hear Douglas's quick breath. "Nothing like what you might be thinking," he added quickly, cursing himself for not being more tactful. He then began to brief the president.

"And that was all he said? Could you determine anything from it? Make something out of his tone of voice? Why didn't Popov call me himself?"

"Only that whatever message he carries is extraordinary and for you personally. He insisted that no one at all should know about it."

"Then there's only one thing to do – just what he proposes. We'll keep this call between the two of us until you go up there and see what in hell this is all about. You're on our turf, so I see no real danger. Stay on your guard, though. Hear what he has to say without significant comment or reaction. Another thing. Call the NSA director and find out if the agency intercepted Stravinksky's call to you; if so, he should seal all copies and keep them in his personal safe until further orders from me personally."

"Good idea," Russell mumbled.

There was a brief pause. "Why don't you rent a private car and a driver – not one from the White House motor pool. Drive back early the next morning so your absence won't be noted on a workday."

"Yes, sir. I'll be back in time for our usual Monday morning session."

"Right, Bill. Until Monday, then. Good luck!"

Douglas leaned his head back on the leather lounge chair and took off his reading glasses. He stared at the decorative ceiling, wondering what the Russians might be trying now, annoyed that he'd misplayed the 16th hole, a par 5 that dog-legged down to the prettiest green on earth. He'd know Monday.

New York, July 16th

On the Sunday afternoon Russell arranged for a private sedan and driver through a friend at a local travel agency, and he and his wife sped north for the day. He dropped Marilyn at her mother's garden apartment in Short Hills, New Jersey. Then the driver took him into Manhattan via the Lincoln Tunnel and stopped in front of the wide revolving doors of the Waldorf.

An imposing edifice, the forty-seven-story hotel occupied the full block between Park and Lexington Avenues from Forty-ninth to Fiftieth Streets. Russell rushed through the Park Avenue entrance's carnival-like doors and trotted up the seventeen steps to the foyer into the main lobby. Turning right, he stopped at the house phones and dialed suite 2900. It was 7:30 sharp.

"Stravinsky."

"This is Bill. I'm downstairs. Shall I come up?"

"Yes."

Russell quickly walked back to the main lobby and took the elevator alone to the 29th floor. *Sunday, the perfect day for secret meetings*, he thought. His weight flushed into his stomach as the silent elevator sprinted up the shaft. He followed the gold arrow into the left wing on 29 and approached the double doors of 2900.

He pushed the buzzer. The door opened.

"Come in, Bill, please," said Stravinsky, waving his visitor into the sitting room. He put out the Do Not Disturb sign, closed the door, and followed Russell. "Please, have a seat."

Bill looked around the large sitting room. Without noticing the luxurious furnishings and decor, he searched for a place to sit. There were several seating arrangements in the room and he chose the one to his right. The sofa was upholstered in soothing light blue. Behind it a mirror covered the wall from floor to ceiling. A marble-top mahogany coffee table sat in front of the sofa, two matching slim tables standing on each side. Russell took the high-back chair to the sofa's right. He didn't want to sink into soft low cushions.

Stravinsky took the sofa. "Bill, thank you. And please thank your president. I assure you when our conversation is over you'll fully understand why President Popov is taking such precautions in relaying our sensitive message to President Douglas." Russell nodded. "Excuse me. Would you like a drink? A vodka perhaps? There's also coffee and tea. Help yourself, please." He indicated the sterling silver tray on the coffee table.

"Thank you," Russell replied as he leaned over and poured himself a cup of coffee from the heavy silver pot. Leaning against the high chair back, he sipped the black coffee and waited.

Stravinsky brought a glass of vodka to his lips. "I want to emphasize the risk my president is taking by presenting a piece of alarming intelligence to your president." He took another sip. "I assure you our intelligence people didn't want to pass this information to your nation. First, as always with intelligence people, they are more worried about their sources than the value of the information they collect. They never want to give information to anybody." He relaxed back, crossed his legs, and glanced at Russell.

"Our intelligence people argued," he went on, "that it would be to our advantage to hold the information for our own unilateral use, or – you might say – for our own protection in the long-term." He looked at Russell pointedly. "And once you know the subject I'm sure you will agree they had a point, and a strong one at that." He paused, hoping to discern a reaction from Russell.

There was none.

"But President Popov, to show his total commitment to frankness and open relations with America, wishes to – how do you say it – lay all of his cards on the table with President Douglas. This was actually my recommendation. And as I said on the phone, President Popov has asked me to pass on this sensitive – even shocking – information to your president."

Russell was becoming irritated. *Get to the point*, he thought.

"We have made a special effort to keep this exchange completely confidential from our mutual intelligence and police channels," Stravinsky continued. "We understand that you will at some point bring your professionals into the picture. However, President Popov insists that the actual exchange of information between our two sides on this matter, now and in the future, be confined to you and me."

"Mr. Stravinsky..."

"Please, call me Andrei. We'll be working together very, very closely on this. We must have total trust in each other." Stravinsky looked straight at Russell, again trying to detect a flicker of reaction.

"Okay, Andrei," Bill said, putting down the bone china saucer. "But so far, I'm unclear what you're talking about. And I'm here with my president's approval to listen only. Whatever this is, I'll pass your information on to the president, exactly as you tell it – nothing more, and with no promises." Russell was starting to feel agitated. He was tired. It had been a dismal drive from Washington and he had to return later. He had put off a pile of work to make this damn meeting. This blasted Russian was going in circles, talking endlessly and saying nothing.

Russell looked at his watch and fidgeted as if about to leave. "How President Douglas handles the message your president sends him is his decision. I'll stress all your points and concerns – including President Popov's desires – and the background you gave me about the attitude at Russian intelligence." He took a deep breath to calm his nerves. "So what exactly is your information?" he asked impatiently.

Stravinsky reddened. *The American shows no signs of gratitude*, he thought. He had been trying to introduce the subject delicately, but decided now he must be blunt. After all, he had flown across the world to help these naive, pompous Americans.

"Very well." He swallowed. "Please advise President Douglas on behalf of President Popov that we know that the Israeli government has recently approved, at the highest levels, a covert-action operation. The objective of this action is the manipulation of your government via your upcoming presidential elections. The Israeli code name for this operation is Hebron." Stravinsky was gratified to see the first glint of surprise in Russell's eyes.

He continued. "Of course, as you will see, there is more to it than that." He prolonged Russell's agony by taking his time to refill his glass and swallow a mouthful of vodka. "The operation involves an American senator who has long been a paid Israeli agent. His Mossad code name is Hebron."

Russell inhaled sharply but didn't dare interrupt.

"Now comes the hard part – the hardest to believe, that is." Stravinsky paused to get Russell's full attention. He leaned forward as if to increase the secrecy. "The Israeli government's highest councils have authorized Mossad to try to get Hebron elected president of the United States of America. Mossad's initial budget for this operation is twenty million dollars." He paused. "The operation is under the direct control of David Tiron, Mossad chief in Washington, who has recently made several trips back to Jerusalem and Tel Aviv to consult with higher authorities there on Hebron. You can check at your end, but we can provide you with his travel dates if need be."

Easing to the edge of the chair, his elbows on his knees, Russell assumed a casual air to conceal his reaction. But shock was on his face, as if he had been struck by lightning. *Shit, this is big*, he thought. Although trying to appear composed, he looked wide-eyed at Stravinsky, able to mutter only, "Is that all?" in an uncharacteristically restrained voice.

"Bill, I know this is hard to believe. It was for me too. Just listen." Stravinsky smiled, his round face creasing into two deep furrows which ran from his flat, pinched nose to the sides of his mouth. "At least we Russians have the advantage of being sure of our source. We have asked our intelligence to make positive identity of this agent Hebron their highest priority. We shall pass it to you if we obtain it."

Russell finally pulled his thoughts together. He was letting himself get carried away with the story, as though it were serious. He'd believe that Mossad had a special relationship, not known to most, with a pro-Israeli member of Congress. But to believe that they'd dare even think of trying to elect an agent as president...this was beyond his ability to imagine. "I'm sorry to hear this," he finally said. "I'll report this to the president, just as you've asked."

"And, Bill, please advise him that he should not entertain any thoughts of our trying to manipulate your government by passing on such extraordinary information. Our motivation is simple – we are concerned about how such a covert operation might affect Russia and its future relations with the United States."

Russell noticed that, although this last comment was accompanied by the merest hint of a smile, Stravinsky's eyes were dead serious, and he truly believed him.

"We Russians know that your intelligence and security services always try to triple-think information they obtain from Moscow. But in this case the information you are receiving comes from the elected head of state, and as such it must be considered seriously. Because of its urgency, your people should not waste their time in checking *how* we learned this. Tell them to check the information instead. It is accurate. Everything our agent has ever told us has proven true, even though Israeli intentions do not always come to fruition. Also, as I'm sure you'll agree, the Israelis have often

211

been more daring than even we superpowers ever were."

"Yeah." Russell knew it was no secret that he was not a special friend of the Israelis, but this type of thing would be hard for the counterintelligence people to handle. "Shit, what a story."

"I'm sorry to be the bearer of such news, Bill. However, I wish the president to know that as a friend of the United States I'm going beyond my official authority in telling you the following – I attended the briefing of President Popov by our intelligence on the Hebron case. I personally listened to the debate and it was exactly as I am telling you. Can you imagine what Russia's relations with your country would become if we really believed that your new president was controlled by the state of Israel? The whole world would pivot from one unstable, unpredictable situation into another. The Balkan and Iraqi problems would be nothing in comparison to the turmoil this Hebron operation could cause. We can't allow this to happen."

"Yeah, I can imagine. Look, Andrei, is there anything else you can give me on this before we break up? As you might appreciate, I have to head straight back to Washington."

"All the details I have, you now have. Except, as I promised you personally, we have instructed our intelligence to obtain the identity of this Hebron agent as soon as possible – for our sake, as well as yours. Once it is in hand, I will pass that directly to you. It will come from no one else." Stravinsky stood and faced Russell. "Also, Bill, you understand how sensitive this situation is for me personally, as well as for our two governments. So please caution the president not to tell your intelligence people about my involvement. I don't want to be approached on this. In fact, if they do, I will rebuff them and simply play dumb, as will our Foreign Intelligence Service. Consider me simply your Deep Throat." He smiled.

"Will do," the American said. *Remarkable how Watergate has muddied the intelligence waters for so long*, he marveled.

212

With a sigh at the weight of the message, Russell rose from the brocaded chair. "Well, I'll say this – when you call for a special meeting, you don't mess around." He smiled unconvincingly, his attempt at comic relief doing little to ease the tension building inside him.

"Good luck, Bill. Both of us need it. With this matter facing us, I'll stay here through most of Tuesday, consulting with the Secretary-General, our UN mission, and the other Security Council members concerning Bosnia. If you want to get back to me, call here at the same times – 7:30 or 11:30 in the evening. I'll make a point of being alone at those times tomorrow evening. I may leave for Moscow late Tuesday, and I would prefer to have some reaction from the White House to take back with me."

"Andrei, at this point I can't promise you anything, except clear and full transmittal of your information to President Douglas no later than tomorrow morning. We'll be in touch. Thank you."

He extended his hand. They shook, and Russell left the suite, pleased that no one was in the corridor. Outside the hotel, his rented sedan was waiting, his driver reading the *Daily News*.

It was past midnight when Russell and his wife reached Alexandria, Virginia, across the Potomac from the White House. He decided to wait until regular business hours to brief the president, even though the events of the past few hours would keep him awake most of what would seem an endless night. He'd review them over and over, trying to make sense of it all. He made a few scant notes to himself, taking care that they would be incomprehensible to anyone else.

Washington, D.C., July 17th

With bloodshot eyes, Russell arrived at the White House at

7:00 the next morning. In spite of his restless night, adrenaline was keeping him as alert as an Olympic sprinter. He was ready when the president arrived at 8:00.

"Good morning, Mr. President," Russell said in his usual tone as he entered the Oval Office.

"Let's have it." Douglas did not wait for him to sit. "What did he say? God, Bill! You look exhausted. Just a second." He buzzed his secretary. "Mary, please hold all my calls. I don't want to be disturbed for any reason, you understand?" He put down the phone.

Russell went to the refreshment table, poured himself a cup of coffee, stirred in three spoons of sugar, and took it to the chair facing the president's desk.

"I don't know where to begin, so I'll just retell it. Chronologically, item by item..."

When he finished his verbatim rendition of what had been said the previous evening at the Waldorf Towers, the president was silent, his eyes narrowed as though anticipating a further onslaught. Nervously, Douglas tapped his pen on the desk blotter.

"Bill, I can't possibly believe this. But what do you make of it?"

"Like you, sir, as I sat listening to this last night, I found it hard to believe. As you told me, I remained deadpan and just listened." He took two consecutive mouthfuls of the hot coffee, nearly burning his tongue. "But this morning, after a long sleepless night, I feel we at least have to bring in the FBI director. Certainly, if it's true, it would be a crime of high treason, so only the FBI is authorized to investigate. Do you agree?"

"And if it's a ploy by the Russians to play some kind of a political game?"

"Then it should become evident soon. Frankly, I think at best it's just Russian intelligence overemphasizing the well-known

214

pro-Israeli sympathies of a presidential candidate like Westlake. That sleazebag has always been in the Israeli camp – never apologized about it to anyone, either. So's Kramer. But to claim Westlake or Kramer or Johnson is an Israeli agent...well, that's just carrying it too far. It's not to be believed."

"Bill, you're not suggesting that in our national history we've never had foreign agents in Washington. Come on, now. Good old Alger Hiss was right here in the White House half the time. No, call Judge Baker right now and get him over here. Him and that woman, his Middle East expert. Straus, I think. She's sharp, and we can use the Sorensson investigation as a cover for our contacts with the Bureau on this."

"Mr. President, may I suggest that we leave that to the judge to decide? We can discuss it with him, but shouldn't it be up to him how the Bureau proceeds?"

"Just do as I say. I'm president till January and meanwhile I'm sure as hell not going to turn this office over to a foreign agent or allow Russia to play footsie with us. Not these good offices. I'm going to manage this one, Bill. It might be my last great contribution to our country...if the story is true."

"I'll call the judge right now," Russell yielded in a slightly apologetic tone. But the president took it upon himself, hitting his intercom button.

"Mary, tell Judge Baker to come over immediately with his agent Ms. Straus. Extremely urgent. I'm waiting." He hung up without waiting for an answer.

Within seconds, his secretary confirmed, "Judge Baker and Special Agent Straus are leaving now. They should be here by 9:45. Should I cancel the rest of your morning schedule?"

"Yes. Then rearrange my schedule on domestic affairs."

He swiveled his chair to look out over the garden. "Bill," he said, his back to Russell, "don't for one minute underestimate the historical significance of this, whatever the truth – or the lies

– behind it. A foreign power – Israel or Russia or someone else – is trying to manipulate us. We've got to decide who's doing what and manage this from the top. I want to reply to Popov personally before your man at the Waldorf leaves."

Chapter Fifteen

Washington, D.C.
July 20th

At FBI headquarters three doors flew open and slammed shut. The next moment three pairs of feet were heard hurrying along corridors. The three agents stepped into the elevator and pushed the fifth-floor button. When the elevator stopped they squeezed out even before the door was completely open. Picking up speed, they rushed down the hall, then came to a halt in front of Special Agent Brenda Straus's office.

A quick rap echoed, followed by a dissonant chord of door opening, feet scurrying, door closing. The agents had finally arrived. They stood before their boss, their eyes riveted to hers, their faces wearing identical puzzled expression.

Brenda rose to lock the door and invited the investigative team working on the Sorensson murder to sit around her small conference table. They looked at one another, wondering what was so urgent that they had to drop everything. Brenda walked to her desk for her notes, then joined her team – Jim Clarkston, the quiet whiz-kid of counterintelligence; Christina Whitinghill, the best analyst Brenda had ever worked with; and Jack Sanchez, the brains of the electronic surveillance group.

"Thanks for coming at such short notice," she said, smiling yet serious. "We've got a problem that makes the Sorensson case look like a minor homicide. This is a top national-security case. It must be investigated posthaste. And this is perhaps the most sensitive issue we'll ever be confronted with."

She swore the team to total secrecy before briefing them on their new burden: the Russian report and the code name Hebron.

After hearing details of the morning's meeting at the White House, the agents were speechless. They just sat there looking at her.

"I know it seems incredible," Brenda said, shaking her head. "But the instructions came directly from the president to the judge and me. We're to take the Russians' allegation at face value and act accordingly – until evidence points to the contrary. The judge says the Hebron investigation will have the highest priority in the Bureau. Nothing else takes precedence until further notice. Not even Sorensson, which will be our general cover for dealing with the White House on Hebron. Questions?"

"Who else knows about this?" Clarkston asked, clearly astounded.

"Very few," said Brenda. She counted on the fingers of her right hand: "The president, Bill Russell, the judge, myself, and now you. Of course, though he's on another assignment, I'll brief Bob. He'll take over the case for the Bureau if anything happens to me."

"No one else?" asked Christina.

"No one else on our side. And that's how it's going to be, at least for now. The reason the White House asked for our team in particular is that everyone in town will assume we're just continuing on the Sorensson murder. Everybody knows that's of top concern to the president. So nothing has changed, and everything has changed."

"If this Hebron really exists," Clarkson began, "we all know who it must be, right? There's only one senator with presidential aspirations who's close to the Israelis."

Brenda shot back, "This may be the most important investigation this Bureau's ever undertaken. We can't afford to assume anything and we can't afford to be wrong. Even the Russians said they had not yet been able to identify Hebron, though I'm not so sure I believe that. But, as I said, we are not going to assume anything." Privately, she thought the Russians were holding back an ace to play if the Israeli operation worked and the US ended up with a foreign agent as prez.

"Okay, you're right," agreed Clarkston.

"And when do we start?" Whitinghill asked, although she already knew the answer.

"This minute. We're going to be busier than ever. Sorensson doesn't go away just because Hebron's in town."

"Sorensson already went away, remember?"

"I always knew it made good sense to keep a toothbrush here."

Everyone laughed, and Whitinghill said, "Okay. So what are our marching orders?"

Brenda looked around the table and focused on Sanchez.

"Jack. Electronic coverage. It's going to be the key to this, with so little else to go on." She consulted her notes. "We must cover the following: one, each of the three candidates; two, the Israeli Embassy, particularly the Mossad station there; and three, the top Jewish organizations in contact with the embassy and with the candidates about the election." She looked up. "You'll probably have to dip into our reserve corps of Hebrew and Yiddish transcribers for all that, though most of the tapes should be in English."

He nodded.

Brenda glanced at her notes again. "Jim. I need maximum surveillance on Tiron."

"David Tiron – consider it done," affirmed Clarkston.

"Give me a check on all his travel and contacts this year. I want a day-by-day picture of the man over the year to date. Cover his phones – office, home, any identified safe houses, lunch hangouts, girlfriends, whatever. If he has a chauffeur, cover him. Don't assume anything he does is innocent. Nothing! I want him covered with a blanket. Any problem with that? Do we have enough teams?"

"What if the Russians are planning something major," Clarkston said, "and they just want us to pull our surveillance off them – so they give us a red herring. I think we have to consider the possibility, regardless of how hot the White House is on Hebron."

Brenda hesitated a moment. Clarkston was a counterintelligence specialist, and he had a point. Finally she said, "That may be true, but bear in mind, I don't – correction, the director doesn't – want anything considered higher priority than Hebron until further notice. Not the Russians nor the Mafia. Nobody! Any manpower problems, check directly with him. Now, concerning the candidates, who are we dealing with?" She looked around. Everyone was with her. "Kramer and Westlake have already been nominated. And the Republican, Johnson, has no opposition now that the president has come out in favor of his nomination. That limits our investigation to the likely suspects."

The others nodded in agreement. It was obvious. Too obvious.

"So," Brenda told Whitinghill, "I want to start putting together everything we have on these three. In particular, any contact each of them has had, does have, and will have with the Israelis, and with the Jewish organizations in the US. And remember that eventually we may have to interview each of the candidates about the Hebron factor. In the highly unlikely event that this intelligence is accurate and one of these senators is a foreign agent, our homework alone could make the difference between cracking this case or not. In other words, the future of the presidency, and by extension the geopolitics of the world over the next generation, is in our hands."

Christina was obviously moved.

Brenda nodded toward Jack.

"We already have pretty fair coverage of the Israeli Embassy," he noted, "though we normally check them and the Mossad guy only sporadically. We'll up that to live 24-hour coverage. We have the transcribers to handle it, no problem. We can institute coverage once we get Foreign Intelligence Surveillance Court approval. If you get me a FISC letter of authorization from the judge for the key Jewish organizations like B'nai B'rith, AIPAC, and so forth, we're in."

Brenda made a note and continued. "The judge has already called the chief justice in his car and asked him to come to his office this evening. I'll get the signatures you need for any technical coverage. God knows where this case will end – privately or publicly – so we're going to do everything by the book, and more. In fact, the judge will be briefing the chief justice himself on Hebron, because of its extraordinary implications – whether the Russians are giving us valuable information or disinformation."

She gave a last look around the table as her team made notes. "Okay, let's get on with it. If you need anything special, get back to me. Don't take any chances."

With encouraging smiles at one another, they broke up and left Brenda's office on their way to begin carrying out these new orders.

Two weeks later

So far, nothing. Nothing had been uncovered by electronic surveillance, or telephone taps, or even physical surveillance. The elections were less than four months away.

Still, the Russians' warning had to be heeded, Brenda

reasoned, even if their goodwill was bogus. To ignore the information could lend itself to fatal repercussions, like those of Pearl Harbor – J. Edgar Hoover had refused to believe his intelligence reports, and they turned out to be dead right, to the perverse delight of the conspiracists. Imagine the outcry if the Hebron story were to mushroom into fact, the FBI had done nothing, and the Russians revealed that their warning had not been taken seriously. Every Monday-morning quarterback in Washington would want to close down the Bureau.

With the Democratic and third-party candidates already selected, and the Republican candidate having no opposition in the August convention, the campaign was vigorously under way. *Which of the three?* Brenda had asked herself over and over. It should not be such a baffling riddle. Yet some anti-Israeli politicians in Washington were arguing that in the United States it was not easy to tell the difference between a friend of Israel and a foreign agent.

Discovering the difference was actually quite easy, Brenda had very good reason to know. It was she who had monitored the telephone taps on the Israeli Embassy and identified the telephone signal from Jonathan Pollard to his Israeli control – the signal indicating his plan to escape. Bureau agents intercepted him outside the Israeli Embassy before he could get inside and claim political asylum.

She was aware that Pollard had passed thousands of highly classified documents to the Israelis. "Enough to fill a basketball court," one counterintelligence officer at the Pentagon used to say in quantifying the theft. So she knew in her stomach that Hebron *could* happen. But would the Israelis risk having a senator double as an agent?

Everyone in the intelligence community acknowledged Mossad as the most daring and operationally-effective intelligence service. No one could forget Entebbe. That was why, to be safe, she had to assume the worst was true, and work on that assumption.

She had warned Judge Baker and Bob Hutchins that the Hebron case could take valuable time away from the Sorensson investigation. "This *is* the Sorensson case," both had insisted.

In a bad way, Brenda wanted, for the Bureau's sake, to make a breakthrough in at least one of these cases. She hoped to make the Bureau look good to the White House. Her idol, Judge Baker, was always noting, "It is amazing what one can accomplish when one is not concerned about who gets the credit."

Corny, she thought, *but so, so true.*

Overburdened with work and the excited pace, Brenda began her day by visiting the counterintelligence desk concerned with Israel. They were not briefed on Hebron, but Judge Baker had ordered them to give her anything she needed. Every agent there assumed that Brenda was connecting their data with the Sorensson case.

"Hey, George," she said to the chief, entering his office without knocking. "Anything for counter-terrorism?"

"Sorry, nothing very sexy today as yet. It'd be easier of course if we knew what in God's name you were looking for, and I can't for the life of me understand what we could dig up that would...Anyway, good soldiers we..."

"Don't you think I'd like to kiss-n-tell, George? But the White House is playing with our minds, trying out their superdick routine on us."

"They did a good job with you in the Ivy League, kid. I'm proud of 'em! I think this Sorensson shit's gettin' to you – or is it that French lover, van den what's his dink?"

"He's Belgian. And he's not my lover. How do you know him?"

"Met him once. Official visit or some bullcrap. Sounded French to me."

"Last time I checked, French was a language, George."

"And he's not your lover?"

"Leave town, would you?"

"Give me a ticket."

"I give you a ticket to help me check with your electronic-coverage people – to see what's on the Israeli Embassy lines these days."

"We're at your service, Miss Brenda," George said in a singsong voice, with a mock-gallant sweep of his arm toward the door. "You know the way."

"Thanks, George. So...you know van den Heuven?"

"It's my job to know him."

At the electronic transcription office, Brenda keyed in her ID number to deactivate the cipher lock. Behind the door, transcribers were working on live coverage of the Israeli Embassy phone taps and audio bugs.

Brenda felt good about returning to the source of her success, where she was always welcome. Many employees there viewed her as an example of how high a smart agent could soar professionally through lucky breaks, acumen, or, best of all, a mixture of both.

"Welcome to the sixth floor," said Jack Sanchez as he pulled open the heavy door.

"Hey. Anything for me today?"

Jack played along, pretending not to know what Brenda was after. "It'd be easier if we knew exactly what you wanted, but you probably have the same problem. You ask – we'll try to answer. That's my best offer."

"Sold. And you're more right than you think about me not knowing what I'm looking for – it could be almost anything!" she said for the benefit of his staff. "Here goes." She took a deep breath. "One, any Mossad coverage suggesting double-talk about anything, local or foreign. Two, any calls into the embassy that sound like coded signals, even by the furthest stretch of the imagination. Three, any calls among Jewish lobbying groups – AIPAC, ADL, B'nai B'rith, et cetera, et cetera – coordinating election activities or support for any candidate in any office anywhere in the States. Four, any special coverage of David Tiron, the Mossad rep at their embassy. Five, anything from the unique audio device we have at the embassy residence."

"Dat all?" drawled Jack.

"Six," Brenda continued, "any reference to any code name or special project of any type anywhere. Seven, any reference to anything in Brussels or Belgium. Eight, any reference to the name Peter. Nine, any reference to US counterintelligence – FBI, CIA, et cetera. Ten, any reference to hookers. That's it for now."

"Phone sex? We'd enjoy the change of pace. Seriously, so this means the Israelis are involved in the Sorensson deal? My God!"

"Jack, and all the rest of you – be patient. I have a lot of pressure on me right now. I can't comment on anything. Just help me with any tidbit here and I'll get you all a raise. You just have no idea of the complexity of it."

Jack rewound the tape and reviewed Brenda's questions. "There are two items that relate to the categories you just mentioned. One's a feisty exchange that took place last night. Let's see, Thursday at 11:37 a.m. from Israel. The assistant to the Mossad director called David Tiron on his direct office line. The assistant was adamant that General Stern wanted daily reports on something that I think was some sort of code. It wasn't too clear and didn't mean anything to us here. But Tiron exploded and told the guy he was *meshuga* to use such a reference. He shut him up and instructed him to cable him at his private cipher. We've never known Tiron to be so hot-tempered."

"That's good, really good. Let me listen."

"You got it. The other's a reference on the bug. It picked up a shouting match between what I think is the ambassador and Tiron. The ambassador says he sniffs something's going wrong with the election and he's not satisfied with Tiron's reaction. Even threatens to have Tiron recalled home if Westlake loses."

"Better still! Give me that one too. Fantastic job. Keep it up, Jack, but keep listening for someone named Peter. It may not be on the Israeli taps but, when you can, review any records of anything. Particularly hit operations. Keep giving me any names that involve Peter, especially as related to contract hits. Also I need photos of any Peter you can find connected with terrorism or professional hits, however old. He's probably southern European or Balkan."

"Give us time. We're finding your Peter character, and if we get any flack from our friends across the river, we'll call you for help with the director. Deal?"

"Deal. Now let me listen to the conversation between Stern's assistant and Tiron. Is it in Hebrew, Yiddish, English, or what?"

"Shifts between French and Hebrew with lots of double-talk in both, but, you know, the transcribers who sift through to these lines all the time claim this was an exceptional conversation in terms of the sensitivity of the subject – whatever it was – to both men. I mean, we know Tiron's a real bastard sometimes but here he's a madman – angry like someone stepped on his dick. All because the aide used an indirect reference to a code word. The aide referred to 'the West Bank town' and Tiron said he'd kill him if he said anymore. It's truly an exceptional conversation. As a former transcriber you'll see that right away. Anyway, you listen and give us your reaction – but to us it's clear there's something going on between Tiron and his headquarters that's rare and sensitive."

Brenda had visibly paled with excitement. *The West Bank*

town, she smiled to herself. This was the stuff that excited spies. And it was the first piece of hard evidence supporting the Russians.

"I want to listen immediately." She stood up abruptly and moved toward the transcription desk they had arranged for her.

As the words resonated in the headset, Brenda came to the conclusion that Stern's aide had started to use the code word, but Tiron had spotted it coming and prevented a disaster by shouting back and cutting off the aide. *Too bad*, she thought, her mind racing. *But 'the West Bank town' is almost as good.*

She then listened to the sensitive tap from the bug in the Israeli ambassador's residence. There was an argument between the ambassador and Tiron stemming from Tiron's lack of reaction to the ambassador's anxiety over Westlake's slipping in the polls. The ambassador became irritated with Tiron's passivity on the subject and challenged him, whereupon Tiron claimed he had no special instructions to get Westlake or anybody else elected. "It was up to AIPAC to do that," he yelled. "Ask them."

"If you don't move your freakin' ass on this it'll be flying home on a El Al cargo flight in November." *Great line*, Brenda thought.

Tiron had replied that he was ready to go home. "I'm tired of the bullshit trivia that preoccupies our embassy." Then there was some garble followed by "Kissing American ass five times a day is not my idea of strategic planning."

Brenda thought the conversation seemed odd, a bit stale. Tiron could be helping Westlake covertly, despite his denial of a covert role in the elections. The Russian had reported that Tiron was in charge of Hebron, and the Israeli ambassador seemed certain that Tiron was playing some covert role. This was too inconclusive to use, but it would be a good idea to have the transcribers on the alert round the clock for any more between the ambassador and Tiron or between either of them and a third party.

The tapes did underscore what her instincts were now telling her. There *was* a Hebron out there.

Chapter Sixteen

Washington, D.C.
August 1st

"Brenda, *mon amie*," Guy van den Heuven's friendly, excited voice sailed over the phone line into Brenda's ear. "I have news for you, but we must discuss it face to face, *non*?" Guy stopped for a moment as if he didn't know where to start. "You must come to Brussels, Brenda. There's only so much you and I can do with these facsimiles and e-mails."

Brenda laughed, and remembered George in counterintelligence. Lover! George was full of shit. "*D'accord*, Guy. But make it worth my while."

She looked around her office with dismay. Mountains of brown files sat on her desk, all related to Sorensson and that West Bank town. Each day the files grew both in number and in thickness. There were files on known assassins and suspected ones; files on two hookers, one dead, one unaccounted for; files on the embassy guard who remained one case's sole witness; and files on every professional hit of political significance over the past five years.

Chronologically stacked, *In* and *Out* files of all the messages generated by her research added to the mass. The sheer amount of invaluable raw evidence warranted special security. Brenda requested a lock on the door with the combination known only to her and her analyst, Christina. Uneasy about leaving such a huge, sensitive accumulation in her office, Brenda changed the combination every Friday at the close of business.

As Guy had said, chief investigators can't do much while thousands of miles apart. Two months of intense transatlantic investigation had elapsed already, producing reams of data but little that brought Brenda closer to solving the murder. A hunch and a theory, but nothing more.

Agreeing to Guy's request, she promised to fly out within the week. Whatever his development was, she prayed it would lead to the breakthrough she was after. In the interim, *keep Hebron as top priority,* she thought, *and don't reveal a thing to Guy.*

Brussels, August 5th

The phone rang half an hour after Brenda checked into her hotel room. "Brenda, welcome back. Meet me at five o'clock, okay? I want to invite you to a new restaurant that I have discovered. You'll love it. Moroccan, where we all sit cross-legged on the floor and drink mint tea. The couscous is divine."

Brenda glanced down ruefully at the standard travel attire she was putting away – two suits, four shirts, an evening dress. "I don't have anything too informal to wear."

"You FBI people never do!" laughed Guy. "You must learn to be – how do you Americans put it? More laid back. Do not worry about how you dress. Come to my office in the Rue des Quatre Bras. I'll be waiting. You remember, number 54, top floor."

The headquarters of the Brussels Judiciary Police was an open-plan, modern building built of glass and steel. *Like a commercial building in New York*, Brenda thought as she waited for the elevator. *Doesn't suit Guy. He should have an office in the grand and classical style of the Palais de Justice.*

She left the elevator at the top floor, walked a few steps down the hall, and tapped on Guy's office door, grinning at the nameplate – his name and title were etched in Gothic letters on a solid brass plaque. Very classy. He opened for her in an instant and greeted her warmly. "Brilliant Brenda! Come this way, please," leading her into a small conference room adjoining his office. Papers were stacked everywhere – on windowsills, floors, desks, tables, chairs, even in piles on the floor.

Projected on a large screen at the far end of the room was a meter-square blow-up of a bulky, mustached man at a sidewalk café. The steam curling upward from his cup of coffee had been caught by the camera, mingling with the steam rising from the coffee of the subject's bearded, austere companion. That the latter's face was partly hidden by sunglasses only added to the clear impression that he was a mysterious figure from the Middle East. *Iranian*, Brenda guessed.

Her gaze never leaving the photo, she pulled up a chair and sat several feet from the screen. As Guy studied the thoughtful expression on her face, she turned and looked at him, her brows slightly raised. He nodded and smiled at her gleaming eyes, and winked.

She blushed. But she realized the implication of the photo. Guy had discovered a key to the case. She whispered, "Guy, you have him...Peter?"

"Perhaps. Two years ago," Guy began to explain, "the French Ministry of the Interior circulated this photo to selected Western police and intelligence services. Your photo library at the Bureau would have one. But the French received no response from anyone."

"I can easily check," Brenda interjected.

Guy walked to the screen, pointing at the bearded man. "The French report, which this photo came with, identified this man with the sunglasses as the Revolutionary Guard representative at the Iranian Embassy in Paris. He is a renowned master terrorist, known as Kavir. He plans and oversees all their operations in Europe. Still, to this day."

"And the other? Let me guess," said Brenda hopefully, leaning forward and pointing at the mustached man.

"It well might be." Guy beat her to the point, his smile broadening. "According to the French report, the waiter at the café claims Kavir called the other guy Peter. But because no foreign police service reacted to the report, it went into Kavir's file, as he was the only one identified. This explains why it has taken me so long to retrieve it. I have been spending seven nights a week since you were here last, looking at reports, photos, double-checking, cross-checking. Maybe now we have it!"

"But what makes you think he is *our* Peter?"

"If you remember," Guy said, returning to his chair, "it was Gérard who told us that one of the two women who came in that night had called the man with the mustache Peter." He gave Brenda a copy of the photo. "Once I had come up with the French report, I showed the photo to Gérard. He positively identified the person as the Peter who was with Sorensson several nights before he was murdered." Guy looked very pleased with himself and basked in Brenda's admiring smile. He had made the breakthrough. She jumped up and cried, "Guy, you're great!"

Blushing a bit from this outburst, she quickly added, "Oh, that wasn't very professional, was it? But...your meticulous research is famous in my world. Now I've seen it with my own eyes. Iran..." she murmured.

Guy responded, "This may explain why the killer apparently dropped a scrap torn from a Baghdad newspaper at the ambassador's. To divert our attention to the hated enemy, Iraq."

"That holds."

While Brenda digested the photo's discovery and its implications, Guy continued, his face slightly flushed.

"Remember, Gérard confirmed that the dead hooker was with Sorensson the same night Peter was."

"But we still don't have any solid information on the other woman? The one who returned the night of the murder?"

"Lamentably, we do not, Brenda. She might turn up dead too." Guy reached for his notepad. "But if she's not dead, she's probably working with our boy Peter. So, *Mademoiselle* Brenda," he conceded, "your hunch that the girl at the residence the night of the murder was directly connected with the assassination may turn out to be quite accurate."

Brenda acknowledged this with a gracious smile. "*Merci*, partner. It's too early to go jumping to conclusions, but certainly the photo and possible identification moves us along significantly."

She raised her head and gazed into space, lost in analytical thought. "But just because a year ago this Peter was talking to an Iranian doesn't prove he was working for them on the Sorensson hit. Even if he turns out to be the assassin," she said to no one in particular before dropping her gaze to the palms of her hands, which were resting demurely in her lap. "The odds are high," she said, "that he's just a professional hit man and only God knows who he was working for when he took out Sorensson."

"Well, that's true," replied Guy reluctantly, drawing Brenda's eyes in his direction. "On the other hand, having this photo, we have to consider the Iranians as his possible employers in the Sorensson killing."

"Guy," Brenda interrupted, "we need to get our hands on him. He'll lead us to the sponsors of the Sorensson hit. If he's really our man." She contemplated the photo. "Let's not send this through to Interpol. I don't want it falling into the hands of terrorist countries – always a possibility with our dear Interpol, leaky sieve that it is. But definitely send it to all the NATO national police and intelligence services. And to the Russians."

Bringing her right hand up, she spread her palm over the image of the Iranian. For a second she studied the shot, then said, "I recommend masking out the half that shows Kavir. We'll circulate Peter's photo only – just a precaution, in case the photo should get into unfriendly hands after all."

"*Oui,* good thinking," replied Guy. "No urgent need to tip off the Iranians we have a photo of their Kavir having coffee with one of his assassins! I will call immediately to get permission from the French Ministry of the Interior to circulate the photo to NATO and the Russians." He hurried into the adjacent office, where he had a direct line to his counterpart in Paris.

Returning to the conference room minutes later, he said, "*Bien, mon amie*, I have French approval to circulate the part of the photo showing Monsieur Peter. And – surprise, surprise – my Parisian friends do not have any problem with us sending a copy to the Russians, so it'll go off to the Ministry of the Interior in Moscow within the hour. Also to the NATO services, your Bureau, and those cousins of yours at the CIA."

As Brenda fixed him with the most serious expression he had ever seen, Guy thought she had not noticed his wink.

She had, but she blurted impatiently, "Okay, my hero, let's get on with it. I'll call the Bureau and get them working right away on a study of all international hit ops within the past five years. I want to see if they can pick up any identification or modus operandi indicators which match Peter. Maybe he has an MO of using bimbos to gain access to a target hit. In fact, this MO reminds me of the infamous Abu Hassan."

"Black September, eh?" murmured Guy.

Brenda stood up and went to the screen, peering closely at Peter's picture. "Guy, I don't know if you have any close buddies in Greek security, but my instincts tell me this guy is Greek – his color, general appearance. I spent two summers there as a student. Give it a check at least."

"*Certainement*! I have an old friend who is vice minister of the Interior in Athens. I'll ask him. Brilliant Brenda, I trust your instincts."

She noticed out of the corner of her eye that Guy was keen to see if she had picked up the light flirtation in that last phrase. But she was concentrating on Peter's photo, burning it into her memory.

"Thanks, partner!" she said, turning around and walking over to face him, with a slight blush on her otherwise serious face. "I don't want anything to prejudice my plan to find the real key to this mess. The other hooker, dead or..." She headed toward the door, flashing a challenging eye at Guy.

"*Cherchez la femme!*" he exclaimed, jumping up. "That we'll do, Brenda. And we'll find her, whoever or wherever she is."

Brenda shot back, "If she's smart, and she must be, she's going to hide right under our noses. She may be there already. Or *here* already." And this time, almost inadvertently, it was she who winked.

Chapter Seventeen

Washington, D.C.
September 1st

George Johnson, New Hampshire senator and Republican presidential candidate, was having a bad day. A very bad day. He had lost the latest round of golf to the president – the-not-so-healthy president. Not only lost, but lost very badly. He loathed losing. The game of golf, the game of politics, any game.

The word "lose" had no place in his family or personal dictionary. His patrician grandfather had been a senator and governor, his father an admiral. From his prep-school days at Choate, he played hard and studied hard, just like his ancestors. Nothing less was expected. *It was the old world*, he often thought. *Like another world.*

But suddenly nothing seemed to be going right. A few weeks before, he had been so confident about the upcoming election. But that had changed. What could be easier, the president had assured him, than to run in the incumbent's place, with the party raising all the money he needed, maybe more. It had sounded so easy.

Now the latest polls revealed that both Westlake and, more surprisingly, Kramer were drawing closer to him. Nearly neck-neck-and-neck. Initially, Johnson had felt that running as the president's choice would allow him to sail through once he had the Republican nomination locked up. But now he realized that he needed a lot more than a mere presidential blessing. He needed to distinguish himself, unleash a knock-out blow.

The country club parking attendant brought the senator's car around. Too upset to observe the customary pleasantries, Johnson swooped into the driver's seat, slammed the door, and flattened the gas pedal. The dark blue Cadillac Seville sprang away and minutes later swung into the circular driveway of Johnson's three-story mock-Victorian house.

The presence of several foreign-made cars telegraphed the presence of his wife's bridge-playing friends inside. Cursing Nicola, her companions, her damn bridge games, and women at large, he scowled his way up the stairs to the door. He was always teased about being Mr. WASP in the US Senate, but at heart, he had long recognized, he was also a raving male chauvinist.

In the front hall he put down his case, slung his coat over his shoulder and, securing a plastic smile on his face, entered the sitting room.

"Darling," gushed Nicola, running to greet him with flamboyant exaggeration. "You're just in time. We were about to uncork another bottle of bubbly. You know the girls."

Johnson graced the women with a well-polished PR grin. "And how are you ladies today? Well, I trust?"

One of the women was quite attractive and she flushed prettily when the presidential candidate spoke. He allowed his glance to linger on her model-like figure for a second or two before turning his attention back to his wife, who was also looking slightly flushed – for, he suspected, quite a different reason. Cursing inwardly, he guessed that this was not her first drink of the day. He'd have to curb her drinking until the election was over, particularly when she was in the public eye.

"Are the boys here?" he asked out of habit.

"They're at their Web programming class. When will you ever

remember their schedule, dear?" Nicola tittered, glancing at her friends. "Here's the man who's running for president and he can't even remember his sons' timetable!"

His inward curses grew stronger. Irritated, Johnson shrugged with assumed nonchalance and walked to the sideboard to pour himself a large vodka on the rocks. As he squeezed the wedge of lime he pictured Nicola's over-made-up face. "Please don't let me disturb you, ladies. I've some paperwork to go over." He gave a small bow before he crossed the room.

"Darling, you should check your messages, too. There are at least three, including one from the White House. Dr. Russell! Sounds important." She winked, with no regard for discretion, loving the idea of becoming First Lady.

"Thanks."

Shaking his head and sighing with relief, Johnson entered his study and closed the door. The first and third messages were urgent. Bill Russell had called twice. He wanted to see him as soon as possible.

"Don't worry, George. It's good news," Russell's second message ended.

Intrigued, Johnson dialed the direct line. Russell picked up almost immediately, as if he had been waiting for the call.

"George, good to hear from you," he said, his voice rushed and breathless. "Listen – three months ago when I was in Europe I visited a Middle Eastern friend of mine. He gave me something I think you'll find very useful in your electioneering. I wasn't going to bring it up, but if what the polls are saying is true..." Embarrassed, his voice trailed off.

"I see," said Johnson, affronted. "And I suppose that's all you're going to say over the phone?"

"Just trust me on this one. I suggest we should meet first thing in the morning – nine o'clock okay?"

"Fine. Can you come to my Senate office, though? With the

campaign at its peak, I'm up to my ass in speeches, agenda, and other crap. And this way there's no official record of your visit. Whereas, if I go to the White House..."

"Agreed. Then, with my dossier, you'll have even more to do! See you at nine."

Johnson tried to return to the speech he was to deliver at a press conference the following day. He was tired and on edge. After a few minutes of failed attempts at creativity he pushed the document aside and picked up the *Washington Post*. According to a lead editorial, his stands on health care and foreign aid were rallying support. However, the editorial went on to say that the senator's past views on foreign policy were inconsistent. And that was something the American people should worry about, the writer cautioned, warning that Senator Johnson would probably continue President Douglas's hard line toward Israel.

"Screw em," Johnson muttered. He had little respect for the media, though he struggled constantly to hide it. He thought he did that well. He wondered how they really saw him. They seemed to report on him so clinically.

The front door slammed. Nicola's excited shout rang out and adolescent male laughter echoed in the house. His boys were home. Hoping for some rare time alone with them, Johnson cast aside the complex world of politics and went to greet his sons, George H. Jr. and Bud.

The next day at 9:00 sharp Senator Johnson's executive secretary showed Bill Russell into the senator's office.

When she left, closing the door, Johnson moved to his office seating area and invited Russell to join him.

"George, my best-informed Middle Eastern contact gave me this file a few weeks back. It's...sensitive. So sensitive that I wasn't sure at first whether to pass it on. But as Westlake's moved up, and even Kramer's closing in on both of you, maybe you can now use this material to some advantage. For obvious reasons, I haven't shown it to the president. This is personal between you and me, okay?"

Johnson opened the plain manila envelope and pulled out the document labeled "The Life and Loves of Wes Westlake, US Senator."

"Is this a joke, Bill?" he asked.

"Read on, my friend. It's no joke – it's dynamite. This road map to his sex life could knock Westlake out of the race if you play it right. I'm sure your media guys can arrange that."

"Okay, Bill. Thanks. Let me look it over. But where do I say I got it?"

"From a European friend who refuses to be named. Literally. It was handed to me by a European woman, in Europe! Look, I've got to get back. Good luck. And remember – the president doesn't know anything about this. We mustn't involve him. He's too sick."

"Right." Johnson wondered if this might be the magic advantage that would push him to the front of the race. But he didn't want to play this card too early. It had to be done just right. And by whom? Suddenly, it hit him – he knew the perfect person.

A few miles away, in Arlington, the Democratic Party's presidential candidate, Senator Wes Westlake, ran his fingers through his hair, his body shaking with anger. He was sitting on the edge of his bed, bellowing into the phone.

"When did this bastard contact you?"

"Some time ago. But of course I didn't say a word."

"Are you sure, Jeri? If you did, believe me, I'll wring your neck," Westlake hissed between clinched teeth.

"I told you, honey bun. Not a word. But tell me this. Exactly how much is it worth to you for me to continue keeping my mouth shut?"

"What?" His bellow rose to thunder. "You bitch! I can hardly believe what I'm hearing. Are you trying to blackmail me? After all this time, and all we've meant to each other?"

"Blackmail is such a strong word, darlin'." In her small Rockville apartment, dressed only in a lacy negligée, the redhead turned from the phone and winked at the man sitting next to her on the bed. He nodded and smiled, encouraging her to continue, as the tape recorder connected to her phone registered every word.

"It may be strong, but it's true, isn't it? Well? How much do you want?"

"Darlin', bein' as I don't appreciate the way I been dumped, a small sum of let's say fifty thousand dollars would be nice."

"I'll meet you outside L'Auberge at 6:30 tomorrow evening. The money'll be inside a two-pound box of Godiva chocolates, which I'll suggest – as a stranger – you've forgotten. There'll be no other words exchanged between us. Understand?"

"Yeah," she replied. "Until tomorrow, then, sugar." She placed the telephone back on the cradle and turned her attention to her visitor. He gave her a thumbs-up signal as he disconnected his recording machine from the base of the telephone.

"So, baby, how much have you made off this guy?" the man asked, squeezing her knee gently with his right hand.

"Including that Austrian woman? Twenty from her and now fifty from him – seventy big ones! He's always treated me like a slut. Now he'll get his due, just when he ain't expecting it."

The man placed the small recorder, wires and all, into his briefcase. He took out an envelope of new hundred-dollar bills and handed it to her. "This ups your take to eighty grand. And wait till we get that telephoto shot of him handing you the chocolates! That'll go great with this tape. Sorry we have to implicate poor Godiva. Great chocolate. Bye now, and have a good day, as they say on The Hill."

Hell, thought Westlake, pacing around his bedroom while desperately trying to think straight. *What a bitch! That's all I need.*

He opened the door to his closet, reached to the paneling at the back, and slid it away. Slowly, he dialed the combination to his safe and took out a large manila envelope, from which he withdrew five fat bundles of hundred-dollar notes from his war chest. Fifty thousand dollars, to be exact. He took an empty Godiva chocolate box that he had saved from the top shelf of his closet, and put the bills in neatly, ready to be delivered the following day. It hurt watching all those portraits of Benjamin Franklin disappear like that, *but when it comes to damage control you can't be cheap*, he thought. *Oh, well, there's no problem that can't be solved by throwing money at it. Daddy always told me.*

Once he had finished his preparations, he tried to put the whole incident out of his mind and returned to work. For the third time that day, he analyzed the poll results delivered by his political adviser. The numbers were a serious blow. In spite of the continual optimistic reports from his campaign manager, and the last-minute contributions, the polls showed that his Republican rival and he were too close to call. And Kramer, the fringe candidate, driven by his conservative New York billionaire father-in-law, was closing in fast. This had all been unthinkable at convention time in mid-July. Then, he hadn't even considered Johnson a serious threat let alone serious competition from a new third-party candidate, albeit a renegade Republican.

It was unnerving. He decided to work through the night. He would analyze the data to try to find out exactly where he was going wrong and where his campaign needed more money. He had the money, cash galore, but it clearly wasn't being used effectively. *That has to be the key*, he concluded. And he picked up the phone to raise hell with his campaign manager.

Brussels

Guy van den Heuven once more read through the computer printout, which now ran into several pages. Thorough and detailed, it itemized every development since the May evening when the American ambassador was murdered. But it didn't give him what he needed – light at the end of the investigative tunnel.

His two breakthroughs had yet to help solve the case. The first was the fact that the murdered hooker, according to Gérard, was one of the two girls who had visited Sorensson several days before his death. The second was the photographic identification of their companion, a suspected hit man named Peter.

Impulsively, Guy dialed Brenda Straus's personal number in Washington. After three short peals a sleepy voice responded.

"Brenda, Guy here. Still in bed? Listen – do you have news for me from NATO, or any other sources?"

Struggling for consciousness, Brenda nearsightedly peered at the alarm clock: 05:06. She might have known it. Guy was hopeless when it came to observing transatlantic time differences. "No," she said. "But today may just be the day."

"*Bien. Bien.* I have this funny feeling, brilliant Brenda, that we are overlooking something important. I have checked and rechecked every piece of evidence. And when Guy gets this feeling, Guy knows he is correct! By now we should have had something solid. I spoke to the Russians. And I get another feeling – I think they know something. When they do not even ask questions, I get suspicious. Are you there, *chérie*?"

Brenda covered the receiver with her hand and yawned. "Yes, Guy," she said. "I'm following what you're saying."

"*Bon, alors*, the Russians didn't ask any questions. But Russians always ask questions! So? If there are links with Iran, they must know. They have good sources there. Why not tell me?"

"Yes, Guy. Right."

"I've decided to see our friend Gérard again. Maybe, as you Yanks say, we have been jumping to conclusions about the second girl. A long time has passed now and she has not turned up in the morgue. Your theory about a female helping the assassin, or even being the assassin, needs more investigating, *n'est-ce pas?*"

"Gee, that's a novel approach, Guy. The second girl. Now why didn't I think of that?"

"*Oui, oui*, Brenda. No sarcasm, please. So you were right from the beginning. Maybe. So, I think, now we must track down hooker number two. Do you want to visit the bars with me, Brenda?" Guy teased, laughing. "A bar crawl *à la Bruxelles*."

They talked for a few more minutes. They agreed to talk again in four hours. Excited, Guy buzzed his secretary. A homely blonde with a big chest and a penchant for short tight skirts, Françoise tapped lightly on the door before entering, notebook in hand. Like most of the other women at the Judiciary Police headquarters, she was smitten by Guy's charm. He knew it, and thoroughly enjoyed their flirtatious relationship, which would lead to nothing on his side but was responsible for her glow on most days. And a readiness to jump when he said jump.

"Please ring Gérard, the guard at the American ambassador's residence. Tell him to expect me in half an hour. The number is in the Sorensson file."

"*Oui, Monsieur*. Is there anything else?" She reddened as he raised his eyebrows a fraction before replying.

"Nothing for the moment. Thank you, my dear. But I will be in touch before you leave for the day to see if there are any messages."

"Right." She scribbled a note in her pad and turned to leave. Guy enjoyed watching her pert little *derrière* and assumed she knew it. *I could never work in the States*, he told himself. *They work well, but where's the fun?*

He gathered his papers, secured his micro tape recorder in his coat pocket and shuffled out. The unmarked car would be better this time. He really enjoyed the drive along the wooded boulevards leading to the ambassador's residence; it was a route he had come to know well over the past few months.

Gérard was waiting for him on the front steps of the residence with the main gates open. Since early summer he had been enjoying the importance accorded him by these sessions with the police commissioner and trusted that his cooperation was being appropriately reported to his supervisor.

Guy's strong legs climbed the steps two at a time. Gérard rubbed the side of his nose and winked before asking whether anything new had come up in the case.

"The information you have given us so far about this man Peter and the dead girl has been invaluable. We are very grateful." Even though Guy did not care much for Gérard, he was getting desperate for more details. "But now I want you to think back to the missing girl. Not the dead hooker, but the other one who returned with the ambassador some nights before his murder. The one you say called the man Peter."

"And who returned on the night of the ambassador's murder?"

"*Oui.* Is there anything else you can add, Gérard? Anything at all you remember about this girl, something which would make her stand out?"

Wallowing in the moment, Gérard was silent for a minute. "Well, no, not really."

"What do you mean by 'really'?"

"Well..."

"Yes?" said Guy, curbing his impatience. "What?"

"It's just that I got a good idea where the ambassador met these girls. It wouldn't have been at a bar around here, for instance."

Guy reflected crossly on the hours he had spent carefully

checking out every bar in the vicinity.

"I only know this because on one of my nights off I got a call from the driver who fills in for me," Gérard continued with relish. "It was two months or so before the murder, and I guess the old man had one screwdriver too many and was harassing one of the bar girls in this dive with topless dancers, dark corners, and some SM types around. This buddy of mine wanted my take on how to handle it."

"I wish you'd told me this before!" Guy switched on the tape recorder concealed in his breast pocket. "It would have saved us a lot of time."

"Well, I'm telling you now, aren't I? It didn't dawn on me before. And not only that, I can tell you exactly where it is."

"How come? You been there?"

"Actually, I have." Gérard was caught unaware, and reddened. "Awful place, called the Parrot's Cave. Stumbled upon it by accident one night. Coincidence, actually. Run by an Englishman. Burned out, over-the-hill rock musician." He tore a piece of paper off the memo pad he kept in his pocket. "Here's the address. They must know who these girls are, especially if the old man was a regular customer."

"Thanks for your help," Guy said, although he would have preferred driving a fist into the man's paunch. "I'll be sure to let you know when we have a real breakthrough," he lied.

He recognized the address. It was in one of the seediest parts of the city, the red-light district near the Gare du Nord. He had never heard of this particular bar but could imagine what it was like. He ran down the steps, crossed the long driveway with wide strides and hurried to his car across the narrow street.

The *patron* of the Parrot's Cave looked like a storybook pirate. His greasy, bleached-blond hair was pulled back in a ponytail. He also sported the requisite gold earring in one ear. The right ear.

But his clothes were from a more recent era – loud Hawaiian-style shirt and purple sweat pants. They contrasted sharply with Guy's immaculate pale-gray Yves Saint Laurent linen suit.

A quick look around gave Guy a fair idea of the kind of business this pirate ran. It was a pickup joint for low-level hookers and SM types. He stood at the bar and ordered a cold beer. When the bartender-owner brought the Belgian brew, Guy began questioning him. Most of the occupants, at least the sober ones, clearly sensed that the *flics* had arrived.

"What's your name?"

"Who wants to know, guv'ner?" the barman said with an accent from London's East End.

Guy had neither the inclination nor the time for pleasantries. He wanted results, fast. He flashed his police ID. The pirate greeted it with a yawn and nonchalant shrug.

"Let's try again, sonny. Your name?"

"Billy Eloy's the name. This here joint's mine."

Hiding his annoyance, Guy questioned the man carefully about the murdered hooker. Eloy checked the photo and admitted that the hooker had indeed frequented the Parrot's Cave. Upon hearing this, Guy fired one question after another at him. "And who was she with? A woman? A man? Always the same girl or man? Or both?"

"I only saw her a few times. Always with another bird an' a guy. Dark an' hairy. A heavy slob, I remember. Mediterranean-lookin'. The bird was high-class. Black hair, green eyes. German I think." He paused to take a long drag of his cigarette, blowing the smoke out just past Guy's left ear. "Is that it?" he asked rudely, turning his back and gathering up some glasses.

"I don't know." Guy's voice, slow and menacing, brought Eloy whirling around quickly. "You tell me. And I suggest you do it fast, or I'll see this place shut down for unlicensed soliciting."

"You can't do that, guv'ner. You got no grounds!"

"Watch me!" Guy leaned over the stale beer and cigarette ash on the bar. "Listen, just tell me what you know about this woman. Did she hang out with anyone else? What was her name? And the man's name?" He stared hard at Eloy.

"I told ya what I know, mate. I never remember names. Don't hassle me."

"Hassle you? I haven't even started," replied Guy with an eager grin on his face. "But I do love that part. Shall we begin?"

"Okay, okay, guv'ner. Just hang on a sec, will ya? Me bird knows more." He opened a small door at the back of the bar, which, Guy guessed, led to the kitchen. "Beautiful, the *flics* are here. This nice police commissioner," he pronounced the words with pointed contempt, "wants to ask ya some questions about one of our customers. That bitch lady friend of yours and her hairy mate."

"Oh, yeah?" The voice was slack and young and burned out. Guy was not surprised to see, when she stepped out into the bar, that she looked no more than seventeen. Probably a runaway, and to top it off she was half-zonked on something. Coke, he guessed. He made a mental note to have someone come by later to check her papers. He suspected she was HIV-positive. She had that look.

"You'll have to excuse me, I got lots to do," said Eloy sarcastically, then, pointing toward his girlfriend, he added, "I'll leave you in the safe hands of our friend here, Rosie."

The young, stoned hooker shrugged and eased herself up onto the bar stool next to Guy.

"So you're Rosie?" Guy asked gently. "Rosie what?" *She certainly doesn't look like a Rosie*, he thought. The girl was sickly skinny. Her flesh was the color of parchment, her unwashed, long brown hair pulled back in an untidy ponytail. Accumulated dirt blackened her blunt nails. Her clothes needed a good wash, and a stale scent of bar wine and tobacco smoke rose from her crumpled clothes. Otherwise, she wasn't bad looking. As she leaned forward, resting her forearms on the bar counter, Guy felt the warm assault of her odor.

"Jones," she answered, staring down at her clenched fists.

With clear disbelief, Guy repeated slowly, "Rosie Jones. And so, Mademoiselle Rosie Jones, what would you like to tell me about this girl's friend?" He slid the photo of the dead hooker toward her. "And perhaps you can recall if she was part of a threesome with a dark, Mediterranean-looking man."

"Don't know about that," said Rosie, examining the picture. "But I know the other bird you're talkin' about. The one who came in with her once." She stabbed a nicotine-stained forefinger at the photo. "Got to know her one night. We'd had a drink and then I went back to her apartment." She colored. "Just for a cup of coffee. You know?"

Guy did know. All too well. But instead of contempt he felt pity for the girl. *She'd be dead in less than five years*, he guessed. He'd seen it lots of times, that look.

"What was her name? Do you remember where her apartment was?" Guy made sure that the barman wasn't looking and slipped her a small bundle of Belgian francs, which she quickly stuck in her bra.

"Just make sure you're telling me the truth. Or I'll be back faster than you can blink."

"I do know where it is. And I don't mind tellin' you one bit," Rosie spat. "That bitch threw me out in the middle of the night and I had to walk all the way back here. She wouldn't even pay for a friggin' taxi! Here!" She scribbled a few lines on a crumpled napkin advertising a local beer. "It's right round the corner from where I used to work."

"Thank you, Mademoiselle Rosie. Now what was her name?"

"Called herself Jay. And around here we don't question people on their names. But when I was in the flat I noticed her passport on a desk. Before I could open it for a look she caught me arm and twisted the passport away. Then she kicked me arse out in the street. My jeezuss, she was pissed off. And tough. She's a lesbian too, that one. Or bi, I shouldn't wonder."

"Rosie, what nationality was her passport?"

"German. I was so bloody shocked by her whackin' me, I can't remember the color. But I remember the bird on the cover. That friggin' German bird scares me, see? Jay's vicious when she's angry. I really thought she was fixin' to kill me. You ever see those cold green eyes of hers? Like pieces of glass stuck in a snake. Just like a snake when she's angry. And she carries a gun."

"You've seen it?"

"I've felt it."

"I'll show you a couple of passports later, Rosie, and maybe they'll refresh your memory. Now, what about Jay's male friend. What was his name? Is he a boyfriend? A bodyguard? What?"

"Peter, and he's a grump. Dunno what she sees in him. No sex machine, him. I think maybe he just pays her to be seen with him, to impress other blokes, or whatever."

Guy quickly downed his beer. "Thanks for your help, Rosie. Keep telling me the truth and it may save your life someday. Now get your boyfriend back out here and fast."

Like a scared child, she ran into the kitchen to get Eloy.

He walked out to face Guy. "Yes, Mr. Commissioner? You happy now?"

Guy replied, "Sure. But I'd be happier if both of you were telling me the truth. And I'm thinking how to get your attention. What do you think would do it?" Suddenly, he leaned over the bar, grabbed Eloy's shirt and shouted in his face, "Would it be a big stick or a few nights in a cell?"

"Hey guv'nor! Take it easy. What's the problem?"

"My problem," whispered Guy, "is that you told me you knew nothing about the hairy guy, Peter. I've decided you know more.

I'm going out to check on an address Rosie gave me and when I return you better be prepared to share what you know about him. It'd be a bloody shame to have to close down such a jolly pub. It's your choice."

He released his steel grip and walked out of the Parrot's Cave, pleased with his tough-guy act. Behind him, Eloy was cursing.

When Guy arrived at the apartment he found the front door locked and bolted. Walking the length of the hallway, looking for another entrance, he discovered a smaller door, which he guessed led to the kitchen. Skillfully he slipped the lock with his Swiss army knife and the door slid open.

Slowly and meticulously, Guy went from room to room. He looked under the furniture, searched the closets, upended drawers, turned hanging frames.

He inspected the bathroom – shower stall, medicine cabinet, toilet tank. He was fast but thorough, probing every conceivable place.

Nothing! Merde.

The flat thoroughly searched, he called on his mobile telephone for a forensic team to search for fingerprints and other clues. But he was already resigned to the probability that it was clean, and done by a professional. Probably the green-eyed woman called J or Jay. *What was she doing screwing around with an item like Rosie*, he wondered. But when it came to human libido there were no surprises. *Everything exists for reasons we can never really know.*

Now was the time to call Brenda. *Just wait till she hears this latest*, he thought as he left the apartment building. *It looks more and more like she might have been right after all.* He walked briskly to his car. It was time to invite the greasy barman to a friendly discourse on a mutual acquaintance, Peter. *The patron of the Parrot's Cave will sing like a canary,* Guy joked to

251

himself, impressed with his own wit.

Moscow

The shower head sprayed needles of hot water on Yuri Borozov's shoulders and back. A sigh of pleasure escaped from his mouth as the water continued to sooth his athletic but overworked body. Turning around, he reached for his shampoo and poured a good amount on his thinning hair, his long, strong fingers vigorously working up a fine lather. *Wonderful.* All his toiletries smelled good and came from duty-free shops in international airports. As he doused himself, he felt ready for the Cindy Crawford in the Omega watch ad on CNN. His blood circulating faster in his veins, Yuri's exhaustion began to peel away.

The phone rang.

"Damn," he swore, stepping out from the shower stall and rubbing suds from his eyes. In the cool morning air Yuri shivered. He tried not to slip on the wet tile floor as he reached for the beige wall phone. He was pleased that he'd installed a unit conveniently in the bathroom.

"Yes?" he yelled in Russian.

A familiar sexy voice answered his outburst. "My sweetie heart, Yuri."

"Yes..."

"I hear a shower running. Are you naked? How I wish I were your bar of soap," she taunted in German-accented English.

Blood, hot and stirring, rushed through his body to his groin. He closed his eyes and took a few deep breaths, gathering his thoughts.

"Jackie! I am so, so glad you called me. Listen, and listen well, *mein liebling*. Your friend – the one with the mustache – I found out yesterday our Belgian friends would like to meet him.

They know his first name. They know what he looks like and they are circulating his picture. A photo of him sitting at a sidewalk café. You follow what I'm saying?"

"Yes, darling. What else did you hear? Did you see that photo? Which café? Do you know?" Jackie's voice was steady.

"Yes, I saw the picture, love. I'm not sure where it was taken. Brussels, maybe. One of my experts says it's Paris. He says the café and the waiter in the background are recognizeable. It doesn't show who your friend was sitting with. I hope it wasn't you, my love! Anyway you should know they're looking for him now as the main suspect in the affair we discussed the other day. Are you listening?"

"Yes, darling. And thinking. Thanks for the tip."

"Well, I hope you realize just how serious this is."

"Don't worry, darling. I'm going to take a long vacation. Away from home base and away from the mustached one. You're right, he definitely is a bad influence. We're splitting."

"You told me that once before, remember? And that was long before your last sales trip. So what am I to believe? Shit, why did I ever fall for a dangerous bitch like you?"

"Sssh, darling, please don't talk like that, you make me sad. You feel for me because we are crazy about each other, and we make great love together. It's nothing to do with your profession, or my little part-time job."

"A long vacation far away from the mustached one would be a great idea. Drop me a card to the PO box." Exasperated, Yuri hung up abruptly without waiting for a response. The post office box was in Vienna, and it was their safest way to communicate in writing. High security was always low-tech and common.

He stepped back into the shower, seeking the warmth of its massaging water, but feeling a chill in spite of the heated spray that pummeled him. A wave of nausea rose in his throat. He pictured the worst scenarios – the police searching for Peter throughout Europe, stalking him, chasing him; finally catching him. If they found Peter, it would pose an indirect threat to Yuri and his rapid rise to the top of Russian intelligence – his sole ambition in life. He turned the shower knob briskly to the left, removing the hot, and braced himself for the invigorating Siberian sting.

As Yuri slowly rubbed himself dry, his mind still followed a troubled path. He recalled the countless intelligent and powerful men around the world whom the old KGB had entrapped with honey-pot operations. Some of the women they used reminded him of Jackie. And here he was, the great intelligence operator, allowing his lack of zipper control to get him into damn near the same situation as an amateur. He caught his reflection in the mirror above the sink and grimaced.

There was no denying the truth. Jackie meant a lot more to him than just another lay. He was crazy about her, and knew he could not replace her easily. For a moment his thoughts flashed to Lina and their vacuous, meaningless marriage.

No, this goes far deeper than lust, he mused while clipping his nose hairs. *Well, at least a bit.* But that didn't mean he was not worried about his professional future. He had to find a way out for her, and for himself. His love for Jackie and his career ambitions were on a collision course. *Stupid bitch. Why couldn't she just knock off penny-ante gangsters and local judges?*

Far away at the Richmond Hotel lobby in Geneva, Jackie was paying the operator in cash, leaving no trace of who made the call. Of all the emotions inflaming her senses after her call to Yuri, anger was paramount. It was dangerous on the open lines even though no names or places had been mentioned. And more dangerous for Yuri than for her. *Who the hell does he think he is?* she muttered to herself as she left the hotel lobby through the revolving doors.

Softening slightly, she walked toward the lake. The problem was that she was in love, or at least seriously infatuated, and, more importantly, she knew the feeling was mutual. *Still, where were his priorities? Protecting his own ambitions, or her safety? Their future? Fuck men! He can freeze his cock off in the Russian winter for all I care. I've got work to do. And major funds to recover.*

Ten minutes later Jackie window-shopped among the most exclusive boutiques along the Rue du Rhône. Yuri had already been stashed away somewhere in the back of her mind. She smiled, losing herself in designer-clothes paradise. How smart she had been not to reveal to Yuri that she was going after her man in D.C. *Well, he'll learn in time, and in a big way! I can be as resourceful as Russian intelligence.* It had been easy tracking the name David Tiron.

Still exulting, she turned down the small side street that led to her apartment. There she collected her car from the underground garage and headed out onto the Swiss *autoroute*.

Peter was waiting for her in the small village of Gruyère, where the cheese of the same name was made and where the police were not likely to look for the world's number-one professional assassin.

This was a crucial meeting, because Jackie wanted to get Peter working on what she now thought of as the Tiron project. She intended to place Peter where the Americans would never think of looking for him – in Washington, D.C. And while hiding there on a phony passport, he could case David Tiron and his habits so she could work out the best way to confront the Israeli about the deception and the debt. Yes, she was about to move the game right under the noses of the people who were looking for her, even if they didn't yet know it.

Guy left the Parrot Cave satisfied. He felt confident he was closing in on Peter and his female companion. He now knew that his man was Greek, feared the temper of the green-eyed woman, had hinted she could kill if provoked, and worried about even being seen with her. She seemed to have money and to be in charge. Peter was more like a tired cowboy than a dangerous assassin. And her name was Jackie. Jay, and other aliases were just minor distractions to keep people guessing.

Jackie.

She and Peter had gone to school together, he claimed. But where? They spoke French together and yet he was Greek and she was German. *So why French?* Guy brainstormed. *They met in France, perhaps. In school? But there was a considerable age difference. Maybe, then, they were in a professional school together. Like an airline training college; she a hostess, he an older steward?* These thoughts ran around in Guy's head till it began to ache. But he was pleased. He had lots of new details, puzzle pieces to push around. He just had to fit them together.

Peter and Jackie were becoming clearer in his mind, even if they didn't yet know it.

It's time for a nice bowl of mussels and shallots and a bottle of Reisling. Guy's body worked like a clock. *Call Brenda*, he reminded himself.

Chapter Eighteen

Washington, D.C.
September 18th

Ever since the night The Five approved Operation Hebron two months earlier at Jerome's farm in Israel, David Tiron's blood had been pumping with exhilaration. The excitement of the challenge, the anticipation of success – the greatest in the history of Mossad – and the challenge of his role in changing the course of history took over his being. Yet the unparalleled risk of the operation also made his insides quiver with unexplained terror. The thought of his participation, coupled with the operation's eventual result, was petrifying. *I'll go down in history.* He slept only in short doses. A good night's sleep would have to wait till after the election – or not – of Hebron as president of the most powerful country in the world. Tiron's obsession became almost demonic.

He had carried both the exhilaration and the dread with him on his return trip to Washington. And they had stayed with him ever since, hurling him from one extreme on the emotional scale to the other. He devoted all his energy to the Hebron operation, neglecting his usual obligation of briefing the Israeli ambassador. His less-than-adequate presence at the embassy gained him a severe rebuke from the ambassador, whose displeasure didn't help Tiron's mental and emotional turmoil.

257

But he really didn't care that his diplomatic superior wasn't happy with him now. One day he would recognize Tiron's supreme devotion to Israel and would give him the credit he so richly deserved. The end justified the paltry means.

Tiron hoped that one day all Israelis present and future, including the children he dreamed of having, would know of his historic role. The very thought made him swell with gloating pride. For although he was a fierce Zionist, and an outstanding intelligence officer, he wanted more than anything to settle down in Israel and raise a family. He'd have a boy first and call him Moshe, after Moses and General Dayan. Then, a girl, Esther, after his mother. Yet, at the same time, he knew he was locked into the most crucial phase of his career. There was no time to search for the right *shöne maitl* to partner with. Well, all in time. *After 5285 years, what's a few more months?*

His meeting with Hebron later that day was another step in that direction. Tiron and Hebron had met rarely since the final phase of the operation had been decided in Israel. Personally, David did not care much for the American agent, finding him arrogant, self-important, and at times paranoid. However, he had to admit that Hebron's loyalties were firmly in the right place, even if always at a steep price. The fact that Hebron was a gentile also made David uncomfortable, but he conceded that ever since being recruited twenty years before, Hebron had played his part well and had produced results – aid packages, arms sales, and the like.

The Willard Hotel at 14th and Pennsylvania Avenue was ideal for their meeting. Its entrance was next to the elevator, while wide pillars and heavy oak screens created a kind of hidden passageway through the lobby. They were to meet in the George Washington Suite, which was booked for the day in the name of one of Tiron's influential pro-Israeli American friends. The friend, who knew better than to ask questions, had given Tiron the key to use at his discretion. Early that afternoon Tiron had sent his station technicians to sweep the room. Although he had faith in their thoroughness, he arrived thirty minutes early to check it out again himself. As a final touch he placed a Do Not Disturb sign on the outside door. If the presidential candidate were to be spotted it would not be hard to justify the hotel visit as a campaign fund-raising call. They all did it, and lobbying in Washington for money and influence was about as unusual as ordering sushi for lunch at a Japanese restaurant.

At the appointed time there was one knock, the door was opened from the inside, and Hebron entered. Tiron's Mossad driver and bodyguard, Abe, had been waiting just inside the suite. He locked the door and remained in the hallway on guard. The two principals in intrigue, Hebron and Tiron, greeted each other and moved into the adjoining salon, closing the partition door firmly behind them.

Tiron helped himself to a glass of freshly squeezed orange juice from the jug on the sideboard, while Hebron poured himself a stiff vodka on the rocks. As they sat opposite each other at the round mahogany dining table without speaking, Tiron handed Hebron a large white envelope. It was filled with cash. US hundreds, as usual.

They always paid this agent in cash. At Mossad's insistence, Hebron kept the money in safes and safe-deposit boxes, never in bank accounts. Mossad wanted to eliminate the risk of Hebron's discovery by some investigative reporter who might obtain a copy of bank statements showing unusually large deposits for which the senator couldn't account. The cash didn't earn interest but it was safe from prying reporters.

Hebron took the envelope, looked inside and nodded. He then looked at the Mossad agent questioningly.

Tiron cleared his throat. "Charles, before we get down to election business I have an unrelated question," he began, using

259

the assumed name they had long ago agreed on for rooms which might be bugged. "Do you know anything about the investigation into your ambassador's death in Brussels?"

Hebron looked at Tiron suspiciously. "Of course I do. From what I've learned, the FBI investigation's continuing – primarily in Brussels – and fingers are pointing to Tehran or Baghdad," he said, putting the money into his briefcase. "In fact, I've heard diplomatic relations between the US and certain Arab countries are becoming more than just slightly strained because of this affair. Which is convenient for us, I must say." Hebron waited for Tiron's reaction.

But the Mossad agent didn't rise to the bait. The prime minister's insistence on absolute secrecy in the Sorensson matter made sense, especially at such a politically sensitive time. Besides, Tiron reminded himself, as one never knew what might break the loyalty of a secret agent, it was always better if the agent didn't know more than necessary to perform his tasks. He confined himself to agreeing: "Yes, it's good news for us, whoever did it. Even with the Arab connection remaining inconclusive, it seems those ragheads are always playing right into our hands. Well, enough of that. Let's get cracking on the business in hand."

"Absolutely. So, how do you read the polls?"

Tiron sighed. "So damn close it makes me nervous. What can we do to give you a push over the goal line?"

Hebron reached into his inside breast pocket, drew out a thick, folded document and handed it to the Mossad chief with a self-satisfied smile. "Look. I've got a copy of the president's confidential campaign plan for the last election. One of my Senate buddies has a girlfriend in the RNC who 'borrowed' it." Hebron winked. "Despite the considerable odds against him, Douglas's strategy worked, particularly in the final few weeks. It's four years old but it should serve as a guideline for us. If they could win an election with it, why can't we?"

As a senior intelligence officer, Tiron always relished the chance to get his hands on a sensitive document, even though he had never before cared about seeing an election plan by any political party.

"Strategy for the Election of Vice President Howard Lee Douglas to the Presidency," he read out. "Very good! My God, you're always ahead of the game, aren't you, Charles?"

"Look at it this way. Some of us run for president, and some of us remain in the background promoting my victory!" As Hebron's tone was lighthearted, Tiron for once wasn't offended by the pseudo-patronizing remark. "But in the meantime it's going to be tough having these meetings with the Secret Service constantly on my ass. Keep that in mind."

"I realize that. But with what's at stake for us all, we must continue to meet no matter what the risks. I'll ensure that reports of all our discussions are passed on to Jerusalem as swiftly as possible. Besides, the Secret Service agents are there to protect you, not to spy on you. They're not going to tell anybody anything. Remember the court cases of Douglas's predecessor."

"I suppose you're right. Okay, let's get to the meat of matters. As far as the polls are concerned, there are indications that my stand on things like abortion and health care is what people want to hear about."

"Charles, I have to leave such matters to you and your campaign team, whom we are also supporting indirectly through our friends here. And don't fret about resources – the lake is stocked." It was Tiron's turn to wink. "That's the least of your worries. Focus on security and winning. Get out there and campaign, please."

"Okay. But, what exactly happens to me if I don't get elected? I mean, will the company retire me?"

"That's not even a consideration," said David flatly. "You are going to win. It's not worth discussing you losing. Just keep us posted on your strategy, so I'll know where we can fit in and help behind the scenes. You remember what Vince Lombardi said, 'Winning isn't – "

Hebron raised his hand, cutting off the pep talk. *Spare me*, he thought, but simply said, "Got it, coach."

He placed his empty glass decisively on the table and spread open a large plan clearly outlining a complicated schedule, with dates and places highlighted in pink and yellow. There were 13 early morning television appearances, twice as many local radio talk shows, a five-state bus tour, and 96 thirty-second paid TV spots on network affiliates. After discussing the campaign layout for nearly forty minutes, he suddenly glanced at his watch. "If there's nothing else, I think I should leave. Otherwise I'll be missed, and anyway I have an appointment. I've convinced my Secret Service guy I'm up here with an internationally famous actress who's backing my campaign, and she wouldn't stand for it if I brought him up with me. So far he buys it."

Tiron nodded, wishing his star agent good luck. He wanted to toast him in Hebrew, but the culture they shared was purely political...and financial. Hebron wasn't even circumcised.

With a cursory smile and a thumbs-up, the senator grabbed his briefcase and left his case officer behind.

Abe checked the hallway, then let Israel's top foreign agent out the door to meld back into the Washington scene as a serious presidential candidate. Despite the all-clear, Hebron was wary, as always; it would take just one prying eye to start unraveling the incredible web he'd spun. And dormant panic perpetually underlay his presidential-caliber poise.

Chapter Nineteen

Mallorca
October 8th

She loved to lie in the hot sun, her sleek powerboat bobbing gently on Mallorca's clear waters. It was Jackie Markovic's favorite way to relax: stretching out nude on the cushions of her boat as she looked out across the azure waters at the beautiful cove of Formentos. While her 42-foot Fountain Lightning was ostensibly a pleasure craft, Jackie's justification of the price she had paid for it was its two 800-horsepower Merc engines. It was easily the fastest boat in these waters – ready-made for escape in an emergency.

On the nearby island of Ibiza, Jackie maintained the first stop for such an escape, a small studio apartment rented under another name. There she kept a false German passport to match the rental contract, identity papers, and spare cash and clothes for a quick change to the new persona, should that be necessary.

Loud music drew her attention to the two topless girls, one black with a swirl of neat braids, the other blonde, who a few moments before had loved Jackie's body. They shook their hips and clapped their hands to *"Uno, Dos, Tres..."* wafting from the CD player.

When preoccupied by a difficult task, Jackie needed to indulge in such pleasure and bask in such luxury. That was when the professional killer in her planned and plotted best. She conceived some of her most imaginative schemes in settings like these. The operation she was planning this time was a personal one. She wasn't hired to do it. There might be no money in it, and lots of danger. But, oh, the reward would be far more satisfying.

Revenge!

Sweet revenge to even the score and restore her good name in the underground world. *No one would ever again make a fool of Jackie Markovic.* The Israeli intelligence official who had played with her as if she were a toy to be used and thrown away – he was going to pay. Jackie had long ago sworn that no man would ever use her again without paying, and paying, and paying...

And now that she was sexually satiated, her usual super-efficiency was at its peak. Her master-plan had been conceived to solve two problems at once. *In today's harsh global economy, one has to be cost-effectiv*e, she reflected.

Her first need was to make certain telephone calls. And if she wanted to keep her life in Spain above suspicion, she must make her professional calls where no one could trace them. Time to fly. She picked up her cellular phone to make plane reservations.

Zurich, October 9th

The next day a Swissair Douglas MD-80 took off from Palma de Mallorca. At 5:40 p.m., precisely two hours later, it touched down on the long rain-swept main runway of Zurich's Kloten Airport.

Chic as a supermodel in her new black suit, Italian leather high heels, and reversible black-and-tan raincoat, Jackie rose from her seat, reached for her black overnight case and a plain, light-colored plastic suit-bag, and disembarked.

Zurich's airport was perfect for her professional requirements. For her, it was the ultimate in efficient stopovers in Europe. While in transit she could conduct her business without having to enter the country or show her travel documents. She did her banking in the huge transit area, made her international phone calls, without leaving a trace, from the large Swiss PTT complex, mailed letters to her Geneva banker, and shopped for duty-free merchandise in the alluring terminal boutiques.

She went into the transit lounge ladies' room to dress down, less like a rich playgirl and more like a working girl on a tour of Europe. She donned a pair of worn-out jeans, a T-shirt that pleaded for Peace on Earth, and black-and-white Air Jordans. A blue beret covering her silky black hair and a Nikon dangling from her shoulder added nice touches. She carefully put her suit and raincoat in the suit-bag which she left in a locker. Thus transformed, she walked to Terminal B through the interior connecting hallways and entered the Swiss Telekom complex, mingling easily with the crowd.

From here she could phone or fax directly to any point in the globe without leaving a trace. These were communications she would not dare transmit from Mallorca. For Spain she needed to maintain the highest level of security so that the local authorities could never accuse her of any criminal activity – not even a minor violation. In her safe-haven of Mallorca she did everything strictly by the book. She paid her taxes, drove carefully, and never used the phone to conduct her true business.

In a soundproof phone booth Jackie picked up the dark red handset, called Washington directory assistance, and requested the switchboard number of the Federal Bureau of Investigation.

"That number is: 324-3000," responded the computerized operator in typically nasal American tones so loud that Jackie had to hold the phone away from her ear. She smiled at the harsh, digital, female voice, making a mental note to practice that accent for future professional use.

She dialed. In heavy, almost unintelligibly German-accented English, she asked to speak to someone responsible for terrorist threats who understood and spoke her language.

"Please hold the line. Thank you," answered the efficient, well-trained FBI operator. The operator rang the counter-terrorism section, where Brenda's analyst, Christina Whitinghill, picked up the phone. "I need someone to take a call in German," said the operator urgently. "I have a 'call-in' who wants to talk to our terrorist experts. We're tracing it. It's probably from overseas, but it's clear."

Christina ran into Brenda's office. "Brenda. Quick!" she said breathlessly. "A call-in, in German, overseas – you speak German. The operator's holding the call."

"Okay, put it through," Brenda said. "And tell the operator to trace the call."

"*Ja, Guten Tag*, *FBI*. How may I help you?" Brenda said calmly in German.

Jackie asked, "FBI terrorist section?"

Still in German, Brenda replied, "Yes, this is the Federal Bureau of Investigation's Counter-Terrorism Section in Washington. How may we help you?"

"Help me? That's a laugh," answered Jackie. "Rather, I will help you. You have some bastards working against you and I know them. One is a former boyfriend, who, I discovered, is a professional killer. The other is under your noses – an Israeli spy. They work together against your nation. You must stop them. They'll kill me if they know I called you."

"Could you give me their names, please," responded Brenda, signaling to Christina to be sure the operator was tracing the call.

"My friend's name is Peter. He murdered your ambassador in Brussels. He is Greek, a hit man, an assassin. A madman. You must know his family name – he hides it from me. His partner –

his name is David Tiron – is the Mossad man in America. The Israelis hired Peter to kill your ambassador. They'll kill more of your people. You have to stop them. I'll try to call you later with more information. It's too dangerous for me now. I must go."

As Jackie knew from Yuri that the Americans had Peter's name and photo and regarded him as a suspect, giving the name Peter would give her call instant credibility and support her claim that the Israelis and Tiron were behind the Sorensson murder.

"Wait – tell us how to reach you. What do you want? Can we protect you? Send you money?" Brenda tried to keep the caller talking for tracing and voice recognition purposes and to draw more details out of her. This type was usually too frightened to call back.

"I'll take care of myself. I need nothing from you people. Just get those bastards who killed your ambassador. They hurt me. If you catch them that will make me happy. *Auf Wiedersehen, Frau* FBI."

Jackie hung up and left the booth. She quickly settled her bill in cash with one of the women behind the desk. As usual, the attendants were too busy to pay any attention to the hordes of visitors coming in and out of the complex, speaking a full menu of languages, and paying their bills in assortments of currencies.

Jackie walked to the large ground-floor transit waiting area of Terminal B. After a few minutes of diversionary shopping in the adjacent boutiques she slipped back into the ladies' rest room of Terminal A to don her chic outfit and reappear as the striking woman who had arrived earlier from Palma.

With the delicate phone call behind her and her switch to stylish clothes, her mood improved immensely. It had not been great since that June day in Paris when she had learned the appalling news that she and Peter had been duped. But now that her plan of revenge had entered its first stage, she was beginning to feel like herself again, secure in the knowledge that, even if the

FBI asked the Swiss police to look for a woman who made a call from the Telekom complex, they would have nothing to go on.

Completely confident, Jackie walked haughtily through the corridors of the big modern airport. With the seeds of her revenge planted, she headed for the departure gate to catch her next flight, to Vienna. She would be in her hometown in time for dinner. She called the maid in her *pied-à-terre* from a pay phone near the gate to confirm her arrival after ten that evening.

Washington, D.C.

Brenda sat motionless, deep in thought, trying to recover from the phone call she had received a few minutes before. "*Mein Gott,*" she murmured, still thinking in German. Suddenly it had come to her, just like that: *The caller was her, the one we've been looking for, the connection between Peter and the murder of Ambassador Sorensson. That was her!* There was no other way to interpret the call. The woman had spoken German fluently, but Brenda's fine ear had detected an accent, Russian or Ukrainian, possibly Balkan. Mentioning Peter, the suspect for whom the entire West was looking, and identifying him as the assassin. The woman had pretended to be frightened, but spoke with such confidence that Brenda was convinced the call confirmed her theory of the mystery woman being the key in the Sorensson murder.

The FBI's high-tech tracers had located the source of the call: the Zurich airport. *But why call the FBI? Afraid of being killed...That didn't ring true.* The caller hadn't sounded frightened; at the end she had seemed more like someone in charge. Brenda focused on the message that the woman was determined to inform on Peter and Tiron to exact revenge.

"They hurt me," the caller had said. "They hurt me." *How?*

One strange point – why did she seem so sure the FBI would

know who Peter was? And what about the Israeli accusation; why did she claim the Israelis were responsible for Sorensson's murder? *That's crazy*, mused Brenda. *That has to be disinformation from someone.* The Russians? But the Russians had made a point of identifying Tiron as the control officer for Hebron. *There must be a Russian link with this woman. And...a link with Hebron?*

This was no accident. Brenda reminded herself what they said at Quantico: "If you believe in coincidences, you shouldn't be a detective." Something was not right here. Or getting to be very right.

Brenda was sure that this call was born of the fury of a woman scorned, if not in the classic romantic sense. Scorned by whom? Peter? Tiron? Had they cut her out of her share of the money? If so, what exactly had her role been? The mastermind, the diversion, or the assassin? Or something else?

The quicker Brenda found that out, the sooner she would close in on her new source of information, her new suspect, an unidentified German-speaking woman calling from the Zurich airport.

Brenda vaulted from her chair and paced around her office, considering the mountainous evidence of her unprocessed hard work. Those files, which she had spent countless hours reading and analyzing, were of no use in identifying the woman's role in this mystery. *Rethink*, she commanded herself. Agitated, she ran her fingers through her short curly hair and walked over to the window. *How about some new hunches?*

Staring out, she contemplated Pennsylvania Avenue without really focusing on the street scene five floors below, but her mind slowly registered the frenzy that laced the usual bustle down there. She frowned at the near-unconscious observation. Election Day was approaching. Then it hit her like a bag of sand. The elections were in less than a month. That realization snapped Brenda into action. She hadn't solved the Hebron case yet. Could this woman possibly turn out to be the key to that as well? "Okay, Frau Whatever-your-name-is. I'm going to get you. You're smart and you're good, but I'm nailing your *Arsch*."

Christina walked into Brenda's office. "That call – do you think it was who I think it was?" She went to stand next to Brenda.

"Hunch says it was." Brenda didn't elaborate and Christina knew her boss was in another world.

"So what are you going to do? Can I help?"

Brenda moved back to her desk, fumbled with a few files, then sat. "Okay," she said distractedly. Christina stayed where she was and held her breath. She could almost see Brenda's mind tossing ideas around. "Okay," repeated Brenda. "Guy said Rosie saw a German passport in Peter's friend's apartment. That won't help, though. She called from Zurich Airport. The Swiss don't keep immigration records on transiting passengers."

Christina didn't make a sound.

"What else do we have? If my hunch is correct and she's a pro, how come we have nothing on her?" She stood up and paced again. "We've overlooked something. A trained killer like that doesn't achieve this level overnight." A light came into Brenda's eyes. She looked up and met Christina's steady, earnest gaze.

"My God," she said slowly. "It's right in front of me. Suppose that what she told me over the phone is true – that the Israelis were behind the Sorensson assassination!"

"What?" cried Christina, her hand flying to her mouth.

"That's what she claims. So, let's assume for the sake of argument that they were. For such a high-profile hit, the Israelis would want the best – a top-notch pro. They'd want to be one hundred percent sure the job was clean. They'd want someone who doesn't leave a trace or anything to chance."

"Right," said Christina, bobbing her head.

"So they'd go to someone with a reputation. Someone with excellent training. Someone thoroughly drilled in clandestine international ops, who over the years had proved his worth. Or hers. And this person would have to be a free-lancer, not immediately connected to them."

"We can check our files for international networks or clandestine operation organizations," said Christina in a rush, concluding Brenda's thoughts.

"You got it. But we have to confine our search to the right time-frame. Gérard the guard and Rosie the hooker both guessed Peter's friend to be in her mid-thirties. So let's say the woman is thirty-five. If she started training in her teens...we should check back twenty years and work forward."

"I'm on it," said Christina, hurrying toward the door. "I'll get back to you as soon as I find anything."

"Thanks. Remember – early eighties and up. We're looking for a female killer or terrorist, maybe German, at least German-speaking. Meanwhile I'll have the computer nerds work on a facial projection from the descriptions Gérard and Rosie gave us."

Two hours later Christina ran into Brenda's office, a file in one hand, a black-and-white photo in the other. "Bingo!" her triumphant voice bounced off the walls. "You and your hunches, Brenda! What would we do without them?"

Brenda ran to meet Christina halfway across her office. "What d'you have? Come on, show me!"

They sat at the conference table, where Christina spread the file. Brenda snatched the photo to examine it and saw a tall, skinny, stooping man. His handsome, weathered oval face wore glasses and a sullen look. He appeared to be showing a young woman how to take a gun apart. In the background were men and women shooting at targets, obviously engaged in a practice session. The young woman was almost as tall as the man, her

271

hourglass body clad in jeans and a T-shirt, dark hair pulled back in a bun. Her face radiated fascination with the weapon. The man seemed to be enjoying instructing her.

"Henri Curiel," Brenda breathed. "The Curiel Communist Organization."

"The numero uno worldwide trainer in terrorism, clandestine communications, sabotage, assassinations...you name it," said Christina.

Brenda's eyes shot from Christina to the file and back.

"We got this from the French years ago," Christina said. "They had a penetration agent in the Curiel organization to gather information about his network. The agent took the photo of Curiel and this trainee in 1983. He reported that the young woman – black-haired, green-eyed, a Yugoslavian – had become one of Curiel's best assassin trainees. She was so good that Curiel recruited her for some of his hits. Her father was reportedly a Serb, a brutal killer, a KGB agent who had been murdered in mysterious circumstances. Her mother was Austrian. And Brenda, are you ready for this?"

Brenda arched an eyebrow.

"The French agent reported that this young woman had developed a strong relationship with another Curiel trainee – a *Greek* guy who went by the alias Bull. A few months after this was taken, the woman and the Greek split from the organization without a trace, much to Curiel's disappointment. He had a high regard for the woman. He called her *Le Valet*."

Brenda was so excited she could hardly speak. She rose slowly and walked back to her desk with measured steps. She picked up the artist's projection which the FBI facial expert had just brought to her, walked back to the conference table, and placed it next to the monochrome photo of young *Le Valet*.

Christina stood up and joined her.

"Take these downstairs and have Mark in the facial projection group take a look. See if he thinks these two women could be one and the same."

Without a word, Christina rushed to the door and bolted from the room, clutching the two pictures to her chest.

Brenda picked up the report and began reading slowly. There were a few facts she could work with. The woman's nationality was revealed – Yugoslavian. This would explain the accent Brenda detected in the woman's fluent German. Second, her relationship with Peter had been established, and her training as an assassin confirmed. Her exceptional talent as an assassin had been documented as well. She was very good. Good enough for Curiel to give her assignments. He reportedly considered her better than Carlos the Jackal, which meant she would be good enough for the Israelis, if they really did hire her for the Sorensson hit.

Finally things were falling into place. Brenda was positive that the facial group would confirm her supposition. She would have to call Guy and tell him of this latest development. But right now she needed to think.

After a walk around the block in the cool October air to help clear her head, Brenda returned to the FBI building and went directly to request that a clerk double-check the files on Curiel's organization. She also wanted files on anyone having any connection with Henri Curiel, no matter how seemingly insignificant.

The next day the clerk hand-carried his findings to Brenda. She summoned Christina to her office, and they began reading through the files. They didn't know what they were looking for, but prayed that something would jump out at them.

October 16th

A week's work had yielded little progress. Nothing of further value had been uncovered; the research seemed fruitless. The FBI had kept tabs on most of Curiel's trainees. Those who were devoted communists and believed in Curiel's tactics stayed with him and did his bidding. Other trainees were youngsters who wanted to make a statement to the world by joining the infamous group. When they grew up they disappeared in the busy halls of life, marrying, having families, severing all connections with their wild youth. And the career-minded who went to Curiel to learn the ropes later went freelance, hiring out to anyone who would pay. But this was all background information, none of it furthering Brenda's investigation. She was looking for a needle in the Curiel Organization haystack.

The needle pricked her in the middle of that night. Her overactive mind jolted her awake. She dressed quickly, phoned a cab, and was in her office by 1 a.m., going through the files of Curiel trainees. She instructed her computer to do four things: First, list all Curiel trainees, from the group's beginnings, by nationality – true nationality, probable, or otherwise. Second, generate a printout of their current addresses, if the FBI tracking had gone that far. Third, indicate if any of them had ever returned to the group, under their original identity or another. Fourth, sort by sex. She hit the enter key and waited.

At 7:00 the next morning, Christina walked into the office. Brenda's face was hidden behind her monitor. Her desk top, cleared of the usual mountains of files, was littered with empty coffee containers. Brenda, impervious to distraction, seemed not to hear Christina opening the door and entering the room.

Christina hesitated to interrupt.

"For God's sake!" came Brenda's muffled, exasperated voice from behind the computer screen. "Come in and close the door!"

"Brenda, what the hell's going on?"

Brenda lifted her head and gave Christina a triumphant smile.

"Archimedes and me – we got it!"

Wide-eyed, Christina walked around Brenda's desk and squinted into the screen. "What are you talking about? Those are the same files we've been analyzing to death for the last seven days."

"Not to death, Christina. And that was our oversight. Sit!"

She dragged a chair next to Brenda's. "Do I get a pat on the head and a nice fat bone for being a good girl?" she asked innocently as she sat.

Brenda burst out laughing, "*Touché*. Okay. Here goes." She explained what she was doing with the information on Curiel trainees up till the time he himself was assassinated in May 1985 and his organization was dissolved.

"...And the computer gave me an Austrian name – C. Bergen, alias Venus. She was trained by Curiel in clandestine operations but refused to get involved with assassinations or terrorist ops. At Curiel's she met and married a Yugoslav communist operative, Risto Markovic. They had two children, a girl and a boy. The boy died at age five, allegedly from a fall – you know what that often signifies."

"Child abuse. And then?"

Brenda frowned. "Markovic, a suspected KGB assassination operative, was found murdered. Case never solved. Venus then introduced her teenage daughter to Curiel to take the mom's place in the organization. Apparently, he wanted to relive her glorious subversive days through her daughter."

"How do you know that?"

Brenda looked down at the computer. "It was in the files." She started to read. "'C. Bergen, married name Markovic, alias Venus, brought her teenage daughter, J. Paula, to Curiel's training camp to have the daughter follow in her footsteps.'"

"What's the J stand for?" interrupted Christina.

"Don't know yet. Anyway, 'The girl, who was given the alias *Le Valet*, took to training so naturally and with such enthusiasm that Curiel recruited her for small operations which she performed with admirable aptitude. He started giving her increasingly responsible and dangerous assignments, which she handled easily. So he promoted her to assassin trainee.'"

"Where'd you get all that?"

"Couple of hours ago. I phoned the French for more material on the Austrian woman who married Markovic."

Christina looked at Brenda admiringly.

"The French police and our guys in Paris, Vienna, and Belgrade are searching for an address for the mother. Once we find the mother we'll find the daughter. Now we have part of our mystery woman's name – J. Paula. She could be using her father's surname, Markovic, or her mother's maiden name, Bergen. Or an alias. We also have a good idea what she looks like."

Brenda fell silent for a moment, biting her lip. "She's my principal suspect, even though I still don't have any proof it's her, not Peter, who's the killer. But if I put out a warrant, God knows where she'll disappear to. If she's our assassin, she's damn clever. So I want to do this as covertly as possible."

"*Le Valet*." Christina rolled the French words on her tongue. "Strange he'd give a girl a guy's name like that. Must've been one helluva trainee for Curiel to call her his servant."

"Not his servant. He didn't call her *Mon Valet*, he called her *Le Valet*, which in French can also mean 'the Jack.' Like in a deck of cards. Hmm...*Jack*, beginning with *J*. Her initial, maybe. And remember Rosie's bitchy girlfriend? She called herself Jay. We've gotta confirm J. Paula's first name," Brenda said wearily, leaning back in her chair and yawning.

Christina gazed at her boss searchingly, concerned by her drawn face. Brenda looked beat. The months of endless hard work had left dark circles beneath her bloodshot eyes. New wrinkles had gathered at the corners of her mouth and her short curly hair was sticking out every which way. Her usually immaculate clothes looked slept in.

"You want another cup of coffee?" asked Christina gently.

Brenda shuddered. "No more coffee, please! What I need's a good breakfast. You too?"

"Who's paying?"

Brenda chuckled. "You've been around Hutchins too long! If you won't tell him I picked up the tab, it's on me."

The computer folded its files and tucked them away, throwing the monitor into darkness. Brenda's office door opened and closed. The tick of its security lock was followed by the clicking of two pairs of high heels. The agents' laughter echoed in the fifth-floor halls of the severe FBI headquarters. Christina was happy to hear Brenda laugh again. Her usually pleasant disposition hadn't been much in evidence since May.

Moscow

This is getting serious, thought Yuri as he fumbled for Jackie's number. *Too serious for my taste. Where the hell could she be?* Exasperated, he thumbed through his private phone book – Palma de Mallorca, Brussels, New York...he never knew her schedule. *She's too fucking professional to let me know her movements,* he thought bitterly. He called Palma. No answer.

Paris. No answer.

Suddenly Yuri got an idea that she might in the United States and dialed her Trump Tower apartment.

She answered.

"Jackie, look..."

"Darling, I don't like these calls, especially here." Jackie's voice sounded sleepy. "First of all, it's risky..."

"Jackie, this is important!" He jolted her awake with his urgent tone. "I just found out they broke into your place in

Brussels. I hope you didn't leave anything valuable there. You know what I mean!"

"You're joking, you big bear. You're just trying to scare me. How could they have found out my address? Probably just a low-life housebreaker." But she slowly sat up in the bed and felt chills run through her.

"I warned you. It's no joke, Jackie. Just think hard. What have you got there that they could get their hands on?"

"Nothing. Nothing at all." Her mind was racing. "Listen. I'm going to hang up now. I've got for an appointment."

"Call me at my city home when you can."

"I will call, darling. But really, there's nothing to worry about."

Jackie hung up and for a few moments remained motionless. She piled her pillows behind her back and leaned on them, trying to collect her thoughts. One thing was for sure: her meeting with Mr. Tiron had to be sooner than later. She could not wait now. And in executing her plan, she would make sure that Peter was more than merely a name on this one. She had to keep the police focused on him.

Chapter Twenty

Tel Aviv
October 19th

Tiron was back in his beloved Israel. Stern had sent him a long cable asking him to return for a final review of Operation Hebron. The American election was now only two weeks away. The clock was ticking and there was no longer any room for error. Tiron knew Eshel and Stern wanted to review every detail face to face with him to be sure nothing was left undone in the final run-up to Big Tuesday. Because of the extraordinary security measures surrounding the Hebron operation, Tiron had been forbidden to send any cabled reports. He had twice sent an enciphered written report by Mossad courier accompanied by two guards, but that was time-consuming.

Although Tiron had been away for less than three months he was overcome by emotion as the El Al aircraft rolled to parking position at Ben-Gurion Airport. Tears moistened his eyes. It felt so good to be on Israeli soil again. He sighed with a mixture of relief and impatience.

He let the passenger herd go ahead of him before he disembarked. He had plenty of time before his meetings and wanted to savor the return to his homeland. Once through immigration control and into the arrival lobby, no sooner had he walked through the barrier separating arrivals from the greeting crowd than he heard, "Over here, Mr. Tiron, please." He followed the voice and recognized Chaim, one of Stern's bodyguard-drivers, beckoning to him, with a broad smile on his face.

"I'll take you to the hotel, Mr. Tiron. General Stern will be calling you there within an hour after our arrival to confirm your schedule. He wants you to keep a low profile and not call any friends or family, please." Tiron grunted in acknowledgement as he climbed into the well-preserved Chevrolet sedan. He had hoped for more time. He needed a rest, a shower, and a decent breakfast, then he wanted to sit down and review the cryptic notes he had carried on him for the debriefing.

Half an hour later the unmarked old sedan drew up outside the Tel Aviv Hilton, where Tiron was lucky enough to just beat a busload of German tourists to the reception desk. Safely installed in his room, he stripped to take his shower and shave. He had to at least look rested. He had been surviving on adrenaline instead of food and sleep as the election drew closer, and he was beginning to show the signs of stress and fatigue. Hebron was the most demanding clandestine operation he had ever participated in, let alone controlled. On top of that, he kept reminding himself that the fate of Israel was riding on the operation's success or failure.

Cleanly shaven, in fresh clothes – a plain white button-down shirt and a pair of khakis from the Gap in Georgetown – the morning sun warming his tired, sore muscles through the open glass doors of his room, Tiron began to review the points of his briefing, which he had not only written in a form unintelligible to any outsider, but had kept in his inner coat pocket during the trip from Washington.

They needed a further injection of money, with the race even – Westlake and Johnson tied at 32% each and Kramer at 30%, now closing to a position where the margin of error in the polls and the undecided vote could push him over the top. Tiron was sure it would be difficult for Johnson and Westlake to raise much more from here on out, and the American press agreed. From Tiron's perspective, more money was the major objective of this last visit to Tel Aviv before Election Day.

The jangling of the phone broke his concentration. He picked up the receiver. "*Shalom.*"

"David, *shalom.* Good to have you here." Stern's voice came through enthusiastic yet businesslike. "Listen. As you can imagine, there's someone coming who's eager to hear your news and views. You and I will talk first. Our friend's driving up from Jerusalem for an evening session with us at my office. Chaim will be waiting for you at seventeen hundred hours in front of the hotel. Take a rest – it may be a long evening." The phone clicked and he was gone.

Tiron could relax now that Stern had confirmed the prime minister would join them for a debriefing and dinner. That would be perfect – secure from other eyes and ears. And he would also have time to rest. He would need every minute of it.

After a breakfast of fresh fruit and eggs, he put out the Do Not Disturb sign, left a wake-up call for fifteen hundred hours, hung up his clothes, and lay down in his boxer shorts. Safe from the attention of American counterintelligence for the first time in months, he fell fast asleep.

The operator awoke him on schedule. He rose and dressed quickly. Hungry again, he had room service bring a club sandwich, slice of cheesecake, mineral water. He flipped on CNN. Another Russian republic was embroiled in a religious war with Moscow. It was all about oil.

About five minutes before Chaim was to be in front of the hotel, Tiron turned off the update on the US presidential campaign. In the past twenty-four hours there hadn't been any major movement; the three senators were still in a near tie. The country had seen close races for two candidates before, but to have a third-party candidate nearly in a three-way tie was unique in American politics. Tiron smiled. He was confident that with a burst of last-minute spending, any of the three candidates, including Hebron, could pull away from the other two and become the next president of the United States. Still, he reminded himself, *It ain't over till it's over.*

Chaim was waiting near the main entrance. He acknowledged Tiron with a nod and motioned toward the black Chevrolet waiting a few yards away.

In the back seat, Tiron pulled his notes from his sport coat pocket to check that everything was in order. He had to force himself not to check a second time. It was a mild neurosis of his profession, this constant checking and double-checking, which he found hard to control. He tried to distract his busy mind by looking out the window to enjoy the passing scenes. The streets buzzed with a blend of late afternoon shoppers and people, his people, all of them, returning from work, peppered with occasional patches of armed soldiers with flak vests. *They all look so young*, he thought.

Mossad headquarters, in Herzliyya on the outskirts of Tel Aviv, was in a large, imposing building constructed entirely from the abundant local sandstone. Abhorring attempts at modern architecture with ageless stone, Tiron had always thought the building unsightly. When he was posted back to Israel, he and his bride would find an old-fashioned house, probably near Herzliyya. The ideal place to live, he always imagined, would be a small suburb where he would be recognized and admired for his position within the foreign affairs-intelligence establishment.

He was mildly irritated to find upon arrival that Stern was not in his office. He had flown all the way from Washington to discuss the most important operation in the history of Mossad, and his boss was not there as scheduled. *Typical.*

Stern's office director offered Tiron a cup of coffee and a seat on the sofa at the far side of the director's large office. He had just taken his first sip when the door burst open and Stern's larger-than-life figure filled his view.

"Sorry, David!" he barked, as if it were a military command. "Got held up in traffic coming over from Defense. Tel Aviv seems to have as many tourists these days as Jerusalem. What're we going to do a few years from now for roads? Oh well, down to business."

"That's why I'm here, Ben."

"So what's going on, and what do you need from the PM? Brief me quickly. That way we can get operations out of the way before he gets here, and I'll give you a hand with how to get what we need from him. I take it that means more cash."

"Yes. But most important, the operation is secure to date. I've stressed security almost above success. Otherwise both Hebron and I would tend to get sloppy in all the commotion and craziness of an American election campaign and make a serious mistake – and neither of us can afford even one. Nevertheless, I've noticed that, as we near E-Day, Hebron's got a case of nerves and tends to lose his cool. It's even shown a bit on television. That worries me some, though I have to admit an election is enough to give most people a nervous breakdown, especially over there where the media pressure is constant – let alone the strain Hebron faces of leading a double life. So I have to remain very low-key to encourage him to keep his cool. As you know, I have a temper, but I struggle to appear serene. God, what a strain."

"You think it's just the stress? Or is Hebron holding back something from us?"

"Just the stress. He has to be both the most public and the most private man in America. As you can imagine, it's intense. These fuckin' musical-show-type elections in the States drain you. Believe me, it's pure stress and fatigue. I've gotten an average of three, four hours of sleep a night for the last month. Hebron's the same, and he's older. Plus, he's the candidate. You saw him on the cover of *Newsweek*, didn't you? And it's going to be worse over the next two weeks and into Election Day. He has a microphone and camera in his face every minute."

"Steady, David! We're almost there. Now, a key question: is Hebron maintaining his agent discipline as he starts to think about becoming president? How does he cope with all those Secret Service types around him? And how is he managing your clandestine meetings with him?"

"It all works because of the suite in the Willard Hotel provided by our American friend. Hebron's convinced his Secret Service detail that he has a mistress with a suite there, a famous star, incognito, who refuses to be seen by his security. And I've put a couple of our sexy birds to work around his security detail to keep them distracted. There's a separate suite if the girls need it to entertain the guards. So far it has worked. I figure we can get by with only two more meetings before the election – except for passing some cash to him via Laurie. She has a safe full of it, right there in the Senate Office Building. Don't you love it? Would the FBI think of looking there for our *shekels*?" He chuckled. "Hebron has a one-way emergency signal device, to avoid the phone. So far he hasn't had to use it. We have the safe haven in Virgina, but it's too risky going out there until all the election smoke settles and we start working with our very own president."

"Sounds okay, David. And supporting intelligence from our other operations in Washington?"

"We have all three campaigns well-penetrated, including Hebron's finance chairman – which Hebron doesn't know, of course. So when I say we need more money, you can be assured I'm not just taking Hebron's word for it. We have independent confirmation from his finance chief and a couple of others in his campaign committee around the country. To be honest, we have so much information on all the candidates, it's become like ENIGMA, the Allies' code-breaking operation in the Second World War. We have to be careful not to give it all to Hebron, for fear he'll say something to a reporter or make some decision which'll show that he's suspiciously, even illegally, well informed."

"Great! How about Whiplash in the White House? My God, she's a beauty! She been any help?"

"Indirectly. She's young, and only an intern, but she's been valuable in keeping us informed about what that bastard president's up to. At least we know when he's about to whack us again. Everybody in the White House is trying to get up her skirt, so she can service our intelligence requirements almost in minutes. Also, with her in the chief of staff's office, nobody dares get in her way. She's too good for early warning on Douglas's moves to risk using her on anything else. In any case all she hears at the White House is the Republican side of things."

"What about our media sources?"

"Still the best. Blowhard and Battlegroup in New York, Whistlestop in Washington, Genius and Garden in Los Angeles, and a few lesser ones. With guys like that, I don't even have to read the newspapers. They're so pro-Israel, they're as good as paid agents. They'll take our spin over the White House's any day. I can place nearly any story with them and pick the date and edition it appears in. Subject, of course, in a couple of cases, to their editors' whims. They keep us abreast of what the rest of the press corps is up to as well. A great early-warning network. Like over-the-horizon radar. And as I advised by cable, we have a new recruit in Defense. I have to tell you more about him, but that can hold till later."

"Yes, David, but what can't wait? What do you need now?"

"Money – my primary objective in coming here! We need ten million in cash. Four directly to Hebron, through me or our cut-out in the Senate, and six million more as official donations through some American friends. It's hardly possible for any of the candidates to raise significant funds these last couple of weeks. The tight three-way race has nearly drained all contributors. With ten million dollars during these two weeks I know we can push Hebron across the finish line, if only inches in front of the other two. So we need that cash, immediately!"

"Okay. Ask Eshel for ten million and if he agrees – which I'm sure he will – make it immediately available. I have a few million more in reserve in the States. I figured we'd need it for this at crunch time. This is the chance of our lives and we're not going to blow it for lack of a few dollars."

"That's great, Ben. We're now so close to November 7th, there's no way the other two could match that much last-minute infusion. No way!"

The telephone on Stern's desk rang. "Fucking telephones. They make my life hell." He picked up the receiver, listened, then said, "Good, Marv. Now hold all calls unless the Arabs attack. And bring in dinner as soon as it's ready. All three of us will eat here.

"The PM's here, David. You've convinced me. Now let's convince him. And let's meet before you leave tomorrow for Washington, so we can review our overnight thoughts on anything that's come up this afternoon or that he brings up. You can also brief me more on our new asset at the Pentagon. I'll be at your hotel at zero eight hundred."

Tiron sighed slightly in resignation. Poor Mom. He'd have to pass her by once more. At least his conscience was clear this time. It wasn't his fault.

Without warning Marvin opened the door and Eshel walked in briskly. He headed straight for Tiron.

"David, welcome home. I could hardly concentrate on anything today, looking ahead to our meeting tonight. Ben, how about a Chivas on the rocks. There are some things that we are not the best at, like making whisky."

"Yes, sir. Coming up." Stern walked to his wall bar, hidden behind a sliding panel covered by a map of the world, and poured scotches for the prime minister and himself. "David, your pleasure?"

"Diet Coke. American style." Tiron's attempt at humor didn't work. No one in the room was in the mood. The future of Israel was at stake. Eshel never joked about that.

With the drinks handed out, Stern opened his desk drawer, withdrew a Cohiba cigar and started lighting it with an old Zippo, a gift from an American Air Force general years ago. Smoking a cigar always made Stern feel the equal of anyone, even a prime minister.

Eshel said, "So, David. Come straight out with it. What are our man's chances? Incredible situation, isn't it? Hard to believe it could be this close, particularly with three running."

"Two major points, sir. First, Hebron wouldn't be in a tie if it hadn't been for our global support. And when I say global, I don't mean international. I mean all the various types – money, intelligence, dirty tricks in the other camps, media coverage, and so on. Second, in one sentence: he *can* win, on one condition – that we inject a final ten million dollars into his campaign at this critical juncture. After the record-breaking spending in the election to this point, the well is nearly dry among contributors of all sizes and shapes. A burst of big money in the last two weeks would be impossible to match by the other two and our boy should edge in front and score."

As Tiron took a long drink of his cola, the prime minister sat poker-faced. "Go on."

"Before you arrived, sir, I briefed General Stern on the security

287

and other aspects of the operation, which we're maintaining despite all the election pressures. There's nothing to worry about there. Operation Hebron is super-secure. So the only consideration you're faced with now is whether to put additional funds into the operation."

"Tiron, I would love to think you're right, but I received an 'eyes only' cable this morning from Ambassador Meir in Washington advising me that our embassy seems to be under heavy surveillance, presumably by the FBI. Tell me, why's that, if your security is so good?"

Tiron smiled confidently. "Sir, Ambassador Meir and most of the diplomats at our Washington embassy have never served in the United States during an election. They have no idea how nervous the FBI and Secret Service can get over the least incident or rumor. In this election two of the three candidates are running with considerable support from the Jewish community, and, as you know, much of that support is being coordinated – some directly – by our embassy. I have to assume the FBI's watching to see if anybody's breaking any laws. But in the final analysis they don't dare move against any American Jewish organization for merely supporting a candidate – that is their American right. So what does the FBI do? It acts heavy-handed and tries to inhibit our people. Fortunately for us, American Jews don't give a damn about this and won't be intimidated. It seems only our novice ambassador and the lambs on his staff are frightened by it."

"Listen, Mr. Tiron. I don't want to get sidetracked on this issue, but Ambassador Meir's a veteran of our armored corps, where he served with distinction. And as a former military colleague of his, I resent the suggestion that he frightens easily. His war record doesn't support your comment – not in the least."

Stern saw the color rising in Eshel's face. Not wanting a personality clash to divert them from Hebron, he interrupted,

"Aharon, please, allow me. Since early this year David's been carrying the full weight of managing this, and from thousands of miles away. He's alone, and tired, and so perhaps inclined to be too straightforward when he thinks of the risks he's been running, compared with the relative non-problems of the ambassador and his staff. So, please let us disregard his regrettable comment, and also keep in mind that Mossad has a thousand eyes in America – a lot more than the embassy. And they're eyes we can count on. If there was a serious security problem we'd know about it. So would Hebron. He isn't exactly unconnected, now, is he?"

"So be it. But remember, I've advised you and David. Don't you forget that, because I won't. Now, the money question. How could such a large amount be injected into the election campaign during the next two weeks without raising security problems? That's my only major concern. We've all been in the intelligence business and we know that historically too much money has blown the cover of some of the world's best agents."

Relieved to have the FBI issue whisked away by his boss's firm defense, Tiron moved to the edge of his chair and looked the prime minister straight in the eyes.

"I'd hand-carry four million back with me and give most of it directly to Hebron. He keeps all cash from us in the two hidden safes our techs built in. One's at his home and the other's in his Senate office. He doesn't deposit any of it in bank accounts – never has. For the rest, General Stern will have to arrange to have that passed to Hebron's campaign through some of our non-Jewish friends there as official or under-the-table campaign contributions. That way it can't be traced to us. We know how to do that."

"Fine. A few more million is nothing compared to what we stand to gain. Consider it done. I'll speak to Yahav later tonight and he'll see you have the full allocation. In the meantime, Ben,

I assume you can provide David with the cash he wants to take with him tomorrow."

"Yes, Aharon. I'll deliver it personally to David tomorrow morning before he leaves. No, in fact, I'll put a diplomatic courier on his flight. It's better if he carries the cash, and this way it'll be escorted. By you," he nodded at David. "I can easily arrange the rest as official loans to Hebron's campaign from a couple of New York banks. I'll just guarantee the credit lines through a cut-out in London with a phone call tonight."

"Good, Ben, that's settled. Now, one last question."

Tiron saw that the prime minister's face was as emotionless as when he'd walked in.

"What's Hebron's mood at this juncture? Toward the election, toward us, toward the possibility of being president of the United States and our agent at the same time? After all, it's the man we are investing all this risk and money in, no?"

"Yes, sir, it is. I'm confident you won't be disappointed. As you know, nearly as well as General Stern and me, Hebron's been a disciplined, productive agent for nearly twenty years. This is not some young kid who's gotten in over his head without realizing the consequences." Tiron stopped to drain his Diet Coke, and Stern went to get him another one.

"David, I know his past. Tell me about now and the future."

"The point I'm making is that it's this past which has formed Hebron and gives us the assurance that he'll cope with this new chapter like a smooth shift of gears. Keep in mind that he's not just an ideological supporter. He receives a monthly salary from us, which, given the expensive lifestyle of most American politicians, gives him a certain edge in social circles, a certain ability to take care of a few people here and there and to entertain better than most. After all, his agent salary is over double what his presidential salary would be. Then there's the bonus we've promised him if he wins – ten million dollars a year as long as he's in office, to be paid offshore in a lump sum when he retires. So, I don't expect any radical change. As long as we pay Hebron considerably more than his own government, we'll control him. There's never been any reason to doubt that."

Eshel grunted, got up, and walked to gaze out the window. He didn't look convinced.

The other two kept silent, waiting.

"David, I've spent my life since the military dealing with political animals from all over the world. When many of them get close to power, or achieve power, they change. And not always for the better. I'm not so convinced that, once Hebron's elected and has all the perks of the world's most powerful office at his beck and call, we'll be able to rely on him to deal with us like before."

"Sir, there's been nothing in his dealings with me during the campaign to suggest he's getting big-headed. And as far as security goes, he's very concerned – always has been and continues to be. In fact, I have to calm him down sometimes about imagined security worries."

"Okay, David. Let's pray we've got a winner! Good God, can you men believe this is happening?" For the first time since he arrived, Eshel smiled. "Okay, Ben, let's bet the final ten million on Hebron. David, you'll be one of the great heroes of Israel's secret history if this succeeds. And after our boy's had a year or so in the White House and we're sure our control of him is still good, we'll replace you in Washington and bring you back for a top job. I promise you."

Tiron nodded in silent appreciation.

The prime minister turned to Stern and asked, "So what's for dinner?"

As the session proceeded, questions about the American political scene and Mossad operations there changed to old Mossad war stories. Tiron was elated as the three enjoyed a private dinner in a spirit of combat camaraderie, past and present.

New York, October 20th

Rolf Hastings of United Press International took out his ballpoint pen and steadied his notepad on his knee, ready for another interview with Senator Dan Kramer, the Reform Party candidate, in his suite at his campaign headquarters, the Plaza Hotel.

"Senator, I've never seen a candidate look so pleased with himself in such a tight race. What's your secret?"

"How could a third-party candidate be happier after what you wrote on Sunday about my victory not being unthinkable any more? You got people wondering and it's had a hell of an effect on my campaign. At least that's what my campaign manager says. He told me promises of new money are beginning to pour in as a result. I said promises – we haven't seen the cash yet."

Head down, Hastings scribbled notes.

"As you said in your column back in March when I ran in the New York primary, it seemed a remote possibility, like with every past third-party candidate. But now Westlake and Johnson are sweating. They're so busy looking over their shoulder at each other, they missed me coming along behind. And the latest ABC-CNN poll, this morning, says we're now all tied – the differences among us are less than the margin of error in the polls. And my friends in the Senate called this morning to say the whole capital is talking about your column. Guess I owe you a word of thanks, buddy."

"Senator, I just wrote the truth, which most of the press covering the campaigns knew but were hesitant to put on paper. Afraid of being laughed at. But I'm used to being right before the other guys, and when I get a hunch and take a chance with it,

I usually hit pay dirt." Hastings doodled on his pad, remembering that he needed an even better story this time.

"First, let's get a couple of good shots. That long frame of yours makes a great photo. Reminds the voters of your days as an All-American tight end."

"Sure, boys. Shoot away."

After the UPI photographer left the room, Hastings settled down for the interview. "Senator, a lot of observers have compared you to the old Tammany Hall politicians of the 19th century. A real pro in smoke-filled rooms. They say that's how you were able to get your new Reform Party effort organized so quickly and professionally in just a year. Could you comment on that, please?"

"First, it was hard for me to break with the Republican Party. I'm a conservative and the GOP had been my home since I entered politics. But frankly, President Douglas is the one with a political machine. And he and his gang of four control the GOP to such an extent that I decided running against him from within the party was not realistic. And then in April, when I heard he was ill and might not run, I realized George Johnson would be his hand-picked alter ego. So I continued on the same road, still nominally a Republican – but scores of advisers, including my father-in-law, Isaac Davidson, counseled me to break with the Republican Party and go with a third-party effort, so I did. Since then I haven't looked back. And frankly, it's been primarily Isaac and the group of supporters he organized throughout the nation that put together my Reform Party candidacy in such a short time."

"Senator, many observers figured Isaac Davidson was a liberal Democrat, especially since he's a big supporter of Israel, and they expected him to back Senator Westlake."

"Rolf, Mr. Davidson can speak for himself on that, but I will say a lot of people feel, rightly, that Westlake tells everyone what they want to hear and has few principles or heartfelt opinions on any question whatsoever. That naturally puts off a lot of Democrats, regardless of his vocal support for Israel. They don't worry about what he says, but they do worry about what he'll do, since his positions on other issues are all over the map. A different position every day. Furthermore, just because President Douglas and his buddies, including Senator Johnson, took some hard-line positions against Israel, that doesn't mean I ever agreed with them. Nor did all other Republicans, for that matter."

The reporter nodded as he wrote.

"I'm a good friend of Israel and will remain so, president or not. And as I am more dedicated to my well-considered positions on key issues than the vacillating Senator Westlake is to his, I think Israel can only prosper in its relations with the United States if I'm elected. Anything else? I've got to leave for a talk this afternoon at Wharton. I took my MBA there, you know, and as an alum I can't be late."

Rolf rose as the Senator did.

"Just one last question, sir. The nation's quite interested in Westlake and Johnson's refusal to debate with you. Most observers say that with your imposing physical presence, good looks, top-flight education, political polish, and debating skills, you'd score an easy knockout in any debate with them. Others figure that your recent TV briefings, the charts you present, the well-known economists accompanying you, are beginning to make up for your lack of a chance to debate. What do you think?"

Kramer walked to his desk to sort out the papers for his next engagement.

"Thanks for the kind words. And yes, it does bother me that the others decline to debate with me. Yes, I have a good grounding in economics and finance, thanks to my education and my experience as an investment banker before entering politics. It's also true that I love to debate. On the other hand, I don't believe the American people are going to be overwhelmed by skills like that if they don't agree with what I'm saying on the key issues of social security, unemployment, taxation, crime, race relations, and welfare. The other candidates are afraid to debate with me because they don't have any real programs or even ideas to answer these problems. And even if I never get to savor the pleasure of dismantling Senators Westlake and Johnson in front of an audience as they repeat their usual superficial answers to these problems, I believe I'm getting my points across in those briefings you mention. That's something the other candidates don't dare to do." He looked up, and stuck out his hand.

The reporter shook it respectfully.

"That's it for today, Rolf. And thanks again for that column – keep up your great work! I'll give you my first exclusive interview from the White House. That's a promise. By the way, after the election, whoever wins, I want to invite you to my father-in-law's digs in the Caribbean. Bring your family. A little thanks for your interest in my campaign."

"Sounds great, Senator. I won't forget. Well, I have a deadline to meet. Thanks for your time, and good luck!" As Hastings walked down the hall, he shook his head in amazement at the political smoothness of Dan Kramer. The man could actually win. *Hey*, he realized, *that's my lead!*

Chapter Twenty-one

Washington, D.C.
October 22nd

Senator Wes Westlake was pleased to see that the leaders of the main American Jewish organizations had scheduled a visit with him en masse. This was an important occasion in his agenda. He instructed his entire campaign staff to be on call in his side offices to provide any statistics or atmospherics necessary to impress these key supporters. *Our victory lies here*, he told them.

Rabbi Weinbert was the spokesman for the assembled group. He greeted Westlake warmly and introduced the eighteen other men and women present.

"We requested this meeting so close to Election Day for several reasons. First and foremost, we wish to reiterate our support for your campaign."

A murmur of approval echoed through the room.

"Second, because of that commitment," the rabbi went on, "we are concerned about the increasingly close race. We want to hear directly from you what we can do over the remaining days to give you the advantage you need to win." The rabbi looked at the other representatives. Receiving their nod, he continued. "Most importantly, we want to know how much in campaign funds you need to finish on top, and anything else we can do to help you win."

"Rabbi Weinbert and friends, it reassures me to see you all here as volunteers to ask what more you can give, what more you can do. With supporters like this, I can't lose, no matter how close the race might seem at this moment. My finance chairman will talk to you immediately after this session." He turned to his secretary, "Linda, get Sidney Straus in here so he can collect their checks." There was mild laughter.

Then the candidate turned his eyes back to the assembled leaders. "Now, before I leave for a TV interview, I'd like to thank you all for what you've done to date and for reassuring me in these final critical days. I know Senator Kramer also promises to support Israel, and receives some Jewish contributions. I also know, however, that no one senator in recent memory has done as much as I have for Israel, or for Jewish immigration from the former Soviet Union to Israel. That's not a matter of debate but of record. Let me add two promises that I'll promptly keep when I'm president. First, I'll reverse the policy of the previous administrations and grant the loan guarantees which Israel requested to build homes on the West Bank." There was applause. "And, and," he built on the mounting enthusiasm in the room, "I'll recommend the immediate move of the American Embassy from Tel Aviv to Jerusalem. I'm firm on these points, and, as proof of the seriousness of my stance, I'm about to announce them to the entire nation. So, listen in. Once again, thank you for your support. Although I must leave now, please stay behind to talk with Sidney Straus, whom many of you already know. Sid!"

With that, Westlake went around the room shaking hands, presenting an autographed photograph to each guest, and finally stopped to pose for a group shot.

An hour later he appeared on the "Today" show, where he reiterated these two campaign promises, this time to the entire nation. He also promised to share the new American YF-22 fighter technology with Israel as soon as the first models rolled off the assembly lines. This offer was a surprise to everybody, as the aircraft, which the Defense Department termed "the fighter of the 21st century," had never publicly been sought by the Israelis, though US Air Force planners knew the Israeli military establishment hoped eventually to persuade the United States to make the technology available to them.

After this public signal to both his American Jewish supporters and to the Israeli government, Westlake was confident that Kramer would not be able to outdo him with this important constituency. Now, he felt, the extra funds he needed for his final-week television blitz were assured. His campaign manager was desperate to top off the campaign budget with some cash, a few million or so that wouldn't have to be accounted for...black money. *And I know just where to get that money!*

Senator George Johnson ordered a vodka on the rocks from the lounge at the Chevy Chase Country Club and looked out the large windows, across the sprawling lawns. His Secret Service bodyguards sat on sofas nearby.

President Douglas had just left the club after their round of golf. Johnson had lost, and it showed. As soon as the icy-cold vodka arrived, he took a big gulp and enjoyed the burning sensation as it hit the back of his throat. Glancing at his watch, he saw that it was already two in the afternoon. Nicola should be on her way now for a late lunch.

At forty-two, Nicola was fifteen years her husband's junior. A high-society figure from Boston, she had brought him elegance, money, and connections, though George Johnson and his patrician family already had plenty of all three. Her father had been a top attorney in Boston with a client list which read like a "Who's Who of the Rich and Famous."

Arriving at the club, Nicola stopped to say hello to friends and VIPs as she passed through the main lobby into the indoor lounge to join her husband. Johnson thought she was a superb consort for a politician and he knew she enjoyed the role. She was also one of her husband's best PR advisers and that was the primary reason for their lunch today. He had suggested they lunch privately to review some campaign ideas his staff had given him that morning.

"Hello, darling," she cooed as she approached him. "Did I miss the president? Too bad."

"Don't worry. We need the private time to talk, Nicola. It's too hectic at home. My staff gave me some bright ideas this morning but nothing that'll help me break out of this deadlock with Westlake. Particularly with Kramer now about to join us at the top. Who'n the hell would've thought we'd all be in a dead heat? A three-way dead heat. Never happened before!"

"Well, George, dear, I talked to Daddy about this very question just after you left the house this morning. Of course you know, everybody's talking about it. At least everybody who matters. Daddy called to say you've got to come out with a major announcement in the last four days before Election Day. A new policy direction, a proposed economic plan, a bombshell – something that will leave Westlake and Kramer gasping for air, and that they'll be unable to counter in so few days."

"Great idea, Nicola. Now does your Daddy have an idea what that might be?" responded Johnson with a smirk of ridicule on his face.

"Now, dear. Please! Daddy's not trying to interfere. Only to give his best advice – as well as, you might remember, a lot of financial support. So I don't think you need to get sarcastic. And if you suddenly don't need my help or his, then I'll just go along and spend the rest of the afternoon with some lady friends gossiping about who's sleeping with who around this town. For the life of me, I don't see why you're so edgy. You're usually so cool, George."

"Darling, I have two problems. Number one, this is my first and last chance to be president. I'm so close I can smell it and I don't want to lose it – and I assume you don't either." He noted her emphatic nod and continued. "Number two, I need money to solve my first problem – how to get elected two weeks from now. My family and yours have poured money into this election, God knows. My campaign people told me this morning Kramer and Westlake are planning last-minute television blitzes, but I don't have the money for that. I asked the president's advice. He insisted I lean on the RNC. I did just that, but they've used most of their money, and since Will's a Douglas man and doesn't expect to be around even if I win, he's not highly motivated to raise more for me."

"Look, this is crazy – my father's just sitting there in Boston, with a Rolodex that goes around the world and back again, waiting to help out. And you know Daddy, he's a fighter and never gives up – which is usually why he wins. Call him this afternoon and tell him exactly what you need. Level with him, George – you're both big boys. Tell him what you need and when. I'm sure he'll deliver."

"Yeah, you're right. It'll be better than feeling sorry for myself. Okay, that's first on my agenda after lunch. For that I owe you a good lunch and a kiss. Let's begin with the kiss."

"Now that's my Georgie!" He leaned over and planted an emphatic one on her left cheek.

October 27th

Silently, Christina entered Brenda's office and handed her an envelope containing the previous day's transcripts of the authorized telephone taps on the Israeli Embassy. Just as silently, she exited. Christina's sense of humor was legendary, but today, Brenda noticed, she was abnormally quiet and seemed preoccupied.

This sent butterflies dancing in Brenda's intestines even before she opened the plain manila envelope to read her analyst's bright-yellow, highlighted text and corresponding notes. She sat back in her desk chair, staring at the envelope as she turned it over and over, wondering what new revelation it contained. *Must be something special!*

A moment later, her mind clear of other details, she took a deep breath, then opened the envelope and pulled out its contents. The top transcript consisted of just two pages, summarizing the attachments. Two entries were highlighted in yellow, one of which caught her eye – Sidney Straus had called David Tiron at the Israeli Embassy.

Brenda's stomach muscles tightened. She was almost afraid to go on. This would be the hardest read of her young life. *My father.*

The summary noted that Straus was advising the embassy that he had been put in charge of budget coordination for Senator Westlake's television and press play for the final week of the campaign. It was clear from the transcripts that the Israeli Embassy press officer and Straus had spoken before. Brenda had of course known that her father was working for the Democratic candidate; what stunned her was how the press officer barked orders at him.

She turned the pages to verify the exact text – "No, you'll *not* do that, Mr. Straus! You will do what *I* damn well tell you. The campaign couldn't be tighter and we can't waste one combined dollar in uncoordinated efforts – in any sort of media play. Got it?"

Brenda turned to the dialogue between her father and Tiron. The call had been placed at 11:21 that morning:

Straus – "Hello, Mr. Tiron. Senator Westlake told me to call you about some extra funds for the last week of media play. I suppose the senator meant funds from major Jewish donors. I know we've not yet met, Mr. Tiron, but you may verify my instructions directly with the senator, if you wish."

Tiron – "Mr. Straus, I do not discuss such matters over the telephone. Come to my office at four this afternoon. In the meantime, I'll check with Senator Westlake. Thank you."

Then Tiron had hung up and cut off any further discussion.

Brenda fought back tears as she swiveled her chair around to look from the window down Pennsylvania Avenue toward the beautiful Capitol building in the distance. If there was one thing she didn't need at this moment, the most challenging moment of her career, it was another clash with her rabidly Zionist father. She longed for a loving relationship with him and knew how much her mother suffered from his refusal to reconcile with his daughter.

To a certain extent, Brenda didn't blame her father. So many Jews of his age felt committed to Israel as though in a fight for Jews around the world. She understood why they identified so closely with Israel, and she respected that. But she could not stomach it when anyone, even her father, put Israel before their own nation or allowed the Israelis to meddle in the American democratic process. She had long known deep in her heart that her father had fallen victim to the disease of confused loyalties. And as a federal police officer, she knew where such a misguided sense of loyalties could lead; it was exactly what smart foreign intelligence officers looked for – to exploit to their advantage.

Brenda's natural human reaction was to call her father and warn him to stay away from the Israeli Embassy. Particularly, to warn him that Tiron was Mossad. Her father had never mentioned to her that he was in contact with the embassy except to attend a few receptions to which many American Jewish leaders were invited.

As soon as that protective thought entered her mind, Brenda realized her professional status precluded her warning him. She consoled herself by reviewing the facts and concluding that her father was not doing anything illegal in the strictest sense of the word, at least so far as she knew.

The conflicting emotions about this incident began to converge in a sense of frustration. She felt overload coming on and decided to seek Judge Baker's counsel. His years of experience on the bench might give her a wider perspective. Certainly a more objective one. A fatherly one, too.

Jamming the telephone transcripts back into the brown envelope she headed to the ninth floor. She waited in the judge's outer office for Kate Sumner to squeeze her into his schedule. As she sat nervously, Brenda was suddenly overwhelmed with the sensation that she must offer her resignation, or at least ask to be taken off the Hebron investigation. *That would be the proper thing to do.* Nothing was more important to her than being the best and most honorable of her profession for her nation. No, there was one thing more important – her personal honor. She would not compromise that for any reason. She would give her life for either cause. Disturbed, confused, she kneaded the letter-size envelope in her hands.

"You can go in now, Agent Straus," Kate suddenly said, putting down her telephone. "I told him you need just five minutes, so please keep it short," she added in a whisper as Brenda passed the desk.

"I owe you one." Brenda smiled an uncharacteristically sad smile. As she opened the door, the judge called out across the room, "Special Agent Straus! I hope this unexpected visit means we have a breakthrough. Am I right?"

"No, sir. Unfortunately not. It means I have a serious personal problem. A conflict of interest has arisen and I think you should consider taking me off the Hebron investigation," Brenda responded in a rush before her courage escaped her. "It's just too sensitive and with the Sorensson murder and the Hebron case...I just don't know." She looked ruefully him. "As you know, I'd planned on interviewing the three candidates this week, in the hope of putting the one who might be Hebron under enough pressure for him to make a false move. But with all the stress of handling two such top-priority investigations, and now this hits me..." She waved the brown envelope in the air. "I just don't know, sir. I need your advice."

"Brenda! You look devastated. Sit down!"

She handed him the envelope and stood facing his desk, struggling to keep control over her emotions. She felt she was on the verge of a breakdown.

"Brenda, I told you to sit down. Relax. Please, young lady. We'll solve your problem," the judge assured her, in just the fatherly style she had sought, as he opened the envelope she had been gripping as if it were her death warrant. He glanced over the transcripts. "These are your father's calls, I take it. You mentioned him and your problems to me once before – you may have forgotten."

He set the transcripts on the desk in front of him and looked at Brenda, who was now sitting nervously. "Special Agent Straus, first allow me to commend you for immediately bringing this to my attention. Others with less sense of professional responsibility might have been tempted to keep it from me. Now the good news – I see no conflict of interest here. Your father is engaging in open electioneering. And like most electioneering, it is not always done with great forethought as to whether the end justifies the means. Your father is pushing the Israeli Embassy to lean on some big spenders. It may be or may not be a bit unethical, but illegal it isn't. So relax and let's analyze this together in the interest of the two cases we have to solve." Baker studied the text further. "The most significant thing about this...yes. It gives us a piece of hard evidence. One of the three presidential candidates, Westlake, knows Tiron and has instructed one of his campaign staff to call him. All we've had till now were the normal diplomatic exchanges between the candidates and the Israeli ambassador. I'd say this earmarks Westlake as our prime suspect. As obvious as it seems..."

Brenda nodded doubtfully.

The judge regarded her with fatherly pride. "As to your concerns about conflict of interest, I must tell you that when the Hebron intelligence was first levied on us by the president, I felt I had the professional obligation to brief Austin Phillips. In that discussion he raised the option of not letting you handle the case so as to avoid a potential conflict of interest for you, and therefore for the Bureau, because you're Jewish. He was concerned about even the appearance, if a conflict of interest should develop, of having a Jewish special agent assigned to investigate allegations of Israeli covert interference in our nation's affairs."

At the look on Brenda's face, Baker raised his hand as if to stem the words he knew were on the tip of her tongue.

"I know what everybody thinks of Austin. I told him that as long as I'm the director of the Federal Bureau of Investigation, I'll assign agents to cases based on the demands of the service and their expertise. I also told him I wouldn't have an imagined or possible conflict affect an assignment – it had to be real. Furthermore, I reminded him of your performance, even on the witness stand, in the Pollard case. I reminded him that you personally had given the Bureau all the protection it needed from media or congressional claims that I shouldn't have assigned you to the case. That's assuming, of course, that the Hebron case ever becomes public, which I tend to doubt, no matter how it ends."

Baker slid the envelope back across this desk to Brenda. "Ms.

Straus, the FBI and its director have the greatest confidence in you. Otherwise, you would not be simultaneously burdened with two of our most important cases. So go back to your office and find me Sorensson's assassin and figure out which presidential candidate is Hebron.

"And keep this in mind. If we can't identify Hebron before the election – and if he, God forbid, gets elected – then our only choice as a nation is impeachment on grounds of 'treason, bribery, and other high crimes and misdemeanors.' Like espionage. Can you imagine the embarrassment and humiliation for our nation in such a case? So, Brenda, it's on your shoulders. Let nothing deter you, or make you hesitate. Just bring back Hebron, dead or alive. Thank you."

Returning to the stack of documents in front of him, Judge Baker started signing those awaiting his approval.

Brenda rose and took a deep breath. "Thank you, sir. I assure you we will find the killer. And soon! The Hebron case is another matter. That's extremely delicate, but I expect Hebron to crack. He'll do something in reaction to our interview gambit. That's our best hope for a quick solution. I appreciate your support on that, Judge. Most directors wouldn't take the political risk."

"Our nation's future is at stake in this Hebron business – it's a political war. What's a little risk to my career compared to that? Nothing! So go out there and get that bastard! Scare the hell out of him. Push him to do something crazy out of fear. Drive him over the cliff!"

"Yes, sir." Brenda left the director's office, light on her feet, her spirits soaring. As she walked by the secretary's desk, she leaned over and whispered, "Thanks, Kate. That made my day."

Kate, phone to ear, winked.

Back in her office, Brenda fell into her chair and let out a big sigh. It was time to think through her interviews with the three candidates. She wanted to make Hebron fear that the FBI was closing in on him. The trick was to do that without insulting any of the candidates – not easy. She would rely on the pressures of the election campaign and the fear of exposure to make Hebron's insides boil.

Just then she noticed a phone message – her mother had called to invite her to dinner that evening. *My God*, she thought. *It's her birthday and I completely forgot.* She dialed her parents' number. "Mom, I'll come by later for coffee and birthday cake. I'm over my head in work. Mom, please...Okay, Mom, I'll be there for dinner, but not before eight." She immediately called a florist and sent her mother a bouquet of orchids. Then she returned to the task of tracking down Hebron. *I'm coming for you, you traitor!* And, for a second, she thought of Jackie.

Chevy Chase Area, That Night

Brenda arrived at her parents' house in northwest D.C. a few minutes after eight o'clock. The beautiful red-brick Williamsburg-style home had been the pride of the family since she was a little girl. Whenever she returned, she had ambivalent feelings. On the one hand, it brought back memories of a happy childhood. On the other hand, she recoiled at thoughts of the screaming arguments there with her zealous father, especially in recent years about her role as an FBI agent in bringing the Israeli agent Jonathan Pollard to justice. *What a shame that I can't ask my father for help.*

He barely spoke to her any more, a situation Brenda felt was probably for the best after the shock she had faced earlier that day, even though Baker had calmed her and reassured her that Sidney Straus was doing nothing illegal. She knew from long, sad experience that he was motivated by what was best for Israel. As always, she could only consider her father's devotion to Israel a mark of her parents' generation. She prayed that her own generation, intermarried with gentiles and less extremist about Zionism, would remain fully integrated into America, its culture and mores, and would consider Israel a friendly nation rather than the fatherland that commanded their loyalties.

As she entered the house she was welcomed by her mother, who gave her a tight hug and a big kiss. "Thank you, darling, for the orchids. They're beautiful." Brenda smiled back. Her father, in his gray cardigan, was watching the evening news featuring the latest election predictions. Westlake campaign literature was piled everywhere around the hallways and the living room. Always the perfect gentleman, he rose to greet his daughter, albeit with a definite coolness and reserve.

Brenda pretended not to notice. She gave him a light kiss on the cheek.

"You look so good, Dad. It must be because you have such a young, beautiful wife. Right, Mother?" Brenda feigned lightheartedness as her mother went back to the kitchen to check on dinner's progress.

Giving his daughter a cold stare, Sidney Straus went back to his TV set.

Tension was apparent throughout dinner. Brenda could see her mother fighting tears as she tried to promote a happier family spirit on her birthday. Finally, while his wife was in the kitchen preparing dessert, Sidney Straus, apparently unable to hold back, fired a salvo in what Brenda thought of as his continuing war against her and what he saw as her gentile anti-Zionist colleagues at the Bureau.

"So, Agent Straus, arrested any Jews lately?"

"Father, please!"

"Oh, don't tell me your Gestapo service has sworn off arresting Jews! My friends at the Israeli Embassy tell me your goons are all over them these days. Are you going to deny that?"

Even though the comment reminded Brenda that, according to the morning telephone taps, her father had had an appointment with Tiron at four that afternoon, she tried to forget it by concentrating on her mother. Also, she didn't want to make a slip and reveal to him that she knew anything more than he said about his Israeli Embassy contacts. "Dad, this is Mother's birthday – can't you at least spare her this for today, if not for me?"

"Ah, you don't want to talk about your Gestapo activities? That's news. You used to be proud to stand up in court and swear before God about all the bad things Jews were doing."

Brenda put down her napkin, rose from the table, and went into the kitchen as though her father wasn't even there. She saw her mother trying to light the candles on her own birthday cake, tears streaming down her cheeks. Brenda hugged her. "The cake is so beautiful. Let me carry it in. You go sit."

Wiping her eyes, Mrs. Straus walked to the dining table, avoiding looking directly at her husband, who, still fuming from the anger he had worked himself into, glared at Brenda with fury in his dark eyes.

"Happy Birthday to you, Happy Birthday to you..." Brenda sang as she carried the cake into the dining room and placed it in front of her mother.

Sidney Straus left the table.

Brenda whispered, "I'm sorry, Mother."

"Brenda, my darling. It's not your fault. Extremism has poisoned your father. He's become a fanatic. Those reform Jews upset him. He thinks Meir Kahane should have been prime minister of Israel. Since Kahane was assassinated, he's become a sort of martyr for people like your father. I don't understand it. I can't talk to him any more. You can't talk to him. It's tearing our family apart. What shall I do, darling? I don't deserve this in my old age."

"Mom, perhaps it'd be better if I stayed away from the house for a while? You could come visit me in my apartment and we could meet downtown for lunch once in awhile. I don't want to fight my own father – I want to love him. But I'm not an Israeli. I'm an American and I won't apologize to anyone for it, even my father. I'm Jewish, yes, but I'm not Israeli. I have no loyalties to Israel and neither does my generation. Only time will heal this. Time. Like another generation or so. I'm sorry for you, Mother. You're caught in the middle. But I love you, and I love Dad."

With that Brenda picked up her purse. As a matter of routine, she checked it to be sure her FBI ID and her revolver were there. The very act reminded her of her professional oath and responsibilities to her nation. At least she had avoided being provoked into saying anything which would reveal her knowledge of her father's contacts with David Tiron. She left the sad house behind and walked to her car. As she pulled away from the curb, she was overwhelmed by a feeling of being alone in the world on the suburban street where she had grown up. She flipped on the radio. More election crap, a sound bite from Johnson. *Are you my Hebron?* she mocked with disgust and flipped off the radio. *Poor Mom.* The pressures from two major cases were cooking her nerves. Once again Judge Baker's voice crept into her psyche. The confidence. The righteousness of his tone. *He's a good man and he believes in me.* That made the difference.

Now, she knew, it was up to her. She was determined to prove that the judge's trust was not misplaced. One day even her father would see. Instantly, she regained her confidence. "I'll bring in Sorensson's killer and I'll push Hebron into revealing himself," she said aloud as her Toyota sped toward home and the Lincoln Memorial, lighted and sober, came into sight in the distance.

Chapter Twenty-two

Washington, D.C.
October 28th

Christina scribbled some notes, put down the phone, and yelped, "Yah-hooo! Kate Sumner just called: the judge arranged all three appointments." She read from her notepad. "First with Westlake in his office at 2:30 this afternoon – according to his secretary, you only get thirty minutes because he's on a very tight schedule. Ha, aren't they all! Johnson's next, also today. His office at 4:30. He'll give you whatever time you need up to when he has to leave for a 6:00 TV appearance. Kramer is tomorrow at two. He'll see you at his New York election headquarters, just after a luncheon speech. His people didn't say how long he could meet with you – his secretary told the judge it would depend on 'media developments.' Think of it, Brenda, you're going to meet the next president of the United States this week, no matter who wins!"

"Calm down!" Brenda tried to be nonchalant and severe but a tiny smile played on her face. She was pleased. "Remember, these meetings are to smoke out an Israeli agent who might be our next president. It's not exciting – it's chilling. I've got to provoke a foreign agent into making a mistake, even a little one, while not pissing off the two candidates who aren't guilty. That's skating on pretty thin ice. So, let's get on with it. And please get

Jack – he's going with me up to the Hill."

Wes Westlake's Office, 2:30 p.m.

Five minutes before the appointed time, Special Agents Straus and Sanchez arrived at Senator Westlake's office on the second floor of the New Senate Office Building. Brenda watched as young aides, intoxicated with the excitement of the presidential campaign, hurried in and out performing small tasks that she knew from long experience around Washington made them feel important. Dreams of working in the White House in January were almost visible.

"Ms. Straus, you may go in now." The secretary's invitation broke into Brenda's moment of distraction. She rose, and Jack followed her into the office of the Democratic Party's candidate – the number-one suspect.

Busy on the phone, he motioned his visitors to the L-shaped sectional sofa occupying the corner next to his desk. Brenda and Jack complied, but refrained from sitting until he joined them. While they waited, Brenda explored what Washington called Westlake's "power wall."

Photos of Westlake sharing special moments with the rich and powerful from America and around the world covered the oak paneling. Some were talking with him, others joining him for meals or a walk. Every photo was signed with a personal greeting. Brenda was fascinated by the pictures of monarchs, presidents, prime ministers, generals, and heads of organizations from the senator's home state of Washington. She caught one of the chief justice standing between the senator and a classic Edsel. On another wall a more modest collection of photographs captured family members throughout the years.

"Yes, Ms. Straus?" came the senator's voice, deep and unfriendly. "Oh, wait a minute – Straus? Do you know Sidney

Straus? He's on my campaign team."

"He's my father," Brenda answered in an almost apologetically low tone.

"Great guy and a wonderful asset to our team. Anyway, what can I do for the FBI? Judge Baker said it was of the highest national urgency. Otherwise, nobody'd get in at this point unless they could help me win the election. Got it?"

Ignoring the rude opening, Brenda smiled and explained that the director had sent her on a most delicate mission, one which called for the senator's cooperation. "We have a few questions to ask you. Your answers, Senator, will help us eliminate a very serious threat to our nation. We would like to ask, first, if you know a man by the name of David Tiron?"

The question shocked the senator. He'd just been on the phone with Tiron. *The FBI must have my phone tapped.* Moreover, he had sent Sidney Straus to see Tiron. Not sure what the FBI was looking for, he had to be careful. *It's too close to the election to risk crazy lies.*

"Yes, I met him once or twice at Israeli Embassy receptions. But I primarily deal with the ambassador, who from time to time comes here to my office. He also visits me at my home. Is there any law against that, Agent Straus?"

"No, sir. We're just trying to ascertain what Mr. Tiron is up to. Do you know he's the Mossad representative in Washington – Israeli intelligence?"

"No. I've met nearly everybody at the Israeli Embassy. As you must know, I'm a great supporter of Israel and I have close contacts with many Israelis, both here and in Jerusalem. What exactly is the problem? Has this Tiron killed somebody, or what?"

"We're not sure yet – that's why we're asking. But we *are* covering him and his contacts in some detail, I must advise you in great confidence."

"Look, young lady, I suppose the hundreds of intelligence types all over this town have to do their thing. Just as you FBI agents have to do yours. But I'm busy running an election campaign. If your questions don't have anything to do with that, can we please put this off for a few weeks? I'll be happy to spend more time with you both later."

"Senator," interjected Jack, "unfortunately, we have reason to suspect that Mr. Tiron does have something to do with a campaign, yours or one of the others. Something illegal in nature. Needless to say, if this is found to be true it could lead to the impeachment or conviction of the candidate involved, whether he is elected president or not."

Brenda stood up. "We are speaking, of course, of illegal involvement in the election on Mr. Tiron's part. We strongly suggest that you and your people stay away from him at least until after the election. And if you recall anything pertinent, here's my card. I can be reached at any time, day or night. We'll be back to see you right after the election, Senator. Thank you for your time." She rose and Jack followed her.

Westlake also stood, looked at Brenda's card with a frown. "Please take care of this yourselves and leave me alone until after the election," he blurted. Without another word, he walked the agents to his office door, his body language pushing them along in front of him. Brenda felt his antagonism sweep over them like a glacial wind as they left. Had they only succeeded in irritating him, or had they triggered fear deep inside him? A few days might tell.

"That was a cold reception, Brenda. If that man wins, I don't think our next president is going to make you head of the FBI."

"I'm only worried about whether our next president will be an Israeli agent. Keep your eye on the ball, Jack. Let's go have tea and cookies with Johnson," Brenda said, moving down the senatorial halls with purposeful steps.

George Johnson's Office, 4:30 p.m.

As Senator Johnson's secretary led the two agents into his office, he came around his desk and shook their hands. "Judge Baker said to see you," he said curtly, "so what can I do for you? I can't give you the full time I promised. Last-minute TV change, I'm afraid. I'm in a tight election, you know. But, the judge said it was a matter of national security, so I'll do my best to help. What's up?"

"Senator, we're facing a threat of foreign intervention in this election. We are asking you and the other two presidential candidates a few questions which might help us in a most sensitive investigation. Needless to say, this is highly confidential and you should *not* discuss it with your staff or the media. If you have any questions after we leave, please feel free to call our director."

Senator Johnson nodded and sat down to face them. "Shoot!" His annoyance was not far from the surface. He didn't have time for this.

"Do you know a person named David Tiron?"

"I don't believe I do. Who is he?"

"David Tiron is the Mossad representative at the Israeli Embassy here."

"Let me tell you something, Agent Straus. As our president and the media can assure you, I'm no friend of the Israelis. That's a pretty well-known fact. You better run over and talk to Senator Westlake – he knows all of them. In any case, no, I don't know this man. Never even heard his name before. Why do you ask?"

"Well, we have sensitive information – known to the president – that Tiron is engaging in illegal financing of one of the election campaigns. We have reason to suspect he is in secret contact with one of the candidates. This is not an accusation, but merely a warning that you should be aware of. Needless to say, if we find this to be true, it could lead to the impeachment or conviction of the candidate involved, even if he is successfully elected. Time is on our side, not his. We expect a resolution, though, within the next few days."

Johnson's face had turned red. He burst out, "Of *course* the Israelis are interfering. Don't be naive. They always interfere. But why would they have to be secretive? It's no secret in America that they interfere in our elections. Why else do you think eighty per cent of the Jews in this country vote Democratic? Ask the president what he faced in the last election."

"Sir, we are not talking about open political interference. We're talking about clandestine funding, illegal subversive activity, Israeli covert action...that's what we're looking for."

"Listen, if I had that kind of information I could use it to win the election – so get to the bottom of it fast. Now, I'm afraid I have to get ready for a TV opportunity in my outer office – some voters from my home state. Call me if I can do anything for you. But the man you're looking for is Westlake. Or maybe even Kramer. Yeah, that might explain how he's come from nowhere in this campaign."

"Thank you, Senator. We'll be in touch right after the election – hopefully with more details. We have Tiron closely monitored so we feel confident we'll pin down something concrete very soon."

"Good. Let me know when you do. If I can help the Bureau on this, I'd love to. I've resisted Israeli interference in this nation's affairs all my life. Good luck."

As Brenda and Jack walked down the hallway, Jack chuckled. "Well, Brenda. I don't know if the senator's a foreign agent, but I would say he's a good, solid anti-Semite."

"Two down, one to go," said Brenda. "Maybe we'll get some reaction from Kramer tomorrow in New York. His whole campaign's always seemed a little artificial, too forced. And too damn successful on such short notice. Hey! Look at the time. I've got to get back. Expecting to hear from Guy. Maybe he's homing in on our wanted killer," she added, only half-jokingly.

FBI Headquarters

Guy rang Brenda with good news. The suspect Peter had finally been identified: Petros Dimitriopolis, a fifty-year-old Greek with an underworld reputation of terrorist connections and contract assassinations. The search for him was on throughout Europe.

"*Mon amie*, Brenda," Guy continued, his voice carrying the unmistakable ring of triumph, "I have even more good news! I took the pictures of the Serbian girl with Curiel and showed them to Gérard."

Her fist tightened on the receiver. "Well?"

"Affirmative. Gérard says she is the prostitute who came in with Sorensson the night he was murdered."

"Was he positive?" Brenda persisted.

"*Oui, oui*. Then I showed the picture to Rosie, the girl at the Parrot's Cave. That checked out too. She identified the woman as, I quote, 'the bitch friend' of the murdered hooker. So one and one makes two again. We have our woman."

"Great job, Guy! Thanks!"

"Brenda, *chérie*," Guy's voice boomed with pleasure at the compliment, "you are, as the Americans say, the eager beaver of this case. You told Guy van den Heuven what you wanted and Guy van den Heuven delivered! *N'est-ce pas?*"

"Thank you, Commissioner Guy van den Heuven," replied Brenda, her laughter filling the office. "Now, what're you going to do for an encore? Catch them?"

"First, we find this Petros Dimitriopolis and question him. He will lead us to his woman accomplice. *Non?* And he *is* Greek, just as you thought. Brilliant *flic* you are!"

"Without you we wouldn't have made it, Guy. Oh, I love the Belgian police! I love Belgium! I love you! What more can I say?"

Guy laughed. "Don't get carried away about the Belgian police. One of our infamous pedophiles escaped today. We are this minute searching for him."

"Well, at least I can get carried away about my Belgian inspector friend." Then her mind kicked back to an unturned stone, the Brussels apartment of the second hooker, and Brenda asked if they'd found anything there suggesting that a J. Paula Markovic or J. Paula Bergen had rented the apartment or had been the occupant.

"Sorry, Brenda, not a trace. The most surprising and even suspicious discovery was that the apartment had been wiped clean of fingerprints; we couldn't find one print anywhere. It was abnormally clean. Whoever she is, that woman covers her tracks," Guy told Brenda with frustration. "But, we are still searching. Hang in there, *ma chère*."

"I'll think of a way, I promise you. I *will* find her!" Brenda said.

"*Mon Dieu*!" Guy breathed. "I wouldn't like to be in that woman's heels."

Brenda hung up and buzzed Jack. "Bring in those follow-up letters we prepped for our senators. Let's get them signed and fax them tomorrow morning just after we see Kramer. We gotta make Hebron pop from stress before next Tuesday. Imagine if we had to lock horns with the president! One fax a day, one phone call every four hours, and two not-so-unobtrusive agents at all times on each one. It's time to turn up the heat."

"I'm with you."

New York City, October 29th

Senator Dan Kramer's campaign headquarters was in total chaos. The scene, Brenda thought, more closely resembled the

New York Stock Exchange during frantic market activity than it did a typical political campaign office. She had a hard time keeping a straight face despite the serious nature of her visit.

A young Kramer aide in a T-shirt came running up to Brenda and Jack. "Are you the FBI people?" he asked breathlessly.

"Yes," replied Brenda with stony look. "We are indeed the FBI people."

"I apologize, but the senator had to leave for Washington today. His secretary forgot to call you. His campaign director, Marvin Goldenberg, would be happy to talk to you right now, if that's okay?"

"No, that's *not* okay," Brenda responded firmly. "Our business is urgent and has to be conducted with the senator himself. Here's my card. Have his secretary call me first thing tomorrow morning so we can catch up with him in Washington. I have to see him tomorrow at the latest." She turned and strode toward the elevator. Jack, always ready with a comment, broke the silence. "Doesn't look like Senator Kramer is very eager to talk to us."

"I suspect you're right. But it's our job to see he has no choice. We need to come up with some fresh ideas before we hit home turf this afternoon."

Washington, D.C., October 30th

"I waited until 10 a.m. When Kramer's secretary didn't call for a new appointment, I called her myself. Her excuse was that she was unable to locate him. But the *Washington Post* says he's giving a speech at a National Press Club luncheon."

Jack laughed dryly. "Strange that the secretary didn't volunteer that information. Is it possible, boss, that Senator Kramer doesn't want to see us?"

"They're toying with us, Jack. Let's go get him – embarrass him, if need be. I have to be honest, I never thought much about

Kramer as a possible Hebron. But looking at his reaction to our interview, and in light of his changing party loyalties and his last-minute entry into the race – yet with loads of money to put him in the running – it all makes me think we could be dealing with a very strange and different politico. A foreign agent usually has a personality flaw. Sometimes it's hidden, other times it's visible though often ignored by onlookers. Well, buddy, I'm not going to overlook his dealings with the Bureau. Or with anybody else, for that matter. So, Jack, it's off to lunch. To the National Press Club. This guy is so suspicious he seems innocent, which makes him even more suspicious."

Brenda and Jack entered the National Press Club dining room about thirty minutes before the scheduled arrival of the guests and speaker. They introduced themselves, showing their credentials to Kramer's Secret Service advance team. Brenda explained that she had important information from the FBI director to give personally to the senator and that she absolutely had to see him in a side room. The Secret Service agents said they would arrange it.

A few minutes later the third-party candidate arrived, talking nonstop to the media herd accompanying him. The head of his Secret Service team pulled him aside for a second to advise him that the agents were waiting, with instructions from the FBI director not to leave without seeing him. They wanted to brief him on something urgent.

Kramer excused himself from the crowd of reporters, stating that he had to review his speech notes. He followed the Secret Service bodyguard to where Brenda and Jack waited. "What in the world is so urgent that you people can't wait a week until the election's over? If someone's going to kill me, that's the Secret Service's problem," he snarled.

"Good afternoon, Senator. I am Special Agent Straus and this is Special Agent Sanchez. Please, we only require a few minutes of your time. The director has asked me to brief you on an urgent problem."

"Okay. Let's have it!" the candidate snapped as he sat on the arm of a leather chair. He appeared as nervous as a cornered animal.

"Senator, the FBI has information that a foreign intelligence service is trying to interfere in this election. This is very sensitive. So we ask you not to discuss it with your staff or the media. Only with us at the Bureau. First, do you know a person named David Tiron?"

"I don't know, Miss Whatever-your-name-is. I meet a thousand people a day in this campaign. But no, I don't think so."

"Thank you, sir, that's all we need. We don't want to take up any more of your time."

"Listen, young lady," bellowed Kramer. "You chased me from Washington to New York and back to ask me that? Then you expect to walk out of here saying thank you! What the hell are you people up to? You're playing games with me and I don't take that shit, from the FBI or anyone else!" He pointed at Brenda. "Either tell me why you've *really* come or I call Washington and have your badge, or your ass, or both. Do you understand?" He paused. "Now. Do you have anything else to say?"

"No, sir. We just wanted to know if you knew Mr. David Tiron, the Israeli intelligence chief at their embassy here. We have him under heavy surveillance on suspicion of being involved in illegal activity in one of the three presidential campaigns. If we eventually prove this, before the election or afterwards, it could, you understand, lead to the impeachment, or arrest and conviction, of the candidate involved, even if he had won the election and were president. In any case, you've answered my question. Thank you."

"Listen here, you two! I'm going to call Judge Baker tomorrow to ask him to put some different people on this case, whatever the case is. You two come in here playing detective with me – do you know who I am? I may be your president next week! Are you're trying to provoke me? Talking about some Israeli because my wife is Jewish and her father is a big supporter of mine? This better be legitimate, young woman, or you can start looking for another job. Got that?"

He rose in a huff and left. Brenda could hear him screaming at his Secret Service agent for letting the FBI visitors see him before his speech.

"I don't think we're invited to lunch," remarked Jack.

"Let's go," answered Brenda. "Now that we've gotten to them all, I have a feeling Hebron will react. Hopefully, before the election. If not, immediately after it. Maybe he's too busy right now, but he will move soon. And Jack, one more thing. From a secure line, leave a message for each candidate's campaign manager. Use these numbers. Don't talk to them; just leave a message."

"Yeah? And what's the message?"

"David Tiron called and it's urgent."

Jack smiled at Brenda's cunning. She shrugged. "Time's running out."

Chapter Twenty-three

Tuesday, November 7th – Election Day
The White House, 7:05 p.m. EST

In a television news bulletin the projected winner of the US presidential election was introduced to the world.

"CNN can now confirm that in the closest American presidential election since 1976, when Jimmy Carter edged out Gerald Ford by 20,000 votes nationwide, Senator George Johnson of New Hampshire has been declared the winner by an even narrower margin. From his Trump Tower apartment, the Reform Party candidate, Senator Dan Kramer of New York, conceded just minutes ago, claiming this as a massive victory for third-party politics in the United States, while Senator Wes Westlake has yet to make a statement. Senator Westlake's campaign headquarters announced that the senator will defer all public reaction until tomorrow morning. He may demand a recount."

As the projected margin between Senators Johnson and Westlake continued into the evening, other political analysts insisted that they must wait for the closing of the West Coast polls before their computers could project a winner. But the major networks and CNN were all calling it a victory for Johnson.

Bill Russell, in his West Wing office at the White House, had been as anxious as a kid going to his first circus as he awaited the results.

"My God. How close!" he whispered aloud as he downed his fourth straight scotch from his office bar. Energized by the news, he ran to his desk and phoned the president's private quarters.

"Mr. President, did you see the news? George won! My God, what a close election. I thought for sure Westlake, with all that Jewish support, was going to rob us. But the results are confirmed now, so, please, rest before your dinner this evening. I'll have your morning schedule canceled, if you wish."

"Great news!" boomed the president. "I had the TV on, but fell asleep in my chair. My worries of the last few days are over. This is all I've hoped and prayed for. What a way to end my political career – able to choose my successor. After Dick's death and this Middle East thing, I needed some good news just to keep going."

The president's voice changed. "And it's thanks, in part, to the help from your Arab friend. Yes, I know all about that. I appreciate it that you kept me out of the loop on that. We all know where that can lead. But clearly every little bit helped. Goddamn pure miracle. The last couple of days I'd almost given up, but the voters were finally put off by Westlake's arrogant liberal manner and liberal love life. I mean, love *lives*. Ha! That Jeri whatever-her-name-is, and those two visits to Paris. And with pictures and the tape, God! That iced it for us. Surprising that the scandal didn't hurt him even more. I hope he has enough money left over to build a shrine to his stupidity. He had the thing in the bag."

Bill Russell murmured his agreement, marveling at the value of his little trip to Mansour's châlet. *How the little details in history blossom out into massive change.*

Douglas couldn't stop talking. "And Johnson, hell of a fund-raiser, isn't he? And that TV blitz at the end! Couldn't help thinking of some of the stuff we did. Masterful, but it certainly cost him some bucks. He must be drowning in debt – I'm just glad it isn't me who has to face paying it back. Well, then again, he'll get that rich daddy-in-law to iron that out," he chuckled. Then he added, "Bill, get George on the phone for me, will you? I want to congratulate our man personally. This is a great moment for me, the party, and the country."

"Will do, Mr. President. Hold still."

Russell pushed a button on his phone and asked the operator to get President-elect Johnson at his Washington campaign headquarters.

"Dr. Russell," responded the operator in just two minutes, "I have President-elect Senator Johnson on the line – at least, that's what they are calling him at his headquarters."

"Hey, Mr. President-elect! Bill Russell here. Congratulations from all of us at the White House. Hell of a job! You did it! And the president wants to give you his personal pat on the back. Stay on the line – I'll pass you straight through." Russell was very proud to be the one to pass the president-elect through to the incumbent.

"Before you transfer me, Bill, I want to thank you for your last-minute efforts. You know, that envelope and all. Every nudge helped."

"Glad to aid a worthy cause, George." There was a tiny pause as both men smiled. Then Johnson said, "I need to discuss with you the transition on foreign affairs, but not tonight. Tonight I'm going to celebrate with Nicola and catch my breath. I'm sure you understand. Okay, now pass me on to the president."

Russell reiterated his congratulations, then pressed a button and Johnson's voice reached Douglas.

"Mr. President, George here. By God, we did it! Not bad, eh? But so blessed close. I've still got a case of nerves and can hardly believe the outcome. You heard that that SOB won't make a concession speech tonight? You don't think he has something up his sleeve, do you?" he asked nervously, then added, "Who cares? We won! And if he doesn't want to concede, that's okay. As far as I'm concerned, the people have spoken and that's good enough for me."

"George, congratulations! I was worried as hell a month ago, but this week you came on like gangbusters! Great work! I would've hated turning this office over to either of those creeps. You saw them sucking up to the lobbies at the end like that. Outright embarrassing for national politics. Moving the United States Embassy to Jerusalem. Have you ever heard such lard in your life! And those stories about Westlake's flings with the ladies of Paris didn't exactly hurt us either, did they?"

Douglas cleared his throat with a swallow of his cocktail. "Your PR people did a great job and I'm glad we were able to help. And if you're worried about the debt, don't. Now that you're president-elect, the resources will pour in. You'll see. Everyone wants to own a part of a winner – especially with the power of this office."

"That's good to hear," said Johnson. "If you like, I'll drop by briefly tonight – although I was planning, I admit, to focus a bit on Nicola after I publically thank my campaign team and supporters and do a couple of one-minute TV spots for the networks. It's been tough on her, all this pressure."

"Of course, of course, George. We're so damn proud of you. Take a night off...! Remember, I was there – I won too. Enjoy it with Nicola and get a few hours' sleep. Come by tomorrow at eight. We'll have a champagne breakfast to celebrate. Just the two of us. And a photo op – I'll be shaking your hand on the front page of every paper in the country. I want to give you a few words of advice on how to handle your new vice president these next few days."

Then in a low tone he added, "Also, as president-elect you should be briefed on a quirky, top-secret national security case laid on us by our Russian friends and piloted by the Israelis, which I'm now convinced was a red herring. There's nothing that can't wait till morning. See you at eight! Okay? And give my best to Nicola. She must be thrilled."

"Good night, Mr. President. See you at eight. And God bless you."

Election Night, Israeli Embassy

"David Tiron!" Ambassador Meir yelled at his empty office, bringing his fist crashing to his desk. "I'm going to have your ass and your job!" He had just heard the CNN confirmation of Johnson's victory. Dismayed at the news of Westlake's close loss, the ambassador zapped from channel to channel, hoping to hear it was not true. But gradually all the channels agreed on the outcome.

"You will *pay*, Tiron!" he bellowed again. But Tiron was not at the embassy. His whereabouts were unknown, according to his secretary, who was still at the office following her boss's orders. "He said he'd be back, Mr. Ambassador."

"I can't believe he's not here," the ambassador shouted at the secretary. "He's probably downing more than Diet Coke to forget this day! Beep him, get Abe on the radio, find him."

"He's not responding to our messages. And, sir, David's car is here. He'll be back shortly, I'm sure."

"He'll damn well face me tomorrow." He slammed the phone down.

Meir fell back in a soft chair, the day's realities sending blood racing to his head, choking his thoughts, giving him a severe headache. He kept telling himself, over and over, that Israel had never come this close to having one of its best friends in the US Senate elected president of the United States. *That bugger snatched victory away from us*, he thought. Any moment his phone would surely ring and his foreign minister or even the prime minister would want an explanation. Where was our political analysis on this? they'd demand. Or perhaps they'd merely send him a cable, which he'd find on his desk in the morning, recalling him home to explain in person.

For he knew, from his many years in a pressure-cooker government, that this was the end of his career. From this day forward, he would be held accountable for whatever bad news Washington sent Israel.

"Damn that Tiron!" he swore savagely. "It's his fault. He fumbled it from the start."

Several minutes before the ambassador called him, Tiron had received a special one-way beeper signal from Hebron demanding an emergency meeting at the safe house apartment in Rosslyn. *Is he fucking crazy!* Tiron screamed in his mind. *Tonight? Now? No!* He had no recourse but to go, but if there was one thing neither he nor Hebron needed, it was a clandestine meeting in Washington on election night. Security was intense, emotions were flaring, the results weren't even finalized, the candidates were in the public eye. The networks were chasing the two losers just as hard as the winner, to catch both pain and triumph on screen. The more intense the mood on the streets, the more dangerous such a meeting. *Let this settle, Hebron*, he thought, unnerved by the horribly close results himself.

I can't not go. That's even more dangerous, Tiron admitted to himself. *But this is fucking* meshuga. *Not now, Hebron, not now.*

Tiron ordered Abe to wear his weapon, and he slipped his own .38 caliber revolver in the back of his belt, under his suit jacket. When he and Abe left the embassy they used the back door. They drove a different car than usual, one with regular District of Columbia license plates. Tiron's senses warned him this was a meeting that should not be held. *We could lose everything right here*, he repeated to himself. *But when your top agent calls, you go*. His nervousness was contagious: Abe felt prickles of anxiety spread though his veins, but he kept his thoughts to himself.

Tangier

Mansour Cherif was in his Tangier palace, far away from his subordinate bases in Geneva and Paris, when CNN Anchorman Ernie Stowes reported that Johnson had won. Smiling with wild pleasure, the Arab multimillionaire ran around in his silk *djellaba*, informing everyone in the palace, including his servants. His household had never seen him this excited.

He was soon bombarded with calls from around the world, congratulating him on his prediction that the original favorite, the pro-Israeli Democratic Party candidate, Senator Wes Westlake, would lose. Mansour's Arab friends, who were convinced that the Jewish lobby in the US could do anything, had been speculating among themselves as to why Mansour was so adamant that Westlake would lose. Of course, they had had no way of connecting that bit of damning news on the Paris scandal to the respected, cultured Moroccan business magnate, a friend of his country's new young king.

"Get me Bill Russell on the phone," he told his son Khaled, a graduate of Georgetown University who had to delay a carnal rendezvous with a certain Leila to help his father handle the flood of late-night international phone calls. "Tonight, Khaled, we make hay. Tomorrow, the lovely ones will be even more eager, my son."

"Hi, Mansour. We did it!" shouted Russell on the line as Khaled passed the call to his father.

"Well, my good friend. You see how we function – we stupid ragheads, as your enlightened ones call us. We have a few tricks of our own, no?"

"You sure do. The president also wants to thank you for everything. Honestly!"

"Thank you, Bill. Give my regards to him and the new president-elect. Enjoy the parties – wish I were there to help celebrate. You lousy American politicians are so in love with politics, you can hardly be aroused anymore. Except for our defeated senator friend." He laughed heartily. "You need a great lover like me to take care of those frustrated harems in Washington. A mere cultural detail, Bill. Okay? Tell them to wait for the inauguration – I'll be over then. *Inshallah*."

"*Inshallah*. Mansour, you're something else. We'll miss you. See you in January. You'll be invited and you shall have a damn good seat, I assure you. And once again – *shukan*, pal."

"Don't mention it, Bill. What are friends for?"

Washington, D.C.

At about 4:00 p.m., Jackie Markovic had decided to go shopping at Tyson's Corner mall in suburban Virginia. The receptionist at the Marriott Motel in Rosslyn, where she was staying as textile consultant Gertrude Schneider, with a false German passport to match, had recommended Tyson's as the biggest, best mall around. "You'll love it, Miss Schneider." She pronounced the German name without the *ch*.

As Jackie loved to do her Christmas shopping in the USA, a trip to America for any reason – skiing in Aspen, or a confrontation in Washington – was always welcome. The Americans, she was convinced, had a variety of merchandise that was just not available in Europe, and the prices were laughably low, even though the Americans went around complaining how expensive everything was. *What if they had to do their shopping in Europe, like on Zurich's Bahnhofstrasse*, she thought, *where the Swiss charge over three thousand dollars for a VCR!*

Nothing brought out the little girl in Jackie like shopping. She bought another green lingerie set with a garter belt at Victoria's

Secret, sure that this would excite Yuri next time. He loved garter belts so, and she enjoyed seeing his cold expression transformed when confronted with such seductive frills. *Poor men – so weak*, she laughed to herself as she imagined the look on his face and continued her shopping with renewed zeal.

Consulting her Christmas list, Jackie started thinking about her mother in Vienna. She had to get her Mama something special this year, as she was fading and Jackie was not sure how long she would be with her. She shuddered. *Liebling, muti.*

Since she had suffered abuse as a teenager at the hand and pelvis of her father – *thief of my virginity* – Jackie couldn't stand the thought of being left in the world without her *muti*. She had never forgotten the risks her mother took to protect Jackie from her abusive husband. Tough as Jackie Markovic was, she felt so alone in the world already, knowing her mother would not be with her long. She would give up her string of apartments around the world if her mother could stay alive as long as Jackie lived.

An announcement on the mall loudspeaker updated shoppers on the latest Election Day news – Senator Johnson was squeezing ahead of Senator Westlake. Although experts awaited the West Coast polls, projections were similar from coast to coast, CNN predicted that Johnson would win by a less than 1% margin.

"Great!" Jackie whispered. While politics were of almost no interest to her, she had concluded from reading the Washington press the past few days that if Johnson won, it would be a blow to the Israelis. And after she finished with Tiron, the Israelis would be hurting from more than just having one of their friends lose an election. Their reputation and relations in Washington would be in shambles. "Mossad Chief Eliminated on Election Night." It was too pretty, she thought, drunk on her scheme. She stopped at a pay phone in the mall and dialed the 800 number for United, which she had commited to memory, reserving a first class seat on that night's late plane to Frankfurt, the last scheduled international flight to leave the East Coast of the United States, 10:50 p.m. At the same time she canceled her reservation on the afternoon flight. Each day this week she had updated her readiness in exactly the same way. Book one, cancel one, not knowing on which day opportunity would knock, which date they'd engrave on poor David Tiron's tombstone. *Patience, my dear,* she told herself. Readiness in this business was everything. This ultimate hit would come to her when it was ready.

She promised herself that.

"Hello, lovely lady. Can I help you?" asked a handsome mall guard in his thirties, coming up behind Jackie. She was about to brush him off when her professional eye caught sight of the sidearm in his holster. It was a Glock model 17, one of Jackie's favorites from her native Austria. That gave her an idea. Quickly assuming that the young man must be bored and had decided to pick her up, she opted to try out a Southern accent.

"Oh, you big, strong man, you. Thank you so much and tell me, where may I find the ladies' room to rest my feet?" She pronounced the phrases as if auditioning to play a Southern belle in *Gone with the Wind*.

"Yes, ma'am. I'll take you there. This way please," said the handsome guard enthusiastically. *What luck*, he thought as he watched the cheeks of her ass sway.

She decided to befriend him so she would know where to pick up a spare Glock automatic in Washington whenever she needed it. She might even need a safe apartment – his. It never hurt to have a backup. "You're a handsome man, are you married?" Jackie asked as she gave him a sizzling, sexy look – a glance which he felt to the bottom of his toes.

That got his attention. *She's a live one.* "No ma'am, too busy to get married – just a lonely bachelor."

"No! Everybody should have pity on poor little me for meetin' such a handsome young brute. Is your place near here?"

"Yeah, ma'am. I got a place in McLean – but I'm on duty until ten tonight."

"Well, honey, let's make it another time, then," she purred, having all the immediate information she needed to exploit this simple soul at a moment's notice. *Just in case.*

After using the ladies' room, Jackie waved a flirtatious good-bye to the young guard and took the nearest exit toward her rental car in the mall parking lot. She drove back to her motel room to wait for Peter's signal from his observation point. There she lay on the bed waiting for Tiron to walk into their trap. It had been days, so what did it matter if it took a little longer. *In revenge, as in sex, anticipation is half the fun*, she thought. She would just fill her days with more shopping, always paying cash, of course. She was patient, and even more determined. She ordered a salad and iced tea from room service, then drew a hot bath to soak her beautiful toned body. Afterward she would remain relaxed, rested, and ready to go at a few minutes' notice.

8:18 p.m.

Senator George Johnson delivered his victory speech from his downtown Washington headquarters. The speech, in which he thanked his staff and supporters and the American public, was telecast on all networks. It was greeted with uproar and applause, while around the country the surprising results were greeted with a mixture of emotions, not the least of which was a sense of relief. Commentators were unanimous in their hopes that the new president would address the key issues which were affecting the economy, and which, it seemed, had been placed on hold during the last weeks of the neck-and-neck presidential race.

8:33 p.m.

Finally, under intense pressure from senior staff and party officials, Senator Wes Westlake gave a terse, one-minute speech stating that he thanked his staff and friends and, out of fierce adherence to his principles, would withhold any concession until the polls were closed and all the votes counted. Privately, he was working on tracing the sex scandal leaks and a few other things. If he didn't redress the situation right now, he was through with public life. Some were saying that he was simply a bad sport, and that was about as un-American as it gets. Following his comment, he immediately rushed out of his headquarters and ducked into the limousine waiting to take him to his suite at the Hilton.

8:58 p.m.

Hebron managed to slip by his Secret Service bodyguards, who had believed him when he said he'd be in his hotel suite with his wife and wasn't to be disturbed. It was always easier guarding a hotel room than a moving target, so they were relieved; every Secret Service member had seen archive videos of the Robert Kennedy assassination. Hebron quickly changed into blue jeans and a light hooded parka, and pleaded with his wife to stay put and cover for him. He had an important campaigner to thank personally. He'd be an hour, not more. "Don't let those Secret Service geeks devour me, hon." He reached over and kissed her lightly. Then he slipped out the service entrance of the suite and down the stairs. In a car he had borrowed from a young staff member, he pulled out of the parking lot unperceived.

Rosslyn

"Get a move on, man," Tiron said impatiently as Abe slowed

to a crawl, stuck behind a group of cyclists riding four abreast. Tiron was furious with the timing of this meeting. *Election night, of all times! Shit!* A string of curses aimed at Hebron for placing him in such a dangerous position paraded through his mind, and a few slipped past his lips.

Abe could hear him. *The boss has gone ballistic!* "The office is beeping you, sir."

"Let them wait, Abe. This takes priority." He was panicked.

They arrived with one minute to spare, parking just around the corner from the apartment building's entrance. Wearing a pair of owlish black-rimmed glasses, Tiron pulled his hat far down over his forehead and put up the collar of his overcoat. He was worried about Hebron's Secret Service bodyguards. A furtive look revealed no one around – just three parked cars, all nondescript and probably belonging to residents.

"Watch the building, Abe. I want to know who enters the lobby. Use the handset to beep me, okay? And Abe, be extra careful tonight. I want no mistakes."

"Are you sure this is a good idea, sir?" Abe looked concerned. "Don't you think it would be safer if I came with you? At least let me check out the apartment first. Please, boss!"

"Don't argue with me. Just do as you're told and be sure to let me know if you see anything out of the ordinary. *Anything!*" Without further discussion Tiron entered the glass doors of the modern building, passed through the vacant lobby and pushed the button for the seventh floor.

Following Jackie's plan like gospel, Peter had been tailing David Tiron and Abe for nearly a week in October before they led him to the Mossad safe house. He had rented a flat and moved in across the hall.

This hadn't been difficult; most apartments in the River House complex were leased by government employees or foreigners working in Washington on temporary duty. Nor had it been difficult to install a tiny laser sensor in the hall to alert Peter when someone entered or left Tiron's safe apartment. If it was Tiron, Peter was to call Jackie immediately. It worked out exactly as Jackie had planned.

She's one smart bitch, Peter had to admit.

In anticipation, Peter peered through the peephole and could just make out the squat figure of Tiron turning to close the door as he spoke into his mobile telephone. A few seconds later Peter heard the familiar whirring sound of the elevator, followed by approaching footsteps.

Try as he might, he could see nothing of the newcomer except that it was a man in jeans and a parka, with the hood covering his head and most of his face. He was wearing gloves. Tiron greeted the newcomer with a curt nod, pulled him inside the apartment, and glanced up and down the hall before following his visitor inside and shutting the door. Although Peter's view was restricted, it didn't seem as though Tiron's bulldog of a guard, Abe, was around. But Peter now knew there was another man in the apartment.

Wasting no time, Peter dialed Jackie at her motel room. "The Chinese food has arrived. Come on over and join the party. There's one plate of food I don't recognize."

"Love to, honey. Be right there," she responded in an exaggerated Southern accent.

Her pulse racing, Jackie quickly dressed in clothes she had prepared well in advance – a man's outfit, including a sloppy hat with full brim, a raincoat, and corduroy trousers. She threw the rest of her possessions into the overnight bag. Then she figured the exact cost of her stay in the motel and left the cash and room key on the night table. Undetected, she took the side door next to the lobby and into the parking lot. Her bag stowed in the rental car, she walked to the apartment building a few blocks away.

Looks like I'll be making my plane tonight, she told herself.

Approaching the building cautiously, Jackie saw a man standing in the lobby glancing from side to side nervously. From Peter's casing report and photos, Jackie identified him as Abe. She quickly changed her path, crept around to the back of the building, slipped through the service entrance, which Peter had taped open, and quickly but quietly climbed the interior fire stairway to the seventh floor.

Peter had left the door of his observation apartment slightly ajar for her. She nodded at him silently. They had practiced the procedure several times. He handed her the SIG-Sauer P228 Silent Stalker 9mm automatic, with dumdum bullets and a silencer. Carefully she checked the weapon, as well as the smaller backup automatic, a 9mm Walther PKK and holster, which she strapped to her right leg just above the ankle, under her pant leg.

Peter drew her aside. "He's not alone. There's someone with him. A man. Don't know who. Couldn't get a good look."

"At this stage, darling Peter, I don't give a damn." Jackie spoke slowly, coldly, decisively. "I'm not going to lose this chance to meet Santa Claus in person, no matter what." *Especially because, after this, I'm going to take a long and well-deserved break.*

Peter knew better than to challenge her at such a critical moment, though he was uneasy at the prospect of an emotional confrontation with a professional intelligence officer which could be could be dangerous for both of them.

"Everything ready to get out of here?" whispered Jackie. "Both your passports?"

"Yes." Peter nodded. "But we have to hurry."

"Do you have the note?" He nodded again and silently handed her a piece of folded paper. "Okay, partner," said Jackie, her green eyes narrowed. "Let's go."

Stretching a pair of black leather gloves over surgical ones, she stepped into the hallway, Peter at her heels. A sudden premonition of disaster overcame him, drenching him in sweat and turning his blood to cold treacle. *Something's wrong*, he thought.

Jackie put her ear to the door of Tiron's apartment. She heard two voices, one apparently Tiron's. The other speaker was unmistakably an American male.

The American was shouting at Tiron in what seemed to Jackie a panicky tone. "David what is it with your system? This FBI agent...they know something. Look at this fax. What's going on? *Tell* me. My political future is at stake here. My life, my reputation, everything! That woman knows. Where's the leak, David?"

"For crissakes, my friend, calm down. What the fuck do you think you're doing? You're going to return to your hotel and follow the flow of events. We'll remake contact..."

"No, you listen to me, you weasel, I'm not..."

Jackie didn't recognize the other voice, but, as far as she was concerned, here was a man in the wrong place at the wrong time. She motioned for Peter to knock on the door.

He had no choice; there was no turning back now. He knocked loudly and shouted in an alarmed tone, "Mr. Tiron, this is the superintendent. Please come! It's Abe. He's in trouble. There's a problem. He has to see you immediately. Quickly, please!"

Increasingly upset as he dealt with the near-hysterical Hebron, Tiron was irritated and alarmed by the unexpected voice. Anger at the untimely interruption overcame just enough of his professional instincts to invite disaster. Instead of checking first, he carelessly unlatched the lock and cracked open the door. "What's this all about? Where's Abe?" he blustered angrily at the man who stood there.

Peter moved aside just enough to allow Jackie to step forward

338

into the doorway. She shoved the silencer hard against Tiron's stomach and gave him a small push back into the room. She said nothing, her face set in a tight smile.

Peter entered behind her and closed the door.

Seeing the glint of the gun, the exercised Hebron jumped to his feet, his eyes open with shock and terror. He looked desperately to Tiron for reassurance. "David, what's happening here? Who are these people? Is this some sort of a joke? I told you..."

"Quiet." Tiron's voice shook with tension. He kept his eyes fixed on Jackie, looking for a way out of this predicament. "What do you want, money? How much? It's not a problem. Name your price."

"How clever you are to guess," Jackie responded, seeing his fear. "But I'm afraid at this stage money won't solve my problem. Or yours," she emphasized, prodding him with the silencer. "I want you, Mr. Tiron, because I understand that you're the one who gave orders not to pay me the rest of my fee for the Brussels job. Well, in my business, I cannot afford to have anyone walking around bragging about not paying me. So, *shalom*, Mr. Mossad."

Tiron, realizing this woman was serious and ruthless, reached for his .38 while making a desperate attempt to vault behind the sofa.

Jackie shot him with the silenced automatic. The 9mm dumdum round hit Tiron near his left arm, drove through his heart, and threw him like a rag doll across the room. In the same motion, Jackie whirled and shot the other man with one bullet to the head, not knowing if he was armed. *Just in case.*

She checked both bodies to be sure the men were dead. Two shots, two dead men. *Haven't lost my touch yet!* Satisfied, she picked up Tiron's .38. As Peter turned from checking the bodies, she pointed the revolver at him. His face registered disbelief for a split second, then his partner shot him once through the heart with Tiron's gun, whispering, "Early retirement, old friend." She then fired a .38 bullet into the wall. These two unsilenced shots would be heard outside.

She would have liked to say a few parting words to Peter before shooting him, but she didn't want to risk him using her name in an uncontrolled apartment where the conversation might be taped, or to risk having him shoot back at her. *Well, he was getting old anyway. Sixteen years ago he was the perfect partner. I didn't have a choice this time. We once worked brilliantly together, but lately, Peter, you'd become a liability. Too soft and timid.* The Americans would have caught him and he'd have delivered her on a platter, opting for a reduced sentence. *He simply had to go. Too bad. In some ways,* she thought, *I'll miss you.* She looked around one last time, and blew him a farewell kiss.

The scene in a flash reminded her of the most horrible yet glorious killing she had ever carried out: shooting her father with his World War II Luger. That was the beautiful part of it. His own gun. Pushing that long barrel right up to him. Letting him feel it. Letting him have a glimpse and a whiff of what he'd get in return for what he'd thrust into her, his own daughter. Those hard fingers grabbing her young chest, grasping handfuls of her. *All those times. Too bad,* she remembered thinking, *I can make him feel this only once.* If only there had been a way to shoot him and then let him live with that recurring anguish for a drawn-out stretch of time. Slow it down. Make him comb his stringy hair in a mirror when it was all over. And then tell him that she loved him. *That's why I'm killing you, my little one.* But, no, he'd be dead when the bullet stopped. Too quick, but just. Her payback with his own weapon, the cruel climax after all that abuse. Fuck you, she had muttered as the hot barrel burned into his flesh. *Fuck, you know what that means, papa.* After that, the murder of others had been easy for her, void of feeling. Murder was the only response. And memory.

The moment came back in focus. Jackie hurriedly placed the .38 near Tiron's hand. Her 9mm SIG with the silencer she laid on Peter's outstretched palm. The homicide detectives would have perfect police-lab matches for the bullets and guns used, as well as their shooters.

She balanced the folded note beside Tiron's thumb and forefinger, making it look as if it had just slipped from his fingers. In neatly typed print, it read: "This is for you and your country, Mr. Tiron, for not paying the Brussels contract. You both pay the price." There was no signature – only Peter's fingerprints.

The assassin coolly and quickly reviewed the situation. In exactly three minutes, she had killed her target and his associate, whoever he was, and had taken care of the growing threat to her personal security that Peter increasingly represented. She had also left Peter, the supposed assassin, to be found by the police. She assumed this would neatly wrap up both the Sorensson and Tiron cases, right there, leaving her free – sooner or later – to resume her profession. At least to make her United flight.

But it wasn't over yet. First she had to exit the scene safely. This was not Brussels but Washington. The police would pour in soon. Highways would be blocked. Airports watched. She had to be as far away as possible before wailing sirens started.

She dashed across the hall to the leased apartment and changed her outer gloves to remove the gunpowder traces. Belting the raincoat tight around her slim waist, she took the stairway to the floor below, to catch the elevator to the ground floor. As she entered the stairway, she heard the elevator bell sound and someone calling, "Boss! Boss!" That would be Abe, having heard the two loud reports from Tiron's revolver.

Abe burst into the apartment. He didn't know, and frankly

341

didn't care, who the other two guys were. But he leaned heavily against the wall when he saw his boss lying dead. Reeling from shock, groaning in anguish, Abe pulled out his secure walkie-talkie and called the Mossad duty officer at his embassy.

Waiting for an answer, nausea sweeping over him, he noticed a piece of folded paper next to Tiron's hand. Swiftly, he picked it up and read it, perplexed.

The phone crackled. "Stay put, Abe," he was told. "We're calling the police now. They'll be there quickly. You return to the embassy as soon as they arrive. But, remember – you have diplomatic immunity. Say *nothing*! Do you have your passport?" Abe replied in the affirmative, turned off his portable and started toward the door.

The note made no sense. But given Tiron's highly sensitive position, it could be incriminating in some way. Before he could think twice, Abe had stuffed the note in his trousers pocket. His eyes darted from detail to detail, dead bodies, circles of blood, a stack of Diet Pepsi cans in the corner. Minutes later he heard the police sirens wailing outside.

Jackie Markovic walked quickly back to the motel parking lot, jumped into her rented car and began to weave her way toward Dulles Airport via the George Washington Parkway, carefully maintaining the speed limit. She had studied the necessary routes well in advance. Shortly after passing CIA headquarters, well marked on her right, she came to a wooded roadside area she had previously cased. She turned off the main highway and parked. Walking a few yards into the woods, she tossed her spare weapon into the Potomac River. She buried her gloves and men's clothing separately, in the underbrush, covering the shallow holes with loose leaves.

Jackie felt considerably relieved but would feel more so once she checked in at Dulles and boarded the late flight to

Germany. Once on board she would change her fake German passport for her real Austrian one and her identity to her real self, continuing on to Palma de Mallorca as an Austrian citizen, J. Paula Bergen – her mother's maiden name, which she used in Spain. *Almost there,* she thought as she dropped off the Hertz vehicle and boarded the free shuttle bus to the terminal. Dulles at this hour was almost empty. Lovely. She grasped her bag with her Christmas gift for her mother and strolled, like a diplomat's wife going on home leave, into the quiet departure area where a few passengers were checking in at the United counter.

Two hours later, safely aboard the aircraft, she began quietly celebrating with a half-bottle of Champagne. She relaxed in her first-class sleeper seat, entirely satisfied with the efficiency of her evening's work.

"That should teach those Israelis to play games with me as though I were a donkey," she mumbled to herself sleepily, a smile on her tanned face. And by placing Peter dead in the hands of the American police, she had, she was sure, ended the global manhunt for the killer of Ambassador Sorensson. A manhunt, which, as Yuri had reminded her, had posed the greatest threat ever to her freedom, even her life.

As she reviewed the events of November 7th from her perspective, she felt that all the risks she had run in going to Washington to take revenge on the Israelis had been justified by the result. Never before had she pulled off such a complex, dangerous hit and seen every detail of her intricate scheme work so perfectly. In fact, it had even worked despite the unexpected appearance of the stranger with Tiron in the Mossad apartment.

As she began to doze, a residual thought flickered across her mental screen: *Who was the man with Tiron?* The one whose faced she had pulped with a dumdum bullet. His light parka and blue jeans seemed like a disguise. *One of Tiron's agents?* She hoped he was important to Mossad. That'd be an ironic bonus. But she hated surprises that she hadn't planned herself, and not knowing ate at her.

In any case, too bad for him, she concluded, finally drifting off to sleep as the large aircraft carried her swiftly away from the crime scene toward her native Europe.

Chapter Twenty-four

Washington, D.C.
November 7th, 10:30 p.m.

The car raced though the capital's streets, wailing and screaming. Its destination, an apartment building in Rosslyn. Its contents, five FBI agents – Special Agent Brenda Straus, her three-person Sorensson/Hebron investigative team, and Art Bosco, a Bureau forensic expert who had been on night duty.

Brenda had been working late when the director phoned and ordered her to respond to an Arlington Police Department call regarding a shoot-out. Baker told her the police had reported three men dead, and the only one so far identified was David Tiron. Tiron's chauffeur was being detained at the scene despite his diplomatic passport and his insistence that he should be allowed to call or return to his embassy. One of the other men was a dark-complected Caucasian male, who apparently had used an automatic with a silencer. The third man was unrecognized due to massive gunfire damage to the face.

"It's obvious, Brenda," said Judge Baker, "that this could involve one of the top-priority cases you are handling. I've ordered the police to touch nothing until you get there. Take charge of this situation from the start. We want to maintain control, for the White House's sake, over whatever international complexities these killings may involve. If we find that this situation relates to one of your cases, then we have the right agent there. If, on the other hand, it turns out to be less than I think it is, we can arrange for you to turn it over to another special agent this evening. Clear?"

"Clear."

"Be careful, Brenda."

"Thanks."

Now Brenda was in the speeding car driven by Jack Sanchez, who obviously reveled in the havoc his reckless driving was causing. She gripped the door handle, glaring at him. Jack grinned and stepped harder on the gas pedal. To distract her, he asked, "So, what'd the old man say?"

That you're a moron, she thought, but answered cautiously, "He thinks whatever happened in that apartment tonight is probably connected with our investigations." She couldn't elaborate in front of Art Bosco.

Jack got the hint. "Between you getting the lead on the Sorensson case," he said, playing along, "and the Mossad rep in Washington being gunned down, I'm not sure I'm going to survive this day. I have a feeling this murder will cause us enough stress to last a lifetime."

At the apartment building, Jack came to a skillfully measured stop that left tire marks on the pavement. He looked out the car window with dismay. "Get a load of all those police cars. And the crowd! Tell you what – I'll talk to those people while you check out the murder scene. Maybe I'll get lucky and find a witness. The killer might even be in this crowd. Anyway, the police up there are expecting Special Agent Straus, not me."

"Fine, Jack. Come straight up after you've finished," replied Brenda, wondering what the murder scene would look like.

Brenda, Christina, Jim, and Art entered the building, showing their credentials to the Arlington police controlling the lobby.

Brenda asked Christina to take the stairs and look for clues. Jim and Art rode the elevator to the seventh floor with Brenda, Jim's assignment being to check out the floor's tenants.

On the seventh floor, a uniformed officer demanded identification. "Lieutenant Ford, the FBI is here – Special Agent Straus!" he shouted. Jim smiled tightly at Brenda before embarking on his chore. Art went to look for the police forensic experts.

Police crowded the seventh floor. A police photographer's bulbs were exploding into a bright display of white light as he diligently tried to cover every detail of the murder site before anything was touched.

"Agent Straus?" asked a man in a brown suit, stepping forward from a group of uniformed officers. "They told me you'd be coming. I'm Lieutenant Bud Ford, Arlington Homicide. I called the Bureau after the chauffeur for the Israeli Embassy – who was armed, by the way – said one of the bodies was his boss, an Israeli Embassy counselor named David Tiron."

"Which apartment is it?" asked Brenda, looking around. "And did the chauffeur give you a statement? Did he elaborate on anything?"

"The bastard," Ford said with disgust. "He had only one answer to every question: 'I have a diplomatic passport. I want to be released.' But he did claim not to know who the other two were. Nor did he seem to be concerned about them."

Ford turned his head and called to one of his men. "Frank? gimme that plastic bag, will ya? Here. We found this on the driver. A .38 Colt short-barreled revolver. Fully loaded, not fired recently. And we took it – diplomatic immunity or not – because it's the same model as one near the dead Israeli.

"You can take a quick look inside now, if you want. But we should have a better view in a couple minutes, when our

347

photographer is finished."

Brenda accompanied Ford down the hall to the open apartment door and stepped in. Her senses were immediately assaulted by the carnage.

Three men lay on the floor, soaked in a mixture of blood and the debris of their own flesh. Chips of white plaster from the walls littered the room.

Through the apartment window Brenda could see a beautiful, preposterously out-of-place backdrop of the Washington Monument and Lincoln Memorial lit and silhouetted against a dark, moonless sky. Death and beauty, mingled in perverse harmony.

Brenda shivered. Then she said, "Please have the photographer finish ASAP. I need to identify the other two right away in case they're also diplomatic personnel. In the meantime, I'd like to talk to the Israeli chauffeur."

"Right this way, Agent Straus."

She had no better luck with Abe than Ford had. If anything, Tiron's chauffeur was even surlier and more antagonistic with her. "I have a diplomatic passport – I am asking to be released!" he repeated after each question she asked.

Once Ford had confirmed his diplomatic credentials, Brenda recommended that they allow him to leave, without his handgun. Ford gave the orders, noting on a small yellow pad the time and details of the authorization. They gave Abe a receipt for the weapon; they had to be sure it had not been used and was registered according to Virginia state law.

Jack Sanchez arrived from downstairs. "Nothing," he told Brenda. "No witnesses. What'd you find up here?"

"Jack, meet Lieutenant Ford, Arlington Homicide. Lieutenant Ford, Special Agent Sanchez."

"Welcome," said Ford. "Agent Straus, my boys tell me the photographer is done. No one else has been allowed in." Brenda asked for the name of the photographer and an inventory of the film shot, which Ford asked Frank to put together. "Just a security measure, Lieutenant."

Keeping out the other officers for the moment, the three of them approached the dead men. The diplomat lay with a gaping bullet hole in his left side. The second body was that of a hairy, swarthy man whose wide-open eyes still registered the angry shock of facing an unexpected death. The third man, lying on his back, had been shot between the eyes, the dumdum bullet leaving his face a messy plum of flesh and blood. He was unrecognizable.

"Holy God, what a massacre!" breathed Sanchez. "Somebody came here this evening with a mission."

"We can take a closer look now," offered Ford. "Why don't you guys get the Israeli and that guy who still has a face, and I'll take the bloody mess over here and see if I can find some ID."

As Brenda and Jack edged closer to Tiron and the open-eyed corpse, Brenda let out a quiet gasp. "Jack," she whispered, "look at this big guy. He's our Peter, I'm sure! I've been studying his file and photo so closely these past few weeks. Look at the mustache. The nose, the chin. I'm 99% certain it's Peter."

"Are you kidding?" Sanchez muttered as he stared at the body more closely. "Then we damn well have to find out fast who the third man is. This could be even bigger than – " Brenda looked hard at her colleague. *Security, man, keep it buttoned.* Sanchez swallowed the rest of his phrase. "One dead Mossad chief of station is already enough to make it a world-class shoot-up. But how in hell do both Tiron and Sorensson's assassin end up in a shoot-out? What's the connection?"

"It's Markovic. She called from Zurich and told us Peter and Tiron were connected. She knew everything," Brenda whispered between her teeth. "I can't get over it. We find the infamous Peter Dimitriopolis right here beneath our feet in Washington, when we're looking for him worldwide. Yesterday, I assured

Judge Baker we'd track him down *soon*. Was that ever an understatement!"

"Holy shit! Agent Straus!" Lieutenant Ford's disturbed voice pierced their conversation in a crescendo. "You guys seen nothing yet. Look at this – the other body. It just ain't possible!" He handed a driver's license to Brenda. He remained riveted, awaiting her reaction.

"My God!" was all she could say, passing the license to Jack.

Brenda, paling, watched Jack study the New Hampshire driver's license. "Senator George Johnson," he whispered, dumbfounded.

"Our president-elect," added Brenda in a low voice. "Shut the door."

The two agents faced each other, a solemn look passing between them. Brenda turned. "Excuse us for a few seconds, Lieutenant Ford. We need a moment to think this through carefully."

Ford nodded and stepped into the next room. "I'll be here when you need me."

Brenda whispered to Jack, "There's only one explanation for Johnson being with Tiron, in a small apartment like this, on a night like this."

Jack nodded. "Johnson is Hebron!"

"He *was* Hebron. Now he's one very dead president-elect."

"What's our next step?"

Brenda beeped for Jim Clarkson and Christina Whitinghill.

"What a mess." "Need any help, Brenda?" they said as she let them in. Brenda told them, still in a whisper, who the three men were. Jim was beside himself, Christina frozen. "Now," Brenda continued, "we have to move fast. Christina, go to the car right away and call the White House Secret Service detail on the secure phone. Ask for an investigative unit and one of Senator George Joh – I mean, President-elect George Johnson's bodyguards to get over here immediately. We need positive identification. Jim, call Judge Baker on the secure line. He'll want to brief the president.

Tell the judge I'm not moving from the scene until we have a full team here and he gives the order. Not for anyone. Now move."

Brenda summoned Ford. "Lieutenant," she began, "we have to keep this discovery to ourselves until the Secret Service gets here for verification. We can't risk a leak and then have it turn out we made a mistake and the corpse belongs to some jerk who stole Johnson's wallet. Let's make sure no one knows about this – keep everyone away from the bodies, especially the press. And I mean *everyone*. In fact, seal off the entire floor. You and the FBI are staying in this room to guard it!"

"Right away, Agent Straus." He immediately moved to the door to block entry until the Secret Service arrived.

Downstairs, in the FBI's unmarked sedan, Jim called Baker, rendering him speechless with the news.

Finally, the director spoke. "Tell Brenda I want her at the White House immediately after she oversees the ID of the body and our emergency crime scene people get there. And tell her I'll call Mrs. Johnson to see if she knows where the senator is. Then I'll go ahead and bring the president up to speed. Brenda must follow me to the White House ASAP with the details – is that clear?"

"Yes, sir. I'm going upstairs right now to give her your message."

The FBI director hung up without comment. He asked his bodyguard-driver to call the Secret Service at the White House and alert the president that he was on his way, on a matter of the most urgent national-security importance.

The White House

Judge Baker was meeting with President Douglas, Vice President Hayes and National Security Adviser Russell when the duty officer showed Brenda into the Oval Office. She reviewed what she had found at the murder scene and confirmed that the Secret Service had identified the corpse as that of the president-elect of the United States.

The national leaders sat in silence.

Brenda concluded, "As unbelievable as it sounds, it looks like the Sorensson case and the Hebron case have both come to an unpredictable, colliding conclusion. We have one of the suspects in Sorensson's assassination, and an Israeli intelligence officer, *and* apparently Hebron, all dead, in the same room."

"So, George Johnson was our Hebron?" blurted Douglas as though coming out of a trance.

"To be precise, Mr. President," Judge Baker said, "he was *their* Hebron. I will sign a warrant and we'll take command of his home and office tonight, immediately, ostensibly as a security measure, but also to search for clandestine communications and hiding places."

Vice President Hayes glanced inquisitively from one person to another. "I don't understand," he said. "He worked for Israel? But he almost always voted against their wishes."

Baker responded, "Well, more of those votes may have met their *real* wishes than we know. Seems as though they were saving him for just such a year as this, when he might enable to them to put a secret weapon in the White House itself." He added, "I'm afraid, Mr. Vice President, that as Johnson's running mate you've inherited a very unexpected responsibility. You'll be the next president."

"Yes, Judge Baker," said Douglas, "you're right. But before we do any congratulating we have to deal with this terrible thing. Dear God! This will make the Kennedy assassination seem clear-cut."

"Allow me, Mr. President," offered Baker, "since you mentioned the Kennedy matter, to recommend that the name 'Hebron' never again be used among us. Thanks to your instructions, no documents exist at this point, and in the national interest none will be created, since the truth about the case will never be fully known. At least, not by us. Bill can explain to the Russians accordingly. And I will separately brief the vice president as we close the unwritten book on the case. Meanwhile, Mr. President, tomorrow you should announce the appointment by the attorney general of a presidential commission to investigate the murder of President-elect Johnson, headed by, let's say, the chief justice of the Supreme Court. It must be done to put idle talk to rest. You and all other government officials can refuse to comment pending the submission of the commission's report to the president and Congress."

Douglas nodded slowly. A close friend, the very man he had selected to replace him, had betrayed his nation. President Douglas was a shaken man. He had lost two close friends within a year – one by murder, the other by betrayal. And both gunned down by the same assassin. He could barely speak to the others. With a formal nod, he dismissed them and left for his private quarters.

It wasn't until Judge Baker and Brenda Straus were securely in the back of the director's limousine heading to the Bureau that the judge broke the silence. "I have to thank you, Brenda, for an incredible job on both cases. Your boss and others have always spoken highly of your work; now I've experienced it firsthand. I've decided that Hutchins will be moved up to assistant director and you'll be promoted to replace him as agent in charge of our Counter-Terrorism Section – if, of course, the various personnel panels agree, and I'm confident they will.

"Speaking of changes, if I'm not mistaken we'll be hearing pretty soon of some changes at the top of Israeli intelligence – a political signal they'll owe us, which will be interesting to await. And Brenda, one of these days, in the golden years of my retirement, I wouldn't at all be surprised to see you in my job."

"Thank you, sir, for your confidence. I'm flattered beyond words. But the Sorensson case is not finished. We don't have our woman yet, remember?"

"What woman?"

"We're convinced that Peter Dimitriopolis was not acting alone, that he was in league with a woman killer, a Serbo-Austrian by the name of J. Paula Markovic – a professional assassin. She is the woman who was with Sorensson the night he was hit. I didn't want to bring this up in front of the president and his people. It would be too confusing when they're trying to cope with Johnson's death.

"You see, sir, it's just too neat to be accidental. She got Hebron – although, how could she have known about him? Maybe an accident? And Tiron, Hebron's control officer. Again, how would she know him? But then there's Peter, the assassin we were after. It's like Peter, Tiron, and Hebron were delivered to us in a package. And if so, she, not Peter, was in control. That would mean she's the effective brain, if not the actual assassin, in these three deaths, plus Sorensson's. The circumstantial evidence is overwhelming. I'm only sorry we can't prove it yet."

"Listen, Brenda, if there's one thing you've earned while working for the FBI, it's our respect for your talent and instinct. I strongly advise you never to apologize, to me or anyone else, for your hunches. Follow them, wherever they take you. You've got my personal authority for that. Understand?"

"I certainly do, sir. Again, thanks for your confidence," replied the new agent in charge of Counter-Terrorism. *So, where's J. now?* she wondered.

FBI Headquarters, November 8th

Brenda declined to move her belongings to a larger office with its own conference room. The suite would complement her new position, but she was troubled by the fact that she hadn't completely solved the Sorensson case. She decided the trappings of status would have to wait until she finished what she had started.

She reviewed the results of her investigations. Peter's death might represent only the removal of someone who had become a liability: another way of saying someone's well-being depended on his being eliminated. The FBI had "caught" one of Sorensson's assassins by default. Peter had been left for them like a bone thrown to calm a barking dog or send him dashing off in another direction. That was just one of the things that bothered Brenda about the episode in the Rosslyn apartment. There was no doubt in her mind that the whole thing was staged to look like a shoot-out. Peter had been killed to close the Sorensson investigation – to keep the FBI at bay. There had been no powder on Tiron's hands, although there were traces on Peter's gloves. The shoot-out explanation was just too perfect to be true.

Exasperated, Brenda flipped the pages of the preliminary report on Rosslyn. Three pieces of the puzzle didn't fit. First, Art Bosco had discovered an electronic device, a laser monitor, in the hall across from Tiron's apartment. It bore Peter's fingerprints. When Ambassador Sorensson's body was discovered in May, the Belgian police found an electronic device attached to his wrist. Both gadgets were top-quality and most likely designed by the same engineer. So, the assassin – or one of his or her people – was an expert in the use of electronic devices. The French police report about the Curiel organization had mentioned the group's displeasure with Peter regarding technological matters; his attributes didn't include a knack for electronics or high-tech gadgetry. But the same report said Curiel's prized female trainee, J. Paula Markovic, also known as *Le Valet*, excelled in this domain, to the point of dictating her own specifications to the manufacturer.

A knock interrupted her train of thought.

"Congrats, Straus," Christina said gaily as she poked her head around the door. "The guys downstairs want to take you out for a big bash. Just say when."

Brenda smiled at Christina's enthusiasm. One would think *she* was the one promoted. "Thanks, Christina. I'll think about it. But come here. I want to try something on you."

"Ooh, noooo! Not one of your famous hunches," Christina gasped in mock horror. But she walked in, closing the door behind her.

"Get this theory!"

"Shoot."

"Exactly!" said Brenda, holding her right hand in an imitation of a gun, then laughing heartily at the look on Christina's face. She lowered her hand. "Three men. Each died of a *single* bullet. Two guns were used. Four shots were fired. What's wrong with this scenario?"

"I don't know. What do *you* think is wrong?"

"In a shoot-out, both parties fire several times in rapid succession, in panic, hoping that one of their bullets hits the mark. Single shots are the mark of a cool professional, in complete control." Brenda held her index finger up. "Tiron was shot, with exceptional precision, straight through the heart. Once. One perfectly aimed shot killed him instantly."

"And?"

"Johnson was also shot once. One bullet killed him instantly." Brenda looked again at the report. "Both Tiron and Johnson were murdered by the same gun. The SIG-Sauer with the silencer."

"What are you getting at?"

"Now consider Peter. He was killed by Tiron's gun. He, too, was hit by one bullet. Another perfect shot." She raised three fingers. "Three shots. Three bullets. Three men dead. Only one stray bullet hit the wall. It doesn't add up."

"Someone else had to be in the room," said Christina excitedly. "Someone who could hit the target dead-center – any target – with the first shot?"

"Exactly. Someone else *was* there. A supremely competent assassin."

"J. Paula Markovic," breathed Christina.

"She knew the FBI was looking for Peter. She gave herself away when she called me from Zurich. By giving us Peter, then killing him, she hoped to keep us from looking deeper into Sorensson's assassination. Why would she want us to close that investigation? Because we have a witness who testified that she was the last person seen with Sorensson the night he was killed."

"Right!" cheered Christina.

"But this circumstantial evidence doesn't *prove* that our suspect – also known as Jay, also known as *Le Valet*, The Jack – killed Sorensson. Or that she was present that night in Rosslyn. I have to go after her, but I can't issue a warrant or alert for her arrest. She has someone somewhere, probably in Europe, feeding her inside information. She'll disappear if we advise Interpol."

"So?" queried Christina.

"I have to get her myself. Personally."

"What about Johnson? Why was he killed?" asked Christina. "He had nothing to do with the Sorensson case."

"Bad luck. Wrong place, wrong time. Professionals don't leave witnesses. Whoever killed Tiron had no choice but to shoot Johnson too. Just because he was there." Brenda raked her hair in agitation. "But I'm afraid *I'm* responsible for Johnson being there in the first place."

Christina looked at her with wide eyes. "How?"

"I spooked him with my interview about his relations with Tiron. We played hardball. The faxes, the phone messages, the tails. Made him suspect that we were onto him, and that I would soon prove who he was. That must've scared him so badly he called Tiron for an emergency meeting. We were hoping to pressure him into making a mistake. We just didn't – couldn't – foresee this result."

"So you're going after J. Paula Markovic? Can I help?"

"Sure. But I need time to think. After I develop a plan, I'll let you know." Brenda walked up to her friend, put her lips close to Christina's ear, and in a conspiratorial whisper asked, "Now tell me: what do the guys downstairs have in mind?"

Over the Atlantic, November 8th

The United Airlines 777 that had taken off from Dulles International Airport late the previous evening glided smoothly over the Atlantic Ocean.

The first rays of sunshine broke through the darkness and early morning haze to embrace the jet in a soft halo. Over the speakers the captain told his passengers he hoped they'd had a restful flight and wished them a sunny morning en route to Frankfurt and a tasty breakfast. Then he broke the incredible news that had reached him overnight from America.

"Senator George Johnson, who won the American presidential election last night, was found murdered in an apartment in a Virginia suburb. The body of an Israeli Embassy officer was also found in the apartment. Both Senator Johnson and the Israeli diplomat were apparently killed by a professional assassin, who also died in the gunfight. The FBI is investigating this tragedy. We'll bring more details just as we receive them. We will be landing in Frankfurt in about ninety minutes. Thank you."

Jackie sat as though frozen in outer space. All around her there was a hubbub of noise as her fellow passengers speculated about the news. "What I wanna know is, what in hell was Johnson doin' with an Israeli diplomat?" she heard a man behind her ask.

"I expect we'll find out soon enough," his female companion answered.

"Or more likely, we'll never find out," the man predicted.

Luckily, with two seats to herself, Jackie didn't have to enter the debate. She was too astonished to speak. *My God!* she thought. *I killed the newly elected president of the United States!* For the briefest of seconds, reality rattled her. Then her resilience and pride bounced back. *Life is certainly full of surprises*, she reflected. *Not only for assassins, but also for presidents!*

She knew exactly what she had to do next: disappear for a long, long rest from her career. With any luck, her gift of Peter to the American authorities would satisfy their professional curiosity and sidetrack their hunt for the author of Ambassador Sorensson's demise. Meanwhile, she would return to Palma de Mallorca, and to her quiet life there as J. Paula Bergen, real estate agency manager.

A fitting end, she considered, *to the most daring revenge of a lifetime. They should have paid me from the start.*

Chapter Twenty-five

Jerusalem
November 8th

Aharon Eshel had been in near suicidal despair since Benjamin Stern awoke him early in the morning with the news about the deaths of Hebron and David Tiron.

Just a few hours earlier, when the election results came in, the prime minister had basked in the glory of the operation's success – an operation which would ensure the nation's security for years to come. Now, their agent of influence lay dead, his face disfigured by a hit man's bullet. Hebron and Tiron were killed by an assassin who, according to Stern, had been hired by Mossad for the agency's wet operations.

What a bitter twist of fate, he moaned to himself, his despair giving way to sharp chest pains. He reached for his medication and took double the recommended dosage.

A few hours later Stern phoned. "A special courier has just arrived from Washington. His pouch carried a note found near Tiron's body by his bodyguard. Thank God he picked it up before the Americans saw it! It's something you must read."

"Come immediately," replied Eshel. "There is another matter I must also discuss with you."

When the Mossad director walked into the PM's office, Eshel impulsively rose from his chair and came around the desk to face him. "Ben. Do you have an explanation yet? How could Tiron let such a thing happen? How could he let an assassin get close to our nation's greatest asset?"

"I'm afraid I might have an answer – at least a part of one. Abe Stiviz, our bodyguard and driver for Tiron, was keeping guard downstairs while Tiron met with Hebron. When he heard shots, he ran upstairs to the safe apartment and found the three men dead. He saw a note by David's hand. Without realizing its full significance – and not knowing the exact nature of Tiron's connection with the other dead men – he pocketed it before the police got there." Stern brought a brown envelope forward. "Abe put the note into this sealed envelope and sent it by courier pouch directly to me. He assured me that no one else in our office in Washington or in the embassy there has seen it." He thrust the note in Eshel's direction. "You should read this."

The prime minister took it, drew a deep breath and read. Then he reread, once, twice, three times. It took a few seconds for the full implication of the assassin's message to Tiron – or better, to the Israelis – to sink in.

"General Stern."

"Sir?"

Eshel turned and took a lighter from his desktop. He handed it to Stern, together with the note.

"Burn it," he ordered. "Burn this last shred of evidence which proves that I was right about that insane wet operation of yours. Do you understand, General Stern?" His voice grew louder and harsher. "Do you realize that your own operation provoked the death of Hebron, the greatest secret agent in our nation's history? Have you any idea of the magnitude of what you've done?"

With bowed head, Stern lit the note and let it fall into an ashtray. Both men watched it burn until there was nothing left but black ashes. Then Stern crushed the ashes with his large, weather-worn right hand until they disintegrated into a thousand tiny particles, which he poured into the brown envelope.

His face turning paler as his chest pains swelled, Eshel sat at his desk and buzzed his secretary. "Bring your pad for dictation."

As Lev Eglon entered, Eshel pointed sharply and rudely at Stern. "General Stern is going to dictate his resignation to you. I will accept it as soon as it is typed and he has signed it. Now – both of you sit here in my office, in front of me, and get on with it."

The envelope of burned ashes now in his worn briefcase, Stern sat with drooping, heavy shoulders and a red face, about to dictate his resignation from the position that meant so much to him and others.

Once Stern had left, Eshel found himself alone once again. He looked out the window over the hills of Jerusalem and watched the early-morning sun drench his capital city in life-promoting rays. New, provocative thoughts raced through his shocked and angry mind. *These insanely dangerous machinations are not the way to protect Israel. No longer. I must sincerely engage our nation in the peace process. That is the only hope for my children and grandchildren. It may cost me my life – we have so many crazies around the fringes. But I've always been ready for that sacrifice for my people.*

Moscow, November 8th

Yuri looked at the Associated Press wire release that was placed on his desk. Frantically scanning the text for any reference to Jackie, he read through the news which had hit the world that morning. Nothing, no reference to a female being involved. Only the report that one Peter Dimitriopolis, an alleged professional hit man, was the killer and had, in turn, been killed in the shoot-out.

Even worse, Yuri had in front of him a decoded clandestine transmission from Volga, Russia's top agent in Israel. Volga, so named because of the endless river of valuable intelligence he had provided to Moscow for years. Volga – Benjamin Stern, in the real world – had just sent a clandestine burst communications signal by satellite, informing his masters in Moscow that he had been fired because of the Hebron and Tiron deaths.

Yuri stared at the message, unable to see anything for the blind fury surging through him. He balled up the news bulletin and flung it across the room. *How could she do this to me? After promising, swearing, she'd stay away from Tiron. It's my fault Hebron's dead and we've lost our best agent in Israel. I'll live the rest of my life fearing this could be traced back to me. She could even blackmail me.*

"I'll never, ever see that, that..." he searched for the word, "*demon* again," Yuri shouted, kicking his desk. "She's death waiting around the corner for every man." She thought she was superwoman, but she had a fatal flaw – the need to revenge herself against any slight from a man. For that she threw away everything she had built up over years, and now she was as good as dead.

Palma de Mallorca, Seven Weeks Later

Smiling, J. Paula Bergen looked up at the couple who had just walked into her real estate agency. Although there appeared to be a good fifteen years between them, they were holding hands and leaning against each other like newlyweds as they began to inspect the photos of villas and apartments on the walls of Jackie's agency. They were speaking German.

"May I help you?" she asked, also in German, remaining at her desk but widening her welcoming smile.

"Yes, please," the woman replied as she turned toward Jackie with a smile full of happiness and fulfillment. "We're interested in leasing an apartment or a villa along the waterfront." She looked searchingly at Jackie. "For a holiday. Some Flemish friends in Brussels recommended your agency."

"Certainly, madame. My name is Paula Bergen. Call me Jackie," she answered. She noticed a hint of an American accent in the woman's German. *Was that a thumbs-up the woman gave her male partner? Why?* "Please, have a seat. Could you give me a few details about yourselves and what type of accommodation you're looking for, and I'll see what we have in my listings. Just fill out this short questionnaire. I'll be right with you."

The woman calmly sat down, took a pen out of her purse and, with great assurance, completed the form, occasionally glancing back at her man with a wink. Jackie took a better look and noted he was exceptionally well dressed – like a Belgian or German aristocrat. The woman showed him the completed form, at which he nodded his approval. She then handed it back to Jackie, who studied it and continued in German, "Right. Let's see. Ms. Brenda Straus, you prefer a large apartment overlooking the port? I'll see what we have. But is your requirement really short-term, or longer? You left that blank."

"A week or two. What do you think, Guy, darling?" the woman asked the man standing behind her.

"A week will be sufficient, sweetheart," he suggested. He looked down at her and squeezed her hand.

"Fine," Jackie said. "We'll start with apartments and see if something catches your fancy. If not, we'll look at a couple of small houses in the port area."

"Thank you, Frau Bergen – oh, I mean Jackie," Brenda Straus responded, suddenly switching to American English. "We're so excited. We've heard so much about you and we know we'll find exactly what we're looking for here. By the way, you have a slight Slav accent, don't you? I'm sure we've talked before – perhaps over the phone?"

Jackie felt a sudden shiver of apprehension as she looked up abruptly from the form. Like early-warning radar, her eyes and all of her intellectual facilities scanned the faces of the couple, one sitting, one standing, both watching her carefully with knowing smiles on their faces. She sensed imminent danger. Like a cornered wild animal, she immediately sharpened her thoughts to shape her next moves.

Have the Americans come for me?

She casually dropped her hand down from the desk to her lap to confirm that her miniature automatic was strapped to her inner thigh, butt to the front, under her pastel blue skirt. Reassured, despite her racing pulse, she reached for the large key chain on the desk, which held not only her car keys but also those to her powerboat and her safe haven in Ibizia. Her mind worked at mainframe speed, assessing her options. Her next decisions would be critical, life-or-death. Of that she had little doubt.

"Monsieur, Madam, I have some excellent properties to show you. What's more, I'd like to invite you to lunch at my house, where you can get a feel for what it's like to live in *paraíso*. Excuse me, but that's what I call it here." Jackie noticed the couple seemed relaxed and pleased with her information. They seemed to have plenty of time and were not trying to control the agenda. *Maybe I'm wrong*, she thought. But she couldn't afford to be wrong. As she gathered her papers the adrenaline surged through her veins. She was like a dangerous big cat now, ready to kill or bolt at a second's notice. She had actually practiced several escape plans, timed them all, knew the pros and cons of each route. The best by far was to reach her powerboat, anchored off the beach below her villa.

"So, shall we go? My car's around the corner. I'll call my housekeeper to arrange lunch."

The couple followed without comment.

An hour later, after viewing four apartments in the port area, she and her clients pulled up in front of Villa del Sol, Jackie's home by the sea. Jackie was even more worried now. The couple had been too quiet, asked few questions about the flats, and only seemed interested in her, her movements, how she talked, her car.

They are casing me, not the properties, she concluded.

Jackie pressed the radio command button and the main gates of her one-acre estate opened. It was like a scene out of Hollywood, a perfect set – a single-story Spanish-style house in the middle an expanse of golf grass, with coconut palms thirty feet high. Only a curved pool interrupted the flow of the lawn to the end of the property, which was the cliff edge overlooking the sea fifty meters below. A stone walkway led down to the small beach. It was a bit tricky and required careful footing. There was also a well-concealed quick route to the beach, which only the owner knew about and had the know-how to use.

As she pulled up in the circular drive, Jackie began to feel in control again. They had not been followed, she was sure, so the danger seemed less than she had imagined. She even wondered if she really needed to act on her determination to go into full flight. She began to reconsider, although all her instincts, so finely tuned over the years, told her – *Run! Run!*

"Your place is beautiful," remarked Brenda. "I never imagined anything like this. Guy, can we afford one like this?"

"Not on our paltry government salaries, my dear."

Government salaries. So, they are police.

"*Buenos días, Señora*," said the housekeeper as she opened the door and walked out to the driveway to see if she could assist Señora Jackie and her luncheon guests.

"Lunch ready, Maria?"

"*Si, Señora*, fifteen minutes."

"Good. Give our guests some drinks while I change," said Jackie as she led the couple to the house. "Please, Mr. and Mrs. Straus, make yourselves comfortable. I'll be right with you."

"Maria."

"*Si.*"

"Please run down to the *mercado* for some limes."

"But *Señora...*"

"A kilo of juicy limes, Maria. Hurry, we have guests."

"*Si, Señora.*"

Brenda and Guy followed their hostess into the spacious salon looking out over the lawn and the tall coconut palms to the sea.

"Ah, this is it! Let's just rent this for a month," exclaimed Guy as he approached the large glass sliding doors opening upon the *terrasse*. He put his arm around Brenda, playing the part well. "A perfect hideaway and love nest."

Satisfied that they were distracted, Jackie headed for the bedroom wing of the rambling house. In her suite, she locked the door, then pushed the button behind the TV which opened a secret door in her closet wall. Playing by the book, she grabbed the small black nylon bag with her escape kit, prepped for moments that were not supposed to come. Watertight, it would float and was fire-resistant. Inside were weapons, cash, false passports and ID, a neoprene diving suit, and a spare set of keys to her Ibiza safe house and several of her apartments around the world. Finally, there was a late-model miniaturized satellite telecommunications kit that could call or be called from anywhere, send or receive digital data, and remote-pilot her office and home computers, all without detection.

Ready, she pushed a code into the "intelligent-house" system she had imported from Miami. It would lock all the doors of her suite, bringing down interior steel shutters from the ceiling to cover the entrance from the main house and all the suite windows. The suite became a protective bulletproof cocoon. She then tapped in a code to prime an explosive device that would demolish the house in twenty minutes, giving her plenty of time to get to the beach and her powerboat. The American and European *flics* would disappear from the face of the earth, along with any possible evidence – though the villa was already clean; she was taking the only compromising article, her escape kit. *Too bad about the lunch*, she thought. *And Maria, she'll thank those limes.*

Jackie opened a sliding door at the rear of her closet which revealed a narrow stairway to a tunnel below, through which she could reach the beach without being observed. Her remodeling of the house had included this attribute for just such an occasion. She had never used it.

Once on the private, secluded beach, free from prying FBI or Interpol eyes, she changed into her wet suit, putting her street clothes in the waterproof escape bag. She waded out to the powerboat anchored in four feet of water, threw her escape kit in, and pulled herself up and over. A quick check of the interior and engine assured her that all was in order, so she took up the anchor and turned the ignition key, still attached to her car key ring. The two Merc engines roared into action.

In the villa, enjoying their drinks, Brenda and Guy looked suddenly at each other as they heard the distant noise of powerboat engines turning over. They jumped from the sofa and ran to the large window to see if they could spot the boat. Suddenly, from out of the cover of the cliff, Jackie's Fountain Lightning surged into view and headed eastward at high speed.

Guy leaned against the window. "That's her, I'm sure. She's on the run!"

Brenda felt a wave of relief ripple through her chest as the realization hit home; it was over for Jackie Markovic. "Well, that's what we wanted." She reached into her large handbag, pulled out a pair of binoculars, and looked through the sharp lens. "Yup, that's her boat." She swallowed hard and braced herself for the shock that was imminent. "Adieu, Jackie Markovic."

"Tootles," chimed in Guy.

Brenda looked at him with a funny expression. "Where'd you

pick up that piece of corn, Inspector? The irony seemed tragic.

"Reruns, my love."

Suddenly, the noise of the explosion ripped through the air. The fleeing powerboat erupted into a fireball.

"Well, I guess our Navy SEALs found her explosives and knew just what to do with them."

"With a bit of help from the Spanish Defense Ministry, remember," Guy added.

"Very cool!" whispered Brenda. "Miss Jackie Bergen-Markovic got herself some surprise. It was the only solution for everybody, particularly for Washington. The judge was right – we couldn't have let her on the witness stand without dismantling the world's intelligence networks. Thank God she went for the extreme solution. It was even easier than we planned. She built her own death trap. We just invited her to her own fireworks."

Maria ran into the room with the limes. "*Señora*! The boat! It's gone!" A look of cruel comprehension spread across her face. *These people hadn't told me everything.* But Jackie had thought to protect her.

"Yes, Maria. And so is Miss Jackie. Thank you for your help; it was critical. Guess we owe you that trip to the United States, right?"

"Yes, *Señora. Gracias.* And my nephew Armando, like you promised. And his MBA in California."

Guy put his arm around Brenda's shoulders as they looked out to sea at the burning debris. There was little remorse. *She was just too big to deal with in any other way.* "Brenda, your plan was *perfecto.* We drove her right into her escape corner, and she bit. She was so prepared, she couldn't even think further."

Just like Hebron, thought Brenda. *Touch the right nerve and the muscle will twitch every time.* Her mind jumped for an instant to her father. *Maybe he'll cut me some slack now.*

"But what if she hadn't?" Guy added as he considered the alternative.

"Well, Guy, I think we'd have had to opt for one of your famous Belgian solutions, and find a way where there is none. Now it's time to get back to our hotel. The judge is waiting for a phone call. And then let's change for the beach. I think we deserve to write our final reports over the next day here in Jackie's *paraíso!*"

"Speaking of Belgian solutions, my brilliant Brenda, it's time you come up with one for us. How will we handle this cumbersome transatlantic romance?"

Brenda turned and looked into Guy's eyes as though testing his seriousness. "What romance, Romeo?"

Guy put his hands around her waist, violating for the first time the distance that their professionalism required, and drew her toward him. He'd been patient.

"You do love me too, don't you, *chérie*?" he asked.

In response, she tilted her head slightly and let him kiss her for the first time, starting soft and then opening with relief after months of anticipation. Moving his lips to her right ear, he whispered, "Some things just begin at the end, *chérie*."

He's so corny, so clichéd, right out of some popular American movie, she thought, and she squeezed herself deeper into his grip.

"Where I'm from, *Monsieur* Policeman," she teased, "you could go to jail for harassment."

"I have the right to remain silent, don't I?"

And he kissed her again as Jackie's getaway burned on the water.